THE
BRAVER
THING

CLIFFORD JACKMAN

RANDOM HOUSE CANADA

PUBLISHED BY RANDOM HOUSE CANADA

Published in 2020 by Random House Canada, a division of Penguin Random
House Canada Limited, Toronto. Distributed in Canada and the United States
of America by Penguin Random House Canada Limited, Toronto.

www.penguinrandomhouse.ca

Library and Archives Canada Cataloguing in Publication

Title: The braver thing / Clifford Jackman.
Names: Jackman, Clifford, author.
Identifiers: Canadiana (print) 20190230835 | Canadiana (ebook) 20190230827 |
ISBN 9780735280212 (softcover) | ISBN 9780735280229 (HTML)
Classification: LCC PS8619.A224 B73 2020 | DDC C813/.6—dc23

Text design: Lisa Jager
Cover design: Lisa Jager
Image credits: (ship) John McDonald, Unsplash; (skulls) OpenClipart-Vectors, Pixabay

Printed and bound in Canada

2 4 6 8 9 7 5 3 1

Penguin
Random House
RANDOM HOUSE CANADA

For Cathy

And if this be madness in the multitude, it is the same in every particular man. For as in the midst of the sea, though a man perceive no sound of that part of the water next him, yet he is well assured that part contributes as much to the roaring of the sea as any other part of the same quantity: so also, though we perceive no great unquietness in one or two men, yet we may be well assured that their singular passions are parts of the seditious roaring of a troubled nation.

— Thomas Hobbes, *Leviathan*

THE COMPANY

The Captain, his servants and allies:

James "Jimmy" Kavanagh, called "the Taoiseach," former shipmate of Blackbeard,
Captain and part-owner (together with the Investors) of the *Saoirse*.

Obiefune, called "Alfie," the Captain's Steward.

Cian Kavanagh, the Captain's son and clerk.

Dobie, the Captain's clerk.

Benjamin, the Captain's servant.

Israel Hands, Kavanagh's enforcer, who put down a mutiny upon Blackbeard's ship
off the coast of Honduras.

The Investors:

Tulip, an Investor, and Master-At-Arms.

MacGregor, who wished to withdraw his Investment.

Alan, who wished to withdraw his Investment, and afterwards reconsidered.

Connor.

The Officers:

Tom Apollo, first mate.

Benjamin Hornigold, second mate, former leader of the Pirate Commonwealth,
afterwards a hunter of pirates.

Alejandros Rios, sailing master (or navigator).

Andreas Yellow, master's mate.

Gérald Devereux, ship's surgeon.

Horace Spry, Quartermaster.

Matthew Lewis, armourer.

Cyrus, bosun's mate.

Quaque, West African canoeman, and coxswain.

Tory, carpenter's mate.

The Factions:

Robert Dickens, radical pirate, loyal follower of Charles Vane.

Harry Ironside, Dickens' chief supporter.

Colin, a supporter of Dickens.

John O'Brien, disloyal follower of Charlies Vane.

Bradford Scudder, formerly a shipmate of Sam Bellamy, a supporter of O'Brien.

Bill Quantrill, formerly a Royal Marine, a supporter of O'Brien.

Davies, a supporter of O'Brien.

Other Sailors:
Harold Hutchins, Able Sailor.
George Beard, Able Sailor.
Obed Coffin, a Quaker.
Kenneth Jacobs, called "Goldie."
Zahir, a Lascar, translator.

OTHER NOTABLES

Pirates:
Sam Bellamy, called "Black Sam" or "The Prince of Pirates," killed in a shipwreck.
Charles Vane, a radical pirate, who deposed Hornigold, then was himself deposed by
Rackham, captured by Hornigold, and hanged.
Edward Teach, called "Blackbeard," former shipmate of Hornigold and Kavanagh,
killed in North Carolina by Governor Rogers.
Bartholomew Roberts, called "Black Bart," a successful pirate and former owner of
the *Saoirse* (when she was called the *Royal Fortune*), killed in North Carolina by
Governor Rogers.
Jack Rackham, captured in North Carolina by Governor Rogers, awaiting trial in the
Bahamas.
George Lowther, captain of the *Happy Delivery*, a radical pirate who escaped from
North Carolina.

The Bahamas:
Woodes Rogers, former shipmate of Kavanagh, Governor of the Bahamas.
Mr. Dennyson, a merchant.

North Carolina:
Charles Eden, disgraced Governor of North Carolina.
Mrs. Kavanagh, Kavanagh's wife.
Rory Kavanagh, Kavanagh's eldest son.
Billy, Kavanagh's nephew.
Joseph Morrison, a cousin of Mrs. Kavanagh.
Mr. and Mrs. Kirkland, neighbours to the Kavanaghs.

THE JONAH

Then the sailors said to each other, "Come, let us cast lots to find out who is responsible for this calamity." They cast lots and the lot fell on Jonah.

—*Jonah 1:7*

Nassau. New Providence. The Bahamas.

April 21, 1721.

1

O bed Coffin sat with his hand on the till and his eye on the sail. The
launch slipped through the shadows of the tall masts of a man-of-
war and beneath the barred windows of the fort, from which some prisoners
shouted invective, and others called out for help, and still others sang:

Did not you promise me
That you would marry me

They glided over the clear green water towards the pier, where the
hangman erected tarry corpses encased in iron gibbets. Past the crowd of
spectators, in the town, it was as if there was a carnival, drunk men wheeling, whores laughing, peddlers shouting, and music.

While the boat was being moored, the master tossed Coffin a canvas
bag.

"Count it, it's all there," he said.

Coffin felt the coins in his hands, raised his eyes, and looked around
the boat. The master did not meet his eye. None of the sailors objected to

him being paid and discharged before the boat was unloaded; rather, they looked relieved. Coffin had served aboard three different merchant ships since his convalescence in the Cape Colony and so it had been every time. He knew (how he knew!) that he deserved their opprobrium, yet how dreadfully it stung, how terrible it was to know yourself a sinner, past redemption, how monstrous it was to be so alone.

"My thanks," Coffin said.

He climbed the ladder and walked to shore. Behind him, the master crossed himself, and a sailor made a sign against the evil eye.

The sharp boys, who lurked in a school by the dock, noticed Coffin. A short, subdued fight took place. Once it was resolved, the victorious boy (a tall, thick lout with a cast in each eye) materialized before Coffin.

"Hello sir, what do you need? Something to eat? Drink? A woman?"

The boy turned his head to accommodate his crazy eyes and look over his prospect. Coffin wore a straw hat, a cloth shirt, duck trousers, no shoes. He was emaciated, except for his jutting stomach, and he was missing teeth. Ill luck radiated from him like heat. In his too-large eyes, nascent tears, wild grief, madness.

"Good afternoon," Coffin said, in a strong Nantucket accent.

"A Quaker!" the boy said, regretting his reference to drink and women. "You must be hungry, Brother."

"Aye," Coffin said.

"Right this way," the boy said. "You don't want to eat down here, sir, they'll cheat you, all the cheats are in town on account of all the hangings. They hang three or four a day, and it's been going on for days, and it will go on for days to come. I don't imagine you heard of the Governor's victory?"

The boy took Coffin by the hand, and he misliked its heat, its boniness, but prattled on.

"Yes, Governor Rogers, him that banished the pirates. Well, them rascals that didn't take the King's Pardon was holed up in North Carolina. Governor Rogers caught 'em drunk and asleep, and killed a score of the rogues, and took three hundred prisoners. They've all been condemned, and now they are being hanged."

As the boy led him through the ribald crowd, a woman threw her arms around Coffin and gave him a beery kiss, and the boy screeched and grabbed her wrist, for she held Coffin's purse in her hand. The whore tried to slap the boy with her free hand, but he bit her arm.

"Oy, you rotten son of a bitch!" the whore cried.

"Let go, you cunt!" the boy returned.

The purse fell, the boy scooped it up and took Coffin (who had made no move to defend his property) by the arm and said: "Lively now."

They skirted a small sea of bloody vomit and dashed past two men kicking a third and came at last to a public house bearing a sign with three ships above the door, inscribed *The Duke, the Duchess and the Marquis*.

"Here we are, mate!" The boy grinned so broad Coffin could see the whore's blood on his teeth, then returned the purse and ushered him through the door.

Inside, it was dark and cool and empty save for one table where three men sat. Their conversation ceased as they looked upon Coffin.

"Hello mate," one of the men said. "How d'you do?"

Coffin took off his hat and nodded and sat.

"What'll you have, sir?" the boy asked.

"I do not know, I . . ." Coffin's throat worked, and he looked as if he would cry. "Perhaps, perhaps I should . . ."

"We've some sea pie," the boy said, cutting him off. "D'you care for some sea pie?"

"I do not know."

"I'll bring you a slice, and we'll see if it answers."

"The whole pie," Coffin said.

"It's quite a large pie."

"Bring it, please."

"Well sir, if you want the full pie, that would be," hesitating, gauging, "a crown."

"Very well."

"Very well, sir."

The boy scampered through a door, behind which he and a woman screamed at each other with shocking vehemence.

The three sailors, each with a tin mug of punch, watched him. He stared at his hands and, after a moment, commenced to weep.

"You all right, Brother?" one of the sailors asked.

The one who had spoken was young and fair-haired and handsome, and though he was slender, he had a powerful voice. The second sailor was older, with a grey-and-red pigtail, and toyed with a fine gold watch in his hand. The last was tall, and powerfully built, and bald, with burn scars around his mouth.

Coffin shook his head.

"There now," the handsome sailor said, and came over and clapped Coffin on the shoulder. "Can't be as bad as all that, can it?"

Coffin only put his hands in his face.

"Can't talk about it?" the handsome sailor said. "I'm sure it will all come right." Then: "Come here about the Cruise, have you? The Adventuring Cruise?"

"Suh-Suh-Scudder," the red-haired man called to the handsome sailor.

Coffin looked through his fingers.

"I . . ." Coffin began. Guilt, self-hatred, choking him. "I am hungry," he said, and looked down.

The boy emerged with the pie, and the three sailors, noticing its size (easily enough for four men), its thick brown crust, the greasy juice that oozed from its edges and pooled in its centre, brightened expectantly.

"There now," the boy said, "I told you it was a large pie. I'll fetch the . . ."

Coffin pushed a golden sovereign towards the boy and then, with a whimper, began to shovel the pie into his face, while the others watched, wincing. In less than two minutes, a time both terribly short and horribly long, the pie vanished, and Coffin (whose stomach expanded visibly as he ate) was overcome with nausea. He pushed the plate away and looked at the men, but they looked away, for Coffin's eyes seemed to ask them for something that they could never, ever give.

The boy vanished with the coin.

The young sailor, Scudder, backed away with a nervous smile and rejoined his friends.

Minutes passed with no sound save for the bustle from the street. Merchants calling, distant fiddles, all playing the same song (*did not you promise me / that you would marry me*), a sudden collective laugh, the screech of a whore: "You will not, John Robinson, you will do no such thing!"

The three sailors leaned in and continued their conversation in hushed tones.

Coffin, bloated, laid his head on his folded arms and made no attempt to listen, but the voice of the handsome youth, Scudder, carried across the room.

2

"We weren't drunk, I tell you," Scudder said. "Every jack aboard was sober enough to answer the call of all hands, but there was nothing to be done."

"There ain't nothing so tuh-tuh-terrible as a lee shore," the red-haired man said. "Must have buh-been horrible, especially for a buh-boy."

"I don't remember too much of it," Scudder said. "A great big jolt, all the rigging went slack, everything came apart, and I was in the water. I got hold of a barrel and washed up with Johnny, a Mosquito Indian who'd been with Bellamy since they was Adventuring in canoes. Sold into slavery, the poor bugger. Eight men were hanged in Boston, but I was indentured on account of my youth. That's where I met Billy." Scudder nodded at the big man. "It was a rough place, that plantation, weren't it, Billy? But we stuck together then, and we stick together now."

The big man, Billy Quantrill, said nothing, but his approval was evident.

"So you ain't nuh-never gone out Upon the Account, then?" the red-haired man asked Quantrill.

"No," Quantrill said. "I told you, I was a marine."

"And you've never met Kuh-kuh-Kavanagh, yourself, then?"

"No, never," Scudder said. "I heard his name once or twice."

"Ah well," the red-haired man continued. "He was never muh-much of a sailor. Buh-but he was always liked by the men, that's how he buh-became Quartermaster for Buh-buh-Blackbeard, and he was clever with his coin. After a successful Cruise, many a Gentleman of Fortune gave him some of their earnings, fuh-for to lay aside for 'em, you understand. And he's duh-done very well for himself, and for all the men who gave him their muh-money. He calls 'em his Investors."

"That's all well and good, Johnny," Scudder said. "But if Kavanagh ain't much of a sailor, then who's to be Captain on this Cruise?"

"He's buh-brought Huh-Hornigold with him," John O'Brien, the red-haired man, said.

"The same Hornigold that turned pirate hunter?" Scudder asked. "How could we trust a man like that?"

"I ain't suh-saying we can, Buh-buh-Brother," O'Brien continued. "I ain't saying we should go on this Cuh-Cruise at all, but we duh-duh-duh-damn well should go to the Meeting. There ain't no guarantee a buh-better Cruise will come along. And . . ." O'Brien's eyes locked with Coffin's.

The other two turned to look as Coffin stood and staggered out the front door into the sun. Outside, he bent over, hands on his knees, struggling not to vomit, the sun pressing on his neck as the shame hit him, wave after wave of it, the shame. For although he knew he was not fit to live, every time his life was in danger, he shrank away. Why? Why did he cling to this shameful life?

The door opened with a bang and Coffin started, but it was only the boy, holding his purse.

"Come now, sir, you cannot leave your purse unguarded on the table!" the boy said, pressing it into Coffin's hand. "Count it, count it, it's all there!"

And so he did, three little golden Spanish coins, each worth, approximately, one pound, and the change provided by the boy.

"I believe the men inside are pirates," Coffin said.

The boy looked embarrassed.

"Thou said thy Governor ended piracy?"

"Well," the boy said, "yes, he did."

"And captured pirates in North Carolina?"

"Well, yes, yes, but here is the thing, sir, the Governor took three ships as prizes, the largest of which you see there in the water. A fifty-two-gun French ship, not two years old. We all believed such a fine ship would be sold into the Service. Instead, as you may have heard, the Governor sold it to Mr. James Kavanagh, who sailed with the Governor during the War of the Spanish Succession, and afterwards went out Upon the Account. As many men did! But he took the King's Pardon three years ago and has been an honest merchant ever since. Some have said that he means to go back out Upon the Account, and so many of these sorts are in town. So many that they outnumber the citizens. Do you see?"

Coffin looked down the gentle slope to the massive ship on the sparkling water.

"Sir, perhaps you ought to come in and have a glass with our other guests," the boy continued. "You could stand them a drink. Then you will see that they are not so bad, and they will see that you are an Honest Fellow."

"How can I get on that ship?" Coffin asked.

"The *Saoirse*? Every man in the Bahamas wants to sail upon her, on account of the rumours, you understand."

"I must get on that ship," Coffin said, and turned his eyes upon the boy, who felt the grisly radiance of the man's ill luck.

"Sir, I must say again—"

"Here," Coffin said, and pressed the purse into the boy's hands.

Three guineas, an unthinkable fortune to a boy who scraped for every farthing. Still, a voice whispered *don't take it, it's cursed*. And yet . . . the heaviness of the little coins.

The boy's off-kilter eyes looked at nothing.

"I implore thee, my friend," Coffin said, tears in his eyes. "Please, I must, I must sail upon that ship."

"But why?"

"I cannot . . . I have nowhere else . . . I must . . . I must be Damned. I am Damned. Only bring me to the ship, I ask nothing more of thee."

Unlucky, unlucky, the voice whispered to the boy, but his whole life, his worldly effects, his person, his past, present, and prospects, were not worth three guineas in ready money.

"Very well, sir," he said. "Come with me."

3

They spent an hour wandering along the wharf, without success. No one would row the short distance out to the ship, even for a golden guinea. They were either afraid of Kavanagh, or anxious to curry his favour, or they did not like the look of Coffin. All they accomplished was to attract the attention of a gang of seedy followers.

"You see it cannot be done." The boy was swinging his head to bring his disobedient eyes to bear upon their pursuers when a red-faced man barrelled up to them.

"I'll take you out to the boat," he said. "I'll take you out for a guinea, and I'll bring you back for free, once they tell you to shove off."

At the man's jolly boat, Coffin paid the fare and made as if to give the boy his last two coins. But the boy only took one.

"Fare thee well," Coffin said.

The red-faced man took up the oars and the boy watched as they made their slow way over the surf out to the ship.

The *Saoirse* loomed, gunports open and sails hung to dry in the calm. She was freshly painted and had a crudely carved shark as a figurehead.

When they came into the shadow of the ship, a man leaned over the rail and shouted: "Bugger off!"

Coffin stood, defeat stamped into every pathetic inch of his person. "Please!"

"No," the man shouted down. "Be off with you."

"Please!" Coffin said. "I will do anything to come aboard."

"No," the man said again, and vanished.

"Well, there it is," the red-faced man said. "Shall I take you back now?"

Coffin pressed his hands into his eyes, gasped for breath, then said: "Bring me round the bow."

"You ain't thinking of going on board, mate?" the red-faced man said. "They'll kill you."

"Bring me around the bow," Coffin said again.

The man grunted and pulled so hard on the oars that Coffin almost fell over.

A scaffold hung beneath the figurehead. Coffin grabbed it and pulled himself out of the little boat.

"Aw, mate," the red-faced man said, "they'll kill you."

"Oy!" came a furious voice. "What in the damn hells do you think you're doing, you whoreson sodomite?"

"Come on, drop down, mate," the red-faced man said. "You can have your coin back."

Coffin drew a knife from his trousers, and as he set to work, carving around the shark's eyes, he felt himself calm.

Feet thumped on the deck, an angry shout, happy ones, laughter.

"Come on, mate!" the red-faced man cried.

"I thank thee, friend," Coffin called down.

"Goddamn lunatic," the red-faced man said, and hauled on his oars, moving to a safe distance.

Coffin carved, and wood shavings dropped down onto his chest or fluttered past him to the sea. A door flew open and a half-dozen men armed with clubs and hatchets came onto the head and leaned over the rail and looked down to where Coffin clung to the wooden shark.

"I told you to bugger off," a man said, broad, big-bellied, missing his left leg below the hip. He leaned on a crutch and held a pistol in one hand. "Now you've gone and done it."

"Please let me join thy crew," Coffin said.

"No, damn you, we've told you, go to the Meeting. No one's allowed aboard until then."

"The boat's left him," another voice said.

The one-legged man pointed a pistol at Coffin. "You can come up here and we shall give you the Sweats and you may go home on the next boat," he said. "Or I'll shoot you now."

Coffin returned to carving. How pleasant it was in this moment to be unafraid.

"All right, then," the one-legged man said, cocking his pistol and aiming it.

A high, unpleasant voice shrilled out. "Put that away!"

"He's a stowaway, Mr. Apollo," the one-legged man said. "And he won't come up."

"Won't he?" Apollo said. "Well, if he won't follow orders, he'll fit in nicely."

"We don't have to take your orders," the one-legged man snapped back. "We're the owners of this vessel. And the Taoiseach told you, on behalf of all of us . . ."

Apollo shoved his way forward, leaned over the rail, and looked at Coffin and his handiwork. He frowned, reached out, and brushed a few shavings away. In the short time Coffin had been at work, the difference was apparent. Before, the shark's eye had been a bulge on the side of a piece of wood. Now it had the glassy, hungry, indifferent glare of the deadliest fish in the sea.

Apollo was a little man, marred by the pox, hair cropped. He had the angry strutting posture of a fighting cock, a spit-and-polish man, a Tartar. "What is your name, sailor?" Apollo said.

"Obed Coffin, sir."

"Coffin, eh? Well, it just so happens that I have a job for you."

A murmur of displeasure from the other men.

"Aren't afraid of hard work, are you?" Apollo asked.

"No, sir."

"Well, I'm not the Captain of this vessel, still less its owner, and I can't promise you a thing. However, if you work hard, I shall put in a good word for you."

"My thanks to thee, sir," Coffin said.

He took Apollo's hand and was hauled aboard into that hostile crowd.

"The Taoiseach said—" the one-legged man began.

"The Captain told me to ready the ship, Tulip!" Apollo shouted. "If you'd help me, I'd have no need of stowaways. Now come along, you, we've work to do."

The sailors parted and Coffin followed Apollo through the door to the upper deck. Directly before them was the stove, set on bricks. Copper pots simmered; impossibly, Coffin was hungry again. Apollo led him down the steep companionway steps to the lower deck, and then down another set of steps to the orlop.

Below the water level there were no gunports, but the hatches were open and the brilliant sun came down in distinct beams in which swam motes of dust. They stooped and wove through the little rough cabins, Apollo quickly, Coffin cautious in the dark, until at last they dropped down through an open grating into the hold, lit by oil lamps hanging from the beams. Negroes stood in the darkness, holding shovels.

Coffin breathed in. The air smelled faintly of smoke and strongly of vinegar.

"We're shifting the ballast," Apollo said.

And indeed they were, digging up the layer of loose shingle and piling it to one side, pulling up the iron bars beneath and hauling them aft.

"Aye sir," Coffin said.

No one offered him a shovel, and so he bent down and lifted a pig of iron and stumbled aft, bent double in the dark.

When at last they came up for their dinner, it was as dark above as it was below. They were served porridge, which Coffin wolfed down alone, for the Negroes sat at a table together and did not invite him. After his meal, Coffin went back to the head and set to work on the figurehead. After an hour or so, Apollo came forward to inspect the work by lamplight, and told Coffin that when he was done he might carve the taffrail.

Coffin nodded. He worked until after midnight, to avoid his dreams. Yet still, when he closed his eyes, they came. He dreamed of horrible screaming from the belly of the ship. Darkness lit up by Hellfire. An emaciated monster on a pile of corpses, gnawing on limbs. Wild and empty eyes staring from his own face. He woke himself with his own cries, as the other men shouted at him to shut up, to shut the hell up or they would damn well shut him up. Other men shouted in nightmares of their own, that the Spanish were coming! the Spanish were coming! And other men, drunk, laughed at all the bedlam.

Coffin gave up on sleeping and went up, gathered the scaffold, and carried it all the way to the cabin at the stern of the ship. The forward part of the cabin was divided into two, the sleeping chamber for the Captain on the larboard side and the dining cabin to port. Past these two rooms was the Great Cabin, a large space with chequered floor and decorations on the walls and a massive table and chairs, all for the Captain's personal use. And past the Great Cabin, through the stern windows, was the stern gallery, a short balcony over the sea. Coffin hung the scaffolding over the side and began to carve a simple pattern of overlapping waves upon the taffrail. He was so entranced in his work that he did not notice the approaching gig until it bumped into the hull of the ship, and he heard the Captain's voice.

4

Two men scrambled aboard, then turned and hauled up a series of heavy chests.

"Avast there!" a loud Irish voice rang out. "Those papers are for the Great Cabin, not the master's. Hang it, man, bring 'em all into the Great Cabin and I'll take care of it tomorrow."

The order was greeted with a hooting noise, the call of a natural idiot.

They had a lantern with them, and from his place in the darkness, hanging from the stern of the ship, Coffin watched them come into the Great Cabin and put five locked chests under the table. There were two Negroes, a white man, and a boy. Once the work was done, the boy hung the lantern from a beam.

"Fetch the whiskey, Cian," the white man said, and pulled a sheet from a large object in the corner, revealing a Gaelic harp. He sat down and strummed the strings.

The boy, Cian, distributed the drinks, and had one himself though he looked drunk already. He and the white man took turns shouting obscene toasts, to the Devil and all his retinue (Beelzebub, Moloch, and Belial), and to the Old Pretender, and to the whores of Kingston and Havana.

One of the Negroes, the smaller, foolish one, who'd hooted, shambled out onto the stern gallery holding a fishing pole and saw Coffin. He pointed, whinnied, and danced. The other men rushed onto the gallery. The white man pointed a pistol at Coffin's heart and said coldly: "I don't know you. Who the Devil are you?"

Coffin's throat worked. Here was the thing he longed for, death, but he was afraid again! Coward, coward, coward, oh God, thou sinful coward.

"I asked you a question," the man with the pistol said.

"Obed Coffin, sir. I was carving thy taffrail."

"Who let you aboard?" the man said.

"Mr. Apollo."

The man narrowed his eyes. "He let you aboard, did he? Don't lie to me now."

"He asked me if I was afraid of work," Coffin said, babbling a little. "He told me to carve the taffrail, he . . ."

The gun lowered, and the man said: "Well, you had better come in and have a drink."

"Sir, I—"

"Leave that and come in. I am the Captain of this vessel. My name is Jim Kavanagh."

And so Coffin climbed over the rail and followed the men into the Great Cabin and sat down at the table. The lamp tilted as the ship rocked. He could not see the other men so well.

Kavanagh poured a drink into a silver cup and pushed it over. "A toast, then. What shall we drink to?"

"I do not drink, sir."

The boy laughed.

"A Quaker, are you?" Kavanagh said, leaning into the lamplight.

"Aye sir."

"A Nantucketer, I take it? A whaling man?"

"Aye sir."

"And you know what sort of Cruise this is, do you? You know this is what some men might call an Adventuring Cruise? A Private Cruise? A ship out Upon Her Own Account?"

"Aye." Here Coffin's eyes flicked down, and Kavanagh said: "Look at me. Look at me when you're talking to me, Coffin."

Coffin raised his eyes. Kavanagh looked to be in his late thirties; his black hair was receding and he had a pronounced widow's peak. The hand holding the silver cup was missing two fingers. The white of his left eye was almost orange (yellow from jaundice and red with broken blood vessels) while the other was clear; Coffin realized it was made of glass. Glass eye or no, the Captain had a very direct, hard way of looking at a man, as if he was trying to guess his weight.

"You ain't never been out Upon the Account before, you?"

"Nay, sir."

"You can hand, reef, and steer?"

"Aye, Captain."

"And row a boat, I suppose?"

"Aye."

"And throw a harpoon, I reckon?"

"Aye."

"Why did you leave off whaling?"

"My ship was sunk," he said. "All hands lost, save myself." Coffin's eyes were down again.

"Whyn't you go back to Nantucket?"

"I can never go back," Coffin said.

"Oh no? Why's that?"

"I cannot."

"Well," Kavanagh said. "That don't mean that this is the Cruise for you. This ain't the Cruise for Quakers, Brother. Ever fired a gun in anger?"

"Nay, sir."

"Killing a man ain't like killing a whale, you know."

At this, Coffin raised his eyes. "Has thou killed a whale?"

Kavanagh kept Coffin fixed with his hard and dirty eye and said: "Can't say that I have."

"There is not much difference."

"Oh no?" Kavanagh said. Abruptly amused. "So it's like that."

Kavanagh plucked out his glass eye and set it spinning on the table in front of him and leaned forward and stared, very hard, at Coffin. Coffin did not think he had ever been so conscious of a powerful mind at work.

The eye lost speed, wobbled, stopped with a clunk, and the Captain smiled; the distant, calculating air was gone. He clapped his mangled hand to the base of Coffin's neck and looked straight into his eyes.

"Well, Brother Coffin, you may stay aboard for now, although I can't promise you'll be selected for the Company. You shall have to attend the Meeting, and sign the Articles, and only afterwards shall the Company be selected, and you've no one to vouch for you."

"I thank thee, sir."

"And you'll have to learn our ways," Kavanagh said, sitting back down. "First, you oughtn't to call me sir. We're all Brothers aboard this Cruise. You may call me Brother Kavanagh, or Captain."

"Aye, Captain."

"And second," Kavanagh said, "you must drink with your Brothers. We cannot trust a sober man. A man who don't drink is liable to be in a Plot against the Company, or, worse, a Presbyterian."

Coffin took the silver cup from Kavanagh. It seemed very full.

"What shall we drink to?" Kavanagh said.

"A successful voyage," Coffin replied.

"Well, that ain't colourful, but it'll get us under way. Gentlemen, to a successful voyage."

Kavanagh downed his rum. Coffin saw that Kavanagh was already drunk, very drunk, and so were the other men at the table. Coffin quaffed half the cup and choked it back up again. Disapproving looks. The boy shook his head.

Coffin got it down, but his throat felt scraped raw and his stomach churned.

"A drink with you," the boy said.

"This is my son, Cian, the ship's clerk, the apple of my eye." Kavanagh leaned back from the table into shadow.

"Your health, shipmate," Cian said, raising his glass, his eyes mischievous.

Coffin drank with him. He drank with Quaque, the big, silent Negro, with scars on his face and great magnificent sharpened teeth, and with Benjamin, the idiot Negro, who'd found him.

After a few more drinks, Coffin went outside and threw up over the rail. Time passed. Eventually he became aware that Kavanagh stood above him, and he started, afraid.

"Ho there," Kavanagh said. "A little jumpy, Brother?"

Coffin leaned on the rail.

"That's fine work," Kavanagh said. "You weren't a carpenter, though?"

"Nay," Coffin said.

"Second mate?"

"First mate."

"Young to be first mate," Kavanagh said. "Must be very 'fishy.' Ain't that what the whalers say?"

"Aye."

"A wife back in Nantucket, I suppose?"

"Aye."

"A babe too, more than likely?"

"Aye."

"But you can't go back?" Kavanagh said. "On account of how you killed a man?"

Coffin was quiet; Kavanagh thought perhaps he had passed out.

"I am Damned, Captain. I can't go back."

Kavanagh did not make a sound. Coffin did not look at him; he did not see him convulse with silent laughter.

5

Coffin slept on the stern gallery, until he was awoken by a loud voice crying: "I specifically told him it was just for show!"

Kavanagh, apologetic: "I know, he knows, everyone knows."

Coffin sat up, his head throbbing, and stood to look through the stern windows into the Great Cabin. A man in a powdered wig sat at the table with Kavanagh; the latter saw Coffin and shook his head. Coffin obligingly shrank out of view.

"I served him with the writ myself," the man in the wig went on, "and I told him our action was only a formality! I told him we would never enforce it against him, personally!"

"I know, mate, I'm sorry, I was only having a fly at you."

"But the shame of it," the voice went on. "The shame of it! The hero of the Bahamas imprisoned for debt! Still bloodied and burned from his famous victory! And as you point out, my name on the damned writ!" The man sounded on the verge of tears.

"Oh, there was plenty of writs," Kavanagh said. "Plenty more than yours, mate. And how was you to know his Investors would leave him in the lurch? And the Crown?"

"I still say we might have done something. We might have appealed to the Crown, we might have taken a collection, we might have done something!"

"Aye sir," Kavanagh said. "It's a shame, it's a great loss for all of us that invested in this colony. Now we're all caught between the Devil and the deep blue sea. For once the Governor departs, who'll stop them damned pirates from coming back?"

"Who indeed?" the man in the wig said, the ingenuous regret evaporating from his voice, leaving his tone quite dry. "Well sir, I cannot speak for you, but as for myself, in the circumstances, I believe I shall seek to liquidate my chattels and retire to my estates upon Harbour Island. Since you need to provision your ship, I thought perhaps I would see whether we could come to an arrangement."

"Well now, what were you thinking?"

Their voices lowered, so Coffin could not hear, until the man in the wig prostested that such prices were little better than piracy, and Kavanagh answered him back that little better than piracy was still better than piracy, and the man in the wig said that he wondered that Kavanagh felt he had time to haggle, and was he sure of his own safety with the Governor gone, and Kavanagh replied that while he was touched by the little man's concern, there were many merchants in Nassau but only one man-of-war to be victualled, and on they went, while Coffin returned to carving.

There were perhaps five fingers between the sun and the sea when the door opened and Kavanagh came out on the stern gallery with the man in the wig. Coffin stood, brushing the shavings off his lap.

"Mr. Coffin, meet Mr. Dennyson," Kavanagh said. "We have just concluded a Bit of Business."

"Good morning, Mr. Dennyson," Coffin said.

"A carpenter, are you?" Dennyson said. He was a fat little man, erect and forceful.

"I know a little," Coffin said. "But I was never a ship's carpenter."

"You were a whaler?"

"Aye sir."

"Well, there's always work for carpenters," Dennyson said. "We're damned short of carpenters aboard my ships."

"My thanks to thee, but I wish to stay with this ship."

"Are you sure? I can pay three and ten a month. Honest money for honest work."

"I thank thee, but nay."

"Thought so," Kavanagh said. When Dennyson looked as if he would say more, Kavanagh said, "Come sir, everyone must go to the Devil in their own way. Let me see you off. Coffin, leave off carving and wait for me here. I should like to begin victualling as soon as the water is aboard."

Coffin waited for Kavanagh inside the Great Cabin. The daylight streamed through the stern windows and the skylight. Two cannons, the stern chasers, were lashed to either side of the room. The walls were panelled and decorated with crossed swords and oil portraits, presumably of the Captain's family. A hutch contained china and silverware, and there were dressers and a chest for clothes. The little boy, Cian, was asleep upon a chaise longue.

Coffin's attention was drawn to a weapon mounted on the wall. It looked to be an expensive musket—blued steel, polished mahogany stock, the hammers carved like leaping dolphins, a silver plate with a man's name inscribed. Only the barrel had been crudely sawn off, so the inscription was truncated, reading: *mes McIntyre, Esq.*

"D'you like it?" asked Kavanagh.

Coffin turned. Kavanagh, standing in the door to the dining room, answered the unspoken question:

"May of 1718, we returned to Nassau, all of Blackbeard's men, divided the plunder and dissolved the Company. As you might expect, the men celebrated, and became rowdy. A friend of mine, Mark Rediker was his name—everyone called him Red Legs—found himself in an argument over a whore, and there was nothing for it but he must have a duel, then and there, though we all Damned him for a fool, and told him to wait till he was sober. Wouldn't hear of it. Only he had no pistols, and I would be Damned myself if I'd give him one of mine. So he took that weapon you see there, which he'd earned when he Gained the Commission of *La Concorde* in the fall of '17, and sawed off the barrel, and the damn fools fought their duel on the beach just before dawn, and they killed each other, though they forgave each other before the end, a man of God like yourself will be happy to hear. Red Legs left to me all his worldly effects, only he'd already spent it all, in one night. The musket was all that's left." Kavanagh smiled. "These are the men with whom you now sail, Brother Coffin."

"Aye, Captain," Coffin said. "Did thou say thou wishest to bring the water aboard? For Mr. Apollo has been shifting the ballast, and I believe—"

Kavanagh grunted. "Come with me."

They found Apollo by the stove, eating some very thin gruel and talking to himself, furious, his face contorted with emotion, as if he was under attack. He mastered himself and said: "Good morning, sir."

"Damn you, Apollo," Kavanagh said. "I told you we must sail as soon as possible. I told you we needed everything ready! I never told you to play around with the bleeding ballast! And now I hear you want to move the damn masts?"

"But sir," Apollo said, "this is not one of your fore-and-aft-rigged Bermuda sloops, she's a square-rigged, fifty-gun man-of-war. If you don't shift her trim, she won't be able to sail as near the wind as a fighting ship must if she hopes to catch anything."

"And I tell you, sir," Kavanagh said, "that we must take our victuals aboard tomorrow, and so we must take our water on board today. Is that clear?"

"Perfectly clear," Apollo said.

Kavanagh turned to Coffin. "Once the ballast is sorted, take a boat and some Negroes and bring the water aboard."

"Aye, Captain," Coffin said.

There followed a frantic scramble down in the dark as Negroes and white men put the pig iron in place and shovelled the shingle on top. Once it was done, Coffin and Quaque and three more stout Negroes took out the boats, the empty casks bobbing behind them. New Providence Island had a fine spring within easy reach, which had been one of its chief attractions for pirates. Soon they had the great casks filled. They rolled them back to the water and then towed the almost-sunken barrels back and hoisted them up the side with rope and pulley. The men aboard rolled them to the open hatches and lowered them down, one after another, into the hold, where they were set up on top of the shingle.

6

In the mid-afternoon, as Quaque and Coffin took their lunch together (Quaque, a West African canoeman, spoke flawless English and had impeccable manners), a boat arrived carrying a dozen townsfolk. A man called out:

"Kavanagh! Damn you, Kavanagh, we know you're in there! You cheated us, you black pirate!"

Kavanagh did not emerge. Instead, the one-legged man, whom everyone called Tulip, poked his head out of a gunport.

"Where's Kavanagh?" the spokesman of the townspeople shouted.

"Be off with you," Tulip shouted back.

"We will not be off! He cheated us!"

"He sold us his enterprises," a woman shouted, "and all the while he knew the Governor was leaving!"

"I'd never have bought 'is warehouse 'ad I known," another added.

"I said be off with you." To punctuate Tulip's words, a cannon rolled out through another gunport. "Or we'll blow the lot of you out of the water!"

"You threaten us, you black scoundrel, how dare—"

The cannon roared, tremendous, the peremptory injunction of a furious god, spraying the petitioners with smoke and glowing bits of wadding. The merchants leapt, and cried, and plied the oars in different directions, yet soon enough they'd turned their boat and fled.

Some of the men on board laughed, and some cursed, and some paid no attention at all. Tulip watched the merchants until they reached the shore, his expression thoughtful.

Eventually Coffin asked:

"Shall the Governor Rogers truly be arrested for debt?"

"Aye," Quaque said. "We dined with him last night, to conclude the purchase of this ship, along with all the charts and logs from his circumnavigation. He has liberated all his slaves and will be leaving in a day or two. From what I understand, his governorship was a private venture. He had all the expenses of putting down the pirates and restoring the fort, and was to make his money off duties and such. But the colony never prospered, for the soil is no good for sugar or cotton. Even the treasure of the pirates, and this ship, was not enough to pay off his creditors."

"Who will be the next Governor?"

"Why, no one," Quaque said, flashing his smile. "Who would want to be Governor of the Bahamas?"

Coffin looked to the shore. There had been no hangings today, but the rotting bodies in the gibbets still spun in the sea breeze.

Kavanagh came on deck. "Good work, lads!" he said. "Let's be off for our Meeting."

7

Apollo and a group of Investors remained aboard, while the rest took the boats due north to Hog Island, a sliver of land a thousand feet wide, fringed with white beaches and curving palms that bounced in the wind. They pulled the boats up the beach and walked to the north shore, where the ocean stretched, a light and clear blue. Fish jumped and birds sprinted just ahead of the waves.

A team of cooks had been hard at work. Bonfires had burned all morning in the sand, and frameworks of wood had been set over the coals to smoke sides of beef and pork in the old buccaneer style. In other places hot stones had been buried with wet leaves and baskets of potatoes, squash, plantains, and living lobsters and crabs and mussels and clams. Great iron pots boiled with hot peppers and shrimp. Long tables beneath canopies of old sails and palm fronds bore bananas, lemons, limes, mangoes, oranges (sweet and sour), and coconuts, along with fresh bread and wheels of cheese, and sacks of pure white sugar. Six hogsheads of rum in great casks had been tapped and half buried in the sand.

At the appointed hour, eight hundred Gentlemen of Fortune crossed the water from Nassau in a great migratory horde. Starved and pinched and wearing rags, they might have been newly escaped prisoners but for their tans. Kavanagh's voice boomed as he wove through the crowd, shaking hands and pounding men on the back and addressing each by name (the Taoiseach had a prodigious memory for names and faces), and all of them ate and drank, frantically, toasting the Taoiseach with all their hearts. Coffin ate, and ate, and ate, until he became ill, shuddering cramps dancing up and down his body, and yet still he ate, and at last he sat down in the sand with his back to the food so he could not see it. As the sunset blazed to the west, crabs came out and marched along the beach, and the pirates sang and danced, pirouetting arm in arm, and some fell down dead drunk into pools of vomit.

Kavanagh climbed on a table and fired a pistol in the air.

"Gentlemen!" he shouted, his powerful voice ringing out above the clamour of eight hundred men. "Gentlemen!"

Eight hundred heads turned, eight hundred men cheered.

"The Taoiseach!" they cried. "Hip, hip, hurray!"

"Gentlemen," Kavanagh cried, "come closer! Come closer! I'm about to call this Meeting to order."

The sun had set, but a nearby fire illuminated his face, and the faces of the men. Kavanagh had taken a drink every time his name had been toasted, and it had been toasted often, and the liquor weighed on him, but he was not drunk.

"Most of you here know me, and I believe I know most of you, but for those of you that don't, Jimmy Kavanagh is my name. I sailed with Woodes Rogers on his Cruise around the world, and I came to Nassau in 1713. I sailed with Hornigold, then with Teach, and I took the King's Pardon in the year '18. After every Adventure I put a little aside, and as I prospered, some of my friends asked me to do the same for them. Now it ain't genteel to boast, but anyone can see how me and my Investors have prospered. So you know, gentlemen, I ain't going to sea because I'm a desperate man. I'm going to sea because this Cruise is the best chance for Wealth and Plunder since the days of Henry Avery. A fifty-two-gun ship, a broadside of 448 pounds. Fully stocked and supplied, with spars and sails and powder and shot and small arms. None of your scrounging and scrimmaging for a crossjack yard. And as for the crew, we'll have caulkers and gunners and navigators, a surgeon with two mates, none of them pressed or forced, and we'll have our pick of Able Seamen. There's never been more trade afloat, and fewer pirates, and all the merchants think we're licked, so they won't be ready! Lastly, my commercial contacts have allowed me to acquire certain intelligence. I can't tell you the nature of this intelligence until we're at sea, but I can assure you the prizes will make the fortune of every man here ten times over. Ten times, I tell you!"

Respectful silence, broken by a man vomiting.

"Now Zane," Kavanagh called. "I did tell you to drink it handsomely, didn't I? Someone lay him on his side. On his side, mind you.

"Well, gentlemen, those are my bona fides, and if there are no questions on 'em, we'll get down to the business of this meeting: drafting the Articles."

"I have a question," a man shouted, "about your fucking bona fides."

The crowd pivoted like a school of fish.

By the edge of the trees, illuminated by a bonfire, stood a small knot of men, every one of them armed. At their head stood a man Coffin did not recognize. He was lean and swarthy, with a thick beard but no moustache, and a terrible scar across his mouth that made his lips look like worms, diabolical in the glow of the fires and the light of the moon.

Silence, save for the growling and snapping of the dying fires.

"I have a question," the man repeated. "How the hell did your old shipmate Woodes Rogers find his way through the shoals off Ocracoke Island? In the dark?"

"Why, I don't know, George," Kavanagh said.

"Oh, I think you do," George Lowther said. "Them shoals move all the time, but you had the charts, didn't you? After all, weren't you selling supplies to every Gentleman of Fortune in North Carolina?"

"Lots of men had them charts," Kavanagh said. "D'you have any proof?"

"Proof!" Lowther said. "Where'd you get that ship floating out there? *Cui bono*, that's my proof."

"*Cui bono*," Kavanagh said, amused. "George, I don't know if you've been following the trial of Charles Eden, the former Governor of North Carolina. A Mr. William Bell testified that Blackbeard attacked him and his son, a boy of eleven years, and robbed 'em of sixty pounds and a box of clay pipes." To the crowd: "Clay fucking pipes, gentlemen. The great Blackbeard." To Lowther: "*Cui bono*? Perhaps Mr. William Bell gave Rogers his bleeding chart. Who could blame him?"

"Aye, he's telling tales now, thanks to you."

"Thanks to me?" Kavanagh said, not to Lowther but to the crowd. "The little folk used to love us. Why wouldn't they? We robbed the Spanish and brought their gold to the colonies, and they'd buy from us at half price and sell to us for double. In the old days they'd never turn informer! By the Powers, that's what we tried to tell you all back in the year '16! But none of you listened. Instead, we sawed off the bough we was sitting on. And then you and Vane and the rest of you, with your dirty tricks. Burning men's fingers with slow matches? Hoisting men up and dropping 'em down and hoisting 'em back up a dozen times? Cutting off their lips and frying them in pans making 'em eat 'em? *Cui bono*? Why, don't you see it, you damned fool? Everyone benefited."

"All that was after the Commonwealth fell!" Lowther cried. "On account of men like you taking the Pardon!"

"Most of the men here took the Pardon," Kavanagh said. "But I suppose we're all traitors to you."

"Aye," Lowther said, glaring. "You're a pack of scurvy dogs, cowards, all of you! None of you care for your liberty!"

"Liberty?" Kavanagh said. "There ain't no forced men here tonight, George. That's more than can be said of many a man that sailed with you. George Lowther never scrupled to force a man if he was short a carpenter."

"I didn't come here to bandy words with you," Lowther said. "I come here to tell everyone that the Commonwealth will be back! Every man that stays in Nassau will be accounted as a true Brother! Every man that goes with Kavanagh is a dog! Begging for scraps!"

"You're the one down with the dogs," Kavanagh said.

"God damn you all," Lowther said. "God damn every one of you!"

Men surged at Lowther, and Lowther ran towards the trees, and weapons cracked as Lowther's supporters, hidden by night, fired upon his pursuers. For a while all was confusion, and Coffin lost sight of who was who in the dark outside the ambit of the fires.

Lowther escaped to his boat, and Kavanagh soon called off the pursuers, shouting: "If there are no further personal reflections, the Meeting will please come to order. The secretary pro tem will read our draft Articles."

8

The secretary was Kavanagh's son, Cian, whom the men greeted with warm applause. He turned his back to the fire and lifted his paper and read:

1) The Captain and his Officers shall have authority when the Ship is in action, but except as otherwise stated in these Articles, the Ship shall be governed by the Majority and every man shall have an equal vote in the affairs of moment regardless of his share.

2) Every man has equal title to the fresh provisions or strong liquors seized from a prize, and may use them at pleasure, unless a scarcity makes necessary, for the good of all, to declare a retrenchment.

3) Every man has the right to the following daily provisions, paid for by the Investors: eight pints of beer, one pint of rum; one pound of salt beef or pork, one pound of biscuit. As well as oatmeal, dried peas, butter and cheese as are traditionally made available according to the Custom of the Royal Navy.

Here the men gave a happy shout.

4) The Investors shall receive one hundred and fifty shares of prize. The Mates shall receive two shares; the Quartermaster, Sailing Master, Boatswain, Gunner, Carpenter, and Surgeon, one share and a half; the Petty Officers one and a quarter; Able Seamen one share; and Negroes one half share.

5) Until each man has earned £1,000, no man shall speak anything tending to the breaking of the Company, or shall by any means endeavour to desert or quit the Company.

6) If any man should lose a limb, or become a cripple in the service of the Company, he is to have 800 pieces of eight, out of the public stock, and for lesser hurts, proportionately.

7) He that sees a sail first shall have the best pistol or small arm aboard her. Otherwise, any man who finds any valuable on board any prize to the value of a piece of eight shall deliver it to the Quartermaster in the space of twenty-four hours.

8) No person shall game at cards or dice for money.

9) Lights and candles to be put out at eight o'clock at night: any drinking or dancing after that hour must be done on the open deck.

10) In the hold, no man shall snap his arms, or smoke tobacco without a cap to his pipe, or carry a candle lighted without a lanthorn.

11) No boy or woman shall be allowed on board the ship, and no man shall meddle with any prurient woman.

12) Private Quarrels to be ended on shore, at sword and pistol.

13) Any man who contravenes these Articles shall suffer such punishment as the Captain and the majority of the Company shall think fit.

14) James Kavanagh shall serve as Captain, and he shall appoint the Ship's Officers, and shall set the watches, messes, and sleeping quarters, which decisions shall not be subject to the will of the Company.

15) In all other respects the Company shall be governed by the Customs of the Coast.

"Now then," Kavanagh said. "Are there any Amendments proposed to the Articles?"

A murmur like a wave through the crowd.

"Brother Chairman," a man said.

"The chair recognizes Brother Lewis," Kavanagh said.

"Who do you propose as the Ship's Officers?"

"I ain't decided on every one of 'em, Brother Lewis," Kavanagh said. "The dear knows there's five or six men here as would have been right welcome as carpenter on many a Cruise I've been on. However, the mates shall be Tom Apollo and Benjamin Hornigold."

Silence, hissing whispers.

"I knew it," a voice called from the darkness. "I knowed there'd be a catch."

"Silence there!" Kavanagh said. "You ain't got the floor!"

"I'm done, Brother," Lewis said, and stepped back.

"Is there anyone else who wants to speak?" Kavanagh said.

A tall, stooped man stepped into the firelight, long arms, big ears, shirtless, intricate tattoos, brands, and lash marks over his body.

"Brother Chairman," the man said.

"The chair recognizes Brother Dickens," Kavanagh said.

"Thankee, Jim," Dickens said. "Brothers, a sweet-sailing ship like the *Saoirse* costs near on ten thousand pounds. I didn't expect no equal distributions. One hundred fifty shares with a crew of four hundred is one-fourth, nearabouts, so all right then. But no elections for Captain? How are we to be protected against Tyranny?"

"Well, Brother," Kavanagh said, "this Cruise ain't the regular thing. I must protect my Investor's investment."

"Well, us jacks have our rights too," Dickens said. "That's the Custom of the Coast, it is."

"Brother Chairman," another pirate called out.

"The chair recognizes Brother Spry."

"Perhaps couldn't we vote on our officers?" Spry asked. "I say nothing about Apollo, for I don't know him, but Hornigold—the man took bounties on Gentlemen of Fortune, I ain't sure it can be borne."

A murmur.

"Oh no?" Kavanagh cocked an eyebrow. "Well, Spry, you listen here. You can vote in your Quartermaster and he'll see about protecting your rights. As for the mates, I need prime seamen, not make-clever lower-deck Sea Lawyers. I ain't going to end up shipwrecked like Bellamy or marooned like England or caught drunk like Black Bart. If you can't bear taking orders from Hornigold, perhaps this ain't the Cruise for you."

Spry suggested that Kavanagh should imitate Bartholomew Roberts, and propose candidates for the approval of the men, but Kavanagh shook his head and said: "Now gentlemen, I've made it clear, the ship shall be governed by the majority. But I'll have none but the best mates. And that's that."

Upon being granted the floor again, Dickens proposed that the Captain and the Ship's Officers be subject to election, as was the Custom of the Coast. No one seconded the motion.

"Why, you're a pack of puppies," Dickens said. And then, more quietly: "Be damned to that, I'll be blowed if I let a man trample on my rights." And then: "A fucking cabin for himself like a lord. I'll let him know who I am."

"Are there any other proposals?" Kavanagh asked.

"Brother Chairman," Dickens said again.

The crowd shifted. A few groans. Someone said: "Oh, why won't he shut up?"

"The chair recognizes Brother Dickens," Kavanagh said.

"Is it only you to have separate quarters, or the officers as well?"

"I shall have the cabin," Kavanagh said. "And there will be separate quarters for the officers."

Dickens objected, saying separate quarters were contrary to Custom and an affront to dignity and conducive to Tyranny, and brought a motion that the practice be forbidden. This motion was seconded by one of Dickens's supporters, but soundly defeated.

"Is there anyone else who wishes to speak?" Kavanagh said. "Now or forever."

None did.

"Are you ready for the Question?"

"Aye!" some men called.

"As many as are in favour of adopting the Articles, say aye."

"Aye!" they called.

"Write it down in the minutes, lad," Kavanagh said to his son. "It's done."

Behind the bar, a crate was opened and the Bibles came out. The men came forward, in twos and threes, serious and electric, and put their hands on the book and swore, and sealed the oath with a glass of rum mixed with gunpowder. Even Dickens came forward, and all of them embraced, and as the last man (Coffin) drank down his draught, the Negroes fired off crackers that exploded high above the island in full view of the terrified town, red and green and blue, lighting up the pale sand and the clear water.

"You fucking lubbers," Kavanagh shouted. "You never asked me about the music! I might have cheated you on the fucking music!"

Their faces flushed in the firelight, all of them grinning and drunk, all of them shouting and clapping and howling, and of course he hadn't cheated them on the fucking music, no, the fife sang out, clear and fey, and the first fiddle sounded, and then another, and then the drums, and then grinning Benjamin skipped through the press of men, slobbering and whinnying, and on his back he bore Kavanagh's massive harp.

Kavanagh sat on a barrel and took the harp against his shoulder and tucked his chin and stared at nothing as his fingers moved to the strings. Everything hushed as he played the first notes, plaintive and homesick and Irish, and the men swayed, and someone sang in a deep voice in Gaelic, and then the tune changed, and he was playing another song, cheap and cheerful, and the men roared, for the song was *Did not you promise me / that you would marry me*, which had been used as the signal in the Green Cay Mutiny, and had been the anthem of the Brethren of the Coast ever since.

The next morning, Governor Rogers left Nassau with his family, along with most prominent citizens. Many soldiers deserted. The tripartite flag of the pirate Commonwealth, red, blue, and black, flew over many buildings. The pirates awaiting execution waved it through their bars, and mockingly sang at their few remaining guards:

Did not you promise me
That you would marry me?

The desperate merchants of Nassau sent their wares to the *Saoirse*. Firewood and coal, salt pork and salt beef and dried peas and oatmeal and butter and cheese, beer and rum, sacks of biscuit, casks of gunpowder, ropes, spars, sails, pitch, oakum, clothes, hammocks, canvas, and all the little things that were easy to forget, lamp oil and candles and the tools for the armourer, carpenter, and surgeon and medicines for the dispensary—rhubarb and grey powder and hartshorn and quinine and portable soup—paint and brushes and needle and thread, paper for cartridges, buckets and mops, muskets and pistols and cutlasses, all hauled up the side and inspected and noted by Cian, as clerk, and then lowered down into the guts of the ship and stored away in their proper place. Last aboard was the livestock, pigs and geese and ducks and goats, some confined to a manger in the foremost part of the lower deck, and the others in coops on the weather deck or tied to the masts.

They'd intended to post the list of men selected for the Company ashore at first light, but the vicious celebration of the return of the Commonwealth raged more dangerously at dawn than it had at midnight. The steady crack of gunfire, men screaming in pain, the howling of dogs. Past eight, the naked and dirty hordes lay prostrate upon the Nassau beach in a vile carpet, and an armed party went ashore and pasted the list upon the wall of an empty warehouse and then fought their way through a crowd of men, shouting with joy or weeping in dejection or begging for someone to read it for them, mate, was their name on the list? Was their name on the bloody list?

The selectants formed a great mass upon the sand, fairly vibrating with joy, most with no possessions other than their clothes. They were brought aboard, boatload by boatload, where Cian sat at a desk upon the quarterdeck, cursing any man who stepped out of line, to the delight of all those assembled, for Cian was a great favourite. Each man was checked off the master list, assigned a mess, and issued two pairs of duck trousers, two chequered shirts, and a straw hat, as well as a hammock and instructions on where to sling it.

Coffin assisted in the disbursement of these items, and he saw that all three of the men he'd met in the tavern (Scudder, Quantrill, and O'Brien) had joined the Company, along with Dickens, who had complained so vociferously at the Meeting.

Voices reverberated through the wood as all three decks filled with men exploring the ship and finding their place. The ship's bell rang, and the band began to play, and there followed a chaotic period of shuffling and shoving, mostly good-natured, as the men rushed to the lower deck in a shambling mob for their dinner, bare feet thumping on wood.

The men ate on the lower deck, on mess tables that hung between the guns. There they sat, jammed shoulder to shoulder, while the chef of each mess went up to the stove. The cook, a wizened Yoruba, gave each chef a bucket with a pound of pork and bread per man, together with a serving of peas, and endeared himself by adding a dollop of slush, the grease that was skimmed from the top of the pot and was by ancient tradition the cook's prerogative.

Coffin's mess was near the bow. The biscuits were hard and dry, the meat was fatty, tough, and salty (despite having steeped for hours in fresh water), but all was free from mould, weevils, and maggots, and there was plenty of it, and it was what they were used to, and the mood was festive.

After dinner, the chefs went up for their buckets of grog. Coffin did not want to drink, but neither did he wish to be thought in a Plot, so he was relieved when one of his sharp-eyed messmates offered to trade tobacco for his grog. Coffin smoked while the others drank.

"Oy," the man said. "Did ye carve that pipe yourself?"

"Aye," Coffin said. "I shall make one for thee, if thou wish."

"Why, I call that handsome," the man said, approving though still wary. "My name is Harold Hutchins."

"Obed Coffin."

"You're a New Man, are you? First time out Upon the Account?"

"Aye."

Hutchins nodded, and turned to speak to his neighbour, a Negro with a cockney accent called George Beard. The conversation flowed around Coffin like water around a stone, until men began to shout for order. The first Meeting was about to start.

10

Matthew Lewis, who had been appointed armourer, began the Meeting by bringing a motion to serve as chairman pro tem. He was older, bald, and had a reputation as a man dedicated to the Custom of the Coast without being overly radical. His motion was seconded by Horace Spry and, with no other candidates, passed by acclamation.

"Thankee, shipmates," Lewis said, while the cows lowed in the manger behind him. "First, a show of hands for every man who fancies running for Quartermaster."

No one put up their hand. Then a dozen men raised their hands. A half-dozen lowered them. Shouting and laughter. Lewis pointed, called names. Told them that according to the Custom of the Coast they must be sponsored by five men, then called a short recess for the candidates to gather their nominations.

In the end there were three: Robert Dickens, Horace Spry, and the handsome boy, Bradford Scudder, only nineteen years old.

The three candidates drew straws. Spry drew short and so addressed the crowd first. He was a plain-looking man, a little grey, and the men at the back had to strain to hear him.

"Brothers, most of you know me. For those that don't, I sailed under Hornigold, Teach, and Bonnet. I was Quartermaster aboard the *Royal James*, right up until we was taken prisoner. It was I who stopped Bonnet from blowing up the ship, and it was I that planned the escape that saved us from the noose—you may ask any man here about my bona fides. I always stood up for our rights, but I always made sure men did their duty. This Cruise ain't the regular thing, but then, what Cruise ever was? We've a sweet crew, and a sweet ship, and we must keep everything running as sweet as can be, until we've made our thousand pounds."

Some applause and whistling.

Spry moved to the side and Dickens stood, stooping beneath the beams.

"Brothers, you heard Spry, this Cruise ain't the regular thing," Dickens said in his harsh voice. "Whoever heard of separate cabins for the officers on a ship Upon the Account? Whoever heard of a Captain who couldn't be removed by the Common Council? Whoever heard of such an unequal Distribution of spoils? And that ain't all, Brothers. Look how he's set out our messes, with the Irish in the waist, just like the marines on a man-of-war. Where's all the small arms? Locked up aft, just like a man-of-war. I tell you, Brothers, you need a Quartermaster who shall do all in his power to make sure that this Cruise don't turn Tyrannical. And, Brothers, who better than myself? I say nothing against Spry, for he's an Honest Fellow, who never poached on a Brother Pirate, but he told you himself how his last Cruise ended up, all of them coming within a hair of drying in the sun. And as for this boy Scudder, I don't know him, but I know John O'Brien who's a-whispering to him, oh yes. It was O'Brien that turned Vane's crew against him, and we all know how that ended. And so, I say, I'm the man to fight for your Rights, for any fool who gives up his Rights for a little plunder or belly-timber shall have neither."

Dickens's remarks were polarizing; a small number of men cheered wildly, but others hissed and muttered, and some few even heckled, asking why didn't he stay ashore if he felt so strong?

Last was Scudder, nodding his head to a final remark from O'Brien, then beaming and crying out: "Brothers, I ain't never been to Nassau before this month, so perhaps some of you don't know me. Bradford Scudder's my name, I went to sea in the year '11 as a midshipman, I was only a little nipper of nine, only my grandfather arranged it, you see. Spent three years in Port and on Blockade duty, and then I was cast ashore, for my grandparents didn't have enough influence to find me another situation. I sailed as a cabin boy aboard a merchant, on'y the damn captain was a tartar, five damned years later and I still bear the marks!"

Here Scudder turned and showed his back, scarred and welted.

"A dozen lashes on three occasions, Brothers! And me only twelve years old. Well, when our ship was taken by Bellamy, what did I do? Well, I said straight away to the great man, take me with you! Don't leave me here, I said. Give me my liberty! The life of a pirate is the only life for any man of spirit! And didn't they laugh to see me, and they told me, nay, they'd have no boy among them, only I cried."

Here Bradford mock wept, and laughter rippled through the men.

"I cried and wept and stomped my feet . . ."

Bradford stomped his feet, and the men laughed louder.

"And in the end they were forced to take me. And so I learned the life of a pirate from the greatest of all pirates, and I mean no disrespect, gentlemen, to Blackbeard or Vane or La Bouche or Howell Davis or Black Bart or any of 'em, Hornigold even, Bonnet, well, perhaps not Bonnet, as Brother Spry could attest . . ."

The men laughed knowingly.

"And gentlemen, I swear to you that I shall be a friend to every man aboard. Irish, English, Negroes, it is all one and the same to me. I shall always follow the will of the Company. I shall always have the will of the Company as my uppermost concern. For that is the most important principle of all. Gentlemen, Brothers, thank you, thank you for your time."

Warm applause, and Scudder shook the hands of a few men, smiling. Lewis gave the men a few minutes to consider.

11

At Coffin's table, Beard and Hutchins dominated the conversation. Beard was for Dickens, Hutchins was for Spry, and they went back and forth, back and forth, bandying the names Bellamy, Bonnet, Vane, Rackham, Teach, until Hutchins noticed Coffin's puzzlement and said:

"Why, I suppose you don't have a damned notion what's going on, do you?"

Coffin agreed.

"It's like this," Beard said, cutting in. "Hornigold was the first Gentleman of Fortune to come to Nassau, back in 1713, with the war over and nobody having no use for us. And that was the start of our Commonwealth, and a merry time of it we had for many years. Only in the year '18 word came that the Crown was offering a Pardon to all men who would forswear the life of a pirate. And it was the question of the Pardon that divided us. Men like Hornigold were all for taking it, while others would have none of it, saying the life of a pirate was the only life for a man of spirit. The leader of those men was Charlie Vane, and Robert Dickens and John O'Brien were two of his closest mates."

"O'Brien was his closest," Hutchins said, shaking his head.

"And at the beginning, Hornigold had more supporters, but more and more of Hornigold's men went off to take the Pardon in other places—"

"Like North Carolina," Hutchins added.

"—and in the end Vane took the town, locked Hornigold in the fort, put him on trial, even. Of course, that all came to an end when Rogers arrived with his squadron. Vane slipped out—"

"Not before he pulled that trick with the fireship."

"—and went out on quite a Cruise himself, for a time," Beard said. "But he lost the support of his Company when he wouldn't let 'em attack a French ship. And he lost a vote of No Confidence to a young man called Jack Rackham, only it was John O'Brien that arranged it all. That stuttering son of a whore is always plotting something or other."

"Vane was put ashore with a few loyal men—" Hutchins said.

"Including Robert Dickens."

"Aye, and Vane was nabbed and hanged. And by who? None other than Benjamin Hornigold."

"He'd gotten a commission to hunt pirates, the rotten traitor."

"Rackham never amounted to nothing," Beard said. "They took one ship, with a load of golden watches, but they was surprised soon after."

"Drunk, more than likely."

"I heard they was frying some of them watches in pans," Beard said. "Anyway, they dissolved their Company and took the Pardon. Now O'Brien's picked up this lad from somewhere and seems he's doing the whole thing over again."

"Dickens is just as bad," Hutchins said. "O'Brien's a Plotter, and Dickens is a damned fool. Spry's the man for this job."

Beard was about to reply, but Lewis called out that it was time to vote.

It was conducted by a show of hands—Lewis stating a candidate's name, hands raising. There were no irregularities, save that an idiot named Goldie voted for all three candidates.

"Spry 117, Scudder 99, and Dickens 94," Lewis announced.

Dickens's supporters cried out, demanding a recount, and this question was put by Lewis to the assembly and it was rejected.

No one had received the required majority, and so Scudder and Spry gave a second speech.

Scudder drew short and went first, and this time, in a longer, more artificial speech, attempted to cast himself as the guardian of the Liberties of the crew, invoking Bellamy's invective against the puppies of rich men. Dickens's supporters mocked him.

Spry's speech was brief.

"Brothers, I've nothing to say against this boy, but if you make him the Quartermaster of a crew of four hundred of the hardest fucking salts ever to sail the seven seas, you will damn well get what you deserve. You damned lubbers were starving upon the beach yesterday. And why? Because you couldn't never think about tomorrow. Well, think of it now, Brothers."

When the vote came this time, there was no need for a firm count. Spry picked up almost all of Dickens's supporters, and a good portion of Scudder's supporters reconsidered once they realized he might actually win.

"Congratulations to Spry," Lewis said. "The Quartermaster of the *Saoirse*!"

"Three cheers for Spry!" Scudder said.

These were given.

12

At the first bell of the first watch, Coffin strung his hammock from the beams with the other men and climbed in (right leg in with the left hand to steady, then jump and twist and watch you don't tumble out the other side, mate) and formed a packed floating carpet of men, snoring and farting and occasionally screaming in terror.

At four the next morning, the Negroes commenced to clean the deck, dumping sand on the wood and pumping up water and on their knees grinding the planks with the big white holystones, before mopping and drying. The bosun's mate shrilled out on the fife and Apollo himself descended to the lower deck, knife in his hand, crying that any man that did not turn out would be turned out, by thunder.

Hundreds of men rolled their hammocks tight in the warm, close dark, then jostled up the companionways to the weather deck and stuffed them in the netting along the rail of the ship.

To the east, the sky lightened with the dawn. The boats were brought aboard, ropes groaning and pulleys squeaking, three boats over the waist and two hung from the stern davits, only the largest, the launch, still in the water.

Apollo shrieked and hectored and the men stampeded back and forth, blundering into each other in the dim light. The bosun rigged up the capstan with long, slender poles, and the fifer played a tune and Coffin took up his place and heaved, stomp and go, stomp and go, tuppenny rum and yo-ho-ho!, and the capstan clicked round and the slimy anchor cable came aboard, redolent of the bottom of the sea. The great heavy bower broke the surface of the water and the forecastle men caught it with the fish tackle and made it fast to the cathead.

Quaque had command of the launch, and he towed the ship, and once she was under way, Apollo took note of the wind and cried out: "Stand by to make sail!" Then: "Lay aloft and loose fore-topsail!"

This command was shouted forward by the sailing master to Hornigold, who was upon the forecastle. "Man the weather halliards," Hornigold cried out, and then: "The fucking *weather* halliards, Jenkins, God rot your soul!"

The sail loosers clambered up the swaying ratlines while the men on deck hauled on the halliards and, far above them, the topsail yard rose up and was mastheaded. Now the sail loosers loosed the sail and kicked it out of the top, the canvas rippling in the wind until it was sheeted home, as some men hauled on the sheet while others eased away on the clew-lines. In the general confusion of cordage and stamping feet, some men hauled on the wrong ropes, or stood unsure what to do, but Hornigold's powerful voice rose above the confusion, directing the men by name to their stations.

Amid all the shouted chaos, the ship passed the mouth of the harbour, coming within two hundred yards of the jail windows. The imprisoned pirates screamed out accusations, threats, curses. Up in the tops and along the rails the men of the *Saoirse* jeered and dropped their pants. And from amidships the band struck up with fiddle, fife, and drum:

Did not you promise me
That you would marry me

And the men sang in unison, deep and lusty, and they waved their straw hats and cheered as they proceeded into the open sea.

The launch let go of the tow line and was itself attached to the stern of the *Saoirse*, and, on Apollo's orders, sail after sail was set, and the ship heeled and the wood and rope tightened and groaned and the *Saoirse* picked up speed, throwing off a great wave from her bow.

Coffin wiped his brow and looked around him. They were off, a wooden world, one hundred and fifty feet long, forty feet wide, crammed with man and beast, a parasitic nation at war with all the world, enemies of all mankind.

ARISTOCRACY

A government in which power is vested in a minority
consisting of those believed to be best qualified.
(Merriam-Webster)

CAPTAIN JAMES (JIMMY) KAVANAGH

The Caribbean.

April 25, 1721.

1

Kavanagh slept little the first night at sea, and he was awoken before dawn by the fife and cries of the bosun's mate. His bed swung with the motion of the ship. He tipped himself out, stumbled into the Great Cabin, stooping so he did not hit his head. The floor rocked and through the window the horizon rolled. Kavanagh went past the cook, who was stoking the portable stove, and into the quarter-galley, his private rest-room, which jutted out over the sea, where he threw up through the seat of ease into the waves.

Nothing in his belly, but it went on, and on, slow, painful retches of thin strands of bile, down into the white water. The door opened and it was the steward, Obiefune, called Alfie, grinning with wide, crazy yellow teeth, holding a silver bowl of steaming water.

"Set it down," Kavanagh said, and returned to his retching.

The Negro did so, patting Kavanagh on the back of his neck before he left.

The cook was Yoruba, and Alfie was Igbo, and so they spoke to each other in an English incomprehensible to white men. Kavanagh planned to invite his officers for breakfast, but breakfast for a dozen men afloat was not a simple matter, as the Captain's stores were three decks below in the hold, and the livestock were scattered through the ship, and eggs had to be fetched and cows milked and biscuits cooked and everything transported over the narrow and crowded gangplanks and all the dishes served warm and simultaneously.

Kavanagh's vomiting slowed. Lifted his face and looked in the mirror. His eye more orange than usual, more broken blood vessels from vomiting. The empty socket looking mouldy. Hair going grey. Prodded his red gums to see how long they remained pale. Wiggled his remaining teeth. Smiled over and over, stretching his face until it looked right. Then he took the warm water in his hands and pressed it along his neck, his ears, over his eyes. Pinched the bridge of his nose.

He'd been sick many times before; it was sickness that would carry him off one day, he knew it. Scurvy, a long convalescence at Juan Fernández. The damned bubonic plague after the sack of Guayaquil. Fever, more times than he could count, all the foul tropical air. One day it would take him; but now he only needed a little more time.

Alfie returned with the razor and the lather, smiling, bobbing, and Kavanagh followed him into the Great Cabin, where he was shaved while Negroes brought in the eggs, bacon, bread, and other soft tack for breakfast. The cook steadied the small stove as the ship pitched and rolled. The smell made him sick again, but he only belched. Other Negroes carried the silver and china from the hutch into the dining room. Alfie brought Kavanagh his clothes.

"Nay, Alfie, plainer," Kavanagh said.

Dressed (with an eye patch, he forsook the glass eye at sea), he went out onto the quarterdeck while the sun was still below the waves, the ship lit by scattered lanterns. By the light of the binnacle, Kavanagh saw that Obed Coffin was at the helm. Above them, a surprising ziggurat of sail.

"Good morning, Captain," the sailing master, Alejandros Rios, said. He and his mate, a cross-eyed little man called Andreas Yellow, stood at the rail with the chip log ready. Rios was a handsome man who prided himself on his grooming and his dress, an excellent mathematician and a conscientious sailor. Yellow was less of a mathematician but regarded by the crew as an Honest Fellow. Between the two of them, they had all the qualities a Gentleman of Fortune might want in a navigator, a rather important and delicate office.

"We're cracking on, ain't we?" Kavanagh said.

Yellow threw the log overboard, the reel spun as the line ran out as if a whale had seized it. Rios kept his eye on the glass.

"Ten knots, Captain," Rios said.

"Jesus," Kavanagh said. Looked up. "Ain't we carrying a lot of sail?"

Rios hesitated. Yellow said, "Apollo's putting her through her paces, Captain,"

"Well, I hope nothing don't carry away."

As if on cue, Apollo's hectoring voice called out, and the men surged up the ratlines to the main yard and began to reef the courses. In a few minutes the ship righted herself, and her speed increased.

"Well, well," Kavanagh said. "Rios, would you care to join me for breakfast?"

"Thank you, Captain," the Spaniard said.

All the officers save Apollo came for breakfast. Hornigold, Rios, young Cian, Tulip, the bosun, the carpenter, the gunner, and the surgeon, an especially amusing Frenchman called Gérald Devereux, part Arawak and almost sixty, with a scarlet parrot on his shoulder who whistled and cried out, "*À borde! À borde!*" and "*Mon Dieu, les Espagnols me le payeront!*" Devereux claimed the parrot was a hundred years old, and she had sailed with all the great buccaneers, and if she were only treated well enough, she could tell them where L'Exterminatuer, Daniel Montbars, had buried his treasure.

Eggs, toast, bacon, and steaming pots of coffee and tea.

Despite his mutinous stomach, Kavanagh cleared his plate, not to hide his seasickness—which was impossible, the attempt would be more shameful than seasickness itself—but to show that he was bearing it.

Toward the end of the meal, there came a knock at the door and Spry entered.

Kavanagh said: "Give you joy of your victory, Brother! Have a glass with us. Gentlemen, a toast! To Horace Spry, the Quartermaster of the *Saoirse!*"

"Thankee, Taoiseach," Spry said. "I don't mind if I do."

They drank punch, Kavanagh smiling, stomach twisting.

Spry said: "Ah, that's fine stuff, that is. Finer by far than the grog down in the lower decks."

"Subtle, ain't he?" Kavanagh said. "Never you worry, Spry. You may spread the word that it's my intention to dine with the jacks each and every day of the week, a dozen or so at a time, so's everyone will get to eat dainty once in a while."

"That'll go over well," Spry said. And then, the inscription on a silver platter catching his eye, he read it out: "*To James Kavanagh, this service is offered by the association of Bahamas merchants in gratitude for his heroism during the War of the Quintuple Alliance.*"

"Aye," Kavanagh said. "They gave it to me in the year '20, along with a hundred-guinea sword." He gestured to where it hung on the wall, gleaming gold, with a diamond in the hilt. "I led the militia when Spanish landed on Hog Island. It was old Benjamin that sounded the alarm."

Kavanagh stood, the ship rolled side to side, pitched up and down, and he clenched his teeth, held back the bile, and sweated.

"Gentlemen, the Quartermaster and I shall have a word, so perhaps you'd best see about your duties. Brother Spry, a cigar?"

"I wouldn't say no."

"Come with me."

In the Great Cabin, Kavanagh took out the cigars and lit them in the portable stove. The pair proceeded to the stern gallery, and Spry looked over the ocean as Kavanagh vomited his breakfast into the sea.

"I've been feeling queasy myself," Spry said, an obvious lie.

"It'll pass," Kavanagh said, now puffing the cigar. "On'y I ain't as young as I used to be."

"None of us are," Spry said. "The crew ain't green, that's for sure. Though you left many an Able Seaman ashore. Dickens says you stocked the crew with Negroes and Irish to keep the Honest Fellows under your thumb."

Kavanagh smiled, an expression that could mean anything.

"It did seem to strike a chord with some of the men," Spry continued.

"Except the Negroes and the Irish, I suppose," Kavanagh said. "The problem with your Honest Fellow is he gets to thinking he's too good to push a mop or even haul a rope, on account of his Honesty."

"I wonder why you brought Dickens aboard at all," Spry said.

"Every Cruise has its Sea Lawyers, you're better off knowing who they are from the first."

"Well, your invitations to dinner will be well received, but I wonder if perhaps you oughtn't to share out the provisions a little quicker. You'd make my life easier. There's bound to be motions."

"There'll be motions no matter what you do, Spry," Kavanagh said. "You can't make it Christmas every day of the year. Even if you could, what then? Why, everyone gets tired of Christmas. God never intended for men to be merry every day; men need both their brimstone and treacle. If a man's life is all brimstone, I'll give him some treacle. But if his life is all treacle, then by the Powers, I'll give him his brimstone, and his soul to the Devil if he don't like it."

"You may expect to hear a great deal about Rights."

"The Rights are set out in the Articles."

"Natural Rights, then."

"Oh, fie, there's another one for you! Natural Rights, for shame, Spry. Have a look at the fishes eating one another, there's the State of Nature for you. There ain't nothing less natural than the Rights—you have to grow 'em like cabbages."

"Ain't cabbages natural?"

"So they are; but then so are caterpillars and aphids. I suppose an Old Salt like you ain't never tried to grow a cabbage. It ain't so easy as it looks, shipmate."

"I suppose you know best, Brother," Spry said.

"You was there with us in Honduras. You saw how it was. You know who it was that kept that crew together."

"Aye, I saw. And you've some hard men aboard this ship what are loyal to you, but you've no one like Israel Hands."

"Why, that's where you're wrong, mate," Kavanagh said. "He'll be coming aboard once we reach Bath."

Spry dropped his cigar; it vanished in the white water.

"Ain't he to be hanged? I thought they'd sent him to Virginia to be hanged."

"None of you've been following the trial," Kavanagh said. "In exchange for a Pardon, Israel testified against Governor Eden and his secretary. Though, as it turned out, Israel'd never seen Teach actually meeting with the Governor or any of 'em North Carolina officials. Only Negroes did, and their evidence was thrown out. Eden was acquitted and Israel got his Pardon anyway."

Smiling at Spry's stunned expression, Kavanagh said, "They say them as are born to hang will never drown. Perhaps it works the other way round."

The Atlantic Ocean.

April 26, 1721.

2

The Company assumed the routine of life afloat as if awakening from a dream. At dawn, or before it, the scraping of holystones and the sloshing of water and swabs, and then the pipe, hammocks up, breakfast, one watch after another, until Rios and Yellow took the measurement and declared it noon.

The men had their dinner and grog, then the officers ate in the gun-room on the upper deck, while twelve lucky bastards joined the Captain in his dining cabin (a Negro waiter behind every man's chair) and were plied with apertifs and wines and liquor and delicacies prepared by the little Yoruba, lobster soup and fresh mutton and greasy lobscouse and trembling puddings. The sound of happy revelry reverberated through the ship, occasionally overborne by Kavanagh's furious roaring: "Oh, you motherless son of a bitch, you've broken my china!" or "Handsomely with the decanter, you monkey-fucking bastard!" The men were even given permission to use the Captain's private lavatory, where they would vomit their rich food into the dark sea, or stick their heads out the window and shout witticisms to their friends: "Look at me, I'm shitting like an admiral!"

Gentlemen of Fortune tend to put more stock in their sailing than their gunnery—they want to capture ships, not sink them—but Kavanagh insisted on daily practice. So, every afternoon, carpenters and Negroes took down the flimsy walls that made the cabins on the upper and lower decks and doused the galley fire and covered the windows with deadlights. All the animals were stowed down in the hold. Five men to a gun, including a captain and a powder boy, with all their tools, rope rammer with sponge, iron bars and handspikes, priming wire. They knocked loose the gunports, cast off the tackles, removed the stoppers, peeled the tallow seals from the vents. The gun's captain motioned with his hands and the crew would aim the gun with their iron tools and then jab the slow match into the vent. Deafening noise, rattling vibration, and the gun jumped backwards. The men sponged the barrel and the powder monkey raced down to the handling room with its dark, damp curtains, where the gunner passed a paper cartridge through a little window from the powder room. The deck filled with smoke, fine ashy strings of oakum suspended, lighter than air. The men injured by the bucking guns were hauled down into the sick bay to receive care from the surgeon and to be cursed in French by his parrot.

After the gunnery, the Negroes retrieved the offended livestock and reconstructed the cabins. Supper was served, and afterwards, during the dog watches of the early evening, Spry presided over the daily Meeting of the Company in the forecastle. After an hour of wrangling, accusations, and motions, the men put their arms round each other's shoulders and sang *Did not you promise me / that you would marry me.*

Topsails were reefed, Kavanagh's great harp was hauled to the forecastle, and there was singing and dancing before the first bell, when the hammocks were strung up and the first watch went to sleep. At last Kavanagh returned to his cabin, joined every night by Benjamin, who took a nip of rum and went upon the stern gallery to fish. The night demarcated by bells and the cries of the lookouts, larboard gangway, all's well, larboard bow, all's well, et cetera.

There is always plenty to do afloat, quite apart from sailing the ship. The rigging must be continually repaired or replaced, or tightened when it becomes slack, and whenever it is tightened in one place it must be loosened in another, to say nothing of all the coverings and chafing gear. Many things used aboard a ship must be manufactured there, especially rope, and there is plenty of cleaning and painting and tarring, and make-work tasks such as picking oakum and scraping rust off chains or cannonballs. But the *Saoirse* had four times as many men than if she'd been a merchant (this was, indeed, the most obvious sign she was a pirate), so many that although there were nominally only two watches, the men soon worked it out so that a third of them slept through the night. The weather was fair, the sailing ought to have been easy. But nothing could be easy with Tom Apollo.

Unlike a merchantman, a ship out Cruising is usually in no hurry to get anywhere in particular. Apollo did not seem to understand this. During his watch he ordered the men to set as much sail as the ship would carry and drove her as fast as she would go. But he was also petrified of carrying away a spar, or splitting a sail, or snapping a rope, and so he would pace the gangplanks, peering up into the web of canvas and cordage and muttering to himself, and was always sending the men up to change something.

By the third day, he began to come on deck during Hornigold's watch, where he found fault and jabbed with his finger and swung his rattan cane so that it made a sinister *zzzt-zzzt* sound, like silk tearing. The men wondered how Hornigold, the great pirate Commodore, could stand it, but secrets are short-lived in a one-hundred-and-fifty-foot ship, and soon all knew that Hornigold was taking laudanum.

Apollo was particularly galled by the *Saoirse*'s tendency to gripe, that is, to turn into the wind when she was sailing close-hauled. This tendency could be ameliorated by setting certain sails (such as the square sails on the main or the mizzen) or by changing the angle, or rake, of the masts, but the problem could not really be fixed without rearranging the ballast, which was now inaccessible. So Apollo took to slapping his thigh with his thin rattan, so that his leg became bruised and cut through his trousers, something sick growing in him, a kind of madness.

Apollo's behaviour was much discussed.

"What is wrong with the man?" Hutchins demanded at dinner.

"I never seen the like," said Beard. "I'd ask whether he thinks he's in the Royal Navy, only I was in the damned Royal Navy and I never saw the like even while I was there."

"I thought he was a-going to start Goldie," Hutchins said. "Raised up his little rattan and I said to myself, by God, he's going to smack Goldie right in the face."

"Is it unusual for an officer to start a man upon a pirate?" Coffin asked.

Beard and Hutchins turned to Coffin, their faces neutral with polite distaste.

"What a question, shipmate!" Hutchins said.

"It is not unusual," Beard said, "it is unheard of."

"Ah," Coffin said as he stuffed his pipe.

The first few days afloat had done little to endear Coffin to his shipmates, or even his messmates. In his favour, you might point out that he was a skilled sailor, and helmsman, and carpenter, and tailor, and rope maker, and might have served as sailing master or the sailmaker or anything in between, and he was a generous man, who would help anyone who asked with anything they might need, whether it was a bit of woodwork or a little sewing.

Yet he was not liked, for he was not merry. Gentlemen of Fortune vary in every particular, but they all know they are doomed from the moment they set their name to the Articles, and they are determined to be merry until the end. A gloomy, solitary, sober man is not only an unpleasant companion but also unreliable, poisonous, an apostate, a recusant. What was he here for, if not for a Merry Life? It was a crime for a man not to be happy, when he had (for such a short time!) everything a man could want, and the world trembling at his feet.

His sobriety on its own might have been forgiven, but combined with his hangdog look, his weeping, his bad dreams, and the favouritism shown to him by Apollo, the men aboard soon regarded him as an unlucky sailor—a Jonah.

As for Coffin, he recognized the men's disapproval, and accepted it. Even here, among the lowest of the low, the worst sinners of the world, he deserved contempt, and worse. It was nothing next to the contempt he had for himself.

Pamlico Sound, North Carolina.

May 4, 1721.

3

I t was, therefore, a perplexed if not yet unhappy crew that sailed from the blue waters of the open ocean through a thin fringe of islands into the green water of Pamlico Sound. The anchor dropped, the ship came to a graceful halt, and the sails were tightly furled. The men gave a perfunctory cheer.

A little rowboat came up alongside and hailed them: "Ahoy there, *Royal Fortune!*"

"Nay mate," a voice called back, "it's *Saoirse* now, Jimmy Kavanagh, owner and Captain."

"Oh ho!" the man in the rowboat replied. "Bad luck comes from changing the name of a ship. As she's christened, let her stay, says I."

Kavanagh shouted over the rail: "Well, superstition brings bad luck, says I. Now you put the word out in town that the men are celebrating tonight. And as my men have not yet received their wages, all bills are to be sent to the Kavanagh estate, north of Pantego."

The rowboat sped off to the shore and the men gave a great cheer.

"Now Brothers," Kavanagh said. "We've stopped here, so I may conduct a Bit of Business. Certain of my Investors are leaving the Cruise and I must pay them out."

"Oy, when did that happen?" Dickens cried.

"Why, before we bought the ship, Brother," Kavanagh said. "You didn't think I'd force any man, did you? Anyway, I shall return tomorrow."

"Three cheers for Captain Kavanagh!"

Kavanagh jammed the uncomfortable glass eye back into its socket and went over the rail and down into the launch with Cian, Quaque, Alfie, Benjamin, and, lastly, the four departing Investors, who took some time to bid adieu to their friends, shaking hands and embracing. As they pushed off, a man put his head through a gunport and sang a farewell to them in Gaelic.

At the mouth of the river, they gave a facetious salute to the first boatload of whores on their way to the ship, and continued up the narrowing waterway, lined on either side with green trees, ancient bald cypress, tupelo, and red maple. Twenty-three miles up the river and at last they arrived in Bath: three streets, two dozen homes, one hundred souls, a gristmill, and a fort. They pulled the boat up through the muck, and Kavanagh said: "Gentlemen, I shall return in a moment."

One of the Investors spoke up: "Damn you, Jimmy, when will we get our money?"

"As I told you, the cash is at my estate," Kavanagh said. "And grousing won't make it come no quicker."

The man who had spoken, MacGregor, scowled.

Kavanagh left them, and made his way to the residence of Charles Eden, the disgraced Governor of North Carolina. A black footman escorted him to the study, where Eden, a portly, red-faced man, awaited.

"Well Jimmy," Eden said, cordial, "it's been a while."

"So it has," Kavanagh said. "And it's a shame I can't stay, but I must reach my estate before nightfall. Are the papers in order?"

"Here they are," Eden said. "The same as when your wife reviewed them."

"They'd better be," Kavanagh said.

"A remarkable woman, your wife," Eden said. "Although she has not endeared herself to her neighbours."

"She don't lack for friends," Kavanagh said. "Here?"

"Just there, Jimmy."

Kavanagh could not read, but he could sign his name, and this he did, page after page, twenty-seven times.

"I shall take 'em all back to my wife and have your copies sent back," Kavanagh said. "It ain't that I don't trust you, mind, but I'll never hear the end of it if I don't let her look 'em over."

Eden wheezed, smiled. "It's all there. A thousand acres, just as we agreed, though it wasn't easy."

Kavanagh's gaze sharpened. "You ain't feeling hard done by, are you, Governor?"

"No indeed," Eden said.

Kavanagh wrapped the papers in oilskin and put them in his satchel. "As I said, I'm pressed for time. Where might I find Mr. Hands?"

"You might inquire in the kitchen."

"Very well," Kavanagh said. "It's been a pleasure, Governor."

"I'm sure," Eden wheezed, amused.

4

In the kitchen, he found a Negress making bread, flour up to her elbows.

"Hello, Molly," Kavanagh said. "Where's Israel?"

"Don't know, sir," she said, looking down.

"Yes you do," Kavanagh said pleasantly. He hooked his thumbs into his trousers and waited.

The Negress kept kneading the dough.

Kavanagh made a noise like: *pfff*. Waited. At last said: "Is it like that? Last chance."

She kept kneading.

"Molly. Look at me when I'm talking to you."

She didn't. But she said: "He's at the end of the lane. Red house, on the right."

"Thank you, Molly," Kavanagh said.

He went out the back door, headed down the road until he spotted the little one-storey red shack. Past it a two-acre rice paddy, brilliant green, in which Negro slaves stooped in the water. Past the paddy, the slaves' sleeping quarters. Kavanagh tramped down a muddy path to the door and stepped into the dark of the shack. While his eye adjusted to the gloom, a voice spoke.

"Taoiseach. How'd you find me?"

Squatting in a corner, completely naked, coated in filth so his hair stuck together in clumps. A livid scar ran through one pinkish-white eye.

"Time to go."

"I ain't ready to go," Israel said.

Kavanagh said nothing.

"I've been thinking. You've done very well for yourself. I seen your family in town. Carrying on. Giving themselves airs. Where's my share?"

Israel Hands had been paid his share, many times over. Kavanagh did not say this.

"A man gets tired of your tricks, Jimmy," Israel said. One fist smacked down into the mud. "That's what I say. A man gets tired of never knowing—"

"We can talk later. There's work to be done tonight."

"Tonight?"

"Yes, tonight."

"What work?"

"You'll know it when you see it," Kavanagh said. "Where are your clothes?"

"How should I know?"

"Come with me."

They walked down to the creek and Israel plunged into the silty brown water. Emerged blowing and snorting and tossing his head like a colt.

"Cut my hair off, Jimmy."

"How short?" Kavanagh said, drawing his knife.

"Short," Israel said.

Kavanagh took a fistful of Israel's clotted, lice-infested hair and cut it and dropped it in the water then took another until an uneven, patchy mess was left.

"Enough," Israel said.

"Damn it, shipmate, you look—"

"Enough, I said," Israel said, and put his head back under the water and dug his fingers into his scalp. When he emerged, he asked: "Is Alfie here? Does he have my clothes?"

They walked along the bank, in full view of the townsfolk, until they came back to the boat. The four Investors were missing. Alfie smiled, bobbed his head, produced a thick bar of yellow soap, which he offered to Israel, and was roundly cursed. The soap vanished, replaced with a set of clean clothes, and Israel dressed himself and sat in the bow. Alfie then handed him a wrapped bundle. Israel gripped it tightly, revealing the outline of a tomahawk.

The four Irish Investors reappeared, smelling of whiskey. They shoved the boat into the water and sailed downstream almost all the way back to Pamlico Sound, before they turned north and rowed seventeen miles up Pungo River and Pantego Creek to a dock in the late afternoon.

As they tied up their boat and unloaded, a group of Tuscarora Indians approached, wearing deerskin and bearing a canoe. The leader recognized Kavanagh and raised a hand in greeting.

"Hello there, Tommy," Kavanagh said, smiling. "How goes it? Out for some fishing?"

Tommy looked grave. "Did you hear the news?" he said.

"What news?" Kavanagh said.

"Your son," Tommy said, faltering. "Your son has died."

"Billy? Billy is my nephew."

But then Kavanagh saw him, little Billy, whom Kavanagh had sent to live with the Tuscarora in the Indian Woods. Hadn't recognized him at first, for his hair was so long and he was tanned so dark and he wore their deerskin clothes.

"No," Tommy said. "Rory. Your son." And then: "I am sorry, Brother."

Kavanagh's friendly smile was fixed on his face. He almost said, You are mistaken, sir.

"Rory?" Cian asked. "Rory is dead?"

Billy was looking at Kavanagh. They were all looking at him.

Consciously, he stopped smiling. "Ah," he finally said.

"It was the Fever, Uncle," Billy said. "The doctor came, but . . ."

Kavanagh raised his hand and Billy fell silent. Cian swallowed and began to cry silently. Alfie put his arm around the boy's shoulder. Kavanagh gathered himself, leaned into the pain. Not even tempted to cry. But so tired. Mosquitoes hummed all around. Crickets and frogs and birds. So loud, all the time, in this swamp.

"Well, I best see my wife," Kavanagh said at last, his voice raw. "Everything well with you, Tommy?"

Tommy shrugged.

"They ain't cutting your timber or cheating you on the ferries or nothing? Mr. Kirkland ain't troubling you none over the easement?"

"No," Tommy said. "I am sorry for you, Brother. My sons, too, have died. Billy is like a son to me now. I went to see your wife, but she sent us away."

The other Tuscarora had the canoe in the water now. All of them still watching Kavanagh.

"I had better go see her," Kavanagh said.

He started walking.

And of course, the idiot Kirkland and his idiot wife saw them and waddled over, and Kavanagh had to stopper the oily black rage that was bubbling up, to keep a calm face and a sensible response when they expressed their condolences, warned him about the state of his wife, offered opinions upon the loss of a child (Mrs. Kirkland having buried seven), complained about the Tuscarora (savages who ought to confine themselves to the Roanoke), and asked to borrow various goods. From behind them stared children, slaves, and livestock.

At last he was able to get away from them and they walked onto the Kavanagh estate. A space had been partially cleared for a great house, and a cellar partially dug, and the foundation partially constructed. For now, they all lived in shacks. Pigs and cows and chickens wandered in a wet and muddy paddock. Dogs ran up and barked. The air was smoky with burning brush. Whites and Negroes, working, watched the party approach.

Joseph Morrison, one of Mrs. Kavanagh's cousins, a tall, intelligent, trustworthy man, left off digging up a stump and approached, wiping his hands on his trousers.

"You heard?" Joseph said.

"Where'd you bury him?"

Joseph gestured past the house. "Underneath the chestnut tree," he said. Then: "Erin is not well."

"*Cian, téigh i do chompord do mháthair,*" Kavanagh said.

Cian broke free from Alfie and ran to his mother's lean-to, still weeping. My bold little pirate, Kavanagh thought, sourly. They can always cry.

"Joseph, kill a pig," Kavanagh said. "And get out some good whiskey."

"We ain't staying," MacGregor said immediately. "Once we have our money, we'll leave you to your grief. I suppose your Negroes will take us back to town."

"Everyone has to eat," Kavanagh said.

"If we leave now, we can return to Bath before—"

"No," Kavanagh said.

"Damn you," MacGregor said, his face flushing. "We've danced to your tune long enough, you son of a—"

"Israel," Kavanagh said.

Suddenly howling, Israel threw himself on MacGregor, a man he'd sailed with under Hornigold and Blackbeard and had fought with, side by side, time and time before. Anyone watching would have thought they'd been enemies, that MacGregor must have done Israel some horrible, unforgivable injury.

One of the other Irish tried to intervene, and Israel caught him with a short, hard elbow and knocked him down. Kavanagh let it go on until MacGregor had balled up in the mud, and then he said, loudly: "Enough."

After one more blow, Israel withdrew, panting, eyes rolling.

Kavanagh left them all and went to the chestnut tree beneath which they had buried his eldest son. He popped out his glass eye and put it in his pocket, and then put his head in his hands.

5

A piece of earth like any other, newly disturbed, and a small pile of stones. Bugs hummed and whined. But he had nowhere else to go. Certainly, he was not ready to see his wife. He sat down. Listened as the pig screamed its last. Smelled the meat cooking. When the dinner bell rang, he found he did not want to leave; a mad part of his mind said to him that as long as he stayed here, under the chestnut tree, and kept his eyes closed, then his son was not really dead.

God damn you, he told that voice.

Roast pork slathered in butter and honey and herbs, wild berries and mushrooms and roots and shoots, fiddleheads and asparagus, potatoes and tomatoes, rice, of course. A great cauldron of punch. The four departing Investors, even MacGregor, had recovered themselves sufficiently to eat and drink; they watched without speaking as Kavanagh conversed with his relatives in Gaelic, accepting their condolences, inquiring about the property.

Towards the end of the meal, Kavanagh sat next to Cian on a stump while the boy picked at his meal.

"How's your mother?" he asked.

He shrugged.

"Will she be all right?"

"What do you mean?"

"Is she broken?"

"Mother would never break," Cian said.

"Everyone can be broken."

"She is not broken," Cian said.

"Is that true? Or do you wish it so?"

"It's true."

"Well," he said, and patted his son on the shoulder.

The evening shadows were lengthening and the bugs grew hungrier. Kavanagh signalled and MacGregor and the three others came over.

"Well gentlemen," he said, "I imagine you'll want to be on your way tomorrow."

"Tonight," MacGregor said.

"Come now, it's almost dark."

"I won't be spending the night here with you," MacGregor said. "Where's our money?"

"I can fetch it for you now, if you like," Kavanagh said.

"Well then, fetch it."

Kavanagh sighed, and walked over to the great fire where a coloured man called Dobie sat with his wife, a Cherokee woman, who was very pregnant.

"I suppose congratulations are in order," Kavanagh said, smiling at them.

"Yes, Taoiseach," Dobie said, smiling back. He was a small, ferrety man, and his wife was too beautiful for him.

"Fetch the books and the money."

"They're with your wife."

"That's why I'm sending you, Brother," Kavanagh said.

Dobie scampered across the muddy earth into the dark. The first stars were emerging in the western sky. He returned with a sack over his shoulder and a ledger under his arm. The money was counted out in four piles of shining gold before the relieved eyes of the Investors.

"Since you ain't a trusting man, MacGregor," Kavanagh said, "you won't be surprised as I'm asking for a receipt."

MacGregor went first, and each of the others also confirmed receipt of 284 pounds, 7 shillings, 26 pence. Dobie waved the papers dry and put them in the accounting book.

"That's done," Kavanagh said.

"Thank you, Taoiseach," one of the men said.

"No need to thank me, Brother, it's your money."

MacGregor looked as if he would say something, but did not.

"Does MacGregor speak for you all?" Kavanagh said.

"What'd you mean?" another of the Investors asked.

"Leaving tonight?"

The man looked at the darkening forest, at all the people around the fire, white and black, smeared with grease and drunk and singing in Gaelic and Fante and other languages of peoples who had been defeated long ago and far away.

"I believe so, Taoiseach," the man said. "We arranged for lodgings in Bath."

"Well then, goddamn you for suspicious fools," Kavanagh said. "You'd risk drowning in the dark rather than spend the night with friends. But every man may go to the Devil in his own way. Quaque will take you. Alfie, fetch a lantern. Gentlemen, a toast."

The mugs were filled.

"To the Devil in Hell!" Kavanagh called, silhouetted against the firelight.

"To the Devil!" they cried.

"*An diabhal*!" another shouted.

They drank.

The mugs were refilled.

"To Baal!" Kavanagh said.

"Ball?" a man asked.

"Baal is a False God, from the Bible," Cian piped up.

Clever Cian. Not like Rory. Slow Rory, plodding Rory, the moralist, the fair-dealer, plain face, plain heart. Where'd he come from? Like a damned Changeling in reverse. Nothing like his father, nor his mother, nor his rebellious father's father, nor his raging father's mother, nor his rakish mother's father, nor his beautiful mother's mother. A plain and simple and ordinary boy, who had been on his way to becoming a plain and simple and ordinary man.

"That's the one—ain't he clever, lads? To Baal, gentlemen, to Baal!"

They drank.

"To King James the Third!" Kavanagh cried.

"Where's your boy with the lantern, then?" MacGregor said.

"I sent for him," Kavanagh said. "Have a drink, damn you. Anyone would think you were in a Plot."

"I ain't in no Plot," MacGregor said, reddening. "I'm not the one playing tricks, Jimmy."

"Enough," one of the other Investors said.

"Yes, enough toasts," MacGregor said. "I gave this man three hundred pounds three years ago and now I've got back two hundred and eighty—"

"And room and board for three years in between," Kavanagh said.

"—and he's got himself a thousand acres, and Blackbeard's dead." MacGregor fell silent, glaring, and no one spoke, and the fire snapped and an owl hooted.

"Is that all, MacGregor?" Kavanagh said.

"Where's Hands?"

"How the hell should I know?"

"Because you're his keeper, or near enough."

"Well, I don't know where he is," Kavanagh said. "I been at the tree with Rory all afternoon." He drank the punch and kept his eyes fixed on MacGregor.

Complete darkness had come suddenly, like ink spreading across the sky.

MacGregor shook with emotion, clutching the knife at his belt, tense, ready to strike.

Kavanagh lifted his mug. "You won't drink with me, Brother?"

A lantern bobbed as Alfie approached.

"See? Here they are. One last toast to send you on your way."

MacGregor threw his clay mug down into the reeds, but the other men drank. "Farewell, Taoiseach," one of them said.

"Now you sure you can't wait until morning?"

One of them hesitated, a man named Alan, looking around at the night. But the other three were already walking towards the dark woods, and so he followed.

"That's that," Kavanagh said. "Dobie, put the books away."

He sat down with two of his cousins and was conversing with them in Irish when the hesitant Investor, Alan, returned. "Taoiseach," he said, then stopped, his mouth opening and closing.

"What're you doing here, Brother?" Kavanagh said. "Don't you want to be on your way?"

"I have changed my mind."

"You want to stay here tonight?"

"No, I . . . I don't want to withdraw my Investment." Alan held out the bag of gold, trembling. "I want to come on the Cruise."

"A little late for that, Brother," Kavanagh said.

"I want to Re-Invest," Alan said.

"Here's the thing," Kavanagh said, turning to the fire. "When a man sets his name upon the Articles of an Adventuring Cruise, he declares war upon the whole world. He becomes the enemy of all mankind. One false step, one wrong word, and it's the noose for the whole crew, stretched out and set to dry in the sun. And so, Gentlemen of Fortune must trust one another. Every man must give his whole self to the Company, with no reservations, nothing held back." Turning back to the man, he asked: "Can I trust you, Alan?"

"Yes," Alan said. "Yes, Taoiseach."

"Can I know?"

"I'll swear an oath, Taoiseach," the man said. "Only please, let me—"

A long, savage wail, undulating and rising, and rising.

"Indians," Kavanagh said. "To arms, to arms!"

Now came screaming, but the screaming did not last long.

Men, women, and children, whites and blacks, all scrambled to fetch their weapons then formed a circle around the fire, with the women and children in the centre.

"You ain't had no trouble with the Tuscarora, have you, Joseph?" Kavanagh said.

Joseph shook his head.

Kavanagh cocked his head, listened. No more sound. Already the bugs and frogs had resumed their chorus. He said to Alan: "Well, Brother, here's a chance to prove yourself."

They started down the path through the woods to the creek. Kavanagh led the way, holding a torch, and Alan followed with a musket. Leaves and branches slapped and snapped. Feet squelched in the mud. After ten minutes they saw a light ahead.

"Who's that?" Alan panted.

"Kirkland, I think," Kavanagh said. "The Indians must be gone."

He turned and gripped Alan's shoulder with his three-fingered hand and looked him in the eye. Alan blinked as the torchlight shone in his face, spoiling his night vision.

"I trust you, Alan," Kavanagh said loudly, to cover the sound of Israel's footsteps. "I do. But I must make something clear."

"What?" Alan said.

His last word, just before Israel's bloody, callused hand clamped over his mouth and his throat was cut.

A little farther along the path, Kirkland and his sons and slaves formed a crowd around the bodies, which were scalped and bloody, hacked apart. A tomahawk was planted in the side of MacGregor's head.

Alfie claimed he had not seen the attackers. Quaque, who looked scared witless, was not so witless as to disagree.

Kirkland blamed the Tuscarora. Kavanagh was skeptical. He told Kirkland of the gold (which was nowhere to be seen), of how the Investors had been drinking in Bath, how robbers often disguised their crimes as the work of Indians. Yet feelings against the Indians ran high, the Cheraw War having ended not three years before. It was decided to send a delegation to Bath, as well as a party to the Indian Woods to confront Chief Blount.

The corpses were carried back to the Kavanagh estate and buried together in one grave.

6

The next morning over breakfast, Kavanagh told Cian he would not be rejoining the Cruise.

"What?" Cian said.

"Your mother needs you."

"But I want to go a-pirating! With you."

"Well, I don't want you," Kavanagh said.

The youth's face crumpled.

"Going to cry, are you?" Kavanagh said. "Cry away."

Everything was wet with dew and smelled of smoke. The Negroes were already at work. They'd been liberated by Blackbeard and then sold into slavery after his fall, and Kavanagh had promised them their liberty again in five years if they worked hard. Though who was to say whether his wife would honour that promise. When he'd proposed bringing in tenant farmers from Ireland, she'd laughed and explained the numbers. Kavanagh was illiterate, but he had a head for figures. His children would be slave owners, like the damned English. So be it. The Way of the World.

If Cian was not coming, he needed a clerk. He went, at last, to his wife's rude wooden shack and entered. She and Dobie sat at a table, drinking coffee. His wife looked at him. Wild and ruined and beautiful, her eyes dead.

"Dobie, you're coming with me," Kavanagh said.

"Beg pardon?" Dobie's eyes widened.

"You heard me. I need someone to mind my papers."

"I thought Cian . . ." He trailed off, making the connections. Opened his mouth. Kavanagh looked at him. Dobie looked down, overcome.

"Get ready," Kavanagh said. "We're leaving now."

Dobie hesitated, but when Kavanagh's expression turned angry, he scurried out, dragging the door shut behind him over the uneven ground.

Kavanagh and his wife looked away from each other. The rude log cabin, windowless and dark, was crammed with their things. Furniture, crates of china and silver, portraits wrapped in sailcloth, musical instruments, except for the harp. He'd learned the instrument while he had wooed her. Kavanagh was only thirty-two. He felt so old.

He leaned against the wall and looked at her. She was still looking down.

"You did it," she said.

"*We* did it," he said.

She waved away a mosquito. She looked at him and seemed at last to see something she liked. She smiled.

"I thought you needed Cian to make it work."

"I don't need him," Kavanagh said.

"What will the other Investors say?"

"What will they do, is the real question. The answer is nothing."

"You can take him. Perhaps you'll come back."

"You shouldn't harbour false hopes, my dear."

"You'll find a way."

"I did find a way," Kavanagh said. "This is the way."

"You'll come back to me," she said. She was so beautiful. He remembered how'd she turned his head. Like pulling a string. His eyes on her while she looked away. His brother laughing, telling him there was no hope. So they'd all said, about everything. He'd done it all. What was this? Just one more thing.

He leaned down and kissed her. "All right," he said.

She clutched his shoulders and squeezed. "You did it," she whispered. "My mother called me a fool."

He kissed her.

"You did it. I knew you would."

One last embrace, and then he was outside, smiling at the men, knocking his hat on his trousers and then putting it on his head.

7

As they approached the ship, they saw the men running up and down the rigging and working in the upper yards.

"Are they shifting topmasts?" Israel asked. "In port?"

It was hard to tell with the glare, but yes, Kavanagh thought that was what they were doing. A delicate operation where the men worked a hundred feet above the deck with complicated ropes and pulleys.

"I thought you gave the men a holiday," Israel said.

They came aboard the ship without ceremony to find the deck swarming, the men obeying orders but vibrating with unhappiness, the mood black as pitch.

Kavanagh did not ask what had happened. He nodded at the men, unsmiling, and said to Alfie, "Go and fetch Tulip." Then he went into the Great Cabin with Israel.

"Where will I sleep?" Israel asked, as he took a stopper from a crystal decanter and filled a mug with whiskey.

"You may have a cabin in the lower deck near Tulip," Kavanagh said, setting his wet boots next to the portable stove. "Where we store the small arms." He rubbed his temples then popped out his glass eye. His head hurt, and even the motion of the ship at anchor turned his stomach.

A knock at the door. Tulip came through on his crutches, together with Rios, the sailing master. Alfie distributed drinks.

"Any whores still aboard?" Kavanagh asked.

"There may be one or two in the cable tier," Tulip said.

"See they're set ashore and no more are allowed aboard. And bring me some water."

"You ain't in a Plot, are you, Captain?" Tulip asked.

"What happened?" Kavanagh asked.

Tulip drank some whiskey before he answered. "The men caroused well into the night, of course," he said, "but Apollo had the Negroes scrubbing the deck at first light. As if that weren't bad enough, he went down below and turned the men out of their hammocks. I weren't there and I didn't see what happened. I gather Rowen cursed him, and then Apollo struck Rowen with his rattan. Dickens shouted that Apollo was starting the men, and Rowen demanded satisfaction. Then Apollo said he would not duel a jack."

"He did," Rios said. "He kept saying how astonished he was that he was expected to duel a common sailor."

Below them, the whores screeched.

"Your man Spry tried to pour oil on the waters," Tulip said. "Said they ought to have a Meeting when you returned. Rowen was adamant that he would settle the matter ashore in the Usual Manner. Still, Spry did his best. He told 'em Rowen hadn't obeyed orders, he'd answered back, now he wouldn't wait for a Meeting, Apollo was your man, Israel Hands was coming aboard. A few stories was told about how you put down that Mutiny off the coast of Honduras. So they rowed off to Ocracoke. Rios here was Apollo's second."

"No one else would do it," Rios clarified.

"So?" Kavanagh said.

"Dickens was Rowen's second," Rios said. "We went ashore, selected the ground, and looked at the pistols, and loaded them, and settled the usual details. But Spry was with us? And he was still 'working' on Rowen, as Tulip said. And in the end, Dickens told me that Rowen would accept an apology, a private apology, on the beach. And I told it to Apollo, who had taken off his shirt, for the duel. Do you know his back is covered with scars? I have never seen anyone so wretchedly flogged, do you know that? His back looked like a . . . a tree?"

Despite his excellent English, Rios worried he was unintelligible, and made almost every sentence into a question, as if that would help.

Outside, the whores shouted bawdy jibes and jokes as they were escorted off the ship. The men did not answer back. A black mood indeed.

"Apollo would not apologize? And, oh! Spry was very angry. Very, very angry. He said that Dickens must have fouled it. He said some harsh words to me, for which he has apologized, and which I shall not repeat. I have never seen Spry so angry! But Dickens and Rowen were not angry. They were, how do you say, gleeful? I would say they were gleeful. So Rowen and Apollo lined up, back to back, and walked ten paces, and Spry dropped the handkerchief. And, um . . ."

Here Rios trailed off.

"Apollo won, I take it," Kavanagh said.

"I do not know how to describe it?" Rios said. "Because Rowen moved so quickly, with such haste, like a blur. And Apollo seemed so slow and careful. But somehow, Apollo's gun fired first. He hit the man in the heart. He was dead in a minute. Dickens was weeping? He'd tattooed the man himself, they'd been shipmates, and so on."

"Word's all over the ship, now," Tulip said. "They're saying Apollo's real name is John Jeffries, formerly of the Royal Navy, as took a twenty-eight-gun French ship with a sloop and then was Flogged Around the Fleet for striking an Admiral."

"How does one contrive to be Flogged Around the Fleet after taking a man-of-war with a sloop?" Rios asked.

"Well, Brother," Kavanagh said, "as you may have observed, the man is a son of a bitch."

8

R ios left, but Tulip remained. They conversed in Gaelic.
        "Where's Cian?" he asked, very blunt.

"I left him ashore."

"I thought he was to be your clerk. What the hell is Dobie doing here?"

"Rory died," Kavanagh said.

He poured himself a very little Irish whiskey in a heavy crystal tumbler. Kavanagh liked nice things. He liked the way this tumbler caught fire with the light.

"Rory died?"

"Fever," Kavanagh said. He set his glass eye on the table and spun it.

Tulip chewed on this, said: "Well, I am sorry, Taoiseach."

"Are you?" Kavanagh said, drinking.

"You told all us Investors you was bringing the boy along," Tulip pressed on.

"Well, Rory died."

"It was a great comfort to us that you were bringing the boy along. It showed you was serious about all this."

"For God's sake," Kavanagh said, making a gesture encompassing the Great Cabin, the ship, the men. "What about all this don't look serious to you? I'm here myself, ain't I?"

"Aye, Taoiseach, you're here, but you didn't put everything you had into this Cruise. The whores was saying you've a thousand acres."

"More like a hundred," Kavanagh said. "And it's all swamp. Ask Dobie, he'll show you the books."

Tulip glared at a spot on the wall for a while, then said: "It always seems like things are never quite like you say they will be. They're close, but you're always changing things. It was a great comfort to have the boy. Cian signed the Articles. Now he left with no Meeting."

"One of my boys died, Tulip," Kavanagh said. "I left Cian with his mother. I ain't asking for permission. Is there anything else?"

"I should ask you that, Brother," Tulip said, glaring. "I should ask you whether there'll be anything else. What else will you change?"

Very well then, Kavanagh thought. He pointed his one angry orange eye at Tulip like a lance.

"What if I do, Brother?" Kavanagh asked, leaning forward. "What'll you do?"

Tulip did not reply.

"Nothing," Kavanagh said, keeping Tulip pinned with his gaze. "Nothing. That's what you'll do. There's three hundred and sixty men aboard this ship with a share each, and thirty-five Investors with a hundred and fifty between you. You need me a damn sight more than I need you. I left my boy ashore, and if you don't like it, you can go straight to the Devil."

Tulip did not reply.

"Be off with you," Kavanagh said.

After Tulip was gone, Spry made a courtesy call, to ask whether the Captain had been informed of the troubles yesterday and whether a morning Meeting would be acceptable.

Yes he had and yes it would, and after Spry left to call the men together, Alfie came with the basin of warm water, razor, soap. When he was done, Kavanagh held the mirror and looked at his face. His eye seemed worse and he thought he saw more grey hairs. He smiled a few times, stretching his face. He strapped on a black eye patch and went out to face the Company.

The facts were not in dispute. Apollo did not speak. Spry recommended that Apollo be punished for his actions.

Then Kavanagh spoke, his voice ringing down the deck.

"Men, I'm sorry to hear what happened. Brother Rowen was a stout lad, an Honest Fellow. I ain't saying Apollo was in the right, though I ain't saying he's wrong neither. It's what the lawyers call moot. Brother Rowen chose to settle the matter ashore, in the Usual Manner. Having done so, the matter is at an end."

"Captain," Spry said. "Apollo struck Rowen with his rattan as punishment for disobeying him. In common parlance, he 'started' him. The Articles state that the Ship is to be governed by the Custom of the Coast, by the Jamaica Discipline, and so Rowen's punishment, if any, ought to have been up to me, or subject to a Meeting. So when Apollo struck him, he violated the Articles. It weren't only a Private Quarrel between two men, but a contravention of the Articles."

"Why Brother Spry, that's quite an argument, but you're forgetting about what the lawyers call *locus standi*, or 'standing' in plain English. To bring a motion against a member of the Company, you need standing. That means you must have been injured. Now in this case, it's clear, Rowen was the injured party, and he had his choice of Remedy and he chose to settle the dispute in the Usual Manner."

"Well, Brother," Spry said, "I can't see how it is a Private Quarrel if an officer on this Cruise starts one of the men, in contravention of the Articles."

A general mutter of agreement from the men.

"The answer to that is that the parties themselves considered the matter a Private Quarrel. That's why they went ashore. Furthermore, I can't see how Apollo must fight a duel ashore and then face a Meeting as well. The Latin term for that, Brothers, is *non bis in idem*—not twice in the same thing."

Gentlemen of Fortune are a singular lot. The *locus standi* business did not go over well, but this argument struck home, many men nodding, some reluctantly. No punishment twice for the same offence, aye, that was for damn sure.

Dickens had not spoken. He was up, way up, on the main topmast yard. Kavanagh was acutely aware of his presence but never once looked at him. Felt, instead, the force of his anger.

It was left to another of Dickens's friends, a short, bristly man called Harry Ironside, to make further angry complaints and objections, culminating in a motion that was defeated.

"Well, Brothers," Kavanagh said. "If there ain't nothing further, let us weigh anchor and make sail. For now, our destination is Cape Verde."

The Meeting was adjourned.

9

Afterwards, Kavanagh met with Apollo in the Great Cabin. Apollo declined a drink and sat very stiffly in his chair.

"I shall speak plainly," Kavanagh said. "You are not in the Royal Navy. You are aboard a Pirate. Discipline is the prerogative of the Quarter-master."

"Well sir," Apollo said. "I do not see how we can trust discipline to an elected man."

"Oh?"

"For he is bound to follow the will of the majority."

"So are we all," Kavanagh said.

"Nay," Apollo said. "Neither you nor I are subject to election."

"I did not say we were, Brother."

"A man subject to election shall not give the men the punishments they deserve, and if the men are not punished . . ."

"Oh, fie, punishment. For shame," Kavanagh said. "A sailor aboard a man-of-war is not kept obedient by whips or rattans or iron bits or leg irons or bosun's mates or marines. The jacks outnumber the officers ten to one and could kill them all in an instant, but if they did, they would become criminals ashore. Every man aboard a Pirate is already a criminal ashore; every man signed his soul to the Devil when he set his name beneath the Articles. The ship is governed by will of the majority, not because of what it says on a piece of paper, but because if the majority of the crew decide to kill us, then we will be killed, and not a soul aboard shall face any hazard they did not face the night before."

Kavanagh waited. Apollo did not reply.

"In any case, punishment is not needed aboard an orderly ship," Kavanagh continued. "If your orders are wise, then the crew will follow them, except in cases of sloth, choler, or drunkenness, which may be left to the Quartermaster. We are fortunate in Spry, and you would be wise not to make his work more difficult."

"Yes sir," Apollo said.

The words were having no effect. Like eight-pound balls bouncing off a ship of the line. So be it.

"Dismissed, Apollo."

Apollo made his way out without a word.

That night, Kavanagh sat with Dobie in the lamplight and went through the papers for hours. Cian was clever but still only a youth, and there was much Kavanagh had held back from him. Many issues had to be properly sorted. Dobie worked, gloomy, pining over his Cherokee wife and the baby he would, in all likelihood, never see.

The door opened, and Benjamin shambled in with his fishing rod over his shoulder.

"Good evening, Benjamin," Kavanagh said.

There were tears in the foolish Negro's eyes as he lifted his nightly cup. Why?

Ah, of course.

Rory.

He had forgotten.

The Atlantic Ocean.

May 5, 1721.

10

Sailing a ship is a complicated endeavour. Setting more sail does not, in all circumstances, make the ship move faster. Windward sails becalm the sails to their lee, and piling on more sail causes the ship to heel, which reduces her speed, and the more sail a ship carries, the greater the risk of carrying away a spar or splitting a sail in the case of a sudden gust or a squall. One must also consider the trim of the ballast, the rake of the mast, and a thousand other things.

Apollo's mind fitted these factors together with a special holistic genius, and the men respected him for it. But day after day, despite the Captain's warning, he grew more agitated. He was miserable if the ship was going too slowly, and so he ordered the men to set a great press of sail, but he was horrified at the thought of the least damage to the spars, rigging, or sails, and so at the first sign of excess strain he would order them back up to shorten sail. At every change in the wind he changed the sail plan, sending the men out along the footropes of the bowsprit to set the flying jib and the spritsail topsail, a dangerous task in even moderate seas. He berated the helmsman, often seizing the wheel; he ordered the watch below to come on deck and add their weight along the weather rail when he felt the ship was heeling; and even when his men were off-duty he had them working down in the hold, for although he could not get at the ballast, he could shift around the stores.

The men were injured (hernias, broken bones, burns, and one man who tumbled from the bowsprit into the cold and hungry sea and would have drowned had not Quaque dived in and saved him). Yet all this might have been forgiven had Apollo not been such an unlikeable, unpleasant man, ugly and scarred, with never a kind word to say, always finding fault, always bleating away in his unpleasant voice. It was not long before the men were answering back.

At first, Apollo brought such incidents to Spry's attention. Spry punished, without fail, any man who "spoke chuffly" to Apollo, typically by assigning him to clean the heads. He also interjected himself into any quarrel before it could start, shouting that he knew his rights and that if they were not respected, he would go before the mast. However, Apollo grew more and more abusive in his language and unreasonable in his requests. The sweeter the *Saoirse* sailed, and the more compliant her crew, the madder and more unreasonable he seemed to become.

At last a man exploded at Apollo after being asked to take in a sail he had set and taken in twice before, and Apollo slashed him across the face with the rattan.

A Meeting was called and a motion was brought. The crew voted to punish Apollo, but not the man he'd hit.

Kavanagh addressed the men.

"I'm sorry to say we ain't in accord," he said. "I trust you know it pains me to go against the Company, but the man admitted he disobeyed a lawful order, though it was roughly made, and in the circumstances I can't say I'm surprised Tom lost his temper. All in all, Brothers, it seems to me a private affair, the sort of thing the parties ought to work out between themselves without calling a Meeting."

The crowd murmured. Someone objected, *But the Company had voted!*

"Aye, they've voted," Kavanagh said. "But that don't end the matter. Don't you remember the Articles? *Any man who contravenes these Articles shall suffer such punishment the Captain and the majority of the Company shall think fit.* The Captain *and* the majority of the Company, gentlemen. Now what does that mean? Well, it means that to punish a man, both the Captain and the Company must agree. And in this case, there's no agreement, and so there's no punishment. The parties ain't *ad idem*, gentlemen. That's the law. Now, if the injured party ain't satisfied, he can request satisfaction. He ain't shy, I know that. Till then, he can mind his duty."

Dickens, in his now-accustomed perch high above the men, said nothing.

Spry said, "Captain Kavanagh, I must object. Your man here is starting the hands. We all know it, and we won't stand for it."

"I heard you, Brother Spry," Kavanagh said. "Only I don't agree."

More motions were proffered. Would not Kavanagh remove Apollo as an officer? Could they not have a respite from the nightly gunnery? Could they amend the Articles? The debate went on for some time, but the malcontents were still a minority, and every motion failed to pass.

The Meeting was adjourned.

11

A day after that Meeting, Kavanagh summoned Apollo, who came into the Great Cabin and found Kavanagh waiting on the stern gallery.

"Come out, come out," Kavanagh called, smiling. "Look at this!" He held a bucket of blood in his hands.

Gunnery practice had just concluded; from below came the sound of hammers.

Behind the ship stretched a long white wake, tinged pink from the bloody scraps Kavanagh was tossing into the water. As Apollo put his hand on the rail, the snout of a hammerhead shark broke through the surface, with its weird flat head and wide-spaced eyes seeming a demon from an alien Hell. It snapped down on the meat and vanished.

"Hell of a sight, ain't it?" Kavanagh said.

"Yes sir," Apollo said.

"Have a drink with me," Kavanagh said.

"No, thank you, sir."

"Come now, what will the men say if they hear you won't have a drink with a Brother Pirate?"

"I don't care for their opinion."

"So I see. Tell me, when did you first go to sea? Was you a boy?"

"Yes sir. I was nine. I was a midshipman aboard a First Rate in the Nine Years' War."

"Nine," Kavanagh said. "I was never aboard a man-of-war till Rogers came to Cork, looking for sailors for his Cruise round the world. I wasn't aboard a ship until I was already a man. You know what surprised me about it?"

A sound from behind. Apollo turned to look through the stern windows. Israel Hands was in the Great Cabin, sprawled in an overchair, his feet, bare and horny, on the table, a tumbler of whiskey in his hand.

The shark broke the surface, seemed to exhale.

"The ropes," Kavanagh said. "All of the goddamn ropes, and every one of them with a fucking name." He laughed, happy, as he sluffed more chum into the water. "The fucking ropes, man! The shrouds, the stays, the slab lines, the sheets, the halliards. And all the mate had to do was sing out and all the men tramped out and laid their hands on just the one. Sweet Saint Patrick, I thought, I'll never learn them all. But I did. I learned them fucking ropes in a week."

Again, that daemonic visage, the crimson maw, the triangular teeth.

Apollo waited.

"So tell me this, Tommy," Kavanagh said. "How is it that an unlettered Irish fisherman can learn the name of every rope in a man-of-war in a single week, and yet here we are, over a month at sea, and a prime sailor like you don't know the name of a single man?"

Apollo was taken aback. "I am learning their names, Captain."

"Are you stupid?" Kavanagh said.

"No," Apollo said.

"D'you think I'm stupid? Is that it?"

"No," Apollo said.

"All I hear is, 'You sir, clean the deck.' 'You sir, look lively.' 'You sir, coil that rope.' If you cannot remember a man's name, call him Brother Pirate, or Shipmate. But we've been at sea long enough you ought to know the name of every man aboard this ship, certainly the ones on your watch."

"I will try, Captain, but with respect, I do not see why they take offence."

"It is a little thing, ain't it?" Kavanagh said. "But if it's a little thing for them, then it's a little thing for you. And there ain't no need to antagonize a fucking ship full of pirates over a little thing."

Kavanagh emptied the rest of the scraps into the sea, but the monster did not show its face.

"As I said, I shall try," Apollo said, peevish. "All those damned fellows need to do is mind their duty. It seems to me—"

"Damn you, sir," Kavanagh said, turning an indignant eye upon Apollo. "Did I ask you for your opinion?"

"No sir."

"Do you like it when the men answer back to you when you correct them?"

"No sir."

"Well, I don't like it when you answer back to me. And I'll tell you right now, Mr. Apollo, your behaviour ain't just impertinent, it's poor seamanship. Poor seamanship, I say. I was only ever a forecastle jack till I bought this ship, and I don't know much. I had to ask what it meant for a ship to gripe. But I know there's three things that go into sailing a ship: the weather, the ship, and the men. You must manage the men as you manage the weather. If the wind is foul, you may tack or you may wear or you may change your course or you may lie to, but you may not sail into the eye of the wind. It's the same with the men. There's always a way to get what you want, but you must know the way to get it. I'm surprised at you, sir. I know you was a spit-and-polish man, but when I heard how you took that French privateer, I could never have thought you was such a poor leader of men."

Apollo's hard, scarred mask of a face twitched.

"Poor fucking seamanship is what it is," Kavanagh said. "It'd be bad enough if you was in the Royal Navy, but this ship is Upon Her Own Account, and you must adjust your manners just as you'd trim your sails if the wind veered. There's a thousand tricks to it, same as anything else, and if you ain't figured them out by now, I don't suppose you ever will, so I'll say this. Keep a civil tongue in your head, keep your fucking rattan to yourself, and for God's sake, call the men by their names."

When Apollo said nothing, Kavanagh turned back to the ship's wake. Apollo walked past Israel Hands and went below.

For a time, things were better. But Apollo, after visibly losing a struggle against himself, once again grew shrewish, waspish, cutting, and insulting. The pirates did not bother with another Meeting of the whole Company, and instead had their discussions in the lower deck, and Spry now spent his efforts fending off No Confidence motions.

When the *Saoirse* arrived at Cape Verde, Apollo fought three duels, two by sword and one by pistol. Two of the men died. Afterwards there were no more challenges, and the ship sailed farther south, her destination still secret, her mood black.

12

At dinner, Beard said: "Well, that fixes it, don't it? Can't stand the man, can't remove him by vote, and can't fight him neither. They'll be rolling the shot below decks tonight."

"Rolling the shot?" Coffin asked.

"Oy," Hutchins said, and Coffin felt him kick Beard under the table. His messmates looked at him, exchanged glances, and finished their meal in silence.

It was a time of hushed conversations cut short. If an opportunity for a Mutiny presents itself in a ship Upon the Account, there will always be a few men eager to seize it, and the Devil with the consequences. The *Saoirse* was no exception (especially with her unequal distribution of plunder) and John O'Brien and Robert Dickens both set to work. But to plan a Mutiny aboard a ship, even a free-and-easy pirate ship where every man has the right to go where he pleases, is a rather ticklish thing. It is impossible to know whether a man is in favour of Mutiny without asking him, but asking can be a dangerous proposition, so a man's feeling must be winkled out through oblique, ambiguous remarks. Such a sounding is best carried out in private, but there is little privacy to be had, and to seek it is to invite suspicion.

Yet it can be done. O'Brien excelled at this work. He would pick his target with care, sidle up to him, making direct eye contact as he would with a woman. After some trivial remarks, he would damn Apollo and wait for a response, and then damn Kavanagh, and comment on the futility of Meetings, and if all these overtures were received tolerably well, he might drop a hint about a further conversation in the cable tier, or the carpenter's walk, or on the foretop, or upon the head in rough weather, or behind the bits.

O'Brien was unpopular, but Scudder had befriended every man aboard. So, during these brief, clandestine meetings, Scudder was brought in to do the talking while Quantrill kept watch. Once he'd sealed the deal, they'd take an oath upon O'Brien's Bible and take a drink of rum mixed with gunpowder.

It was a difficult, slow business, but after two weeks in which the ship tacked into unfavourable winds and was driven westwards by storms, making little progress, O'Brien informed Scudder that he did not believe it was worth the risk to approach any more hands than they had recruited, and they ought to open discussions with Dickens.

A conference with Dickens was set for four bells of the middle watch. It was yet another dirty night, strong winds and warm rain and high seas. Scudder was the captain of the foretop, and every man there had taken their oath. Quantrill stood watch at the foot of the mast, but the only man out on the deck in this weather was foolish Benjamin, clinging to the rail and hooting at the black, rolling waves.

The bell rang, and the lookouts cried out, "Four bells and all is well," from the tops and the chains and the bow and the stern. In turn, Scudder cried: "Foretop, all is well." O'Brien ascended the shrouds, and half a glass later Dickens followed him with his supporter, Ironside. Last came Quantrill, through the lubber's hole.

"Buh-buh-Billy, we nuh-need you to kuh-keep a lookout," O'Brien said.

"Damn you," Quantrill said. "You always make me the lookout. I ain't stupid."

"How would it luh-look if Kuh-Kuh-Kuh-Kavanagh's men find us like this?" O'Brien said.

"You keep a lookout, then," Quantrill said.

"Keep it down, damn you," Ironside said.

"Pack of lubbers," Dickens muttered.

"It's all right, John," Scudder said. "We don't need no lookout on deck."

"How many men can you speak for?" Dickens said.

"Fuh-forty-one," O'Brien said.

"Forty-one!" Ironside said. "That's too many."

"Every one of 'em's sound," Scudder said. "I brought 'em round."

"Aye," Dickens said. "You're a talker, I'll give you that. I don't doubt you can turn a man's head with your tongue. As for this one"—Dickens jerked his thumb at O'Brien, refusing to look at him—"he's a deft hand at this work. I don't deny it. How could I? I seen him do it to Charlie Vane."

"That wuh-weren't nuh-nothing like this," O'Brien said. "That was a vuh-vuh-vote."

"Now you've found yourself a new talker," Dickens grumbled on. "Haven't learned nothing."

"Now Robert, we ain't here to go over that," Scudder said. "We'll never get rid of Apollo unless we work together."

"Duh-don't you know thuh-that Kuh-Kavanagh's counting on us fuh-fighting with each other?" O'Brien said to Dickens. "He thinks you and I cuh-can't work together because of what happened wuh-with Vuh-Vane. That's why he's duh-done everything the way he duh-did, buh-bringing both you and me along and duh-dividing the Company between his Investors and the Nuh-Negroes and the puh-petty officers. He duh-don't want us to be united."

"What I can't see is why he don't get rid of Apollo," Scudder said.

"Kuh-Kavanagh duh-don't want his officers to be puh-popular," O'Brien said. "Wuh-why would we need him if they were?"

"I suppose," Scudder said.

"I don't care what he's thinking," Dickens said. "I'll be damned if I let that martinet stamp all over me. And I'll have my revenge for Rowen."

"How muh-many men can you speak for?" O'Brien asked.

"Seventeen."

"Fifty-eight," O'Brien said. "Muh-more than enough."

"I'll tell you what we'll do," Dickens said. "We'll cut his fucking throat when he comes onto the forecastle to play his harp."

"Uh-aye," O'Brien said. "And suh-send men uh-aft to tuh-take the small arms."

"What about Apollo?" Scudder said.

"With Kuh-Kavanagh duh-dead, it's a *fait accompli*."

"Damn you," Quantrill interjected. "What's that mean?"

"It means a done deal, Billy," Scudder said.

"And as for that turncoat Hornigold," Dickens said, "I'll wring his fucking neck myself."

"And after?" O'Brien said.

"New Articles, new vote, new everything," Dickens said. "All by vote, all in accordance with the Custom of the Coast."

"And equal shares," Quantrill grunted.

"Tuh-tomorrow?"

"Tomorrow night," Dickens said, and at last locked eyes with O'Brien, and the two men nodded, and spat in their callused hands and shook, and Scudder produced the flask and they all drank. Quantrill was first down the shrouds, followed by Dickens and Ironside.

"It's duh-done," O'Brien said to Scudder. "My lad, by tomorrow Kuh-Kavanagh and his Investors will be guh-gone, wuh-we'll be on equal shares, and you'll be Cuh-Cuh-Captain of the *Saoirse* to buh-boot."

Scudder shook his head and smiled, nervous. "Many a slip between the cup and the lip," he said.

"It'll be cuh-close," O'Brien said. "Israel Hands is duh-deadly, and the Irish will fuh-fight to the last man. But when the Tuh-Tuh-Taoiseach hits the deck, the whole thing comes apart." He clapped Scudder's shoulder. "Tomorrow night."

One hundred twenty miles off the Pepper Coast.

June 20, 1721.

13

The pipes shrieked through the darkness of the lower deck, the bosun called, "Turn out! Turn out!" and the men hit the deck and carried up their hammocks, the sun smearing the horizon to the east. The water was the colour of nickel, the Negroes in rows on their hands and knees grinding the stones into the wood, Apollo on the quarterdeck, pacing, sleepless and vile with secret anger, his rattan hissing through the air.

In the general confusion, men climbing ropes and coming down, water splashing on wood, buckets of tar lifted aloft, and men moving along the yards, the conspirators exchanged significant glances, muttered, winked, signalled.

Today was the day.

A sullen, tense breakfast as they wolfed down their biscuit and drank their beer.

The weather had grown warmer and the men worked shirtless, brown bare backs showing puckered white scars, and tattoos, some crude and mangled, others intricate and beautiful. They trimmed the sails in accordance with Apollo's hostile instructions.

"Yap away, mate," a forecastle hand said from the top, looking down at the little man so far away. "Yap away, while you can."

And then time came for dinner, and the men gathered at the quarterdeck to learn who would be dining with the Captain today, and the list was announced, and there were mutters of discontent and dark looks, for among the names were John O'Brien and Bradford Scudder, though Scudder had already dined with the Captain upon this Cruise, and there were men who had not yet had their turn.

Alive in their unhappiness to any favouritism, the men cursed and spat and shook their heads and the news spread like a virus down the companionway and forward on the lower deck to where O'Brien and Scudder sat at their mess, in anticipation of their modest dinner.

"I already had my turn," Scudder announced to onlookers. "That ain't right."

O'Brien sat frozen on his bench, his mind spinning. An oversight? A coincidence? The guilty flee where none pursue. A trap? Could the invitation be declined?

"I don't think it's right," Scudder said. "Was there a mistake?"

Scudder looked to O'Brien for help, but O'Brien's face was blank.

When they arrived at the forward companionway, the cooks were already on their way down, bearing salt horse with peas, and cried at them to make way there, you damned lubbers, and so they went aft instead, and ascended the companionway to the quarterdeck, where waited the Negro steward, Dobie.

"Dobie, there's a mistake, I think," Scudder said. "I already had my turn last week, and—"

"Ain't no mistake, Brother," Dobie said. "Come in, they're drinking."

"I don't feel right—" Scudder began.

"There you are!" came Kavanagh's voice, so effortlessly loud. "Get in here, you dogs, and have a drink like an Honest Fellow!"

Scudder and O'Brien went into the dining room. None of the other diners were conspirators, and quite a few were Irish, large, raw-boned fellows. Behind each chair was a Negro with a bottle of wine. The men were drunk, having already given many toasts, and they toasted Scudder and O'Brien now, their flushed faces grinning.

Israel Hands sat next to the door to the quarterdeck with a tin cup of water. He did not take part in the toasts, and he did not smile, but watched them as they took the empty seats at the far end of the table, next to Kavanagh.

The toasts went on, one after another, Kavanagh standing stooped and calling them out, the Devil, the Old Pretender, liberty for Ireland, confusion to King George, the Pope in Rome, and if he saw any man leave so much as a drop in his glass, he jabbed a callused finger and cursed his soul and asked him whether he was in a Plot against the Company.

By the time the food arrived, some men had slid beneath the table and had to be carried away by the Negroes. A suckling pig roasted over the stove, the meat falling off the bone, the crackling skin on a separate platter, blood pudding, soused pig's face, trotters, fresh vegetables from Cape Verde, and cheese and butter and bread and pickles and delicacies from glass jars.

When the meal was finished, O'Brien made as if to leave, but Kavanagh called him a whoreson and produced another bottle, and there was nothing for it but to take another round of toasts, great huge cups brimming with brandy, and some men vomited on the table and others collapsed on their plates and they were carried out until the room was empty, save for a few of the largest and most hardened Irish, Kavanagh at the head of the table, and Israel Hands by the door.

Scudder, from drink and native gregariousness, was talking a mile a minute, laughing at his own jokes, waving his cup in the air. The man to whom he spoke was smiling a smile that did not look right to O'Brien.

"Well Captain," O'Brien said, "that was quite a feast. I can't see how you could eat like that every day! I'll be cuh-content with my buh-biscuit tomorrow." He rose to his feet.

"Stay," Kavanagh said. "Come with me upon the stern gallery, and we'll have a smoke. Scudder, you too."

Scudder's flow of speech dried up. He looked from the smiling Irishman to O'Brien's wooden face to Israel's eyes, as empty as a squid's, and tried to think of something to say.

But Kavanagh had already moved into the Great Cabin, leaving the door open behind him, telling them to bring a light, bring a light!

Israel Hands leaned back in his chair so it rested against the exit.

They lit cigars with a candle and Kavanagh took up a thick green bottle and they went onto the stern gallery. Between the motion of the ship and the alcohol, O'Brien staggered. Kavanagh drank deeply from the bottle and passed it to him. O'Brien pressed his tongue up against its mouth and only pretended to drink.

"I'm a plain-speaker, so's I'll cut to the chase," Kavanagh said. "You lads know why you're here."

"Why no, Brother," Scudder said. "I can't say that I do."

"Come on," Kavanagh said. "There's no need to pretend."

Through the windows, they saw Israel Hands come into the Great Cabin.

"Ain't you going to be straight with me?" Kavanagh said. "Come on, man, no need to be coy."

Scudder's friendly, puzzled smile did not falter.

Kavanagh sucked on his cigar and watched them both. "It don't do you no credit to play these games. I asked you here because I thought you'd give it to me straight."

"I'm sorry, Captain," Scudder said, "but—"

"It's about Apollo," Kavanagh said.

"Apollo?" O'Brien asked.

"Devil take you!" Kavanagh said. "Yes, Apollo! I know you ain't happy with him! Do you aim to deny it?"

"No, of course not," Scudder said. "We already brought motions."

Kavanagh leaned against the rail of the ship so that his back faced the sea.

"Well, what's to be done about him?" Kavanagh said.

"What do you mean?" O'Brien asked.

"What I mean is, d'you think a demotion'd do it, to second mate, or should we turn him before the mast? Or is he to be made the governor of an island?"

"Duh-don't know," O'Brien said.

"Whyn't you ask the Quartermaster?" Scudder said. "Or call a Meeting?"

"I have my reasons," Kavanagh said. "I brought you here. Ain't you got nothing to say?"

"If you ask me, Captain," Scudder said, "if he was able to mend his ways, he'd have mended them before now. He must be put ashore."

"I suppose so," Kavanagh said. "Who's to replace him?"

"Rios, perhaps," Scudder said. "Or even Coffin. He was first mate aboard a whaling ship, you know."

"Is that so?" Kavanagh said.

"Or perhaps, Brother, we ought to put it to a vote."

"Hmm," Kavanagh said, taking back the bottle and drinking. He looked over the water, appearing thoughtful. Then at last he said, "Of course you're right."

He signalled to Israel through the stern windows, who disappeared.

"No time like the present," Kavanagh said.

"Now?" Scudder asked.

"Yes, now," Kavanagh said. "I'll confine the little viper to quarters. And I'll put together some loyal hands before I do it, for the man has his supporters, and there may be trouble. I trust I can rely on your support?"

Through the window, they saw Israel re-enter the Great Cabin, but now he held a musket. Behind him thumped Tulip, looking like business, and behind Tulip were more Irishmen, all of them armed. O'Brien turned back to Kavanagh and found in his ancient eye an expression that was not even contempt.

"Of course, Captain!" Scudder was saying, smiling. "But I don't think you need worry about any supporters of Apollo on the lower deck!"

"Better safe than sorry," Kavanagh said.

14

Tulip handed each of Scudder and O'Brien a musket and hustled them onto the quarterdeck. When the waiting bosun saw them, he called down the companionway: "All hands on deck! All hands on deck!" and the bosun's mate blew his fife and from all over the ship came the sound of feet.

The Irish, together with Scudder and O'Brien, formed a solid wall between Kavanagh and the Company. Scudder was grinning. O'Brien turned to him, but before he could open his mouth, a knife dug in between his shoulder blades.

"Eyes front," Israel whispered, "and don't say one fucking word, my love."

"All right, Brothers," Kavanagh shouted. "It's all over, Brothers. I know all about it. John and Bradford have told me everything. Once I promised there'd be no hangings, they told me everything."

Scudder's mouth fell open.

"Yes, Brothers," Kavanagh said, waving a piece of paper in the air. "Forty-one men swore an oath to John and Bradford here, and another seventeen swore with Dickens. They was to murder me when I went on the forecastle to play my harp, and they was to kill Apollo, and Hornigold, and the bosun and the carpenter and the gunner, and some other men, and after that they thought the rest of you would fall into line, a *fait accompli*."

Kavanagh put the paper away and shouted louder. "Don't you know, you damn fools, that you've put your neck right into the noose? We ain't even committed an act of piracy yet. I could throw the Articles overboard, sail into any port in the world, and within a fortnight every damn one of you would be drying in the sun. And besides that, how could you think these silly Sea Lawyers would get the better of me, the Taoiseach? Didn't you hear how I handled them mutineers in the Bay of Honduras in the winter of '17? Ask your elected Quartermaster about that one. He was there, he saw. Did you really think Dickens and O'Brien would get the better of me and Israel Hands?"

He waited, and looked at them, and shook his head.

"Now, no Cruise is perfect, and this one ain't no exception. But ain't I been fair with you? Ain't I kept my word? I'd said you'd eat every day like the Royal Navy, and didn't I keep my word? I said there'd be drinking and dancing, and didn't I keep my word? And now the men I brought into my own cabin on my own ship was plotting to murder me when I came down on the forecastle? For what? A few blows? A few curses? A Mutiny over that?"

Changing tack, Kavanagh continued: "What would the Bastards say if they could see you now? Hmm? All them lords and judges and bishops, what would they say? I'll tell you what they'd say. They'd say: *this is why we always win and they always lose*. Well, gentlemen, they aren't going to win this time. We're going to thump the Bastards, and make our fortune, and then it'll be us that's laughing, and every man here's going to be riding in a carriage, you have my word of honour on that. I been close with our destination, but I'll tell you now. We're on our way to Corso Castle. Yes sir, gentlemen, Corso Castle, the greatest factory of the Slave Coast, chock full of gold dust and other loot, and thanks to my intelligence I know it's ready to be plucked."

A murmur as the men looked at each other.

"Would I be here if I weren't sure?" Kavanagh asked. "Now gentlemen, before you're dismissed, I must say a few more things. Although there'll be no hangings, nor any whippings, there'll be no more dinners in my cabin, nor will I play my harp on the forecastle. And you all know that, in accordance with the Custom of the Coast, there ought to be no private conferences or communications. That rule's often observed in the breach, but no more. If you have something to say, call a Meeting. If you want to write something down, then you best nail it to the mast once you're done. Any secret communications shall be presumed mutinous. I'm sorry to do it, men. I thought I could trust you, but you've proved me wrong. Brothers, you're dismissed."

Kavanagh went back into his cabin and closed the door, and the rank of Irishmen broke up. The knife left O'Brien's back and Israel Hands patted his shoulder. O'Brien presumed the gesture was ironic, but when he turned, Israel's face was unamused, even bored. Tulip took their muskets and went down the stairs with most of the Irishmen.

Scudder stood stock-still, pale and green, and shocked.

15

Kavanagh sat in the Great Cabin, moody. Below decks he heard the predictable shouting. O'Brien and Dickens at it like hammer and tongs, Dickens having a natural advantage because he did not stuh-stuh-stuh-stutter, and the rest of the men shouting about losing their dinners and the dancing. He could not be sure, but it sounded as if that boy, Scudder, was weeping. He felt no triumph; it had been too easy for that. In the morning he had thought his tongue looked unhealthy. The surgeon had said it was nothing, but Kavanagh had insisted upon a bolus and had spent many hours groaning in his quarter-galley.

Apollo, Hornigold, and Quaque sat around the table with him. Apollo, for once, looked ashamed of himself. Hornigold was confused, addled with laudanum. Alfie distributed drinks. The door opened and Spry came in, escorted by Tulip.

"Mr. Spry," Kavanagh said. "Have a drink with us, if you ain't in a Plot."

Spry accepted a crystal tumbler of punch.

"How are the men?"

"They vary," Spry said.

"They always do," Kavanagh said. "Dobie, get the charts."

Dobie took them out, one at a time, unfolded them with care.

"Cape Coast Castle," Kavanagh said.

As it appeared on the map, the Castle was roughly diamond-shaped, divided into two by a central wall. The landward gates were on the north-western wall, and the seaward gate was at the eastern tip.

"You want to attack a Castle?" Spry asked. "High walls, dozens of guns, soldiers?"

Kavanagh gestured to Quaque.

"I was a canoeman at the Castle for many years," Quaque said. "There are very few soldiers. When they die, which they often do, the Governor leaves them upon the books to collect their salary. They sell gunpowder, powder, and shot, which fetch a high price in gold from the natives. The cannon are exposed in the damp air and are corroded; they are mostly used for firing salutes and signals. Finally, the Castle itself is flimsy. Those high white walls are made of small stones and mud and lime. Rubbish painted white. While I was there, a tower collapsed when a salute was fired. A twenty-four pounder would put a ball clean through."

"Are you sure about all this?" Hornigold said, seeming to sober. "Edward England tried to cut out a ship from under the Castle's guns and he found their firing rather hot."

"Come now, Commodore," Kavanagh said. "Would we be here with-out confirmation? Quaque, show them what you showed me."

"See the chart," Quaque said. He leaned forward and tapped the paper. "Three sides face the sea. There are many guns along the south wall, and along the east wall, where is the sea gate and where the canoes land. There is no gate on the west wall, and there are only two guns. They are set up high, so the ships can see them from afar, but they cannot point down at the beach. A few barrels of powder would bring them down."

"Who will land the boats?" Hornigold said. "That's some of the most dangerous surf in the world."

"Quaque, for one," Kavanagh said. "Then there's Coffin, our whaler. He's no stranger to the tiller. Last is Israel Hands."

Hornigold took a closer look at the charts.

"The Castle's a great storehouse, where the ships keep their gold while they're trading up and down the coast," Kavanagh said. "They ain't ready for us, gentlemen. Not for a fifty-gun ship with twenty-four-pound guns that can pound down their walls from a mile away. They think we're finished, us pirates, and they don't think we have the nerve. Now, we've all the charts we could ever want, and Quaque knows that anchorage and the beaches. It can be done."

He was talking to Spry.

"One heated round shot in the powder locker and we're all blowed to kingdom come," Spry said. "But I agree, it can be done. A pretty piece of piracy that would be."

"I'll drink to that," Kavanagh said, and lifted his glass. "Now go and tell the men."

Without music, the evening was sombre. Kavanagh enjoyed the silence and solitude, broken only by Benjamin's soft hooting and humming as he fished off the stern gallery.

16

By now they could deliver three broadsides with reasonable accuracy in five minutes, but Apollo raised his standards. During their exercises, he would tap a man with his rattan and say that he had been killed, and another man would have to take his place. He would call away the sail trimmers and other skilled sailors and take the ship through difficult manoeuvres with reduced crews while the guns were firing. He ordered the men to fire the guns on the lower deck in heavy seas, so the water sloshed inside and they had to time their shots perfectly.

Although he was always finding fault, Apollo was less abusive than usual. His gloom and rage had given way to a frantic mania. With the prospect of assaulting a British fortress before him, he rubbed his hands, and made creaking chuckling noises, and even shouted out compliments when something was well done.

However, the *Saoirse* now entered the doldrums, without a breath of wind. The sails, trimmed to almost nothing, sagged slack from the yards, and the ship barely moved at all, rolling on the slow, greasy waves, and the men became seasick, and the water around them grew filthy with refuse and human waste. Stultifying heat. Tar melted from the ropes and dripped to the deck. Caulking oozed from between the boards. The ship smelled rank and close.

Apollo did all he could to speed their progress. All the boats were lowered and, with ropes, turned the ship, trying to catch faint movements of wind. When that failed, they simply towed her, and Apollo took his turn at the oars along with the men. They carried buckets on their shoulders up the stays to dump water down the canvas, making the fibres swell to tighten the weave and catch more wind. He even indulged in superstition: the men whistled for wind and scratched the backstays and carved hex marks into the masts and put coins beneath the mast, and Apollo had long discussions with the older forescastle hands on matters both technical and spiritual.

At last, after days of calm, a hot and sluggish breeze came from due east, carrying the dust of Africa. A foul wind is better than no wind at all. They sailed on a bowline, east-southeast, and tacked every watch, every time with Apollo on the quarterdeck and Coffin at the wheel, and they never once missed a stay, as they inched along that brown and scorched coastline. They rounded Cape Three Points in a thick rainstorm and the wind began to smell like trees, and they could see it, fading in and out through the rain, the Gold Coast, a thin strip of bleached white sand, and past it, the vastness of the jungle.

Cape Coast Castle.

July 11, 1721.

17

On the dawn of the second day after they rounded Cape Three Points, they saw the smudges of white sails against the green of the shore. "Two sails in the roads!" the lookout cried from the foretop.

They had disguised the *Saoirse* the night before. The deck was cluttered with coops and barrels, and the animals roamed free among the coils of rope and spare sails and timber. Her guns had been hidden under tarps and her real gunports had been covered with canvas on which fake gunports were painted; the *Saoirse* was disguised as a merchantman disguised as a man-of-war. The hammocks had not been brought onto the weather deck, and none of the men had slept, for the lower decks were cleared, fore and aft. They'd eaten their breakfast before dawn, but the galley fire was still lit, so the smoke was visible. She was towing all six of her boats—the launch, the two cutters, the pinnace, the jolly boat, and the gig—and each one of them contained a hidden crew.

Apollo ran forward, through the mess of barrels and cordage, and scrambled up the foreshrouds to the top. The lookout pointed and Apollo raised his glass. Sure enough, two ships, a brig and a sloop, both at anchor. A mile past them he saw the shining Castle, whiter still than the white sands of the beach.

"There it is, men," he said, and his face creaked into a grin. "Furl topsails," he said, and the men (led by Bradford Scudder) climbed up the topmast shrouds to the crosstrees and ran out along the yards and set to work hauling up the canvas. The main and mizzen topsails were also furled. The work was slow, for it was done by only a dozen men.

At the quarterdeck, two men held the wheel, while Rios had the con. Kavanagh stood upon the poop with his hands behind his back. The sails shivered as the ship turned into the wind, but the helmsman kept them on course. After the topsails were furled, the men stayed on the yards, demonstrating to the Castle that there were no men below to work the guns.

So here it was, Kavanagh thought. That time again. A tingling feeling ran through him. Before, he'd always been a jack, a forecastle hand. Now there was so much waiting, and always up here on deck, exposed. Soon they would be dead, or rich. There'd been thirty thousand pounds in ready money aboard the *Whydah*. How much more in a Castle?

Apollo was frenetic, bouncing up and down. Kavanagh thought about speaking to him, but no, it was his moment. He watched as Apollo shoved aside the yeomen who might have carried his messages and shouted down into the waist to fire the salute!

The *Saoirse* fired seven cannon, one after another, *boom, boom, boom, boom, boom, boom, boom*. The tang of gun smoke.

The Castle, after a ponderous delay, returned the salute by firing five guns.

The *Saoirse* responded with three.

It was half an hour's sailing to the ships anchored in the roads. The men below, crammed up against their guns, unable to see, hissing questions to the men up on the weather deck, waited. The men in the boats, lying down, wetted by spray and bounced on the waves, waited.

The leadsman in the chains hurled the lead, which sank to the bottom, and he called out his measurement of the depth. "By the mark, eighteen. By the mark, seventeen."

The *Saoirse* behaved exactly as if she were a slaver, except for one thing. She had come too close to the coast. A thousand-ton ship would normally anchor three miles out to be safe from the rocks and shoals. The Castle would be watching curiously, if not anxiously.

Eight hundred yards from the brig, a man shouted to them: "Ahoy the ship!"

The *Saoirse* was downwind and Kavanagh could smell her human cargo.

"Silence fore and aft," Apollo hissed.

The injunction whispered up and down the ship like a forest breeze.

Five hundred yards.

"From whence the ship?" the man cried again.

Four hundred, three hundred, and the men on the brig knew something was wrong, they were rushing now, some at the windlass, some running below, some climbing the shrouds up to the yards.

The man yelled: "Ahoy, from whence the—"

A pirate screamed from somewhere below: "From the seas, you dog!"

"Fire when ready," Apollo called.

The men on the yards let loose the topsails and then rushed to the crosstrees and scrambled down the shrouds to the tops, where they took up muskets. Men came from below and grabbed the ropes to set sail, and cleared the weather deck, carrying the supplies below or throwing them into the sea, barrels and rope and cages, sometimes with their unfortunate occupants inside. The galley fires were doused, the deadlights installed over the windows.

The *Saoirse* came within a hundred and fifty yards of the brig, and the men in the tops, the best sharpshooters on board (including Bill Quantrill), delivered a crackling, popping hail of musket fire. A half-dozen men aboard the slaver were picked off, their bloody bodies tumbling from the rigging.

The pirates reloaded buccaneer-style—biting the top off the cartridge and pouring the powder down the barrel and jamming in the paper and ball and, instead of using the ramrod, thumping the stock of their weapon upon the wood to push the shot in place and prime the gun. The quicker ones refired in ten seconds; in the minute it took to sail past the brig, they fired five times.

Then came the twelve-pound guns on the upper deck, loaded with chain-shot. They mauled the rigging of the brig, bringing down the mainsail yard in a mass of rope and wood.

Apollo shouted over the gunfire, his ugly face turning an unnatural prunish colour, and the *Saoirse* leaned away from the wind and threw up a white bow wave. The men pulled the tarps off the bow chasers and the hammocks were passed up and stuffed into the netting by the rails, providing some protection from small arms.

"Run up the black flag," Apollo said.

Kavanagh looked up. The Union Jack came down, squeaking, and two flags ran up in its place—one the tricolour of the Pirate Commonwealth, blue, black, and red, the other the colours of the *Saoirse*, designed by Dickens and adopted by the Company, a white skeleton upon a black field, with a sword in one hand and a judge's gavel in the other.

At the sight of the flags, the sloop struck her colours. The jolly boat went to take possession. Three of the boats sailed for the western beach, a cutter, the pinnace, and the launch, fully loaded with men, muskets, cutlasses.

Now that the *Saoirse* sailed due north instead of northeast, the wind came in a broad reach, a sailor's breeze. Apollo called for more and more sails to be set, and they dropped down, filled out, and were sheeted home, and the *Saoirse* sailed faster and faster. They were only a mile from the coast, closing on the dark masses of rocks that poked through the shallow white water.

The leadsman cried out from the chains, by the mark, fifteen! and by the deep, thirteen!

Kavanagh gripped his wrists behind his back. His heart thumped, roaring blood in his ears. He kept everything off his face and watched as guns on the great southern wall of the Castle began to fire, one after another, the sound clear and distant, *boom, boom, boom.*

Then a crash.

The Castle's southeast tower exploded in a fine spray of white powder and black gun smoke, and a sheet of crumbling masonry slid down onto the black rocks and showered into the sea.

"There it is," Rios shouted, relieved. "I did not credit it?"

Kavanagh grinned, wolfishly, and some of the men cheered.

The *Saoirse* did not present much of a target, for she was pointed straight at the Castle, but the range was very close and the water exploded all around her. A ball smashed through the hammocks upon the bow and knocked a cannon askew. Apollo shrieked down into the lower deck and the word was passed and men charged up the forward companionway as the gun rolled with the motion of the ship. One daring man jammed a marlinspike in its wheels.

"Well done, sir," Apollo cried. "Upon my word, well done!"

They came closer. The rocks loomed larger.

The Castle kept up its fire, and its shots fell closer. A ball arced and smashed into the main top yard, knocking it askew, and the bosun and his men climbed up towards it like a fat mother spider with her brood.

Ashore, a cannon exploded. Another shower of lime and pebbles rose up into the air.

Closer, closer, so that any closer was madness.

"Hard to larboard," Apollo cried.

The helmsmen spun the wheel, the ship turned, directions were shouted, feet stamped, the sail trimmers turned the yards, the men climbed the mizzen-mast and furled its sails.

Apollo opened his mouth to shout for the men to fire when ready, but they were already firing, in reasonable order, the twelve-pounders of the upper deck and the twenty-four-pounders of the lower. The timbers shivered with the recoil, a great cloud of smoke enveloped the ship, the cannonballs soared into the distance. When the smoke cleared, Kavanagh saw that the Castle's wall looked ragged, but its defenders were still firing.

"Hard to larboard," Apollo cried, "bring the larboard guns to bear."

The ship turned southwards now, exposing its stern to the Castle, and a shot smashed into the taffrail. She turned farther till she was sailing southeast, and the gun crews below (who had rested for a moment, drinking water out of the scuttlebutt and conversing as well as they could in their temporary deafness) rushed to the other side of the ship.

At the maximum range of the twelve-pounders now, the guns rang out, twenty-four times, an irregular cacophony of smoke and vibration, and this time when the smoke cleared, the Castle's south wall was in disarray. Great masses of shattered white masonry had crumbled, painting the black rocks white, and the guns lay askew in the ruins.

Corso Castle, smashed by two broadsides.

Kavanagh grinned, clenched his fist, and looked over to Apollo, but Apollo looked disappointed.

Madman, Kavanagh thought, and turned his eyes to the boats.

18

C offin sat at the stern of the cutter with his hand on the rudder and his eyes upon the sail, a single mast bearing a fore-and-aft rig. The boat was twenty feet long and carried ten men, their weapons wrapped in tarred canvas. Ahead of them was, first, Quaque, in the launch, and then Israel, in the pinnace. With its fine lines and narrow stern, the pinnace was easier to handle in surf; the issuance of the cutter to Coffin was a compliment.

He sailed due north, the little boat heeling, the men sitting windward to balance her, and when the waves slopped aboard, the men bailed. The water was dark blue, and the waves were high, and the boat rolled, up and down. Coffin watched Quaque's boat; she hesitated at the edge of the surf, where the waves broke and crumbled into cold white foam and rumbled towards the shore.

Coffin gave the order and a man furled the sails and took down the mast.

A gun roared from atop the western wall. Coffin saw the shot plunge into the sea, twenty yards from Quaque's boat. Still Quaque waited.

A great wave lifted the stern of Coffin's boat and pointed the bow straight down into that dark-blue void. When they righted, Coffin saw that Quaque had ordered his men to ply their oars and they were riding on the back of the great wave as it disintegrated, all the men hauling and hauling and Quaque's faint voice crying, and the moment they were in the shallows, the men leapt out and seized the gunwales and carried the boat up the rocky shore.

"There it is, I suppose," Coffin said. "When I give the word, thou must pull with all thy hearts."

Ahead of them, Israel's pinnace caught a wave and his men pulled, pulled, with all their hearts, driving into that chaos of froth. Coffin turned and looked behind and counted, and the waves came in, each three feet high, and then finally the seventh wave, twice the size of its antecedents, leaning and trembling, only held upright by its forward momentum, came upon them, and he cried out for them to pull, pull, pull, and pull they did, and as their bow rose, they raced along with the living wave under them, faster, faster, the bow wobbling, and Coffin knew that if they lost this wave, the next would broach them. The oars of the men plunged and rose, plunged and rose, and the boat skidded and pitched.

Ahead of them, the pinnace had somehow gone a-kilter, and Coffin could see, but not hear, Israel screaming at the men, and their rowing grew uneven, confused, and the boat slowed and they lost their wave and the following one struck them upon the quarter and that was it, she was gone.

"Pull, pull!" Coffin cried. "For thy lives, for thy souls, pull!"

They did. He counted, three, two, one, cried: "Stop!" and they stopped as one, the broken water racing onwards, and they grasped the gunwale, and then they were past the swamped pinnace (now bobbing up to the surface) and Coffin jumped clear and grabbed the stern and the men jumped too and all of them ran, ran like madmen, the water sucking at their legs, till they had hauled the cutter up onto the beach and laid it down next to Quaque's boat.

Coffin ran back towards the water. The waves had dropped Israel's pinnace hard upon the shore and then sucked it back, and the pirates were shambling up out of the water, coughing and gasping, and Coffin ran past them to where Israel wrestled with the boat. He grabbed a hold of her and together with some other men they waited for the next wave and ran with the water carrying them, so their toes scarcely touched the earth.

"Did all the men make it ashore?" Coffin asked once they were ashore.

"Fuck them," Israel grunted as he unwrapped a bundle of muskets.

Coffin counted. Two men missing. He ran back to the water, where the waves pounced with enough force to break bones, and he timed his entrance and dived down and swam in the calm dark beneath the disorder. The current sucked him out to sea and he broke the surface and for an instant he held himself above the white water and he caught the merest glimpse of a man struggling, and he swam to him, ducking under the waves, and he saw the man in the dark and grabbed his hand and gripped him under the arms and turned onto his back and kicked perpendicular to the beach until they were out of the riptide. The man was still in his arms. Light, calm. Coffin thought he was in shock, or exhausted. It was only when he hauled him out of the water and saw that the man's leg was missing, bitten off at the hip, that Coffin realized he was dead.

Coffin let the corpse drop, and a wave took the body back. The other pirates had their weapons and they were charging the western wall, which, as Quaque had told them, had no cannon that could point towards the ground. Coffin followed, but slowly. He did not wish to kill anyone, and in spite of everything, he was still afraid of death, though this life had become a plunge into bottomless sin.

19

The landing party blew up a barrel of gunpowder by the western wall, which crumbled like a chalk waterfall, and then rushed to the attack. Still, Kavanagh could not believe that seventy pirates could take a Castle. Through the grimy spyglass he watched hordes of men running back and forth, but very few red coats. At last he put the glass away. He fought the urge to pace, leaving it to Apollo, who now ran down the deck to the forecastle to scream at the men for some perceived deficiency of the rigging. Despite the easy victory, or perhaps because of it, his poor mood was returning with a vengeance.

"Look there!" Kavanagh called.

The Union Jack was coming down from the Castle.

"They've done it!" Kavanagh shouted. "We've gone and bloody done it!" He whipped off his hat and slapped it on his knee. "Don't you see you've done it, you fucking dogs! You goddamned sons of the everlasting whore! Look! Look!"

The flag was gone. They waited, as the *Saoirse* rose and fell. Then at last, slowly, slowly, another flag rose above the Castle's shattered walls. Red, black, and blue. The tricolour of the Commonwealth.

The men watched, disbelieving, and then cheered, cheered, cheered.

Kavanagh went among them, Tulip at a discreet distance, shaking hands, slapping backs, grinning. We've done it, we've done it! Bloody Corso Castle, mate!

The *Saoirse* sailed back to the roads, a safe distance from the surf, where awaited the captured brig and sloop. Dickens and his men had been sent to take the brig, while O'Brien and his lot had taken the sloop, except for Scudder, who was in the foretop, and Quantrill, who was ashore with Israel Hands. If the mutineers wanted to run, they would be given every chance.

Now Kavanagh sent Dobie for Scudder and relieved himself in the quarter-galley while he waited. The seas were choppy and rough, and his stomach troubled him. He did not much relish the prospect of landing in all that surf, and the air around the Castle was deadly, but he needed to be ashore to make sure all was in order. He looked at himself in the mirror. Pale gums, yellowish eye. Just as well. When he came back into the Great Cabin, Scudder was waiting, looking eager to please, as well he bloody might.

"Bradford, do you wish to go ashore?"

"Certainly, Captain," Scudder said.

"I'm going ashore myself to make sure all is in hand, but I ain't well."

"Sorry to hear that," Scudder murmured.

"You've a loud voice, Bradford, and I'd be grateful if you'd do the talking for me."

"Oh yes, Captain," the youth said, brightening. "Only, what would you like me to say?"

"Don't worry about that," Kavanagh said. "If you step wrong, I'll set you right. Only remember, we don't use our real names ashore."

Scudder winked, gave a brilliant smile, and left.

Kavanagh went onto the stern gallery and looked at that magnificent sight, the ruined Castle, the tricolour snapping in the jungle winds. Allowed himself to enjoy it.

After an hour, Quaque and Coffin returned with their mostly empty boats. The men gave them a lusty cheer as they came alongside.

"Well done, well done, damn well done," Kavanagh said. "A toast, gentlemen, to your famous victory!"

Coffin looked uneasy at the prospect of a drink. Quaque said, "Perhaps we should take it ashore, Captain. The surf is rough."

"Why, damn you for a lily-livered Presbyterian," Kavanagh said. "Have it your way."

Kavanagh jammed his glass eye back in. Apollo, Tulip, and Hornigold would remain on board and the boats filled with men eager for a holiday. They sailed to the eastern beach, with the seaward gate and the gentler landing, but the surf was still wretched, and Kavanagh was grateful he'd eaten no breakfast. When they landed, Quaque and Scudder actually carried Kavanagh ashore, like an officer's wife, and set him down with dry feet on the white sand.

"Thank you, lads," he said.

Cocked his head.

Listened.

A noise rose above the roar and smash of the surf.

Drums.

He looked at Quaque, who said, "The news will be up and down the coast in a few hours."

They walked up the beach to the plain brown double door. It was unlocked.

"The Door of No Return, they call it," Kavanagh said. "Yet here you are, Brother."

Quaque smiled, but looked sick.

"Strange to be back?"

"Shall I return to the ship for more men?" Quaque asked.

"Nay, the rest shall stay afloat," Kavanagh said.

Quaque hesitated as the others went through the door.

"What now?" Kavanagh said. "You ain't thinking of visiting your village?"

"No," Quaque said. "I would only be enslaved again. I was convicted, now I am a pirate. My wives will have other husbands, my sons will be men. I can never go home."

"Well then, come on in," Kavanagh said.

It was startlingly dark in the little tunnel.

20

The Castle had been constructed by the Swedish in 1650, then taken by the Danish, then the English. Because of the surf and the rocks, all contact between ship and shore was done by canoes. Quaque had been only a boy when he began to work as a canoeman upon this coast, as his father had done so before him, and his grandfather, and on, and on. The canoemen were well paid in tradeable goods, along with whatever they could steal. Quaque could speak six languages, and in his most successful year (the one before he was enslaved) he had earned gold dust worth two hundred pounds, more than three times the salary of a merchant captain. His sons were being brought up in his trade, and one of his daughters, his favourite, a laughing, beautiful girl of thirteen, had been taken as a wench by one of the Castle's factors (a union made according to local custom) and had produced at least one mulatto grandson, who had been baptized in the Church of England and would learn to read and write.

Then: disaster. Quaque was arrested for stealing. The usual procedure was for his family to pay a redemption price, which they could easily afford, but the Governor, frustrated with thievery, decided to make an example of him. And so Quaque had been marched out through the Door of No Return in chains, rowed out by the same canoemen with whom he had worked, and sent west, across the ocean.

Now his mind was indeed taken up with memories of how he had walked in chains through this door, and of how he had been rowed to sea and stuffed in the hold, of how he had told everyone who would listen, and some who would not, in English, how he was a wealthy man, an important man, how he was a skilled canoeman, and not a slave like these others at all, how he would pay a great price for his own freedom, how his entreaties had seemingly fallen upon deaf ears, but only seemingly, for he had eventually earned a tense interview with Jimmy Kavanagh, who had many questions about the Castle and its defences and the tides and the rocks.

Yes, these memories flooded through him as he walked through the dark tunnel. But what haunted him now was not the memories of that bizarre, dreamlike day, but all its pedestrian counterparts. All the other days, the regular, normal days, when he had not walked through the Door of No Return but waited with his canoe down by the sea. When he had ferried the slaves through the surf to the waiting ships, day after day, week after week, month after month, year after year.

How many had it been? Quaque could not read or write, but he could perform, without effort, complicated arithmetic in his head.

How many had it been? Why, perhaps ten thousand. Ten thousand slaves he had ferried out to the ships before he was ferried out himself.

They came into the light, into celebration and song.

21

The parade ground was roughly triangular, surrounded by white walls. The mood was jubilant but somehow a trifle off, and the men were not in good order, rampaging through the officers' quarters for loot. The men behind Kavanagh surged past to join in. Spry jogged over, looking concerned.

Nothing can ever be easy.

"Scudder," Kavanagh said. "See about bringing these men to order. Call a Meeting. Make arrangements for dinner."

"Won't the Negroes do that?"

"Free Negroes coming ashore at Corso Castle? Ah ha ha! No, Brother. Set the Castle slaves to it."

"Yes, Captain," Scudder said, and sprinted forward, roaring in his boyish voice. A few of the men looked to Kavanagh, startled, but he nodded, and they obeyed.

To Spry, Kavanagh said, "You look troubled."

"There's no gold," Spry said.

Kavanagh tilted his head, waited.

"I asked the Governor. He said the doldrums are bad this year. Said he was surprised we didn't notice. Said the ships are worried about pirates."

"No gold?" Kavanagh said.

"Five hundred ounces only."

Kavanagh hissed involuntarily. "Go with Scudder. Once dinner's started, see what you can do about the evening's entertainment."

"Entertainment?"

"Something judicial, you see," Kavanagh said.

"If you think so, Captain," Spry said.

"I do think so," Kavanagh said. "The boy Scudder shall be the Defendant."

"Should I inform him?"

"Keep it a surprise."

Spry left, and Kavanagh turned to Quaque. As no one could see his face, save the canoeman, he indulged his choler.

Quaque visibly paled.

"Captain . . . Taoiseach . . ." he began.

"Thirty thousand pounds at least, you told me!" he said, his voice very, very quiet, so Quaque had to strain to hear over the booming surf, the shouting, singing men.

"I couldn't . . . I didn't . . ." Quaque said.

"You owe me thirty thousand pounds," Kavanagh said.

"Captain, sir, I do have an idea, I do."

Kavanagh looked at him.

"I need a hard man," Quaque said. "Hands? Or do you . . ."

"Hands."

"It will not be pretty," Quaque said. "If you had any thoughts of a Pardon . . ."

Kavanagh made a face and chopped the air with his two-fingered hand.

Behind him, Scudder was calling the Meeting to order. The men were cheering, whistling—they seemed delighted with him.

"Hands will be indulging himself," Kavanagh said. "Where are the slaves?"

In the corner of the parade ground, a great trap door. The lock had been smashed and the door thrown open. A short, crude spiral staircase. The ceilings were low and arched, it was dark, hot, humid, the stench powerful, shit, sweat, death, tactile as much as olfactory. The yellow glow of the lantern on the black bodies, all of them chained, all of them with weeping brand marks on their flesh, but dissimilar in every other particular. Men, women, thin, fat, tall, short, young, old, farmers, fishermen, blacksmiths, gunsmiths, soldiers, priests, tiny babes, debtors, prisoners of war, kidnappees, literate Muslims from far north, those who had been convicted of witchcraft, those who had made their living on the sea and those who had never seen the sea, those with tattoos and scars and sharpened teeth and those without.

Israel grunting over an old woman, her face scrunched in misery. When he finished, he spat in her face.

"What?" he asked.

"The battle?" Kavanagh said.

"It was just as they said," Israel said. "There weren't above seventy white men in the Castle. Thirty were sick."

"Nothing notable?" Kavanagh asked.

"Your man, the big one, what's his name?"

"Quantrill."

"Aye," Israel said. "First over the wall, first in the fight, first in everything. Spry granted him the Commission, first pick of everything. He's a stout one. You ought to cut his throat."

"Noted," Kavanagh said. "There's no money in the warehouse, Israel. Go with Quaque. I believe he wishes you to put a gentleman to the Question."

Israel pulled up his pants and nodded at Quaque.

The Meeting was in full swing. Scudder stood upon the stairs, paced back and forth, telling them he was the appointed representative of Captain Poseidon, who was feeling unwell. The men laughed.

Kavanagh sniffed. The air here was noxious, redolent with Fever. He had brought with him a cloth sack of potpourri, and he pressed it to his nose and breathed through it.

Israel and Quaque stepped past Scudder on their way to the Governor's apartment.

The first motion was whether to liberate the slaves, which passed unanimously. The Meeting dissolved into disorder as men rushed to give the news to the slaves, who came up into the sunlight and were met by Matthew Lewis, the armourer, with a cigar clamped between his teeth and the tools of his trade set before him.

"Liberty for all!" he cried, already drunk, and he set to work with a hammer and chisel, tap tap tap, freeing one after another.

Scudder had moved on to other business when they all heard the Governor scream, a long, horrible, warbling noise, like he was coughing or laughing. Then, "Quaque, please! Please!"

The expression of confusion on Scudder's face produced dark and derisive laughter.

The Meeting was adjourned, and Scudder fled down the stairs to see about dinner.

22

Liberating the slaves was long, hot work, and it dragged on for hours, until Lewis was too drunk to continue, and then others took up the tools. The parade ground filled with unchained Negroes, and yet more and more came up from the holes.

Quaque came down, and the slaves crowded around him, but all he could do was to shake his head and shrug, and eventually he pushed his way to the boats, where the sober and sensible were stacking the most valuable chattels. Some slaves approached the white men and tried to speak to them, but they could not make themselves understood, and having performed this grand liberation, the pirates had little interest in conversation.

Eventually Scudder led a group of slaves to the landward gate, where Quantrill was drinking in moody solitude. He brightened at the sight of his friend, the only one he had aboard the ship, and proudly showed him the weapon the Quartermaster had given him, a magnificent rifle inlaid with silver. At Scudder's command, Quantrill lifted the bar and threw open the door, dramatically, and the pirates upon the walls cheered.

But beyond the gates of the Castle was the town, rows and rows of houses inhabited by the Fante, the legal owners of most of the slaves. The villages from which the slaves had come were hundreds of miles away, and between there and here was no succour. Some slaves ran, but most hung back, confused, unsure, talking to each other, looking around, as if someone would help them. Some went out over the shattered western wall, while others went down through the Door of No Return to the eastern beach, there to be confronted by a short strip of white pebbles, high black rocks, and a steady train of waves.

One of these was a tall woman. Older, handsome, naked save for a loincloth. She returned to the parade ground, with purpose, and addressed a group of slaves in a high, theatrical voice, almost as if she were singing, and gestured towards the seaward gate. Many wept. Some shook their heads. A young woman clutched a little baby to her breast, very tight. The older woman took the young one by the shoulder, but the younger pulled away and wept and shook her head and squeezed the babe, who began to scream. Finally, the older woman kissed the younger on the head, brief but tender. Most of the slaves in her group, perhaps fourscore, followed her as she walked back to the seaward gate.

The young woman cried out. Some of the departing slaves looked back, but the others did not. The older woman was singing as she led them out the Door of No Return. As the last ones vanished into the darkness, the young woman with the baby followed.

Coffin, together with a crew of twenty men, was loading the launch when the Negroes walked into the sea, flinching and weeping. He did not realize what they were doing until a powerful wave knocked them down and the insatiable water pulled them into the deep.

There were so many. It was madness. It was sin.

One after another damning their souls.

Last was the young woman with the baby, and he could not bear it; at least the child must live. He rushed down to her, screaming and mad. She flinched away and neither of them saw the wave, and they were both knocked down and tossed back and forth at the mercy of the power of the sea.

The crew of the launch watched. Some of them had been slavers themselves, and only shrugged and spat and said, aye, the Negroes often did thus if given the chance, and who could bloody well blame them, but others had no experience with the trade, and of those most were shaken, and solemn, and quiet. When Coffin at last crawled from the hungry surf, all of them went back to work.

23

Kavanagh climbed upon the ruined seawall where the air was better, but when half an hour passed and he did not smell cooking fires, he went to find Scudder. In short order the Castle slaves were routed out of their hovels, and bullocks and goats and pigs were butchered and fires blazed and meat turned on the spit. This accomplished, he threw his arm around Scudder's shoulder and brought him back to the seawall for fresh air, for the youth was looking green.

"Something troubling you, Brother?"

Scudder smiled, embarrassed. "One of the Castle slaves told me there was some preserves in the Governor's apartment, and when I went up there, well."

"Hmm?" Kavanagh said. "They gave him the matches?"

"No, it was his eye, his eye, you see, it . . ."

"Sort of popped out, did it?" Kavanagh said, pleasant.

"What did they do to him, do you think?"

"I imagine they woodled him. Didn't see none of those tricks with Captain Bellamy, I suppose?"

"Ha ha, no," Scudder said.

"The Prince of Pirates, they called him," Kavanagh said, holding the sack of potpourri to his face. "It was a different world then. It ain't the year '17 no more."

Dinner was late, by naval standards. Eighteen men were posted sentry round the Castle, by the seaward and landward gates, and by the hole in the western wall, and by the slave holes, where the prisoners were held. Perhaps another dozen were insensible from drink. The rest of the men, over fifty, crammed into the great dining hall, with its long tables and chandeliers. The portrait of the King had been defaced and hung upside down, and the usual toasts were given, as well as those to the heroes of the day, Quaque, Quantrill, Lewis (who had struck the chains from so many slaves), and Kavanagh, the founder of the feast.

He sat at the head of the table with Israel at his right hand, laughing, red-faced from the heat and drink, slapping at mosquitoes and matching every man toast for toast. The Castle slaves brought in food by course, leaving as quickly as they could, turtle soup and fish and meat and bread and cheese and pastries. Howsoever many dishes they piled upon the table, they vanished just as fast, and the pirates pounded their fists and demanded more. Wine stained the linen and the men began to punctuate their toasts by hurling the dishes against the wall. A man of Scudder's party fought one of Dickens's, and they had to be separated.

At last, Kavanagh said: "Gentlemen! A moment of your time. Gentlemen!"

"Speech, speech!" they cried. "The Taoiseach! A speech!"

"I'll be brief, Brothers," he said, rising to his feet. "You've done it, you goddamn Devil dogs, you've gone and bloody well done it, you took Cape Coast Castle, with only the loss of two men, and them drowned! Toast your fucking selves, mate!"

They did, howling. A chair was hurled into a chandelier and it crashed onto the table and a cloud of shattered glass exploded into the air.

"Now then, you son of a bitch, what was the need for that? It might have got in someone's eye," Kavanagh said, brushing his shoulders. "Anyway, men, they'll be talking of this in London, in the West Indies, all over the world! The finest stroke since Morgan took Panama. And I'm damned sorry the ships weren't in. We didn't do as well as I hoped, I'm the first to admit it. Why, I imagine our take is only, what would you say, Israel?"

Kavanagh tilted his head towards Israel, made a show of listening to him, turned back to the men, his face grave, and said: "Only . . . twenty-one thousand pounds!"

Grinning, he motioned behind him, and two slaves stepped from a shadowy corner and set a small chest on the table and threw it open, so the gold dust piled therein sparkled in the light.

The pirates shouted, kicked away their chairs, and surged forward, and Kavanagh's voice rang out: "Handsomely, oh handsomely, you fucking mules!" The slaves ploughed through and dropped chest after chest on the table.

"Had it hidden away in the walls, they did," Kavanagh said. "Rotten swabs. Twelve thousand the Governor had, the thieving whoreson! And they call us pirates! Anyway, you've Hands and Quaque to thank for this. Let us, gentlemen, drink their health!"

This was done. Quaque rose and bowed. Israel was too drunk to stand, but he nodded, and then took out his member and pissed under the table.

"Now gentlemen," Kavanagh said. "Ask your Quartermaster about the watches—we must keep watch at all times. And if you see anything you want to bring back to the ship, get it down to the parade grounds. The Quaker ain't drinking, he'll get it aboard for you."

"Three cheers for Coffin," Scudder said, very drunk, waving his cup.

"A toast from a mutineer," Kavanagh said, his tone suddenly changing, his gaze turning cold. "Why, I call that handsome, don't you, gentlemen?"

An awkward silence.

"Thought I'd forgotten about that trick, did you?" Kavanagh asked.

Scudder smiled, uncertain, and opened his mouth, and then a hood dropped over his head and he was jerked off his feet.

Chaos, screaming, a tussle, sharp blows. Scudder felt himself dragged away, heard the noise die down.

His heart raced in his chest. Caught! He was caught! He was going to die, right now, it was another one of Kavanagh's tricks, lure them off the ship!

"Billy, Billy!" he screamed, terrified. "Billy! Save me."

"Silence there!" Kavanagh shouted. "Order in the court!"

Strong hands forced him onto a chair, though he was so stiff he lay atop it like a rigid board.

"Order!"

The hood was jerked from his eyes.

24

The light from the firepit was at first blinding, but he soon saw he was in the courtyard before the landward gate, surrounded by pirates and freed slaves. Kavanagh sat at a wooden desk. He wore a scarlet uniform with golden epaulettes and a powdered wig and he was pounding upon the desk with a carpenter's mallet.

"Order! By God, you scurvy dogs, I'll have order or I'll clear the court!"

The sun had set and it was very dark, but he saw everyone in the light from the fire, grinning, shouting abuse, laughing.

"Order! Order!" Kavanagh cried, and the unruly crowd quieted.

Scudder felt a hand on his shoulder and he whipped around. It was the Quartermaster, Spry, also wearing a wig and a stolen uniform. He smiled very kindly at the youth, and called out:

"May it please your Worship, and you Gentlemen of the Jury, here is a sad dog, and I respectfully submit that he ought to be hanged. He has committed piracy upon the high seas, plundering and burning and sinking many a ship, he has overthrown powerful forts, and he has ravished innocent women, children, and small dogs."

Laughter, jeering.

It was a joke, a game.

Relief, relief, relief.

"I never ravished a child," Scudder piped up, his voice still wavering. "And as for the dog, it weren't innocent, it was of loose moral character."

The men around the fire roared.

"Moreover," Spry continued, "we shall prove, your Lordship, that Scudder has been guilty of drinking small beer, and as your Lordship knows, there never was a sober fellow but what was a rogue, and he has used his comely looks to seduce his helpless shipmates into unspeakable acts of indecency in the lower decks."

"By God," Scudder cried. "Who's playing the informer? Was it you, Cyrus?"

"Silence there," Kavanagh cried. "How do you plead?"

"Not guilty, your Honour," Scudder said.

"Not guilty?" Kavanagh said. "Say it again, and I'll have you hanged without any trial."

"Sir," Scudder said. "May it please your Honour, I am an honest young man, and I only ever meant well, but I was forced into piracy by one Horace Spry, a notorious pirate and a sad rogue, and he forced me."

Now the men howled.

"A likely story, you wretched little catamite," Kavanagh said, as he smacked his mallet into the table. "I've heard enough."

"But your Honour, I haven't had a chance to speak," Scudder said.

"If you are allowed to speak, you may clear yourself, which is an affront to the court."

"But I hope you will consider—"

"Consider? I've never considered anything in my life."

"But if you will listen to reason—"

"We don't go according to reason, you little son of a bitch!" Kavanagh cried, waving his gavel. "We go according to law! And so you shall hang for three reasons. First, it is not fit that I put my wig on and nobody be hanged. Second, you have sailed across the ocean and not drowned, and as everybody knows, those who were born to hang shall never drown. And third, you shall be hanged because you have a hanging look. Take him away!"

The hood dropped back over Scudder's head, and he was hauled out of the chair, and everyone around him was screaming and shouting. Back into the Castle, propelled up the stairs, and then out into the warm night air again, and he could feel the drop before him as the noose went around his neck.

Wait, Scudder thought, they won't really . . .

A hard shove between his shoulder blades and he was falling, his lungs empty, and then he hit the pond.

25

Kavanagh slept in the Governor's bed, for the Governor had no need for it any longer. He woke at dawn and slapped at a whining mosquito. He was sweating, but despite the smothering wet heat, he felt chilled. Something was wrong. After a moment, he realized: the drums had stopped.

Israel came in.

"They're here," he said.

Kavanagh rolled out of bed.

"Get the boy, Scudder," he said.

Kavanagh waited by the fetid pond in the courtyard. Vultures everywhere, great big awkward things, waddling and croaking. At last, Scudder appeared, rubbing his eyes, and they walked to the landward gate and climbed the stairs to the top of the wall, where Billy Quantrill awaited, still sullen, but now alert and interested.

Below them were the Castle gardens, oranges, lemons, bananas, pineapples, and mangoes, and past them was the town, and past the town were two fortified hills, Phipps and Smallpox, each with a little tower. Past these was the pathless forest, green and complete.

The Fante army numbered at least a thousand men; the Asafo, as they were called, dressed in white cloth and bore muskets. They had taken both the hills, and their tents and bivouacs filled every empty space.

"They don't have cannon," Israel said.

"Neither do we," Quantrill grunted. "Why didn't these people put no cannon facing the land?"

"They didn't need to, that's why," Kavanagh said. "The Royal African Company has permission to be here, it pays rent, it pays for water, it pays for wood and supplies, it pays canoemen. Thousands of pounds a year over to the Fante. And, of course, the Fante buy Negroes a hundred miles from the coast, and sell 'em for five times what they paid. The poor white men sail 'em all the way across the ocean and get twice what they paid if they're lucky."

Kavanagh spat over the wall.

"Bloody good racket they've got going on, the Fante!" Kavanagh said. "But ain't nothing as easy as it looks. Got to protect it, for one thing. And so you have the Coalition of the Coast. A thousand men mustered in a night."

"I sent for Quaque," Israel said. "But he's out in the canoes loading the ship. I know you talk some Fante, Taoiseach, but—"

"We ain't going to need no interpreter, Brother."

And they did not. When ten minutes later the messengers approached the gate under a flag of truce, one of them called up in perfect English: "What flag is that?"

Kavanagh nudged Scudder, who said: "It is the flag of our Commonwealth."

The messenger was a man of high status, a caboceer or a braffo, and he wore a colourful necklace and gold jewellery. After speaking to his entourage, he said to Scudder:

"Here is my message. The Fante have a treaty with the King of Great

Britain. The British use this Castle with our permission. You have no treaty with the Fante. Also, you are not a real nation but only pirates. You must leave the Castle before noon. If you do not, we will attack, and because you are only pirates, you will be killed or sold to the Moors."

"We need a day," Kavanagh said to Scudder.

"That is not enough time," Scudder called down. "First of all, the men are drunk. Secondly, we are not finished with our robbery. Lastly, as I told you, you ignorant savage, we are a Commonwealth, and I have no authority to negotiate terms without a full Meeting and a vote."

"It is not much time," the messenger agreed. "May I speak to you informally, unofficially?"

Kavanagh nodded. Scudder said, grandly, "By all means."

"You understand I have no authority to say what I am about to say?"

"Please, speak freely," Scudder said.

"We are not a Commonwealth," the messenger said, smiling. "But we have no king, either. Some men have come from afar and they have no slaves in this Castle and they wish to loot as much as you. We cannot offer you much more time, pirate. In truth, I do not think you will even have two hours."

Kavanagh whispered to Scudder.

"Now you listen here, you heathen savage," Scudder said. "As you can see, our men have no interest in your slaves and if you let us finish our business, we will return them to you. However, if you attack us this morning, I swear by God that we shall kill your slaves, every one of them."

The messenger nodded, and said: "I shall convey your message. But I think that if you have not left by noon, those that die will be the lucky ones."

The messenger and his party left. Kavanagh said: "Scudder, stay here. If they come back, stall 'em." To Israel he said, "Come with me."

They went through the Door of No Return and found Quaque on the beach, loading the launch. He came to meet them. "Yes Captain?"

"Get all the slaves out onto the beach," Kavanagh said. "Tell 'em the Castle's surrounded and we'll take 'em somewhere safe."

Quaque did not reply.

"Getting soft on me, mate?" Kavanagh said, and in his eyes something truly dangerous stirred. He caught Quaque by the neck. "I don't know if I've mentioned. My father was Barbadosed after the Williamite War and died on a sugar plantation. Most white men do, within five years. Negroes last a little longer, but not much. All the slaves here are already dead. So don't you be getting soft on me now, shipmate. Too fucking late for that." He released Quaque. "Once you're done, take me out to the *Saoirse*."

Within moments, Quaque returned, followed by crowds of Negroes, revived and buoyant with hope. They clogged the narrow tunnel and the thin beach. Kavanagh looked over the water to the canoes. He knew the Fante could see. Would they believe he would go through with it? Would they care if he did?

Once Quaque returned, he stepped aboard the launch, heavy with cloth, bottles of wine, other valuables. Kavanagh had begun to shiver, and his head ached. Fever. He was sure of it.

They were just away when they heard a crackle of musket fire, the pops dimly audible over the roaring surf.

"Goddamn it," Kavanagh said.

Whether they were driven, or they had panicked, the slaves surged through the tunnel and Kavanagh saw them trip and fall and trample each other. The foremost ones were crowded forward by the hindmost, and some of them were smacked down by the water, which came with such force that even an ankle-high wave might knock a man down and drag him out.

26

The attack had only been an exploratory push. W_____ ___ was met with musket fire and grenados, the Fante retreated, leaving behind their dead. It took hours for the boats to return to the ship, and to unload all their cargo, and then more hours to return to the Castle. There were under fifty pirates still ashore. Quantrill and Scudder waited on the wall above the landward gate. It was intensely humid. Vultures circled. There was plenty of time to think.

"I expect you've never been in a real one," Quantrill said.

"Ah ha ha," Scudder said. "Not ashore, no."

Quantrill grunted. "You'll be all right."

The drums started a little before noon. The Fante milled around, chanting and cheering, then advanced in a column, waving their flags.

Quantrill opened a box and handed out grenados, small, hard metal balls with short, stiff fuses. "Wait till they're close," he said.

Bullets slapped into the white mortar and kicked up powderized stone.

The Fante broke into a run, closer, closer.

A candle was passed down the line and each man lit his grenado. Scudder watched the wick sizzle and retreat into the shell and then he stood and hurled. The first grenados had already done their work and he saw men blown apart, looking strange and unnatural with pink tubing hanging from them or missing legs and all awash in blood. After his own grenado exploded, Scudder aimed his musket into the mass of men and pulled the trigger, and though he was shaking, trembling all through, he must have hit something, for he could hardly have missed. Yet the Fante pressed on, close enough he could see how young they were, almost boys, eyes glassy.

He fumbled at his cartouche, took out a cartridge (others spilled on his feet), bit through the paper, poured the powder down the barrel, rammed the ball and paper home.

The young Fante were at the gate below them and more grenados were dropped upon them, the explosions so close that the vibrations crawled spider-like up Scudder's legs. Farther back, the older Fante aimed and some pirates along the wall were hit.

Here Scudder's vision became disconnected into a series of images that no longer formed a sensible narrative. Blood flashed out on the white wall. Bits of stone rained down on his head. A Negro holding his severed arm tiptoed from the battle. A white man clutched his neck, his expression calm while blood came out of his nose.

Dozens of muskets fired every second, and the walls fractured and exploded, pebbles skittered and white dust showered, so the defenders seemed a pack of ragged bakers.

"We need more time!" someone cried. "The bloody boats are still a half an hour away."

The Fante fled, and at first the pirates cheered, till they saw that a barrel of powder had been left by the gate, connected to a flaming, shrinking line of gunpowder.

Quantrill jumped twenty feet to the dirt below, rolled expertly, and popped up none the worse for wear. He cut the line of powder with his hand and then reached up and grasped the rope that was dropped for him. Bullets whined and smashed the wall around him, but he came over the top unharmed. The pirates roared. Below him, men opened the gates and brought the barrel inside.

Scudder began to laugh, and once he'd begun, he could not stop. Never before had the world seemed so alive, and he noticed so many little things, the movements of ants and shimmering vibrations in the dust. Below them, the path was choked with mangled bodies. Beyond them, the Fante prepared for another push. The pirates reloaded and passed a flask of rum.

The Fante shouted and charged, this time bearing ladders and ropes. The pirates' grenados were exhausted, and they were only able to fire one volley before a ladder smacked into the wall next to Scudder's head. He stood up, wielding a hatchet, and a bullet blew off the bottom of his right ear. He sank the hatchet into a man's forearm and it stuck there and the man pulled the hatchet out and screamed, in rage not pain, before his face shifted into a pulpy mass, smashed by a pistol shot.

"Get down, you bloody lubber!" Quantrill shouted.

The Fante fought the pirates hand-to-hand above the gatehouse, while others scaled the walls where there were no defenders. No one called a retreat, but they were all running, running, abandoning the wall and falling back to a rude barricade.

The gate bulged inwards as the Fante smashed it with their weapons. But next to it was the barrel of powder, with a flame approaching.

Quantrill laughed. It was the happiest that Scudder had ever heard him.

The barrel exploded. The gate was open, for a moment, offering a non-sensical view of shattered wood and rock and men, and then the gate-house came down, blocking the scene. A wave of white dust washed over them as the pirates screamed in victory.

But then the Fante came over the shattered gatehouse in a wave. Hundreds. How many pirates were still fighting? Twenty? Thirty? The muskets rattled, but had no effect. Scudder lifted his weapon and pulled the trigger, but it was not loaded.

It was over. The Fante were in the Castle. From their ranks a knowing roar.

Scudder snapped. He threw down his musket and ran. People bumped and jostled him, but he didn't know who they were, he might have knocked them down and stepped on their faces as he ran, he had no idea. He was racing to the shattered western wall and trying to breathe, that was all. A pirate beside him stumbled, blood blooming from his leg, and Scudder moved to sidestep him, but the fellow caught his ankle, almost tripping him. He jerked his leg free and kept running. A sound that had been happening now stopped happening. After a few steps Scudder realized the sound had been a man screaming.

A small group of pirates stood at the western wall with cutlasses drawn, mostly beating back the terrified slaves. Scudder climbed over broken stone and fallen bodies with panicked agility, warm and smooth skin under one foot, rock under the other.

He was on the top of the wall. Two of the approaching boats had turned back to the *Saoirse*. Only one of them, the launch, was still coming. A huge wave threw it up on the beach, and Coffin and the oarsmen jumped clear and hauled it away from the surf. A panicked swarm of white men formed around the launch and turned it around.

"Wait!" Scudder screamed, terrified. "Wait."

And wait they did, for agonizing seconds, as the waves rushed up, crashed down, and slipped away, and Scudder joined them and grabbed the gunwales, until at last Coffin said, "Now!" and the men sprinted at the ocean and they dropped the launch in the water and jumped aboard and began to haul on the oars.

Water jumped beside Scudder: a musket shot. He looked past Coffin to the beach and the Castle. Some Fante fired their muskets from the wall, but most of them had remained in the Castle. The beach was lined with slaves and some white men, crying alike for rescue.

Behind him, he felt the bow rise.

"Pull, pull, for thy lives!" Coffin shouted.

Now the bow tipped down, and they dropped so fast Scudder's heart stopped, and there was a noise of water and his feet were wet and the whole boat pitched, wobbling like a slowing top. Scudder pulled his oar. Each time a wave struck the bow, he was soaked. But the beach receded, and at last the surf too was behind them.

"Ha ha!" he laughed, crazed. "Ha ha!"

He looked around grinning at the crowded boat, at the man at the oar beside him.

"Ha ha ha!" he laughed.

The cannon of the *Saoirse* rang out one last time, smashing into the sand and rock. A Fante warrior stood upon the wall, waving a spear. The pirate colours came down. Coffin gave the order to set the launch's sail.

27

Kavanagh watched from the quarterdeck as the men from the launch were hauled aboard, pounded on the back, mugs of punch pressed into their hands. Everyone was laughing and shaking.

"Well done, well done," Kavanagh called. "Let's have a count. How many men did we leave ashore?"

The count established that twenty-two men were missing.

"Christ," Kavanagh said. He took off his hat and wiped his brow. The sun beat down. He did not feel well. "Well men, here's what I propose. Let us make sail to the east, to Whydah. There ought to be prizes there. Does any man object?"

None did.

"Then let us be off before the drums bring the news up the coast."

Kavanagh went into his cabin, while the men hauled ropes and set sails. He had a glass of rum, though he did not want it; rum was the thing for his Fever.

He had not brought them far enough. He could not die yet. He would die soon, yes, he knew it. He would not last another year on this wretched ship in these toxic climates. But he had not brought them all far enough, nor taken near enough treasure.

The *Saoirse*, together with her two prizes, sailed to the east. By noon of the following day they arrived at Whydah and found nine ships in the roads. At the sight of the black flag and the firing of a gun, every one of them hove to. Kavanagh's health had worsened. He called Scudder into his cabin.

"You can see for yourself I ain't well," Kavanagh said. He was shaking and sweating. "God! I feel so cold. Can you believe it? I ain't suppose you ever had Fever."

Scudder shook his head.

"Well, my lad, you did well at Corso Castle. Now you take in these ships, see what ransom you can get for 'em. One trick is to give the captain a receipt. Make sure you use a false name, mind."

Scudder nodded.

"And you may draw up a Letter of Marque as well," Kavanagh said. "Sometimes that does it. Draw it up like it was from the Commonwealth in the Bahamas."

Kavanagh leaned back in his chair and gave Scudder paper and ink. He dictated a flowery commission, and the two of them laughed like old friends as Scudder wrote that they had a Letter of Reprisal from the Commonwealth of Eleuthera, whose mission was to spread liberty to the four corners of the earth and which was, accordingly, at war with all nations. Once the rough draft was done, Scudder prepared the final document, using exquisite penmanship on soft vellum, and adding a wax seal. He forged the signatures of George Lowther and Jack Rackham, calling them "Consuls." Then he left in the launch, under the command of Spry, and sailed to the ships in the roads. Kavanagh waited in his room until Dobie came in.

"Here's his writing," Kavanagh said, handing him the draft.

Dobie looked with a critical eye, licked his pen, and wrote a few lines. By the fifth, his writing was indistinguishable from Scudder's.

"I'm sick, Dobie," Kavanagh said. "You keep all these papers safe. If there's any trouble, you go to Israel, not Tulip. Understand?"

Dobie nodded.

Only one captain refused to pay the ransom. Spry returned to the *Saoirse* with the loot, while Scudder went to the recalcitrant captain's ship to unload and burn her. Removing the crew was easy; there were under twenty white men and many were very ill. But there were eighty slaves in the hold, and unshackling them was tedious. There was some mix-up, so that while Scudder lounged in the captain's cabin with Quantrill, drinking Madeira chilled by the sea, like liquid candy, and giving out toasts to all the False Gods he could remember, there arose panicked cries of Fire! Fire! And greedy fire ran up the tarry ropes and wolfed the furled canvas and leapt from yard to yard and rained down on the deck. Scudder and a confused pack of men leapt onto the boat and hauled hard on the oars. A few slaves stood on the deck, pleading for help, until the heat drove them into the sea, where awaited the sharks, and the dark water turned white in their frenzy.

Kavanagh watched from the stern gallery, shaking his head.

28

The little convoy sailed southwest, with the trade winds, until they were out of sight of shore, and the *Saoirse* signalled for the prize crews of the brig and the sloop to come back aboard, together with a handful of new men. O'Brien and Dickens were called into the Great Cabin along with some of their supporters.

"Gentlemen," Kavanagh said. "You've all done well. I reckon we'll keep the sloop as a consort, but I can't imagine we'll have any use for the brig. I know some of you ain't happy, and so I wanted to make an unofficial offer. Any of you that wants to leave the Company may do so."

"The Articles say the Company shall not be dissolved till we've made a thousand pounds a share," Dickens said.

"I know what they say," Kavanagh said. "Here's what I say. You ain't happy, I'll give you forty pounds in ready money and you may take the brig, and go to Nassau, or North Carolina, or Britain, or straight to the Devil. This is your last chance, now, for we sail for Madagascar."

O'Brien glanced at Dickens, who scowled.

"Go think on it," Kavanagh said. "And tell your mates, or else I'll tell 'em for you. It's irregular, I grant you, but it ain't a secret."

Think on it they did, and the matter was not put to a vote. Neither O'Brien nor Dickens accepted Kavanagh's offer, though twelve of their supporters did. Israel Hands shepherded them to the brig while Rios was given command of the sloop. The two ships sailed southwest, following the wind.

29

A hundred and three men had set foot ashore at Corso Castle, and eighty-one returned. Forty-five were infected with the yellow jack.

Kavanagh lay in his bed, shivering, suffering. The surgeon hung over him, wearing the large, ornithological mask of a plague doctor, the snout stuffed with potpourri and herbs. When Kavanagh's vomit turned black, the surgeon pronounced him hopeless. Kavanagh damned his soul and sent him away and called for Alfie.

"Don't let me say nothing when I'm Feverish," Kavanagh said, his teeth chattering. "Gag me."

Alfie, smiling and unsentimental, put a rope between Kavanagh's teeth.

Kavanagh's mind raced into the past, dim memories of his family losing all after the Battle of the Boyne, his father gone, his mother broken, his brothers fishing in the River Lee. The cold, grey poverty of it, the illness, the hunger, the bitter tales of better days. He had sworn that such a life was not for him, that the universe would not trod him under, that he would never be defeated. Now he was so close, he could not die. Alfie

need not have bothered with the gag; all he said, over and over, was *níl fós,*
níl fós, níl fós.

The doctor pronounced it a miracle. His harp was brought to him and
every day, to prove to the Company he was still alive, he played that jaunty,
saucy tune:

Did not you promise me
That you would marry me

By the time he was well enough to leave his cabin, they were in the
southern latitudes where wind and waves roared around the earth with no
land to slow them. The cold seeped through the cracks between the planks
and poured down the hatches. Cockroaches turned white and died and
their corpses were found in every dark corner. Before the *Saoirse* at last
turned east, the wind howled all day, and the ship was tilted so far that
Apollo had the men line up upon the windward rail, yet still the cold sea
sloshed over the lee chains. The waves lifted them up high, so they could
see for miles in every direction, then set them down in the trough, so they
were surrounded by dark walls of water and their sails slackened for want
of wind.

Finally, she turned, the wind now howling from behind like a wolf
in pursuit, and they raced up the waves and then plunged down and the
gunner secured all the guns with preventer braces and Coffin made sure
of all the boats. There was neither drinking nor dancing upon the forecastle; as much as possible, the men stayed below in their snug, smelly
deck with the hatches closed. Topgallant masts were struck, and they
sailed beneath double-reefed topsails, no more, yet still they cracked on,
flying before the wind.

They arrived at the mouth of the Mozambique Channel in September,
after the stormy summer but before the end of the favourable monsoon.
They encountered nothing but pirates, nimble little sloops and galleys
that darted from green and secret shores with decks jammed with swarthy

men. It became a callous and profitless game upon the *Saoirse* to attempt to lure the little pirates close enough to blast them with grape. Encouraged by Apollo, they disguised the ship and kept the greater part of the men below deck, and spilled the wind from their sails and sailed sluggishly and feigned panic when the local pirates appeared. Then they would wait as the little ships closed the distance, firing their pitiful little guns and massing their sailors upon the forecastle. Most of the pirates, upon getting close, would grow wary, and turn away, but some, brave or stupid or desperate, would keep coming, and then the men below decks, drunk and giggling, would throw open the gunports, run out the guns and spray them with grape, and laugh uproariously at the butchery.

Other than this entertainment, it was a dull time. The soft tack was long gone; even the Captain was down to salt horse and biscuit. The pirates were tired of each other and eager to make landfall at the pirate Commonwealth in Madagascar, called Libertatia. Few of the men had ever been there, yet it did not stop them from regaling each other with tales of how there were plenty of fresh provisions, rice, fruit, fish, everything held in common, no slavery, no kings or captains, every white man living like a sultan, with his own seraglio. Last anyone heard, a man called Horatio Darby was the big man ashore, and Dickens told anyone who would listen (and some who did not want to listen) that Darby was an Honest Fellow, a true Gentleman of Fortune, who did everything according to the Custom of the Coast.

They sailed up the straits, rounded the great island of Madagascar, larger than Britain, and came down the eastern coast to St. Mary's Island. In the little Baie de Tintingue, to the lee of the island, the wind slackened, and they dropped an anchor and fired a gun. No one appeared. The only sign of the pirate colony was a wrecked hull against which visitors might careen their ships. Past it was the beach, and past the beach were the trees.

A Meeting was called, and Kavanagh, still thin, emerged from the cabin.

"Now gents," he said. "I know you're anxious to go ashore, and we'll all get a holiday, but when it's time to get to work, every one of you whoresons better do your duty. After our holiday, any man who don't do his duty will be made a governor of this island and that is a stone fucking fact. And we must keep watches—our Brothers here have been known to get up to some tricks. All right? Mr. Hands and Mr. Spry shall make contact, and when we're sure all is well, why, I shouldn't think one week's leave would be out of place."

"Three cheers for the Captain!" Spry cried, and the men gave it with a good will.

Kavanagh smiled. He was feeling better. Perhaps he would not die. Perhaps they would take a great Indiaman groaning with jewels and he would return home after all. Anything was possible. But if not, well, they had come far enough there was no going back now. He had done it. He had won.

Libertatia, Madagascar.

October 9, 1721.

30

S pry returned with unwelcome news. The pirate colonists had sold
some of their local allies into slavery and been caught out, and they
were now all dead or slaves themselves far in the interior. No maritime
stores were available.

Still, the Malagasy came aboard the *Saoirse*, bringing fish and fruit
and game, and they smoked Kavanagh's tobacco and negotiations of
respectful length took place. For a fixed price the pirates were permitted
the use of the bay, to take water and firewood, and they were provided
with fresh provisions and women. The natives had no rum, powder, shot,
cordage, or spars.

Kavanagh gave the men their week off, and they roamed up and
down the coast and hunted turtles and caught fish and rowed up the
rivers to the Malagasy villages and propositioned the women and traded
for jewellery and blankets and other crafts, and they caught an enormous
saltwater crocodile they called Blackbeard and failed to catch a bigger
one they called Black Bart. They dove for pearls and built huge fires upon
the beach, and the Malagasy children screamed and laughed and played

with them. Butterflies and dragonflies of riotous colour. Green lizards, ring-tailed lemurs, fish that glowed at night.

And here Kavanagh made his fatal mistake. Hearing that the famous pirate Edward England, one of Vane's Abominable Society, was alive and free in a Malagasy village a few miles up the river, he and O'Brien and Dickens and Tulip and Israel and a few other men made the trek to visit him, finding England on a stool before a small hut with a fat child upon his knee and a pretty wife of about nineteen. He was desperate for tobacco and rum but otherwise perfectly content.

His men had marooned him here for being too "gentlemanly," but he bore them no ill will, and had no desire to ever leave Madagascar. Kavanagh and the others spoke with him for hours, getting drunker, reminiscing, telling stories of comrades gone under, Bellamy, Vane, Blackbeard. Dusk came and the mosquitoes multiplied and Kavanagh, who had enjoyed his visit, suddenly grew cold. To him the air abruptly smelled foul, like rotting eggs, or a corpse. Vapours and humours. Fever. He made his excuses and left.

By the time he crawled into his bed, he was shaking and chilled all the way to his core. The pain smacked into him in waves.

Goddamn it. Death was here, for certain, slipping into him, little by little, like a knife shucking an oyster. He was afraid, afraid. Yet he gritted his teeth and held back the screams. He told himself he'd won. The universe had ripped away his birthright, but he had restored it to his sons. A thousand acres. Rice, tobacco. His lineage was secure.

But the universe, and his sickness, never fought him fair, when he was healthy, himself. It insinuated and then retreated and waited for him to weaken. It showed him memories of his childhood, happy ones, his mother and his brothers laughing, and it contrasted them with the swampland in North Carolina, Rory's grave beneath the tree.

Did anything really change? Did it make any difference, all the fighting and struggle, in the end?

He was only thirty-two years old.

In his last moments his mind turned from his own legacy to the men, and warm affection spread through his wasted body. He truly loved them all and felt no guilt for how he had treated them, not the Investors, not even MacGregor and the three others he'd buried in the swamp. He'd always taken care of them in his way, as a pirate. Without him, every one of them would be dead from drink or drying in the sun. They would see for themselves when he was gone.

In the end he faced down the fear, and the regret, and in the morning, when Benjamin found him dead, a prideful look was etched into his wan face.

TIMOCRACY

A government in which love of honor is the ruling principle.

(Merriam-Webster)

CAPTAIN TOM APOLLO

1

Apollo was a light sleeper; he was awoken by the sound of footsteps and the lantern shining through the canvas walls of his cabin. His hand went to the loaded pistol on his chest.

But it was only Dobie.

"He's dead," Dobie whispered. "Come up, come up."

Israel Hands, Tulip, and Hornigold were waiting in the Great Cabin. Israel was drunk. "The Captain is dead; long live the Captain," he said, raising a bottle.

"You intend for me to be Captain?" Apollo said. "Will not the men request a vote?"

"They will request," Israel said. "But we are aboard, and they are ashore."

"How many men are aboard?"

"Thirty."

"Thirty men?" Apollo said, dubious. "And all our provisions are ashore?"

"Aye, and the loot too, you damned mad bastard," Israel said. "Had to mess around with the ballast again, didn't you?"

Apollo had assumed that if Kavanagh died, he would die too, and was surprised to find this was not the case.

"You leave the election to us," Tulip said. "D'you hear me now? You leave the men to us."

"Hornigold shall take the news to the Company under a flag of truce," Dobie said.

Apollo looked at Hornigold, who had a fine, leonine profile, long hair, and a great beard of mixed red and grey. He seemed to have awoken from a deep sleep.

"And if they say no?" Apollo asked.

"They shall not say no," Tulip said.

"But Brother Tom," Dobie said, "we need a prize."

Apollo cocked his head. "What of Kavanagh's intelligence? I thought there was more than just the Castle."

"Well," Dobie said. "The Mughal fleet will be returning from the hajj. They say the Archbishop of Goa is moving his fortune. But we don't have no real intelligence. Not like for Corso Castle."

Hornigold spoke at last. His voice sounded thick. "There's no one aboard that can replace the Taoiseach. Not me, not Spry. Not you. We need to bring the men together, and no one here can do it. The only thing that could bring them together is a big prize. D'you follow me?"

"Aye," Apollo said. "I believe I do."

Captain Apollo went down into the hold with a lantern. The ship had been unloaded. Yesterday he (together with a few petty officers and Negroes) had caulked up the hatches and lit a slow fire of green palm fronds and pasted over everywhere smoke leaked out. Apollo himself had gone on his hands and knees and attacked stains with a holystone and vinegar. Now he took up a shovel and dug through the ballast, the foulest parts of which were dumped in buckets and hauled up to the weather deck to be tossed into the sea, and then worked to shift the pig iron. The work was slow because Apollo would often call everyone to a halt, and think, think, think, and then order them to undo and redo work already done and undone before.

They came up in the afternoon, the work almost finished, Apollo exhausted and irritable, and he was called into another meeting with Dobie and Hornigold.

"It's done," Hornigold said. "All of the Taoiseach's shares are to be distributed to the jacks. You shan't receive no more than you was going to anyway. In return you shall be Captain."

"Can they remove me?"

"According to the Articles?" Hornigold said. "No. There are ways, though, Brother."

Apollo was caked with grime and sweat. He felt no triumph.

"Spry has been removed as Quartermaster," Dobie added. "Dickens was elected."

"Shall I have to deal with him?"

"I am afraid so," Dobie said.

"Don't worry about him none," Hornigold said. "Him and O'Brien'll be at each other's throats. Only get us a prize. No one'll want to make trouble once they have a good thing going."

"Very well," Apollo said. "Start bringing them aboard."

The men came one boatload at a time, signed the revised Articles, and were returned to shore. The mood was calm but brittle. Two-thirds remained ashore for an extended holiday, while the rest (the Irish, the Negroes, the older, more skilled, and sober sailors) stayed aboard. At last the ballast was sorted and the masts were adjusted to Apollo's satisfaction. All the seaweed and barnacles and other unwanted passengers were cleaned from the ship's bottom; wood and water were brought aboard.

The Irish Investors buried Kavanagh in a private ceremony in the Pirates' Cemetery on St. Mary's Island, beneath a tall white stone carved with flowing Gaelic script. Their mood was inscrutable to the rest of the Company. To be sure, they grieved, but they were also blackly angry, and thoughtful.

Seven men took the opportunity to defect. The rest returned, and the *Saoirse*, together with the sloop (rechristened the *Piranha*), set sail for the Gulf of Aden.

2

Kavanagh's clothes were auctioned off before the mast, but in a show of goodwill Apollo distributed most of Kavanagh's private stores to the new Quartermaster, including wines, liquor, and preserves. Dickens made them generally available, and they vanished instantly; the crew became very drunk. Dickens declined to enforce any discipline, and he instituted the practice of daily Meetings (the "Common Council," a Custom of the Coast, as he said). These Meetings were largely pointless. Attendance began poorly, then declined. Mostly they were an excuse to get drunk, since Dickens now had a key to the spirits room and always set out a barrel of rum. The result was a steady stream of non-binding requests; and occasionally Dickens or O'Brien attempted to force through a motion directed at their enemies.

Apollo hated these Meetings; they caused him genuine anguish. He stalked in the Great Cabin, unable to avoid hearing, striking his leg with his rattan. Though he held the pirates in contempt, he was morbidly sensitive to their opinion. He could not credit the insults he was required to countenance. Tulip and Dobie would not even allow him to issue any challenges.

"Damn it, Brother," Hornigold said to him in the Great Cabin (which was much altered, as all of the small arms had been brought inside and stacked in piles). "How many times must we tell you? As long as you keep your temper, Dickens will make himself out to be a bloody fool. Discipline to the dogs, the ship's a sty, and already most of the Company are sick to death of Meetings. The only reason O'Brien is blocking a motion of No Confidence is he don't want Spry to win. The moment you break up their Meetings or argue with them or hit them with your bloody rattan, you'll turn it all around."

Hornigold was now quite sober, having gone through a painful period of chills and pains, and Apollo found him to be a capable sailor. He knew Hornigold's advice to be sound. But he was the prisoner of a poisonous Voice that chattered, nattered, nagged. Sometimes the Voice was useful, so that he knew that the ship would gripe. But it would never stop; it saw imperfections everywhere. When the ship was in action, the Voice was silent. Otherwise, it might be silenced by hard work. But, alas, there is little to do in fair weather upon a sailing ship as heavily manned as the *Saoirse*. Add to that a crew of disobedient, rowdy sailors, decent seamen, to be sure, but men who took a special pleasure in spitting on the decks and dirtying the brass, and Apollo's mania grew, and grew, and grew, so the Voice was shouting, rather than whispering, and he would strike his leg, again and again, until it was purple and bloody, the pain of the self-flagellation somehow quieting the Enemy.

Kavanagh had understood him; his rebuke about poor seamanship had struck home. But alone in his cabin, Apollo fell prey to waking dreams, argumentative fantasies. He would imagine himself in a coffee house in some free port where he would be recognized and suffer some slight to his reputation. In these imaginings, he would confront his accuser, and a heated argument would follow, and he would rebut every criticism, and then challenge his accuser to a duel. Sometimes a challenge would be shamefully declined, other times it would be accepted, and he would fight the duel, too, all in his mind, pacing in his little cabin, swinging his rattan like a sword and crying "Ha!" with each thrust.

These fantasies always ended with his complete vindication, yet they made him sick, nervous, unhappy. And when he emerged from his cabin and saw tar upon the deck or the mess a goat had made or the sails trimmed improperly or ropes dangling slovenly from the yards or a drunken man wheeling down the gangway singing and waving a pewter mug, the Voice would whisper that if They could see this ship, They would say how far he had fallen, a common pirate, exposed to slights and insults and disrespect, and his rage would overwhelm him like the rising tide.

Eventually, Kavanagh's rebuke became more ammunition for the Voice. *Jeffries never could get the men to do as he wished, an indifferent seaman at best.* And Apollo argued with his secret enemy, refuting each one of its specious arguments, and battered it into silence, but he could still feel its leering presence, melting away into mist every time he attacked, only to re-form the moment he turned his back.

A prize, he told himself. A prize, a prize.

Off the sandy shores of the Gulf of Aden they parlayed with native boats. The boatsmen were invited into the Great Cabin, where Apollo and Hornigold interrogated them.

Regarding the towns and settlements: How many lived there? And what race? And were they rich? And what did their riches consist of? If fortified, how many guns? Was it possible to come upon them undetected? How many lookouts? Where to make the best landing?

Regarding the shipping: When did boats pass? How many were there? What colours did they fly? How many guns? How did they sail before the wind? Upon a bowline? What goods did they carry? What languages did they speak?

Wind, weather, navigational hazards?

Apollo spread the word that local pilots were wanted, as well as sailors to replace those who had died or deserted. There was no shortage of volunteers. The dusty towns of the Horn of Africa were home to many small bands of pirates, and soon forty men had been brought aboard, a mixture of lascars, Turks, and Negroes, some with turbans and some with bald heads and some with curved swords and others with heavy Turkish firearms. Their induction into the Company was a raucous, obnoxious affair, with much grandstanding by Dickens, but most of the men favoured their admittance, particularly O'Brien, who knew full well that Scudder was popular with coloured men as well as white. And indeed, Scudder spent many days working his charms with the new-comers, showing them the ropes and learning a few words of their languages and offering them any help they should need.

Apollo heard that a great convoy from Surat had passed through on the way to Mecca a month before and was expected to return any day. Hornigold was given command of the *Piranha* in anticipation of the battle, for Apollo did not respect Rios. For three days the *Saoirse* prowled the mouth of the Mandeb Strait. On the morning of the fourth, the lookout bawled out at dawn.

3

The wind blew from the east and so the convoy sailed upon a broad reach, a sailor's breeze, as it came south through the Mandeb Strait in a great straggling line. At its vanguard was a massive galleon in the Spanish style, three decks and eighty guns, sixteen hundred tons if it was an ounce.

The *Saoirse* was sailing due north when they saw her, and Apollo shouted to wear ship. The pipes sang out for all hands on deck and the men rushed up and climbed the ropes and the *Saoirse* turned away from the wind, heading west, then south, then southeast.

The galleon fired a single gun. A salute or a warning? Apollo watched on the poop deck through his spyglass. Its rigging swarmed with men, and yet she moved like a fat cow. Her crew, on deck and upon the yards, seemed to be getting in each other's way, and the yards were slow to turn, and uneven, and the sails moved up and down raggedly.

The *Saoirse*, on the other hand, now sailed beautifully upon a bowline, making almost no leeway. Yellow heaved the log and measured the ship's speed and announced that they were making five knots, in faint wind and close-hauled. Apollo looked up at the sails, all of them filled, nothing flapping or loose, and closed his spyglass with satisfaction.

"Spill some wind from the main course, if you please."

His command was relayed, and the waisters loosened the appropriate ropes. The speed of the ship lessened, although she still outpaced the sluggish galleon, retaining the weather gage (that is, the wind blew from the *Saoirse* towards her prey) while keeping out of range of the galleon's guns. The rest of the convoy came through the straits, five smaller ships, and another galleon bringing up the rear.

"Well guarded," Rios said, shaking his head.

"They're lubbers," Apollo said. "D'you see how long it takes them to furl their spanker?"

"If they stay together, we haven't a chance," Rios said.

"Then we shall separate them," Apollo said. "Signal the *Piranha* to sail to the east."

For ten days the *Saoirse* and the *Piranha* kept ahead of the convoy. On the third day a storm rolled in, and the convoy sheltered in the port of Aden, while the *Saoirse* rode it out, topgallant masts on deck. When the weather settled, the convoy came out, and the *Saoirse* took up her position ahead of them, beating to windward, sometimes allowing the galleon to close the distance before making a show of spreading all the canvas the masts could bear and pulling ahead. In fact, not only was the *Saoirse* spilling her wind, she was dragging a spare sail underwater. She also brazenly flew her pirate colours, as well as the tricolour of the Commonwealth, so there could be no doubt about her intentions.

The wind came from the east, sometimes veering northeast. A square-rigged ship may sail about six points from the wind, and when her destination lies in the direction from which the wind blows, she must either beat to windward (build up speed, and then bring her bow through the eye of the wind) or wear ship (turning away from the wind and taking the long way round). The slow, top-heavy galleons huffed and puffed, changing tacks with great difficulty, and sometimes missing stays by failing to bring their bow through the wind and having to wear instead. When this happened, the smaller, nimbler ships in the convoy reduced sail and kept in formation.

On the tenth day, the convoy left the Gulf of Aden and turned northeast; passing them by, it crept along the Arabian coast into the teeth of the wind. Now if the *Saoirse* was to attack, it would be from downwind. If the galleons turned to fight, there was no guarantee the *Saoirse* could outrun them, for as fat and clumsy as they were, they could spread a great deal of canvas. The thought of this, the risk of it, lit Apollo up with joy; he grinned and tapped his feet and sometimes even whistled, and both confused and infected the men with his mad happiness.

The next day, the Captain ordered the men be served their dinner for breakfast and provided them with cocoa from his private stores, and then the galley fires were doused and the ship was cleared for action.

By noon, the gap between them and the convoy was only three miles, and Apollo gave the order to fire the bow chasers. Time ticked by. The gap shrank and shrank.

The galleon's stern chasers fired.

"Steady on," Apollo said. "Wait for my command."

Boom! Boom! Boom!

The glass turned. The minutes stretched into hours. The gap closed.

Boom! Boom!

The guns cast great clouds of black smoke, through which the *Saoirse* glided, blind, all aboard smelling that tart brimstone smell.

Three miles became two, and two miles became one. Two thousand yards. Eighteen hundred. Rise and plunge. Apollo climbed to the mizzen crosstrees, peered through his spyglass. How large they were now! Crowds of brown men around the guns, shouting and waving their hands. Disorderly.

"Is everything ready?" Apollo called.

"Ready sir," the bosun cried from the maintop.

Apollo gripped a tarry backstay in his callused hands and slid down to the deck, landing with a thump on the rolling wood, and as he did, he heard the bosun call out to be ready, boys! Here it comes! A moment later the sound of the cannon. Apollo watched a ball sailing towards them, dropping, dropping, and whizzing through the tangle of rigging to the larboard of the main top yard. The bosun called out and ropes were let go and the top yard came plunging down, bringing the sail with it, and the *Saoirse* slowed.

They were three-quarters of a mile behind the galleon. Perhaps two-thirds.

"Two points to windward, Coffin," Apollo said.

"Aye sir," Coffin said. "Two points it is, sir."

Coffin turned the wheel two ticks and the ship turned into the wind and her remaining sails shivered and the ship slowed and bobbed on the waves. The pirates surged up and down the shrouds, creating the appearance of confusion, although the waisters were ready to hoist up the yard at a moment's notice.

A sharp eye looking through a spyglass might have noticed the deception, but Apollo was tolerably sure there were no sharp eyes aboard that galleon. A pack of musselmen and their idolatrous slaves, Apollo thought, the commanders the favourite catamites of some oriental despot. The question was whether they had any spirit at all.

"Put her in irons, Coffin," Apollo said.

"Aye aye, sir," Coffin said. He spun the wheel, and the bow of the ship turned into the eye of the wind and lost her momentum and the wind gently pushed it back upon its original tack.

"Wear ship," Apollo said.

"Wear ship," Rios shouted through a speaking trumpet.

"Lay it on thick, men," Apollo said, his voice measured, not its typical disagreeable screech. "The captain of that fat tub hasn't the spirit of a court eunuch, I'll warrant."

The *Saoirse* turned from the wind, the sails going up slow and crooked, the ropes tangling, the yards a-kilter. Apollo watched the galleon.

"Oh, come on, you geldings," he said. "Remember your lost testicles!"

The galleon's sailors were packed along her stern rail, cheering, but she seemed to be making no attempt to pursue. Probably she was under orders to stay with the convoy, but it was to Apollo evidence of a sickening lack of pluck.

And then. Aboard the galleon, the bosun's mates thrashed the gawkers with rattans, drove them back to their stations, and the sailors climbed the shrouds, and horns blew, and drums drummed, and the galleon fell away from the wind.

"She moves to chase!" Apollo shouted, and stowed his spyglass. "Handsomely, handsomely now!"

The *Saoirse* had now turned to the west-southwest, still feigning to have lost her main top yard, still spilling her wind, still with the drag sail underwater. Sluggishly, then, she sailed with the wind at her stern, while the great Leviathan pursued, one sail blooming after another, a great dingy wall of canvas.

Sailing large, she would run them down in an hour. But in that hour, she would put five miles between herself and the rest of her convoy.

"Start the water," Apollo said to Rios. "And throw a cannon or two overboard."

"Is that really necessary?" Rios asked. "They're already—"

"I would do it if this ruse was real," Apollo said. "So we will do it now."

In the hold, the great casks of fresh water were opened and poured down into the ballast and the men went to work at the pumps. Jets of water spurted from both sides, and two guns upon the quarterdeck were thrown over the side, along with empty barrels, other rubbish, and an unfortunate goat.

Apollo watched the sailors aboard the galleon wave their curved swords and howl.

"Cut away the drag sail," he called.

One, two chops with the axe and the cable snapped and whipped off the deck. Their speed increased. Still the galleon gained.

"Set a course due south," Apollo said.

Coffin adjusted the wheel. The galleon still outpaced them. Apollo ordered the main top yard restored, and it was hauled up. Anyone but a damn fool would know something was up now, but Apollo could sense that the galleon had wholly swallowed the bait, the way a fisherman might feel it through the line. They raced south, every inch of sail set, all the men back down below at the guns, and then Apollo turned them a little east, and then a little more, and then a little more, until at last they were sailing close-hauled. The convoy was over the horizon, out of sight. The galleon pursuing was only eight hundred yards behind, close enough to do real damage. Her bow chasers were massive brass pieces that could knock down a mast.

"Bring us through the wind," Apollo ordered.

The command was shouted up and down the deck, Coffin moved the wheel, steady and slow, the sails luffing up handsomely so as to lose no way, but the wind was dying, and she slowed.

Boom!

A cannonball sailed towards the *Saoirse*. Apollo, seeing the ball hurl towards him, planted his feet and braced himself, stood to his full height. Too low. It smashed through the deadlights, shattered the stern windows, and thudded inside his cabin.

Now the *Saoirse* was through the wind, picking up speed and heading east-northeast.

"Put the helm up," Apollo ordered.

The galleon was faced with a choice: follow the *Saoirse* through the wind, and risk missing stays, or wear ship, allowing the galleon to fire a broadside but surrendering the weather gage and allowing the *Saoirse* to cut her off from the convoy. Eventually she chose the latter, turning south, bringing her guns to bear, and firing them in a disordered series of explosions. Apollo gripped the rail and watched the metal fly. Two sails were holed, and a topgallant yard tumbled down in a tangle of tarry hemp. That was all. The *Saoirse* went north, the galleon south.

While the galleon turned from south to southwest to west to northwest to north to northeast, the *Saoirse* sailed on a bowline, easy as kiss-my-hand. Finally, she turned, cut off the galleon, and fired down the length of her deck from a range of seven hundred yards, snapping rope and killing men. The galleon turned north, seeking to fire its broadside and escape the *Saoirse*'s guns, but the *Saoirse* wore too fast and headed northwest, the rigging all trembling, the canvas straining, threatening to split. She cut off the galleon again, and fired another broadside, this one with chain-shot at closer range. The galleon's sails and rigging were shredded, and there was a groan like a dying god and a cracking like the birth of the world, and the foremast, with its long yards and gun platform and miles of rigging and blocks and sails, all of it, came smashing down into the sea.

The pirates cheered. Apollo's heart thundered in his chest. Now was the time. Though hamstrung, the galleon had her teeth and claws, to say nothing of the hundreds of fighting men aboard and the reinforcements that might arrive at any moment. He looked at the flags to gauge the wind, but he could not think for all the cheering, and he turned to Rios, furious, to tell the men to be silent, for God's sake, but Rios was cheering too.

"Hurrah, señor!" Rios cried, dancing, grinning. "What a veectory! I give you all the joy in the world!"

"Damn you, sir," Apollo replied. "Save your joy until after we've won."

"We have won!" Rios cried. He pointed. "Look!"

The galleon had struck her colours. All along the side of the ship, men were jumping, panicked, into the sea, while others ran below, and still others tried to lower the boats. Passengers had come up on the deck, old men and children and women, crying and rending their hair.

Apollo felt the adrenalin turn sour, wine into vinegar.

Pathetic.

Eight hundred men aboard that ship, at the least, and help not six miles away.

In his head the Voice whispered, no real victory at all against such lubbers. Just like Corso Castle. He knew the visions that would come when he was alone in his cabin, the imaginary sarcastic remarks, and his stomach turned.

"Clear the decks with grape," he said roughly. "And send over the launch with sixty men. Mr. Rios, you shall lead them."

"Ah," Rios said. "That is the prerogative of the Quartermaster?"

"Fine," Apollo said. "Only tell Dickens to be quick about it. I want to be after the convoy."

"The convoy?" Rios said.

"Yes, damn you!" Apollo cried. "We've still a few hours of daylight left."

Dickens assembled his boarding party, selecting his most loyal followers and choosing the rest based on seniority and ideological affinity, including a lascar called Zahir as a translator, a handsome man with a long beard and wild eyes. They climbed into the launch and rowed over to the galleon under the cover of the *Saoirse*'s guns. Once they were safely aboard, the *Saoirse* sailed northeast in pursuit of the convoy, Apollo pacing and scowling upon the quarterdeck, every now and then striking his leg with his rattan.

4

S ometime before midnight, the pirates came upon the hindmost brig under the pale light of a full moon. Not spotted by the lookout until they were within three hundred yards, the *Saoirse* fired a broadside and the brig hove to and struck her colours. Rios was sent aboard with a boarding party. They locked the crew below decks, doused the lanterns, and fled into the night.

The *Piranha* attempted to board the next ship, but they had at last come upon some men with pluck, and the pirates did not have the weather gage, and as the other ships in the convoy turned upon them, Apollo signalled for a retreat.

He had kept detailed hourly notes of the ship's speed and her course, and he had a mind like a golden astrolabe, and he navigated by the crisp glow of the stars and brought them back to the captured galleon before dawn.

Dickens had not posted a lookout. This alone would have angered Apollo, for his mind was polluted with imaginary criticisms of the action, the lubberly motions of the galleon, her slow, inaccurate cannon fire, the panic of her crew. But worse was to come, for across the dark water came the sounds of drunken singing, screaming and weeping, glass breaking.

Apollo ordered the cutter lowered, shrilling at the men when they fumbled in the lampless night, and striking one with his rattan when he answered back. Coffin was coxswain, and went aboard with a crew of Irishmen and Cyrus, the bosun's mate, an enormous mute Negro, and they crossed the gap between the ships without a sound. Apollo's scarred countenance was emotionless, but he flexed the rattan in his hands, over and over.

They boarded the ship at the waist. The foremast had been hacked clear and tossed overboard, and the other sails were abacked, occasionally flapping against the masts. Chests and goods were piled upon the quarter-deck; past them, lamplight and the sound of singing came from the cabin. Apollo walked through the door.

"Captain!" a drunken man cried. "It's the Captain!"

The dining room was crowded with pirates. Despite that the ship was Islamic, they had found casks of rum, and all of them were very drunk. The pictures on the walls were knocked askew and the crockery was broken.

"Get out on deck," Apollo said. "And get the plunder into the launch."

"But the loot ain't all ready," the drunken man said. "We didn't expect you till dawn."

"Do as I say."

From the Great Cabin came a brief, despairing cry. Apollo shoved through the pirates and threw open the door. Here he found a great room lit by a single lantern and dominated by a huge bed, and a crowd of women huddled together. The smell of rum, vomit, blood. Fear. Sex. At least three rapes were in progress. Apollo drew his pistol, levelled it, and fired. A man's head snapped back and he fell dead on top of his victim and she commenced to scream.

The pirates wheeled, drunken, unsteady. A man came towards Apollo with a drawn sword and Apollo drew his other pistol and fired it and the man sat down and said: "Oh!" And then: "Oh God! I'm shot!"

"Get out on deck," Apollo said. "All of you."

They complied, stunned, one or two muttering, only to be silenced by the rattan.

Dickens rushed up from below decks.

"Murderer!" he said. "Damn you, you'll hang for this!"

"Is all the plunder on deck?" Apollo asked. "Have you prepared a list of everything taken?"

"I ain't ready yet," Dickens said. "Goddamn you, we didn't expect you so early."

"You are relieved of command," Apollo said.

"Oy!" Dickens said. "I'm the Quartermaster of this ship! You can't do that."

Apollo motioned to Cyrus, and Cyrus caught Dickens by his pigtail and threw him down and straddled him.

"I want everything of value on this galleon upon the deck in half an hour," Apollo said. "Any man too drunk to work can go back to the *Saoirse*, and goddamn you for a lubber."

Dickens's party outnumbered them, but Apollo's men were armed and sober. A few chose to leave with Dickens, still shouting threats and warnings, but most stayed, hoping to curry favour. In an hour they had transferred the plunder to the *Saoirse*. When a sail was sighted upon the horizon, Apollo gave the order to flee, leaving some bulky items behind, together with the brig.

In total they had taken over seventeen thousand pounds in specie. Gold dust, gold and silver bars, coins of all shapes and denominations, Portuguese and Spanish and Mughal, doubloons and pieces of eight and silver rupees and gold mohurs, inscribed with Arabic calligraphy and zodiacal signs and portraits of distant rulers of fabulous wealth. In chattels they took silks, spices, gems, ivory, India cotton, trade goods, kitchenwares, lumber, ingots of iron and tin. Yet all the talk was of the murdered men.

The Gulf of Aden.
December 7, 1721.

5

At the Meeting the next day, Ironside, Dickens's chief supporter, levelled charges of murder against Apollo, describing how he had shot and killed the two men.

Apollo waited with difficulty. His head was throbbing, for he had not slept, and he was weakened by sundry terrible imaginings. When he was granted the floor, he described, with considerable agitation, the scene that had greeted him upon boarding their prize. Most of his audience (who had spent the night not in drunken revelry but in frantic pursuit of, and then desperate flight from, a convoy of superior force) was rather more opprobrious than might be expected. Scarcely a man aboard would not have acted in the same manner as the boarding party had they been given the opportunity, but they had not been given the opportunity, and that was the whole thing.

Dickens defended himself, at length, but did not find a sympathetic audience, and was reduced, in the end, to insults. He did find one supporter in Scudder, who had been advised by O'Brien that if Dickens lost his position as Quartermaster it would surely go to Spry. Scudder argued that the Captain ought to have brought charges at a Meeting, which was true, but it was also true that Apollo had tricked an eighty-gun galleon into abandoning her convoy, retaken the weather gage, demasted the monster in two quick passes, then run off after the blessed convoy! It was the boldest stroke any of them had ever seen. And all the while that whoreson Dickens, always going on about the Articles, had been flouting them aboard a prize. Apollo was acquitted by a show of hands.

Charges that they had "meddled with prurient women" were brought against Dickens and some of the members of his boarding party. Dickens argued, on behalf of himself, that he had never touched any of them, which was borne out by the evidence (he had, in fact, stayed sober). On behalf of his men, he argued that they had only taken liberties with the slave girls. This evidence was rejected by the translator, Zahir, who made it clear (in English, as well as Marathi and Gujarati) that the pirates had attacked passengers, young maidens and married women and old grand-mothers, and many had drowned themselves afterwards out of shame.

Dickens next made several technical arguments based on the lack of direct evidence from the women on the question of consent, and the difficulty of identifying those who had attacked prurient women, not slaves. When the charges were brought to a vote, everyone was narrowly acquitted. However, that did not end the matter. Spry called a vote of non-confidence against Dickens, which passed, and then he handily defeated Scudder in the election for new Quartermaster.

Afterwards, Apollo stalked into his Great Cabin, where he was informed by Dobie that it was customary to offer the new Quartermaster a drink, which he did, without taking one himself. Spry did not bother to point out this breach of the Custom of the Coast. Instead, he said, plainly, that if Apollo could not govern his anger, he would find Dickens back as Quartermaster soon enough. Apollo, looking haggard, only nodded.

Matters improved. The life of a pirate captain suited Apollo, in that he bent his considerable naval genius to the task of taking as many prizes as possible, and his mind was wholly occupied. For months they Cruised the

Indian Ocean, the Mozambique Channel, the Gulfs of Oman and Aden. They gathered intelligence and waited outside ports and in shipping lanes and raided small towns. In thirty days they took seventeen ships, carrying mostly bulky and illiquid goods, timber or metal ore or textiles, and belly-timber. The best Cruising grounds were infested with native pirates, and twice the *Saoirse* had to fight them off while taking a prize.

Fresh food they had aplenty, but the ships they took were Islamic, and the supply of rum declined. The ship would soon need to be careened, and men spoke of breaking up the Company, though as things stood they'd receive a hundred pounds a man in specie, plus whatever they could get for the trade goods. More than ten years' salary in the Navy, but they'd all blown through greater sums before.

One night they were set upon by a powerful storm; the scuppers were buried in foam and lightning danced wicked and free, bleaching the ship then dipping it in darkness. Six points off the lee bow was the coast, the dreaded lee shore, with no time to wear. The men waited at their stations, soaked, afraid. Apollo screamed his commands into Yellow's ear, and Yellow passed them on, all the way forward, where the forecastlemen, led by Coffin, made their way across the slick and hung over the side of the plunging ship and unfished the anchor and dropped it into the blackness of the sea.

As the cable jerked taut, the men at the windlass screamed and shoved and the windlass jerked around a tick. The ship jerked, and then her bow swung through the wind, for a moment meeting the storm head-on, the wind shrieking down the length of the deck and the bow dipping and smashing into a wave, and then she was through to the other side, pointed away from the shore, and the cable was released and the anchor left behind, and sailors trimmed the yards and set the sails, balancing a hundred feet above the deck, fumbling with slick tarry ropes in the pitch-dark and hauling canvas soaked with rain, and the ship continued her turn, away from the wind, turning, turning, till the wind was on her quarter, and she raced away under a few scraps of canvas, all she could bear.

Apollo stayed on deck all night, his heart thumping in his chest, alive with the triumph of it, and then the Voice chirruped in his ear, luck, that was all, was he to take credit because the anchor didn't drag?

In his cabin, he cut himself on the shoulder with a dirk, so blood dribbled down, and he felt the strangest relief.

The next day, they came to the Comoros islands off the coast of Africa, and as they glided through the warm seas, they saw a ship at anchor in the great bay of the island of Juanna.

Juanna, Comoros Islands.

January 6, 1722.

6

Apollo climbed to the foremast crosstrees and peered through his spyglass. The ship was a galleon, four decks, a hundred guns, and anchored with her broadside facing out to sea. She had been mauled by the storm. Had she thrown her guns overboard? One could hope.

"She ain't got a single fucking mast, Brothers!" Scudder cried out from the foretop, below him.

"Sharp-eyed fellow, aren't you?" Apollo said, then called, "Do you men know of anyone who might pilot us through this bay?"

"I'll find you a man, Captain!" Scudder said.

In the small Master's Cabin, on the port side of the quarterdeck, Apollo and Rios consulted the various charts bequeathed to them by Rogers, as well as the ones they had taken on their own, but they found none for this little island. Apollo went on deck and ordered the leadsman into the chains to sound the depths, and reduced sail. The galleon, after all, would not be running away.

From below came the usual banging as the cabins were disassembled, the tumult as the livestock were stowed.

The leadsman called, "By the mark, seventeen."

Zahir came into the Master's Cabin with another of the lascars, a clean and toothless fellow with an intelligent expression. They gathered around the table where Apollo had sketched out a rough map of the bay. The lascar marked down the reefs, but as for the shoals, he shrugged and looked heavenwards and said, "*Allāhu 'a'lam*."

The wind blew from the east-southeast and they sailed southwest, upon a sailor's breeze. The galleon came into focus against the white beach. Coffin, at the wheel, watched the sails. Apollo waited with his hands behind his back on the windward side of the quarterdeck.

"By the deep, twelve," the leadsman in the forechains called.

"Signal the *Piranha*," Apollo said. "Engage from the east."

"Shall I run up the black flag, sir?" Dobie asked.

"No," Apollo said. "Portuguese colours."

The *Piranha* sailed close-hauled to the other side of the bay, to come upon the galleon from the east.

Rios conversed with Zahir and the other lascar, and gave instructions that were relayed to the sail trimmers, and the yards were adjusted.

Three miles became two, and two miles became one.

"By the deep, eight," the leadsman called.

"The damn galleon got in there somehow," Rios said. "Shall I reduce sail?"

"Yes," Apollo said. "And let us lower another boat."

"By the mark four!" the leadsman suddenly screamed.

A horrendous crunch as the *Saoirse*, sailing at three knots, ran aground. The men in the rigging and the yards were hurled into the sea, except for two unlucky ones who smashed onto the deck. The masts lurched, groaned. The wood made an animal noise of pain. Ropes snapped and whipped.

"Back the sails!" Apollo screamed. "Lower the boats, all of them!"

The deck filled with men, bumping into one another, struggling to their stations.

And then the galleon began to fire, fifty guns, the largest of them forty-two-pounders, a full broadside from a man-of-war at anchor, carefully aimed by the soldiers of a great power.

"Oh God," Rios said.

"Down, down, everyone down!" Apollo screamed, and led by example.

Most of the shots fell short, smashing the glassy, turquoise sea, sending up hissing spirals of clear water. Others punched through the sails, or thundered into the *Saoirse*'s hull. One crashed down into the forecastle, and the men there simply exploded, arms and legs cartwheeling through the air, a shower of blood, screams.

"The boats, the fucking boats!" Apollo screamed. "Get them in the water!" And then to the men fiddling with the pulleys: "Cut them loose, cut them loose! Get them round the stern!" To Dobie: "Signal the *Piranha*, engage the enemy more closely." To Rios: "Start the water over the side!" To Coffin: "Take the bower anchor! We must warp the ship at once!"

The boats were cut loose, tossed over the side without ceremony, oars thrown down. Dobie scrambled with the signal flags, getting them in the correct order. The kedge anchor, ready at the stern, was lowered, connected to a great hawser cable.

The galleon began its second broadside, in perfect order, less than three minutes after its first. Puffs of smoke, then the booms. Iron balls rising, rising, rising, in the air. Then falling, one after another. The *Saoirse* was struck again, and again, and again. The hull, the yards, the sails, the rigging, cracking and snapping and dropping down to the deck and catching on fire. Another crowd of men liquefied. Everyone sliding on blood, screaming, splinters flying, men trapped under blocks of wood and sheets of canvas.

At last it stopped.

Apollo gripped Rios by the shoulder. "Get in the longboat," he said. "Take soundings. You shall have to lead us through the shoals."

Rios was trembling with shock.

Apollo struck him and was going to do it again when Israel Hands caught his arm.

"I'll do it," he said. To the lascar and Zahir, he said: "Come now."

"Go to the capstan," Apollo snapped at Rios, and he fled.

Apollo looked at the *Piranha*. Sailing into the wind, she had not made it out of range of the galleon's broadside, and she too had been mauled. But now she was sailing straight at the galleon, and Apollo saw, with great surprise and gratitude, that Hornigold was turning her into a fire-ship. The men had formed a human chain and were handing bucket after bucket of tar up from the hold and dumping them over the decks and the rigging and sails, the ship now black and dripping and reeking, and all the guns were rolled into their ports, loaded with two shots each.

The galleon's guns thundered, and the men flinched, but no shots fell upon the *Saoirse*, for she was firing, desperately, at the *Piranha*, from which the pirates were leaping. While it was still well short of the galleon, the *Piranha* exploded. Tremendous noise, and smoke like a tree bending in the wind, and burning wood and hot metal raining down in a pittering shower.

And then Apollo took a deep breath. Looked up at that perfect sky. In a moment he would need to do something. For now, he basked in the marvellous knowledge that for a few hours his mind would be silent, and soon he might even be dead.

While Coffin and his crew fumbled the enormous bower anchor over the side of the ship into the sea, Apollo drove men to the capstan, rigged and waiting, till it was fully manned, on the upper deck, on the lower deck, clutching the bars up against their chests, and then when the chant began, stamp and go, stamp and go, the lady comes from Mexico, they heaved, waited, heaved, waited, and the capstan clicked around, and the hawser snaked aboard, running nearly two-thirds of the length of the ship from just behind the foremast to the stern.

Stamp and go, stamp and go.

The ship groaned, and groaned, and the men shouted. The hawser wavered and trembled.

Stamp and go!

The ship rocked upon the shoal.

The thunder of cannon fire, that fucking galleon, her aim getting better every time. Apollo watched the balls rain down. If they were demasted, it was over. They were not, though the balls smashed down another yard and shredded more rigging and pounded the hull. And one sinking, sinking, so that it almost fell short, but did not, and instead smashed through the grating above the galley stove. The capstan stopped, the shivering motion of the ship stopped, and the air filled with screams.

If they have wrecked the capstan, it is over, Apollo thought, and he sprinted down the aft companionway, together with Dobie, others, a press of men, and they saw the damage the shot had wrought to the men at the capstan on the upper deck, dozens blasted to pieces, lying in a tangled pile of their own guts and severed limbs, and they were dragged away by their grey-faced Brothers, the worst of them thrown still living out the gunports into the indifferent sea. Those who might live were carried aft, those too shocked to work shoved out of the way, and new men took their places, and the chant rose up, *fifteen men on a dead man's chest, yo-ho-ho and a bottle of rum!*

The *Saoirse* pulled on her cable, rose, then settled.

Heave!

She tilted.

Heave.

She tilted again, almost free, pushed back upon the shoal by the tide.

"One more fucking time!" an anonymous man screamed.

Heave.

And the *Saoirse* was free.

The oarsmen in the cutters pulled hard and towed the bow to starboard. A single sail was unfurled and roped and filled with wind and was sheeted home. The hawser cable was severed with a stroke of an axe, the two anchors abandoned, and they sailed southeast, close-hauled, towards the galleon.

Ahead of the cutters was the longboat, where Israel Hands heaved the leadline, sounded the depths, and shouted back through a speaking trumpet to the cutter. The *Saoirse* was in a labyrinth of shoals; she needed to sail first southeast and then cut back to the southwest.

"Six feet of water in the well, sir," the carpenter called to Apollo.

"Man the pumps. And man the guns. Where's the gunner?"

"Dead, sir," the carpenter said.

Apollo nodded, his eyes sparkling. He looked ahead. They had two forward-facing cannon, the bow chasers, little nine-pounders. Tulip worked one and Quantrill and O'Brien the other, taking shots every three minutes, little peashooters against that monster.

Now, as the *Saoirse* glided through the channel, Quantrill waited with his slow match poised above his cannon's touch hole, waited, and waited, as the ship pitched up, and down, and some deep part of his brain made calculations. At last, as the ship rose, he fired.

Apollo watched the shot rise up, and up, and arc down, and down, and smash into the side of the galleon, sending great splinters of wood spinning through the air.

A good shot, Apollo thought—it may have dismounted a gun.

It was better than that.

A loud, flat boom echoed across the bay and flames leapt out of the gunports and the hatches.

"By the Powers!" Apollo cried. "The lubbers had their powder on the gun deck!"

The *Saoirse* shivered with the news, and the men popped their heads out of the hatches to look and cried out, savage and hysterical, and the *Saoirse* glided on for a minute, two, three, ten, and the galleon did not fire a single shot. Apollo cried out, the cutters turned, the wheel was spun, the yards trimmed, and the *Saoirse* cruised to the southwest.

At last the galleon resumed its fire, ragged and less accurate. A ball skipped twice on the water and smashed through a porthole into the lower deck. Another shot brought down the mizzen topgallant mast only ten feet in front of Apollo. But that was all. Apollo shoved away the helmsman and took the wheel and deliberately ran the *Saoirse* aground upon a reef due west of the anchored galleon.

Now she could bring twenty-four guns to bear upon the enemy, who could only fire four in return.

Apollo looked at the sun. It was mid-afternoon. He wiped the blood and sweat out of his eyes and spat out something hard and sharp—wood, metal, bone, tooth? The boats took shelter behind the ship and their men climbed aboard.

"Gentlemen," he said to them all. "Today we fire our guns. Tonight we board."

8

Fire the guns they did, and though their twelve- and twenty-four-pounders did little to the thick hull of the great beached monster, they shattered her windows and gunports and brought down her jury-rigged masts and raked the decks clean and drove the gunners from her stern chasers.

All the while the wounded screamed from the sick bay, the loblolly boy trumpeted *you're all right, mate, nearly there, nearly there, eight hundred pieces of eight for that chicken wing, Brother.* Devereux amputated limb after limb, and these were gathered in baskets and carried up and thrown into the sea, turning the turquoise water pink, attracting dozens of little reef sharks.

They fired, and fired, and fired, and when the Portuguese put up nets to repel boarders, they switched to chain-shot and ripped the nets to shreds and fired grape down the length of the deck to keep her men below.

The Negroes ran up and down the stairs until the cartridges were gone, and the pirates drank deep draughts from the scuttlebutt, and the overworked gunners' mates, exhausted and dehydrated, stumbled up from the powder room and blinked in the red evening sun. Biscuits were distributed, together with kegs of rum and everything that remained of the private stores, rounds of cheese and jars of pickles, breads, smoked fish, and the band struck up a tune, and some of the men, even in that extremity, began to dance, tanned and tattooed, thin and scarred and crazy, deafened by the guns and black with gunpowder and scarlet with blood.

Their casualties were heavy. Without the men from the *Piranha* they had fewer than three hundred. The boats could not carry half that number, and Apollo appointed captains for each of them, and apportioned the crew between them, leaving Rios behind to make sure the guns were not fired until he gave the signal.

Lewis, the armourer, was at work, and the grindstone spun and sparked, and the weapons whined as they were pressed to the blurry stone, the swords and axes and pikes. Each shining blade was blacked with tar and distributed. Tulip had charge of the muskets and pistols, and he passed them to the sharpshooters together with cartouches packed with paper cartridges. Each boat was issued a box of grenados and a smoking slow match.

Thus armed, the men loaded into the boats till they were jammed with hairy, blood-soaked bodies, and waited for the moment of startling darkness after the sun set and before the moon rose. When it came, Israel whistled the jaunty signal (*did not you promise me / that you would marry me*) and the men rowed.

As they passed through that warm dark, lit only by distant stars, the *Saoirse* continued to fire. Each oar stroke quiet, quiet, the darkness almost complete, everything obscured, except for the lights of the galleon, growing closer.

"Hss, hss," Apollo said from the lead boat, and the rhythm of the oars slowed, slowed. He turned the rudder and the launch sailed to the north, the seaward side of the galleon, and was followed by one of the cutters, while the other three boats made for the landward side.

Now they were hardly rowing, only gliding, black faces, black weapons, everything dark, silent, silent. Closer, closer, till the great dark galleon blocked out the stars. There had to be at least six hundred men aboard her. At the very least, they were outnumbered two to one. Oh, how Apollo loved this moment! How he loved this beautiful, beautiful world and everyone in it! How limpid and dear and gentle was this soft silence in his mind!

From the galleon a panicked cry, the sound of hundreds of feet.

"Send up the signal!" Apollo cried, and a rocket was fired, lighting the whole world an unnatural red, and the grenados flew, dozens at once, sizzling and sputtering, bursting in the air and upon the deck. Ropes thrown, men jumped and grabbed the portholes like demonic monkeys with knives in their teeth.

A rail gun fired into one of the cutters and the ball smashed through the hull and blew a man apart, and the boat rocked and filled with water. Apollo lifted a musket to his shoulder and in the garish red light of the rocket aimed and pulled the trigger, killing a man preparing to fire another rail gun. Dobie handed Apollo another musket and he lifted that one and fired as well. So too all the sharpshooters; musket fire battered the ship.

Now the first pirates wormed aboard, squirming through the holes in the rails and the netting. First aboard was Dickens, and he fired two pistols into the packed men before him, driving them back for an instant, and then he flung the guns down and lifted his hatchet. "For the Seas!" he cried, and this cry was taken up.

For the Seas!

"*Para deus, o arcebispo eo Rei!*" a Portuguese screamed. The grenados had scattered them, but they re-formed near the stump of the foremast and fired a volley of muskets, in good order, and pirates screamed and dropped and tumbled back into the water, and a haze of gunpowder hung over the deck.

Screaming, Dickens led the charge. For a time, he and his men bore the full brunt of the mass of Portuguese, but then more pirates came over the landward side, a great scraggly crawling mass, and the pressure receded, and the men fell into the routine of parrying, swinging, thrusting, and dodging. At last Apollo came over the rail, and he was cheered as he had never been cheered before, and he charged forward into the mass of men with a brace of rapiers, one in each hand, and their thin blades flicked quick and precise, probing and lancing, each independent of the other.

"*Saoirse!*" he cried as he carved his way into the Portuguese, too far, and they closed around him.

9

Coffin and another man steered the launch back to the lights of the *Saoirse*, where Tulip waited with an impatient crew. As Coffin brought the launch alongside, the men jumped aboard. Some had come up from the operating bay—men with bashed-in heads and missing eyes and crushed ankles, wrapped in white bandages stained red—and when the launch was full, Tulip cried to go, go, goddamn you! And the men hauled on the oars and the launch fairly flew over the water back to the galleon.

As they approached, they saw pirates falling into the water, but because of the dark they could not tell how the battle progressed. Yet retreat was impossible, the only hope was to press on, and so Tulip raised his sword and cried in his rumbling voice: "*Saoirse, Saoirse!*" And when they reached the galleon, the men grabbed a rope dangling from the rail and climbed aboard.

Coffin would have remained with the boat, but Tulip would not allow it.

"Get the fuck up there," he growled, "or I'll bloody well kill you myself."

What dangers had he not faced upon the sea from the wind or waves or the whale? Yet now Coffin found himself afraid, deathly afraid. For here was another transgression—the violation of the prime Commandment. Surely this sin did not matter in the face of all he had done, yet how awful it was! The cries of men, their fear, their pain, so unlike what he had imagined!

Tulip cursed him again and he joined the battle.

Coffin was soon surrounded. He advanced, tentative, and lifted his sword, and thrust, half-hearted, and he knew it was not in him to stab a man to death. He could not do it. Something hit him from the side and Coffin was on the ground with a man on top of him, powerful and stinking of salt beef, a long, bristling beard jutting into his face. The man was bringing a knife down and Coffin was fighting him, but the man was stronger.

"No, no!" Coffin screamed. "Don't! Please! Don't! Don't!"

The Portuguese man's eyes were filled with tears.

"No!" Coffin screamed.

"*Eu devo*," the Portuguese said. "*Eu sinto muito.*"

The knife slid into Coffin's chest and hit a rib. A bright bloom of pain.

"No!" Coffin screamed.

"*Morra, por favor!*" the Portuguese cried, and then the top of his head disappeared, and Coffin's face was coated with blood, brains, hair, and bits of skull as the corpse pressed upon him.

Quantrill had saved his life.

The big man fought with his usual cold fury, his axe humming through the air, smacking down a man on each stroke. Alone, he fell upon the flank of the Portuguese and drove them back, and the pirates regrouped, calling out the name of their ship so that Quantrill did not kill them by mistake.

The lanterns had been shattered and fire ran up the rigging and blood glowed upon the dying men.

From the forecastle came a voice crying, "For the seas! For the seas!"

It was Hornigold.

The men of the *Piranha* had boarded the galleon at the bow, stroking the tits of the figurehead for good luck and climbing onto the head and hopping up upon the deck, where they fired a volley of small arms and attacked.

The pirates began to shout *rendemos* and *tradução* and Israel Hands struck the Portuguese colours. Though they were outnumbered, still the pirates fought, and fought, and fought, and the blood splashed and the fire spread and the moon rose and the pirates fought. All of a sudden, for no obvious reason, the Portuguese began to throw down their weapons, and genuine cries of surrender outnumbered the ruses of the pirates, and the virus spread through all the soldiers, and the battle was over.

10

Though suffering from dozens of wounds, Apollo took charge. He found the Portuguese captain (actually a Frenchman), ritually accepted his sword, and gave it back. The two men conversed stiffly in French while the pirates whooped, and the wounded screamed, and the captain's small son wept without making a sound. Before the sun rose, and the Portuguese could perceive their numerical advantage, the soldiers were disarmed and locked in the hold. The Portuguese surgeon came on deck with his mates and together with Devereux went through the wounded, sorting them, while they begged and wept.

Apollo could not find Spry; instead, he addressed Scudder.

"Search the ship, but mark me—any man who mistreats a prisoner or a passenger will be strung from a yardarm, trial or no."

Scudder nodded.

Apollo followed the captain into his cabin, an enormous space twice again as big as the Great Cabin of the *Saoirse*, and the captain poured out Madeira, but Apollo did not drink. Already he was beginning to feel low.

Already the Voice chattered: did not they surrender too easily? Was there really any honour in taking a demasted ship?

"Forgive me," the captain said. "You said your name is Apollo, but I must inquire. You are not the famous John Jeffries?"

"In another life," Apollo said.

"I thought so," the captain said. "I was in the West Indies during the last war, and your exploits were much admired. My name is Louis Burgevin. I drink your health." Then to his son: "This man took a man-of-war with a sloop. His country treated him shamefully."

"Another life," Apollo said.

Burgevin, a little man, evidently did not feel the normal shock and confusion of defeated captains. He was bright and lively.

"You will show my son how you accomplished this feat?" Burgevin said. Taking a set of chessmen from a drawer, he arranged them on a table. "Your ship was here? From where blew the wind?"

Apollo set up the chessmen, and was beginning the story when below their feet men screamed.

Apollo put his hand on the hilt of his rapier. "What's that?"

"And then?" Burgevin asked. He and his son were looking at the chess pieces.

The screaming changed to laughter and cheers.

"What's happening?" Apollo asked.

Burgevin leaned back in his chair. "They have found the treasure."

"What treasure?"

"Aboard this ship," Burgevin said, "are both the Bishop of Goa and the Viceroy. And with them the fortunes they amassed during their respective tenures."

Voices growing louder and intelligible.

"I can't hold it!" someone shouted.

"Turn it to the side, Jesus!"

"Ha ha ha ha!"

The door to the cabin burst open and pirates came in, bearing a cross of solid gold so large it took three men to carry it. Diamonds, rubies, emeralds caught the light, winked, sparkled. The cross fell to the ground with a crash.

"That's bad fucking luck!" a man yelled. "That's Holy, I don't care if it's Papist, it's a Holy cross."

Apollo knelt. Three, four hundred pounds of solid gold?

"It's nothing but gold and silver down there, Captain!" a pirate cried.

"Give me the manifest," Apollo said.

Burgevin produced it from his desk.

Apollo flipped through the pages.

"How much is there?" Scudder asked.

"I don't know," Apollo said. And after a pause: "I am very tired."

"Give it here." Scudder took it and read it. His eyes bulged. "Captain . . ." he began.

"A million of your English pounds," Burgevin said. "Give or take."

Silence.

"A million . . ." one of the pirates managed, and then choked into silence.

"Shall we drink?" Burgevin asked.

11

At dawn the water churned as the sharks worried the dead. The pirates hauled box after box after box of silver bars out of the galleon, along with all manner of gems, rubies and pearls and emeralds, and little velvet-lined chests filled with gold coins, and rowed them across to the *Saoirse*, which had been towed off the reef and anchored in the bay. To make room, they unloaded chattels from the *Saoirse* and rowed them back to the galleon in a kind of exchange.

Throughout all this feverish, anxious work, Apollo remained in the cabin with Burgevin and his little boy. A servant cooked them breakfast, eggs poached in red wine, with fish and mustard and fresh bread and coffee, and after they had rehashed Apollo's famous victory in all its particulars, Burgevin said, "And after all this, to be treated so shamefully, by a Port Admiral at that. Shameful. Disgusting."

Apollo said nothing. The unaccustomed rich food made him feel ill.

"You will forgive me if I am indelicate. But your current career, Upon Your Own Account, it is a matter of honour for you? Revenge? Necessity?"

"Perhaps both," Apollo said.

"*Mais monsieur*," Burgevin said, smiling. "It cannot be both. It is your choice, or it is not."

"It doesn't matter now," Apollo said. "The die is cast."

"With the English, perhaps," Burgevin said.

Apollo pushed his bread around in the yolk and wine.

"I will speak frankly, sir," Burgevin said. "Should you surrender your ship to any ship flying the flag of Portugal, you shall be pardoned and rewarded, far more, I suspect, than whatever share you are allotted under the Articles that govern your Cruise."

Burgevin sipped his coffee; his lively eyes never left Apollo's scarred face.

"And then there is also the possibility of a command. In the Portuguese navy, or perhaps the French. Nations who prize courage and honour above the complaints of little people."

"How can you make that promise?" Apollo said.

"It is not me who promises, but the Archbishop."

Burgevin's servant, a sallow, intelligent-looking man, laid a sealed envelope upon the table.

"Signed by his hand," Burgevin whispered.

Apollo took up the envelope. Surprised by its heaviness. The paper inside crinkled.

"Otherwise, monsieur," Burgevin said, "I do not foresee that you will ever spend one *livre* of that money. Not one *sous*."

A knock at the door. The knocker came in without waiting. It was Spry.

"We're done," he said.

"Any recruits?" Apollo asked.

"Aye," Spry said. "Almost forty, and a caulker and the captain's cook among 'em."

"*Mon Dieu*, you do not even leave me my cook!" Burgevin exclaimed.

A press of men stood behind Spry.

"What's that letter?" Spry said.

"A private matter."

"A what?" Spry asked.

"Leave us," Apollo said. "I shall be out."

Spry hesitated. Apollo put the letter in his jacket and made a shooing motion.

The door closed.

"Well Captain Jeffries," Burgevin said. "Shall I say, *à bientôt*?"

Apollo stood, his wounds stinging, and shook the hand of the French captain, and of the boy, and then he went out.

12

The *Saoirse* leaked so badly that the men were obliged to keep at the pumps day and night. It took nine days to return to Libertatia. The winds would be unfavourable until the changing of the monsoon, which would not be for another three months. The Company had a great Meeting upon the beach. Spry had done the accounting; the specie alone came to £2,785 pounds per share. The Company agreed to dissolve at the earliest opportunity; how this was to be done was left to the next Meeting. The last item of business was a motion brought by Dickens requesting the Captain to explain what he had discussed with the French captain, what was in the letter that had been upon the table in the captain's cabin, and to reaffirm his loyalty to the Company. Apollo declined, saying it was a private matter, and he also rejected a request for him to repeat his oaths as an insult to his Honour.

The curses, insults, and threats Apollo received were all empty wind; after the triumphant Cruise, his position was unassailable. Still, they maddened him. His mood sank lower with the knowledge that there would be no more battles. He went back to the ship and, together with a small faction of men, worked eight hours a day, six days a week, on repairs. In the evening he visited the wounded, with whom he was patient, and he and the doctor took turns reading to them from the Bible and the complete works of William Shakespeare.

The Voice lurked in the back of his mind, chanting over and over that there was no honour in taking a demasted ship, that he had been lucky, that he was now a common pirate. He saw the faces of the dying Portuguese, the men he had killed, and the Voice told him how those men could say they had died with Honour, for their King and Country, while he could not.

And even apart from the maleficent Voice, practical questions threatened him. Where would they go now? After they broke up the Company, what would he do?

For now, he did his best to stay busy and avoid these questions. But at last the repairs were completed, at the cost of almost all their supplies; if they lost a yard, they would have to whistle for it. Some few days were spent pretending there was more work to be done, and his mood turned sour.

Then one morning they were awakened by the cry of the lookout.

"Sail ho!"

Libertatia, Madagascar.

April 3, 1722.

13

A twenty-eight-gun schooner with fore-and-aft rigging, flying the colours of Old England. A black flag rose to join it. The wind picked up, and the black flag fluttered, and Apollo saw an anatomy, in white, and a heart with a knife through it.

"Do you recognize the ship?" Apollo asked Hornigold.

"The ship, no," Hornigold said. "But I believe those are Lowther's colours."

"The fellow from the Meeting? On Hog Island?" Apollo asked.

"Aye."

Apollo grunted, put away his spyglass.

"What shall we do?" Hornigold asked.

"Let us rather wait, and see what they do," Apollo said.

Lowther's ship dropped its anchor at the mouth of the bay and fired a gun. A jolly boat was tossed over the side and a few men, including Lowther, climbed inside and rowed ashore, waving a white flag of truce. Lowther grinned at them, showing scarred lips and missing teeth, and bellowed out greetings. He came aboard the ship and was received in the Great Cabin by Hornigold, Spry, Tulip, and Apollo. A bowl of punch was produced, the usual toasts given, and all drank.

"Where's the Taoiseach?" Lowther asked at last. "Ashore with Darby?"

"Kavanagh is dead," Spry said. "And so is Darby."

"Blow me down!" Lowther said. "Who's in charge of Libertatia then?"

"The Malagasy," Spry said. "They killed everyone before we arrived."

"So there ain't no supplies, no provisions?" Lowther said. "No merchants?"

"All gone," Spry said. "You can see for yourself."

"Well, well," Lowther said, and drank his punch. "And they elected you Captain, did they?"

"Ah, no," Spry said. "I am Quartermaster. Tom Apollo is our Captain."

Apollo inclined his head, not quite a nod.

"Well, I give you joy, Brother Pirate," Lowther said, and took up the ladle and poured himself more punch.

"What're you doing here?" Apollo asked at last.

"Come to provision my ship and sell some booty, same as you, I expect," Lowther said. "This is still a free port, ain't it, shipmates?"

His eyes roamed. No one spoke, so he continued: "Perhaps you gentlemen are wondering what's happened in Nassau since you left."

They all listened.

"Well, mates, it's our Commonwealth come again. Vane's tricolour above the fort. No Governor, no redcoats, no Royal Navy. A fleet of ships, all flying the black flag, and merchants of every nation buying and selling without no taxes. And we're offering a Pardon, just as King George did."

"A Pardon?" Dickens asked.

Lowther removed a document from his pocket and it was passed around. It was a proclamation, setting out what he had told them.

"You pirates and your fancies," Apollo said. "Why do you bother?"

"Well, I suppose our ways seem strange to you, as you're no true pirate," Lowther said. "I'm surprised to see you the Captain of a Company of Honest Fellows. Then again, you'll see some rather hard men keep on as captain as are lucky in respect of prizes. And I heard you've been lucky."

"What have you heard?" Spry asked.

"Cape Coast Castle," Lowther said. "Heard about that one when we swung by the Guinea coast. Best believe they was talking about it. And ever since we came up through the straits of Mozambique we've been hearing about a galleon, the *Nossa Senhora do Cabo*. They were saying you took a million pounds of loot. That can't be right, though I'm sure it was a fine haul."

He waited as if for an answer.

"We've been lucky," Spry said.

"Give you joy," Lowther said. "But, Brothers, what's this about one of you flashing around a Letter of Marque saying you was from the Bahamas? Handing out receipts, even?"

"Ah, that was Kavanagh's doing," Spry said. "I ain't sure what he was playing at."

"When word gets back to the Commonwealth," Lowther said, "I don't reckon they'll be happy." A pause. "Still, if you were to go back, and pay the Commonwealth its share, them Letters of Marque might be ratified, *ex post facto*, as the lawyers say."

"Back to your Commonwealth?" Apollo said.

"Why, what else will you do with the stuff?" Lowther said. "You'll have to fence it somewhere, won't you? Why don't you take it back to your Brothers? We could even escort you back. What do you say?"

"What do we say?" Apollo said. "I say that sailing a great treasure into a nest of pirates is the height of folly."

"Well, we'll need a Meeting," Spry said.

"There will be no Meeting," Apollo said. "Should you wish to take your portion of the treasure back to an island founded upon thievery, that is your choice. But we will go elsewhere to divide our plunder." Apollo stood. "You would have us believe you are alone, Lowther?"

"What?" he said.

"You heard me," Apollo said. "You are accompanied by no other ships?"

"I'd have said so, wouldn't I?"

Apollo smiled thinly. To Hornigold, he said: "Take charge of Lowther's ship." Then to Lowther: "You will not leave until we do."

"Oy!" Lowther said, and started to his feet. "This is a free port, this is! Brothers, will you . . ."

He stopped.

Apollo was pointing a pistol in his face.

"What?" Apollo said. "What was that? Brothers, will you . . . what?"

Lowther's eyes went cold. He nodded. "All right," he said.

14

Despite Apollo's injunction, Lowther repeated his proposal to the Company at a Meeting ashore after Apollo's men took charge of his ship (the *Happy Delivery*). It met with little favour, other than some intrigued questioning from Dickens and his supporters. The motion was never brought to a vote, and the decision on their ultimate destination was adjourned again. Lowther and his men spent the night drinking and feasting with Dickens and his mates, and the next day the Company boarded the *Saoirse*, and she sailed from Madagascar, leaving the *Happy Delivery* behind.

All day, and most of the night, Apollo stalked the quarterdeck with his rattan, striking himself on the leg and muttering retorts to the Voice. The men, spoiled by their long vacation, were unruly and lazy and frequently answered back. On the second day, Apollo struck a man in the face so hard that he ripped open his cheek and bounced his head off the gunwale, and then had to be dragged to his cabin, screeching and cursing, by Alfie and Dobie.

Another Meeting was called, and from the start it felt different, as if some bond had been cracked now that their great triumph was an established fact rather than a bright prospect. Three months in that Edenic port, fresh food and liquor and warm, gentle rains, now traded for this reeking, leaking wooden world, infested with cockroaches and centipedes, and Apollo's fault-finding and bullying. Amazingly, he still did not know the men's names; he had addressed the man he had struck as "You Sir."

Dickens brought a motion that Apollo be removed as Captain. Sensing triumph, his speech was moderate:

"Now Brothers, while Apollo ain't quite the demigod as some make him out to be, there's no dispute he's a fighting Captain. And perhaps that's the problem. For we ain't got no more fighting to do, at least not till there's a Distribution of Plunder. And why he's lording it over us, acting the tyrant, is because you puppies don't have no notion of your rights."

Apollo exploded with wrath, ignoring Spry, who shouted that Dickens had the floor.

"Goddamn your souls, you mutinous devils, every one of you signed the Articles that said I am not subject to your wretched voting! Goddamn you to Hell for all your complaining."

He struck himself far harder than he'd struck the man.

"I can't for the life of me understand you lot! When we attacked that galleon, there wasn't one of you that didn't do his duty. There wasn't one man who was not champing to go over the top! Yet you can't coil a rope or swab the decks or man the pumps or do any other thing. Well, until the Company is dissolved, I am the Captain, and I feel I have shown my worth and I shall not suffer any further disrespect, and if any man here doesn't like it, we may settle it ashore in the Usual Manner."

"I've got the floor! I've got the floor! You see how he lords it over us, Brothers!"

But Apollo had many supporters now, especially among those who had done all the work to refit the ship. Even those who did not like him had grown used to him, a man larger than life. The motion fell well short of a Simple Majority.

Next on the agenda was their destination. This was not an easy decision. It was one thing to acquire a fortune, it was quite another to spend it. Was it better to go to a large settlement, like Batavia, where they might do their business in relative anonymity? Or was a smaller port better, where they would outnumber the lubbers and could bully the authorities? They settled upon Batavia, though it was still a subject of discussion that night at dinner.

At Coffin's mess, Hutchins said to Beard, "I don't hold with it, myself. A small port is the thing. You come up with a few hundred men and thousands of pounds of gold and silver, no one makes no trouble. There may be great ships at Batavia."

"Aye," Beard said. "But at a small port, what happens after the Distribution? At Batavia you may find passage to anywhere you want to go. Besides, we've done no injury to the Dutch, and they always say that Jesus Christ is good but Trade is better. And I don't believe Dickens and his lot have any intention of giving up the Pirate's Life, no matter how much loot they've taken."

"Why not?" Coffin asked. "Why would a man stay a pirate with two thousand pounds in his pocket?"

Hutchins looked at him. "Well, what is a man to do when he leaves off being a pirate? What will you do, shipmate? Hmm?"

Coffin had no answer; he felt cold at the thought of the end of this Cruise. He had wanted to end his life, but lacked the courage to do it, and he had joined these men as a way of escaping the pain of life while staying alive. He gave up everything, or so he thought, and sank all the way down to Davy Jones. But he had found fellowship, humour, tragedy, courage, all the stuff of life, even here, among the worst. All of them caught up in the thrum of the current, save him. To be cast ashore, alone but for his gold—what a horrible fate.

The Indian Ocean.

April 5, 1722.

15

I f the winds were fair, it was only a month's sail to Batavia. However, the winds were foul, and Apollo was faced with the choice of sailing to the east, and tacking into the wind, or taking an indirect route. If Apollo had truly known the men, he would have chosen the former, so that the hard work would shake them out of their torpor. However, Apollo's genius did not lie in that direction, so he chose the latter, in a futile attempt to placate his shipmates and extend the Cruise.

In consequence, he was miserable. The *Saoirse* sailed sluggishly, and there was nothing he or the men could do about it. He grew insufferable, and undermined Spry to such an extent that Spry was defeated in a motion of No Confidence and replaced again by Dickens (who once again narrowly defeated Scudder). The daily Meetings recommenced, and day after day Apollo had to listen to the men insult and attack him.

A few weeks out of Madagascar, they caught a glimpse of topsails over the horizon to the west. The *Saoirse* turned, but the ship, if ship she was, slipped away. Was Lowther following them?

That night, Apollo stood for hours on the stern gallery, rigidly at attention, staring blindly at the ship's bioluminescent wake, a marvellous fluorescent-green ribbon, looking without seeing, in his head the Voice refusing to submit despite being defeated again, and again, and again. All at once he became sure that he had made an error in the ship's log. The calculation appeared in front of his eyes. They had today travelled 109 nautical miles, but he had written 106. His stomach, always delicate, twisted. He stalked to the Master's Cabin, where the log was kept. Benjamin, fishing off the lee quarterdeck, let out a surprised bray. Apollo found the door of the Master's Cabin locked. He rattled the handle.

"One moment," he heard Dobie squeak.

There was something in that tone that Apollo did not like. He hit the knob with his knee and the wood splintered and the door opened.

Dobie's hand jerked, overturning an inkpot.

There were two logbooks in front of him.

"What the hell are you doing?" Apollo cried.

"Shh . . . shh. . . . shh!" Dobie said.

"Don't shush me, you insubordinate whoreson! What the hell, what in the hell, are you doing with my papers?"

"Captain, please," Dobie whispered, "I can explain."

A crowd of curious onlookers gathered around Apollo.

"Shut the door, shut the door!" Dobie cried.

A strange and horrible light in Apollo's eyes. He drew his pistol and cocked it while he shut the door with his foot.

"What?" he said.

Dobie, panicked, endeavoured to communicate through looks and gestures. Apollo studied the two logs, written in two different sets of handwriting. One was Apollo's. This was the logbook in which he wrote every day. The other logbook was written in another handwriting. Not Dobie's, another hand, very fancy, familiar.

Scudder. It was Scudder's hand.

"What are you doing?" Apollo asked.

"Shh! Shh!" Dobie said.

Apollo ripped the duplicate logbook away from Dobie and flipped back to the beginning. The first few entries were in Cian Kavanagh's handwriting. After their visit to North Carolina, the entries were in Dobie's handwriting. And then, a little after the visit to Cape Verde, the handwriting switched to Scudder's.

But the entries were all wrong. Apollo stood, baffled, as Dobie held out his hands for the return of the book.

Apollo's direct, honest mind took some time to make sense of what he was seeing.

And then, all at once, he understood.

"Faugh," he said, disgusted.

He took both logbooks from Dobie, along with all the rest of the most important maps and charts, and opened the door. A crowd waited at a respectful distance. Apollo shouldered through them and carried them to the Great Cabin.

The Indian Ocean.

May 12, 1722.

16

After reading the false logbook, he shut it up in the writing desk. Alfie came in with his breakfast, thin gruel, water from the scuttle-butt mixed with vinegar. The daily Meeting started up and Apollo stayed in his cabin to avoid it, feeling like a miserable prisoner upon his own ship. Soon there came a knock on the door.

"Brother Captain."

It was Spry.

"The Company requests your presence, Brother."

Apollo came out, scowling, blinking at the light.

"We've passed a motion," Dickens said. "We understand there was some dispute with your clerk last night and all the papers were taken out of the Master's Cabin, where they must be stored pursuant to the Customs of the Coast. Therefore, the Company requests that they be returned as soon as possible."

Dickens delivered this request without his usual vim, without even making eye contact.

"No," Apollo said.

Dickens looked up. His eyes widened, like a child about to receive a present.

The Company did not shout. It gasped.

"What did you just . . ." Dickens began, his voice rising with each word.

"Brother Captain," Spry said. "You cannot keep the books and records of the Cruise in your private cabin. They belong to the Company, not to you."

Apollo lifted his rattan, held it horizontal, and fetched his calf such a savage blow that the men in the gangplanks heard it and winced.

"I have had enough of this nonsense," Apollo said, hissing. "None of you, not one, have bothered to check the papers before I moved them. You only ask for them to be put back to be defiant. It is I who sets the course. It is I who drafts the charts. It is I who sets up the sail plan and adjusts the ship's trim. You—"

"No, no, no!" Spry was saying. His face horrified, as it dawned upon him that Apollo was serious. "You do not understand!"

"—only ask for them because you wish to hector and annoy and bully!" Apollo punctuated each verb with a blow upon his body.

"But Brother," Spry said. "We must have access to the logs, because we must know where the ship is going!"

"Why? So your Mutiny shall be easier? You have already resiled from sworn oaths and attempted to remove me with one of your double-damned votes. Why should I trust you? I have had enough of this nonsense. I shall act as navigator. Rios and Yellow are dismissed. Leave off these Meetings, and see about your duties, and if you have a reason to see the Captain's log, you may speak with me."

As he closed the door, the Company let out an astonished roar.

17

Apollo's action provided him with no relief. He sat in the Great Cabin, shaking, on the verge of tears, and carved a line into his forearm with a penknife.

A knock at his door.

He did not say anything, only rolled down his sleeve and waited, as the door opened and Israel Hands came in, followed by Dobie and Hornigold.

"Tulip, are you there?" Apollo cried. "Come in as well, Tulip." He clicked open the latches on his pistol case and took a duelling pistol in each hand.

Israel slowed. His eyes turned gentle with interest.

"Tulip, man, come in here," Apollo said. "Should not the Investors be represented?"

"Are you mad?" Dobie hissed.

Hornigold raised his hands and spoke calmly and carefully.

"Captain, I know you're worried about the men, but we're a few weeks from the largest free port in the Orient . . ."

Tulip thumped in on his crutch. Two burly Irishmen followed him.

". . . the men won't Mutiny. Don't worry about their Meetings, don't listen to Dickens. Only one thing can make 'em Mutiny now, and that's the fear that you'll give us up to the—"

"That I shall give you up?" Apollo arched an eyebrow. Blood leaked through his sleeve.

"Something happen to your arm, mate?" Israel asked, his eyes growing bored.

"For Christ's sake, Captain," Hornigold said. "Just put the books back."

A flick of his wrist and the logbook was spinning through the air. It hit Tulip in the chest.

"Can you read, sir?" Apollo asked.

Tulip looked around, confused.

"Apollo," Hornigold said. "You should hear 'em out there, they're going on about the Portuguese letter, they're saying on this northerly course we could be heading for Goa, we ain't seen land in weeks, the jacks don't know where we are, for the love of God put the books back in the—"

"This ship has two logs," Apollo said. "The real logbook, the true one, and a second logbook, a false one, which states that there was a successful Mutiny at Cape Verde and Bradford Scudder was elected Captain and the ship turned to piracy. Dobie maintained the false logs until yesterday. You will see that he went so far as to imitate Scudder's handwriting."

Tulip muttered something in Gaelic, and one of his companions shouted, and more Irishmen swarmed into the cabin.

"Until yesterday," Apollo repeated. "Why write a false log? Well, 'Brothers,' if the ship was captured, Kavanagh and Dobie would have presented it as evidence that they were 'forced' into piracy. That is why Kavanagh had Scudder do all the talking at Corso Castle. I suppose Dobie has been maintaining it as a sort of insurance policy. You will note, Tulip, that both you and I are listed as having been killed. This document would have been no help to us. In fact, for it to be of any use to Kavanagh, we would need to be dead. In contrast, Israel, Dobie, and Hornigold are all listed as having been 'forced' into piracy."

"Oh, by all the Powers, who cares now?" Hornigold broke in. "We've a million pounds in gold and silver in the hold of this ship. Let's throw all them forgeries overboard and give the men the proper log back and be on our way!"

Tulip made no move. "Why didn't he have me down as a forced man?" he asked at last, lifting his eyes. Trembling and raw.

Apollo shrugged.

"There ain't one Irishman in the list of forced men," Tulip went on. "What's in the rest of his papers?"

"I have not read them, for I do not have the key," Apollo said.

"We'll throw 'em all overboard," Dobie said. "I'm . . . I'm damned sorry, mates. I didn't want no part of this."

"What's in the papers, Dobie?" Tulip said, looking down. Not angry.

"It didn't have nothing to do with me!" Dobie said. "My wife's had my child back in North Carolina, I didn't want no part of this Cruise! All right? I didn't want no part of it!"

"So MacGregor and them was right," Tulip said wonderingly. "They was the smart ones after all, and I . . ." He trailed off as a thought occurred to him. "Did he pay them off, though? I saw the receipts, I . . ." He shook his head.

"We have a million pounds in the hold," Hornigold said again. "A million pounds. I don't know nothing about all these papers. I swear by all that's Holy."

"All that's Holy," Tulip murmured.

"Whatever it was, the Cruise is a success, don't you see?" Hornigold said to Tulip. "He turned the Investors' seven thousand pounds into a million. A million, Brother! All this, I can't say nothing about it, it was just his plotting, you know what he was like."

"No," Tulip said flatly. "I know what you're like, Benjamin. And I know what Hands is like. There ain't much to know about you, is there, Israel?"

"No," Israel said.

"And I know this martinet, I think," he said, with a dismissive wave towards Apollo. "But I don't know the Taoiseach. I never did."

"And me, Brother?" Dobie said. "You know he forced me? I have a wife, Brother, he forced me."

"What happened to MacGregor?" Tulip asked.

Dobie hesitated, looked at Israel.

"He . . . he paid them," he began.

"I killed them," Israel said. "All of them." Abruptly, a knife glittered in his hand.

Apollo raised his pistols.

"No, no, no," Hornigold said, throwing himself into the middle. "No, don't!"

"You son of a bitch," Tulip said to Dobie, angry at last. "You god-damn—"

"Gentlemen," Apollo said, his pistols steady. "That is quite enough."

"Just give them the true log back," Hornigold pleaded. "Brother, there's only one thing that can unite this crew against you, and that's it, that's it! Give them the bloody log!"

"No," Apollo said. "The log stays here. Tulip, confine these gentlemen to the orlop. Post a guard outside my cabin."

"Tulip, mate—" Hornigold began.

But Tulip and the Irishmen dragged him out of the cabin and down the companionway. Outside, there was shouting, but the Irish barred the men from the Great Cabin, and the Meeting ended in chaos.

18

A pollo felt some fleeting satisfaction. Finally, he had gotten his way! But it melted away, and he spent the next night pacing on the stern gallery, flexing his rattan, muttering, arguing, arguing, arguing with the Voice.

A little before dawn, Tulip laid a hand on his shoulder.

"Brother, a word?"

They went into the Great Cabin.

"Something surprising will happen," Tulip said as he poured himself a drink. "Don't cry out."

The door opened, and another man came inside. At first Apollo did not recognize him, then he did, and clicked his teeth shut to stay silent.

"They've made plans to Mutiny," the spy said. "Scudder and O'Brien brokered it between Spry and Dickens. Hornigold is to be made Captain. The books are to be restored. A full Meeting postponed until we reach Batavia. You are to be confined in your cabin."

Having passed along this message, the spy went on his way.

"We don't have much time," Tulip said.

Apollo twisted the rattan in his hands so that the leather bucked and cut the flesh of his palms.

"I thought about letting 'em do it, you mad bastard," Tulip said. "But I won't stand for Hornigold as Captain. Are you listening, Brother?"

"Yes," Apollo said, sweating, muttering. He stood up and whipped his back with the rattan. No release. He did it three more times.

The nerve of those mutinous dogs! After all he'd done for them! Only a fortnight out of port!

"Brother, listen to me," Tulip said.

"I am listening!"

"Whatever the deal betwixt all these Sea Lawyers, if this Mutiny goes through, it's majority rules, and that's bad for the Investors. Even shares, at best, but they won't leave it at that, they'll be looking to settle scores. I think, if you give them the books back, that would do it. Not for Dickens, he's out for your blood. But Spry won't Mutiny if you restore the books."

"No," Apollo said, his heart hammering, a funny taste in his mouth. "No. Enough giving. It's over."

"We're twenty days out of Batavia."

"No," Apollo said. He had not slept properly in weeks, his body was criss-crossed with scars, he started at every sound. "No, no, no, no, no. No. No."

"Damn you," Tulip said. "You're mad, you know that? Horace Spry turning mutineer? O'Brien and Dickens working together? Dickens agreeing to Hornigold, the man that captured Charlie Vane, as Captain? You are mad. You are a madman."

"Yes," Apollo said. As soon as he said it, he knew it was true. "Yes. Yes. I am mad."

Tulip paused, disgusted. "What were you talking about with that Frenchman?"

"Nothing."

"I . . ." Tulip began, then stopped. Pinched his nose. If he let the Mutiny happen, Hornigold would not be able to hold the crew together. A single share would still be nigh on twenty-five hundred pounds, but then you were trusting the Company to pay you out.

On the other hand, he could try to keep the mad bastard in power.

If only there was someone else! But there wasn't. On top of being, far and away, the best seaman aboard, Tom Apollo was still Tom Apollo, the most successful pirate captain who had ever sailed the seven seas. If you let the men replace him, anything was possible, anything was permissible. You'd never be able to draw a line and say this far but no farther. The circle of order would crumble, the welter would rush in and follow its own instincts down into the very heart of the thing. Tulip had seen it in Honduras. The same thing would happen here, twenty days out of port or no.

He found himself, strangely, missing the Taoiseach. The extent of the man's perfidy knew no bounds, yet you could not doubt his head in a crisis.

Well, he was not here now. Tulip went onto the quarterdeck and spoke to a few men in Gaelic. None of them protested or gave any sign. They were old hands. They'd been through this before. Just one last time.

19

The Mutiny took place as mutinies usually do: a sudden rush aft by a press of men on the lower deck, intending to seize control of the rudder and then surge up through the companionway. However, as they sprinted towards the bulkhead, a dozen muskets jabbed through rude loopholes fired, and then withdrew, and fired again.

Dozens of men dropped, bleeding and screaming, and the progress of the mob was checked, and a pack of armed men, led by Cyrus and wielding pistols and cutlasses, came up the forward companionway from the orlop and jammed up the spaces to either side of the foremast, trapping the men in the waist of the ship. The jacks outnumbered Apollo's men four to one, but they were surrounded and could not make use of their numbers, and in two minutes they were shouting for quarter.

"Fight to the death, men!" Dickens cried. "It's your only hope!"

But it is a hard thing to ask a man to get off his knees when he has a bayonet in his face. The mutineers were ordered below while the forecastle was searched, sea chests smashed open and their contents dumped out, anything in writing seized. Finally they were brought up to the weather deck under armed guard. Scudder, Spry, and Dickens were stripped to the waist. Scudder was tied, spread-eagled, to a grating rigged by the mainmast.

"You see?" Apollo said. "You see why I cannot allow you to have access to the logs, the charts, the navigational instruments? How can I trust you swabs, when you would seek to murder me, after all I've done for you?"

Apollo paced, his rattan slashing back and forth, spittle in the corner of his mouth.

"I am tired of being a prisoner of your motions. I will not allow discipline to break down. Men, I tell you for the last time, we are going to Batavia. I will bring you there safe and sound."

Most of the men were stunned; so much had happened in so little time! But a few of Apollo's supporters were grinning, lording it over the Sea Lawyers who had been whining and shirking for months.

"In a well-ordered ship, everyone knows their duty, and the duty of the men around them, and everyone knows their place. From this moment, we will have order, and discipline, and you will stop complaining, and do your duty, and everyone will be satisfied."

"You're mad," Scudder said.

"One hundred and fifty," Apollo said to Cyrus.

The silence grew more silent. Even Cyrus hesitated, his smile cracking.

"One hundred," Apollo said. "And fifty."

Cyrus delivered the first blow upon Scudder's bare back. Scudder stiffened but did not cry out.

Cyrus, the mute, held up one finger to the crowd.

Then everyone waited twelve seconds. One. Two. Three. Four. Five. Six. Seven. Eight. Nine. Ten. Eleven. Twelve. The whip whistled, struck.

"Ayeeee!" Scudder screamed.

Cyrus held up two fingers.

Every time Scudder was struck, his heart faltered in his chest from shock and pain.

It was a spectacle with which every man aboard was familiar, though none had seen it in a long time. It was a slow, difficult, awful thing to watch. By the twentieth stroke, Scudder was bleeding. By the thirtieth, he was weeping. By the fiftieth, Cyrus, exhausted, gave the lash to Apollo. By the one hundredth stroke, when Cyrus took up the lash again, Scudder was silent, and took each blow on his mangled back with as little response as if he had been a side of beef. When the beating was finished, he was doused with salt water, provoking one last cry before he was thrown down on the deck. The beating had taken a half-hour.

Dickens was rigged up in his place. Hardened to floggings, he shouted invective at Apollo and the crew, until he was battered into silence.

It was Spry's beating that had the greatest effect upon the assembled crowd. Unaccustomed to the lash, terrified by the hour-long spectacle that had preceded his turn, he was reduced to begging, and pleaded for Cyrus to stop after every stroke. And though perhaps some of Dickens's supporters smirked and exchanged glances, the greater part of the Company was profoundly affected. A ship where Horace Spry might receive one hundred fifty lashes was a troubled ship indeed.

After the floggings, Apollo said: "In light of this attempted Mutiny, there shall be no more Meetings, public or private, until we arrive in Batavia."

20

The corpses were thrown into the sea. Spry was carried below, while Dickens and Scudder walked to the forecastle under their own power, stiff-backed and slow.

Apollo paced upon the quarterdeck. The floggings had given him no satisfaction. He wanted to go into his cabin; he did not think he could sleep, but he would have liked to put a cool cloth on his brow. But he would not do it, he would not allow anyone to think him shy. His teeth were gritted, and the Voice was whispering, there, you've done it, you've lost them now, what kind of a captain loses his men after such a Cruise.

Images of all the men who had ever slighted or insulted him ran through his mind.

Scudder came back on deck in a clean shirt and sat on the forecastle picking oakum with shaking fingers, teasing fibres from segments of old rope.

"You there!" Apollo cried. "What are you doing on deck?"

"Picking oakum, sir," Scudder said.

"Why don't you go below decks, for God's sake?"

"It's my watch, sir."

"You just had a flogging—go below decks."

"I can stand my watch, sir."

Apollo stalked forward, out of the safety of the quarterdeck, so he was among the jacks. They parted.

"Making a show of yourself, are you?"

"I'm standing my watch, sir," Scudder said. "I'm picking oakum. If you want me to go below, just give the word."

"Suit yourself," Apollo said.

After another hour, just before the watches were to change, Apollo ordered the fore-topsails reefed. As the men moved to take their places, he cried: "Scudder! Take your position! On the double!"

The men paused. Scudder was the captain of the foretop and his traditional place was upon the extremity of the yardarm. But two hours after receiving one hundred and fifty lashes, he could barely stand. His muscles were pulverized, his internal organs leaked blood, his heart fluttered, irregular and weak, and his ribs jolted in pain with each breath.

Yet he stood.

"Scudder, Scudder," O'Brien whispered to him, "just go below."

Scudder made his way to the rail. The ship rolled and Scudder fell. When he stood, stripes of blood had appeared on his shirt.

"You can go below or you can climb the mast," Apollo said.

Scudder stepped over the rail, down into the chains, stumbling as the ship rolled to larboard, lifting him up from the sea. He held the ratlines as tightly as he could, but all the strength in his grip was gone, leaked out of the wounds in his back. Before the ship could roll back to starboard and dip him into the water, he swung his leg around and, using both arms and legs, dragged himself onto the webs of the shrouds, where he hung, panting and bleeding, like a seasick old lady upon her first voyage, or a lubber scared of heights.

"On the double, you son of a bitch, or I'll have you flogged again!" Apollo shouted through a trumpet.

Scudder climbed. His arms next to useless, he made his way by stepping up with his feet until his body was crouched double and then straightening his legs. As his shredded back flexed, his body was shocked with pain and he let out little gasps of agony that sounded like: "Shh! Shh! Shh!"

"Faster!" Apollo roared. "Or make way for another man."

He climbed, and climbed, his heart stopping and skipping, sweat running into his eyes, behind him a friend murmuring: "Easy now, Brad, one two, one two, easy there now." At last he poked his head through the lubber's hole and friendly hands pulled him up. Before them was the white expanse of the fore-topsail, full and curved and straining against the ropes. The ship was heeling to larboard, everything sloped.

"You can't do it," a voice said. "Wait here."

Scudder shoved the hands away, swung his leg over the rail, and pulled himself up.

Below him, Apollo screamed at him to go faster.

Scudder climbed, up, and up, and up, towards the foretop yard, from which the sail hung, and then, waiting for the ship to rise, he let go of the shrouds and caught the yard with one hand and then another. There was no strength in his arms, none, yet at the top of the rise he leapt and grabbed the footrope between his legs, and as the yard dipped back down, he sat on the rope and then stood.

When the yard pointed towards the sea, he shuffled along the footrope, gasping now, getting as far as he could before the rise of the yard checked him, and he clung and waited. The wind shrieked and struck him, but at last he came to the very tip of the yardarm. Every movement of the ship caused him pain, and so he kept his body rigid, straining down and forward and gripping the wet, heavy canvas of the sail.

"All right, mate, you're all right," the man next to him said. "Hold fast now."

The man bent over the yard and began to haul up the sail, hand over hand.

"Oh God," Scudder cried. "Oh God!"

"Steady on, steady," the man whispered.

The wind blew harder, and the sea grew rougher, and the ship bounced unexpectedly, and Scudder was lifted off the yard and missed it on the way back down. For a strange eternity he hung, disconnected, and then he caught the footropes with one hand as the ship started her starboard roll.

Work stopped on the yards, on the deck, everywhere. Every man saw what came next. No one breathed as Scudder held on with one hand and dangled above the hungry, heaving sea.

Every man on that ship had been flogged, and all knew that no man who had received so much as a dozen lashes could hang from the footropes in rough weather. It could not be done, and Scudder would fall, and that would be that, it was over.

Scudder fell, and fell, and then the ship came to the end of the starboard roll, stopped, and Scudder was jerked tremendously, and he screamed, but there was no pain in that scream, it was nothing but fury.

And he did not let go. The sea rushed towards him and his heart lurched arrhythmic and his arms were airy and weak, and he had a vision of all the men and women swallowed and forgotten by history, and he knew that now he would join them, that no one would remember, no one would mourn, and he filled up with so much anger, there was no limit to it, this anger, like a scalding subterranean ocean, endless, and his hand clenched with such force that it would break before it came loose, and he did not fall, he rose with the yard and the sea receded and his shoulder lurched and almost separated and the lacerated muscles of his back exploded, but he felt no pain, only a burning, smokeless rage.

At the top of the roll, he caught the yardarm and stamped down hard on the footrope and he was safe and fast again.

Every man watched and every man saw and a restrained, wordless hum passed through them.

They hauled up the sail and reefed it, and then Scudder inched his way back along the footrope to the crosstrees. He did not feel able to climb back down, even to the foretop, so he sat there at the very top of the very front of the ship and looked down at the white bow wave and empty blue sea.

But then the glass was turned, and the bell rang, and Apollo shouted at him, and Scudder did climb down to the foretop, with the help of his fellows, and then he went down to the chains, slowly, slowly, and then he rested again in the chains, the cooling sea spray wonderful on his back, and then he climbed over the rail and he was back upon the deck.

Apollo was waiting for him. Scudder looked him in the eye and saluted. Apollo, whose face was without expression, fetched him a savage blow to the temple. Scudder crumpled to the deck and did not move.

Since Scudder had begun his climb, the ship had been silent. Now the silence became appalling, broken only by the wheezing laughter of Cyrus, the jerky, airy laughter of a tongueless former slave, and whether he was laughing at Scudder or Apollo none could say.

21

Unnoticed in the confusion:
O'Brien made his way aft, his heart pounding, into the waist, where Benjamin leaned over the gunwale with his fishing rod.

"It's yuh-yuh-you, ain't it?"

Benjamin saw the knife in O'Brien's hand.

"Don't you cuh-cry out," O'Brien said.

Benjamin made a confused bleating noise.

"I've suh-smoked you, you son of a buh-bitch. It cuh-could only be you. It's all an act, all of it, you've kept it up for yuh-years. You go wherever you puh-puh-please, no one takes note of you, and then on your way to do your fuh-fuh-fishing on the stern gallery you spill everything to the Cuh-Captain. Well, you scurvy son of a buh-bitch, unless you do what I say, you're duh-dead. I've already given your name to one of my mates and we'll get the wuh-word out on you and you'll never be safe again."

O'Brien leaned in.

"You meet me upon the head at four bells of the first watch. If you ain't there, you're duh-dead."

The men were silent at dinner, and at night there was no dancing, singing, or other music. The *Saoirse* sailed on into the darkness. Benjamin shuffled to the upper deck and walked forward to the head, feeling his way through the dark. The cook nodded as he passed, and in reply he smiled and gibbered. Then, he went out into the night.

Here the motion of the ship was most pronounced, rising, and falling, and thin sheets of dark spray soaked the men at the latrines. Benjamin dropped his pants and sat down at the foremost seat of ease and waited. In a few moments O'Brien came out and sat next to him. There was no moon and the only light came from a lantern upon the bowsprit.

"It's been you, the whole time?"

Benjamin nodded.

"Speak puh-properly."

"Yes," Benjamin said.

"No other suh-spies?"

"None."

"You're sure?"

"I'm sure."

"All right," O'Brien said.

Benjamin watched a man come out to relieve himself.

"Tuh-tuh-tomorrow," O'Brien said, "I will drop a buoy into the water attached to a rope. When you are alone aboard the stern gallery, bring it up and tie the rope to the rail."

Benjamin did not reply.

"Did you hear me?"

Benjamin's face slackened, drool glistened at the corners of his mouth. His gaze diffused, and he shuffled away.

But O'Brien knew that he had heard.

22

Apollo slept little, and came onto the quarterdeck before dawn. A group of Irishmen armed with swords leaned on the windward rail. One of them spat and shook his head and the disrespect made the Voice shriek. He was so tired of it. He was run ragged.

The log was heaved, the line run out. Eight knots. The *Saoirse* tore through the sea, casting up a fine bow wave and holding a firm line. Yet all was not well. Even Apollo could sense it. The easy manner of the sailors was gone. No one sang, no one joked. They were not free, and neither was he.

At breakfast, the cook brought him eggs poached in sea water together with weak tea, but even this gentle fare was too much for his stomach. Inside his cabin, on the poop deck, or by the wheel, everywhere he looked, he saw some fault, some further example of shoddy seamanship or carpentry.

During his usual fantasies of meeting someone from his old life, and of being accused, he could no longer think of anything to say. In the past this blue feeling might have been dispelled by some victory. But in a simple moment of revelation he understood that victories had never made him happy, and they never would. His whole life he had followed a false compass. Now he was lost.

At lunch, he took out the Portuguese letter, reviewed it again. He looked at the maps. If they did happen to encounter a Portuguese ship, he did not know what he would do. He thought he would probably fight. He could not surrender to the Portuguese any more than he could surrender to the men. He imagined one possible life after another, and each one was burdened with shame. To betray his men for a Pardon was tawdry, murine. To live as a pirate despicable and shameful. His whole life he had thought of nothing but his honour, yet somehow or other it had been trailed through the muck. What then was his life worth?

A knock at the door; Benjamin shuffled inside. The spy drank his tot of whiskey, licked the inside of the silver cup with a deft pink tongue, and looked Apollo in the eye.

"Nothing," he said.

"I find that surprising," Apollo said.

"Nothing of consequence," Benjamin said. "They're cursing your name. And some of the bolder ones are saying they'll settle their scores ashore. But none of them are plotting anything afloat. They know there's a spy. And so, I better be out for my fishing."

Benjamin left the Captain's cabin and leaned up against the rail. He cast his line and waited. The ship's wake trailed into the distance. To larboard the sun sank towards the waves. For the benefit of any who might be listening, he made a garbled noise and jittered his head.

What a life he had lived.

Darkness came, and the *Saoirse* ploughed through a great strangeness of luminescent jellyfish, glimmering pale under the dark and empty sky. Benjamin waited until he heard the buoy clunk against the side of the ship. He reeled in his line, set down his rod, and gathered his fish, and in so doing looked for anyone who might be watching him. But there was no one, and so he lay on his belly and reached over the side of the ship and grasped the rope and tied it to the rail. The buoy twirled away behind the ship. He went back into the Great Cabin, pretended to lock the door, but did not.

Apollo did not look up.

"Do you want a fish, Captain?" Benjamin said. "The flesh of the tunny is very light."

"No, thank you," Apollo said. "Good night."

"Good night," Benjamin said.

23

Night.

The door to the stern gallery opened and shut, quickly, and quietly, but not quietly enough for the troubled sleep of Captain Apollo.

"Who goes there?" he said.

A sudden blundering noise, banging, papers falling. Apollo grabbed the loaded pistol by his head and when the door to the Great Cabin smashed open, he pointed and fired. In the flash he saw it was Quantrill, soaking wet from the sea, and the bullet, meant for the head of a normal man, smashed his collarbone.

It was dark, very dark, only a little light leaking in through the window, and Apollo threw aside the spent pistol and drew his knife. Quantrill barrelled forward, and Apollo cut out, deft and precise, and hit Quantrill three times, jabbing for a vein, but Quantrill twisted his body to deflect the blows, and now he had his hands on the Captain, first one on the knife arm and the other on his throat, and Apollo was shoved up against the hull and Quantrill smashed him with a head-butt, once, twice, thrice, and then stabbed him, very hard, no subtlety to it, and blood rushed out, down his trousers, between his toes, the deck slippery with it, everything going grey.

At last, Apollo began to scream.

The door rattled. It had been rattling for some time. Finally, it banged inwards, and Quantrill withdrew as the light of the lantern revealed the bloody, tangled scene.

"Murder!" Apollo cried. "Mutiny!"

An Irishman knelt next to Apollo, pushed his hands upon his wounds, and the Captain was lifted by many hands, the lantern jostled, the light danced. Quantrill fled aft, took up the rope, and jumped into the sea. Tulip rushed after him, lantern in one hand, pistol in the other, and fired a shot down into the dark water.

Apollo, jostled and jammed, wheezed and bled. His mind raced with a thousand disconnected thoughts. And then they stopped. At last a vision came to him, a fantasy. Dawn comes. The lookout cries. It is a galleon, a hundred guns, flying the colours of Portugal. Escape is impossible; the enemy has the weather gage and runs them down. They turn and fight. All old enmities forgotten. All striving as one. But it is no use. The enemy cannon bring down their masts, and the ship is raked. At last the galleon ceases fire; it cannot risk sinking such a prize. Yet her boarders are repulsed, again and again, until at last the pirate known as Tom Apollo falls to his death, pierced through with swords and musket ball alike. The crew surrenders. After searching the cabin, the Portuguese find the letter. They are amazed! This Captain could have saved his own life and retired a rich man. Yet he chose death rather than break his oath! The pirates, in the little time they have before their executions, reflect upon the greatness of this man, whom they never appreciated.

He smiled, closed his eyes.

24

While the guards rushed to the Captain's cabin, the mutineers freed the cannonballs from the garlands, rolled them along the deck in a great iron tide, skipping and bouncing, and followed them in a silent rushing pack. A few muskets snapped and a few men dropped and then the pirates, unarmed save for marlinspikes and small knives and iron cookware, smashed into the Irish, knocked them down, killed them, and broke down the bulkheads into the armoury.

Tulip heard them. On the quarterdeck with a rapier in one hand and his crutch under the other arm, he knew all was lost. Yet he shouted: "Batten down the hatches. Batten 'em, nail 'em shut!"

The aft companionway was easy enough—the hatch slammed and canvas stretched over it—despite the pleas from the officers in the gun-room. Once this was done, Tulip cast aside his crutch and hopped forward, from rope to rope, like a monkey swinging in the jungle. His men initially followed, but took cover when muskets snapped from the foretop.

"Goddamn you cowards," Tulip cried at his retreating supporters. "The hatches, damn your eyes!"

Below him, he saw the mutineers climbing the stairs, armed now, and he slammed the hatch shut himself, and sat upon it, but it was no good. Six men smashed it open from below, and he was knocked into the rail of the ship, and the jacks were on the deck.

"Damn you," Tulip shouted. "I'll see you all in—"

But he never said where they would see him, though they all could guess, for a pistol was fired, and the ball struck his throat, and he fell into the sea.

Below, on the upper deck, the mutineers smashed through the canvas cabins and stabbed the officers in their hammocks, a chaos of blood and shredded cloth, chairs overturned and furniture broken, chests looted. Men shouted at one another, gestured, cried. Some had broken into the spirits room.

The Irish abandoned the quarterdeck and took refuge in the Great Cabin. But the mutineers climbed upon the roof, shattered the skylight, and threw grenados, which burst with tremendous noise and light, smashing the windows and sending clouds of black smoke into the sky.

At last they broke down the door and rushed in, howling, and overcame the defenders. Axes and swords chopped down and mangled bodies were hurled out the windows, where they vanished in the wake. The men danced and howled and waved their bloody weapons. The Mutiny was over; the *Saoirse* was a free ship.

DEMOCRACY

A government by the people.

(Merriam-Webster)

CAPTAIN BRADFORD SCUDDER

The Indian Ocean.

May 13, 1722.

1

Scudder had not taken part in the fighting; now he ran aft on the upper deck.

It was very dark, above and below; a lamp swinging from a beam alternately revealed arms, legs, panicked faces, splashes of blood. Someone shouted, "Fire!" A cannon fired. All of a sudden a blue, ethereal flame, like a will-o'-the-wisp. Someone had set alight a barrel of rum.

"Put a lid on it, you fuckers!" A furious voice. "Just put the fucking lid back on."

A crowd of men stood round, plunging their hands through the flames and laughing. The crowd surged, the barrel tipped dangerously, a lid clapped down, and the flames vanished.

Scudder went, limping, up the companionway, almost out of breath by the time he was on deck. Men rushed everywhere. No one was in charge. He went aft. O'Brien was shouting and pushing his way inside the Great Cabin. Here was an abattoir, fortunately barely visible in the dim light. The grenados had blown the rooms apart. O'Brien was guarding the iron chests of papers with Davies, one of the new men from the slavers. Davies was one of the few men aboard whom Scudder could not bring himself to like. There was something revoltingly soft about the man, weak but not kind, like a dead jellyfish on the beach that still might sting.

The ship rolled and Scudder slipped to his knees in the blood. The wounds on his back flared.

"Is it over?"

"Duh-duh-do we have the puh-puh-puh-puh-POWDER room suh-suh-secured?" O'Brien asked.

"I don't know," Scudder said.

"Duh-Duh-Davies, guh-go and check."

Davies gave his usual smile, showing more gums than teeth. Scudder smiled back. But before he left, Dickens came in, shouting, waving his hands. Most of the men in the cabin were nominally his followers, but they paid him little mind.

"Ruh-Robby, do we have the puh-puh-puh—" O'Brien asked.

"Aye," Dickens said. "It's over. I don't know but we killed every man jack aft of the mizzen-mast."

"Juh-Jesus Cuh-Cuh-Christ," O'Brien said. "How muh-many men left as cuh-can sail the ship?"

"Yellow," Dickens said.

"Other than Yuh-Yuh—"

"I don't know," Dickens said.

"Well, no more kuh-killing tuh-till we suh-settle that," O'Brien said.

"Agreed," Dickens said.

"Huh-who is sailing the guh-goddamn ship?"

They went out and found Coffin was at the wheel, illuminated by the lantern in the binnacle, looking past the chaos, up at the sails, keeping them full, luffing and touching. He glanced at them once, his eyes large in the dark.

"Oy," Dickens said, motioning to two of his men. "Take a trick at the wheel." Coffin flinched. But Dickens said: "You're the Captain, mate, until further notice."

"Me?" Coffin said.

"Aye, until we've had our Meeting," Dickens said.

"Qu-Qu-Quantrill will help you," O'Brien said. "Guh-Go find him, he's on the fuh-forecastle."

Back in the Great Cabin, a group of men cleaned the mess, while Davies and O'Brien went through box after box of the Taoiseach's documents by candlelight. Scudder lay down on a chaise longue, his back in agony. Quantrill arrived, indifferent to his wounds, dripping wet, to confirm his instructions. He was fêted even by Dickens. Below decks singing, dancing, thumping, cannon fire. Every now and then a scream. The revelry did not end until noon. The galley fires were out, the Negroes were not at work, and there was nothing to eat. Coffin and a skeleton crew sailed the ship for twelve hours.

At last a drummer was located, and all hands were called on deck. Many were not sober enough to answer the call, yet the gangways were packed with men who whistled and cheered as Lewis, the armourer, addressed them.

"Well Brothers," Lewis said. "While you've been having your fun, a Committee has drafted a revised set of Articles. I propose that I shall go through 'em one at a time, and vote yay or nay. I shall chair the Meeting and I shan't run for any office. What do you say?"

The motion was acclaimed.

2

The first Article was unchanged:

The Captain and his Officers shall have authority when the Ship is in action, but except as otherwise stated in these Articles the Ship shall be governed by the Majority and every man shall have an equal vote in the affairs of moment regardless of his share.

It was passed without debate. Next up was an Amendment to the Article regarding provisions:

Every man has equal title to the provisions and strong liquors, and may use them at pleasure, unless a scarcity makes necessary, for the good of all, to vote a retrenchment.

This too was seconded and acclaimed. Spry suggested an Amendment concerning drunkenness but was shouted down. The next Article was amended as follows:

The Captain, Quartermaster, and the Ship's Officers shall be elected by
the Company.

The men let out a throaty cheer at this, and some threw their hats in
the air, and danced around in circles, arm in arm. When the cheering
ceased, Scudder asked, waggishly, if any man had any objection, and
none did.

"Now Brothers," Lewis said. "We come to a difficult matter, and that
is the question of shares. We did not reach an accord, in the Drafting
Committee, upon this matter, and so I shall put the question before the
Company. How should the duff be divided?"

"Mr. Chairman," Dickens said.

"The Chair recognizes Brother Dickens."

"I will grant the Captain two shares," Dickens said, "but no more!
And the Quartermaster a share and a half! But every Able Sailor shall
have one share and no more, and the Negroes and other landsmen
shall have the half share for which they contracted."

A rope maker was granted the floor, and said that he had signed on
for a greater share, and 'tis only fair, if you will pay an Able Seaman
more than a Negro, that you shall pay a petty officer more than an Able
Seaman. The debate dragged on, and at last Scudder (after a discussion
with O'Brien) proposed a compromise: The Captain to receive two shares,
the Quartermaster one and a half, and everyone else one. However, the
warrant and petty officers would receive an additional ten shares to
divide amongst themselves, while the Able Sailors would receive twenty-
five. After puzzling over the arithmetic for a few minutes, the Company
accepted the proposal.

The previous Article governing the dissolution of the Company was
now irrelevant and was deleted. Regarding duelling and punishment:

Any man who contravenes the Articles or who fails in his duties shall
suffer punishment as the majority of the Company sees fit.

Dickens addressed the Company as follows:

"Now Brothers, we all seen the trouble the goddamned duels caused us on this Cruise. We all seen it. A skilled duellist could lord it over the others like a tyrant. And as for giving the Captain a veto on punishment, we seen how the Captain used it to protect his favourites. So put everything before the Company, says I, bring it before a Meeting, put it to a vote, says I."

Spry said:

"Brothers, it's one thing to make a man clean the heads or stop his grog, but it ain't right for a man to be shot or hanged without meeting some higher standard than a Simple Majority."

Dickens did not agree—majority rules, he said—but the Company was rather leery about every Meeting becoming a matter of life and death. And so the Article was amended as follows:

Any man who contravenes the Articles or who fails in his duties shall suffer punishment as the majority of the Company sees fit, save and except that no man shall be shot or hanged absent a two-thirds majority vote.

There being no further Amendments, the men fired off the guns and toasted each other as free men at last.

Next was the election. Scudder, Dickens, and Spry put themselves forward for Captain. As usual, Spry put great emphasis on good governance while Dickens warned of Tyranny. Scudder spoke last.

As he stepped forward, the Company gave a great cheer. Scudder's face almost split with his grin. How it warmed him through! They loved him! They loved him! He remembered after the failed Mutiny how they'd spat at him, sneered. Look at them now! It was mother's milk to him, ambrosia, the stuff of life, their cheers! Heart brimming, he began:

"I'll admit, Brothers, I ain't the most experienced man aboard this ship. But one thing you know about me is that I'm a friend to every man aboard. Every one of you, yes, even the Negroes and the lascars and the skilled sailors and the Sea Lawyers and all. I'll stand up for every one of you, even the least of you. I won't let no one trample on your rights, and I'll always follow the will of the Company. That's what a Captain ought to do, upon a Cruise such as this, full of prime seamen and men as value their freedom. If a Captain follows the will of the Company, he won't go too far wrong. As for my Brother Spry and my Brother Dickens, well, if you elect either one of them, we'll be at each other's throats, you know we will. We need a man to hold the Company together. Brothers, that's me, I'm your man."

Thunderous cheers. Stomping. He carried it without need for a second vote. There had been, perhaps, some question of his pluck, hanging towards the back during battles and such, but he had more than answered that with his defiant performance on the foretop yard. And he had O'Brien for advice and Quantrill for strength. The Company did not doubt but he was the man for the job.

"Three cheers for Captain Scudder!" O'Brien shouted, joyfully, and it was given with goodwill.

Scudder held back his tears.

3

The election for Quartermaster was more competitive. A dozen men put their names forward. The final two candidates were Dickens and Spry. But Spry's faction was much reduced, since many had been killed in the Mutiny, and Dickens carried the white sailors almost entirely, and was confirmed to the office.

Next was the trial of the surviving collaborators, including the Investors, many of the petty officers, and Hornigold and Israel Hands, who had been confined below. (Rios and Yellow were not charged, as they had been sent before the mast when Apollo took charge of navigation.)

Lewis granted Davies the floor to explain what he and O'Brien had found in the Great Cabin.

"Errr, um, shipmates," Davies said, smiling, "we haven't quite been through all of 'em, and we ain't, um, sure how they all fit together. It seems that Kavanagh betrayed Teach and Roberts and the other Adventurers in North Carolina to, uh, Governor Rogers. Um, uh, furthermore, although Kavanagh told his Investors the price of this ship was six thousand pounds, it seems he only paid one hundred."

Cries of astonishment.

"Well, um, ah, Kavanagh used his Investors' money to purchase thousands of acres of land in North Carolina, although he did not even pay full price, for he was blackmailing the Governor there as well; he, um, had evidence Governor Eden was fencing the duff brought in by Teach and them."

More shouting.

"I ain't, um, sure why he brought all them papers aboard," Davies continued. "I suppose if we'd been taken he'd have turned, mmm, on Rogers and Eden as well." He then explained about the false log and presented the letter from the Archbishop of Goa, and invited the Company to look at all the papers themselves.

Reactions to these revelations varied. Some men cursed and spat. Some men were shocked, almost driven to tears. Some men laughed cynically at the sheer perfidy of it all. And some shook their heads, and muttered that you could curse or cry or laugh, aye, or all three, but say what you would about the Taoiseach, he was the sort of man for a Cruise like this one, and, by thunder, a few men here might have cause to miss him yet before they were safe in port.

Dickens cross-examined the Defendants, showing both an excellent memory and an unforgiving character as he brought up slights and insults from weeks and months before (and, in Hornigold's case, years).

The bosun, superficially wounded, was near tears. The carpenter's mate cast down his eyes. The gunner's mate, a wicked man, sneered. The surviving Investors were silent. Hornigold's great head shrank back into his shoulders, as if he was expecting a blow. Frightened, but calm, knowing. He made no excuses or speeches and gave short answers. His bearing was that of a man who was looking for a particular moment, like a prospector panning for gold.

Only Israel Hands was unmoved. He'd caught three rats down in the hold, killed them and tied their tails together, and he held them at his side, bouncing them off his thigh in boredom as he answered questions.

Yes, he'd known the Taoiseach had cheated his Investors. Yes, he'd known about the business in North Carolina. Yes, he'd killed the dissenting Investors (this information was volunteered, no one had asked). No, he hadn't known about the log, what did he care about that? They would all swing sooner or later. No, he hadn't known about the Portuguese letter.

One question came up over and over again.

"Who is the spy?" Dickens demanded.

"I don't know," Hornigold said.

The other Defendants pleaded ignorance too, though a careful observer might have noticed a little flicker in Israel's eyes.

"Twice our mutinies were betrayed by a goddamned spy," Dickens demanded. "He must be caught! I ask you again, gentlemen—who is the spy?"

No one spoke.

"Step forward, sir," Dickens said.

None did.

"I give you my word of honour, as a Gentleman of Fortune, should the spy step forward now, I'll bring the motion myself to put him ashore, not at no civilized port but not too out of the way neither, with powder and shot and a hundred golden guineas. That's as handsome as you can ask for, handsomer than you deserve. But if you don't speak up now, when we find out who you are—"

"And we will find out," Scudder added.

"Right you are, Bradford," Dickens said. "We will find out. Then it's death. And you won't be strung up by no yardarm, neither."

Still no man stood forward.

"So be it," Dickens said.

On O'Brien's whispered advice, Scudder proposed a compromise when it came to the Defendants. Rather than hang the most valuable of them, they would be put on half shares, and forbidden from voting or holding any position of authority. This was Hornigold's fate, along with the bosun, and the last carpenter's mate, but the last bosun's mate (Cyrus had been killed in the fighting) was sentenced to be hanged, along with the gunner's mate, as well as most of the Investors, save two for whom someone spoke up when Lewis asked: "Does anyone have anything to say in this man's favour?" One was a massive but gentle brute called Connor, who had a lovely voice but could not speak a word of English, and the other an affable fellow called Ryan.

The most surprising acquittal was Israel Hands. He'd been Upon the Account since the year '13, and he'd saved the lives of many men aboard, and they spoke in his favour, starting with Dickens. There was no doubt that he was, in his particular way, an Honest Fellow, as demonstrated by his forthright testimony during the trial. And when it became possible that he might be acquitted, the Company became afraid—who would want to have voted death if he lived?

The gunner's mate spat and shook his head and prophesied they'd all drown, all of them, head straight down to Davy Jones's locker. The nooses were prepared, the doomed men accepted their last drinks, and they were lifted, kicking, up into the air, by their fellows.

4

Now that the matters of import had been resolved, only trivial issues remained regarding the sailing of the ship. Scudder proposed that the men elect their officers, but Dickens objected, asking how the men were to be divided into watches. Scudder suggested that the Quartermaster perform that function, but Dickens said it ought to be a decision of the whole Company. The matter dissolved into a tedious debate, which was resolved by granting the authority to set the watches to the Quartermaster but gave the men the right to trade places with men on another watch, should they wish to do so, and for the whole thing to be subject to the will of the Company.

The Meeting was adjourned while the men organized themselves into watches, another long process, with much haggling and arguing, and when they reconvened, half of the crew had gone to the forecastle to dance or was drunk and insensible below decks. Almost the entire day had been taken up with this Meeting, and although the weather remained fair, the ship made erratic progress, for Coffin and his men were exhausted.

Once the watches were set, Dickens moved that each watch elect its own officer, and the motion was carried. Dickens had arranged so that one of the watches was composed almost entirely of his followers, and they swiftly elected Yellow as their officer. The other watch would be controlled by Scudder, so he met with O'Brien and Quantrill by the wheel.

"Well then," Scudder said. "Who is to be our mate?"

"I am," Quantrill said.

"Come now, Billy," Scudder said.

Quantrill scowled and said, "I don't see why not. I killed Apollo. It's my turn."

"The officer needs to be quite a seaman, Billy. He needs to decide which sails to set and so forth."

"I don't think there's anything to all that," Quantrill said. "Anyway, I can ask Coffin."

"Well why don't we just make Coffin the mate then?"

"Because I earned it," Quantrill said, and glared.

Scudder looked at O'Brien for support, and O'Brien said, "How about this, Buh-Buh-Billy. Suh-Scudder can't make you the muh-mate, on account of how it would luh-look puh-putting his best friend in the juh-job. Luh-let's make Coffin the muh-mate, buh-but you don't have to do nothing he tells you to do. And muh-me and Scudder'll duh-do something for you. All right?"

Quantrill did not answer. O'Brien and Scudder had a hurried conference and a runner was dispatched. The Meeting resumed, the officers were appointed, and Scudder called out: "One more thing and we'll adjourn. I would like to recognize the great bravery of William Quantrill, who last night swam aft, climbed aboard the stern gallery, and killed the tyrant Apollo. Every man here's a hero in my book, but I believe I may say with no fear of dissent that the Company is especially grateful to him. And in recognition of his bravery I should like to present him with a token of appreciation. What do you say to that, men?"

The applause was surprising in its warmth and duration. Even Dickens called out, "Hear, hear!" And why not? It was a bold stroke, none could deny it, and every man was flush with rum and liberty. Best of all, the fucking Meeting was over at last.

Quantrill shuffled his feet and looked down, unsmiling.

With a flourish, Scudder produced Kavanagh's one-hundred-guinea sword.

"This here was presented by the merchants of Nassau to Kavanagh," Scudder said. "And now we, the Adventuring Company of the *Saoirse*, present it to you. All yours, Billy. Well earned, well earned."

"Hear hear!" the men cried.

"Now gentlemen, perhaps one toast and then the Meeting shall conclude. Does everyone have a glass? You there, where's your cup? Yes, you too, Coffin, one drink and you may be off to bed. Is everyone ready? To liberty, gentlemen! To liberty at last!"

The men cheered. The band began to play:

Did not you promise me
That you would marry me

5

Bradford Scudder walked into the Great Cabin brimming with an airy feeling. He pulled up short at all the blood. Lord, it was horrible. The Negroes streamed in after him, nodding, unsmiling, carrying their buckets and swabs and holystones, and set to work.

He did not like to see all the blood, so he went onto the stern gallery and looked over the ship's wake. All of a sudden, he felt lonely. How could that be? How absurd! They loved him! He was the Captain, for God's sake. The Captain of a great ship!

Still, the feeling persisted. He went back into the Great Cabin. It was certainly very large. A man had eighteen inches to sling his hammock on the lower deck. Up here there was plenty of space to stretch your legs. But by thunder it felt a little queer.

"Alfie, there, lend a hand," Scudder said. "I believe we shall auction a few of these things off before the mast."

Alfie's face went from smiling obsequiousness to polite disapproval. He did not quite disobey orders, but he seemed to suddenly have difficulty understanding English, or hearing at all, and lingered over many things, the china and silverware and the heavy metal globe, and some of the decorations, so that somehow not quite everything made it out onto the quarterdeck.

The pirates happily abandoned their work and rushed aft. Scudder led the bidding, in his element again, particularly when it came to auctioning off Kavanagh's strangest memento, the musket that had been sawed down to a pistol, and which bore the truncated inscription: *mes McIntyre, Esq.*

Foolish Benjamin was desperate to acquire this item, and kept raising his hand no matter the figure quoted, and certain wags noticed and entered a number of bids, so that the final price was over nine hundred pounds, almost all of Benjamin's half share. When the bidding was complete, Scudder, having somehow acquired a rather grave and commanding air, said:

"Oh, Brothers, I believe there has been a mistake! For as you all know, Benjamin is a fool, and therefore he is . . . what do you call it, Johnny?"

"*Nuh-nuh-nuh-non compos mentis,*" O'Brien said.

"Thank you, Brother, yes, because he is a fool, he cannot enter into a binding contract. And so, I shall accept the second-highest bid. Brother Trevor. Your bid—nine hundred and ten pounds, was it?"

The man blanched.

"Nine hundred and ten pounds, Brother? Or would you care to withdraw your bid?"

"Oy, that ain't right!" someone said.

"Don't you tell me what's right, you poxy-livered son of a goat!" Scudder thundered, his voice carrying the length of the ship. "Damn you for playing tricks on a simpleton. He only wanted something to remember his Captain by, Lord knows how long they'd sailed together . . ."

"He knowed the Taoiseach's father!" someone called.

"That's right, he was slaves together on Barbados with Kavanagh's father, and he wants something to remember him by, and it's a goddamned dirty trick, and I won't have it. I said I'd be a friend to every man aboard, and I meant it. Benjamin," he called, lifting the ruined weapon. "You may pick it up whenever you like."

The auction over, his departure was greeted with more applause, and he felt that warm feeling as he went into his Great Cabin. But the applause soon ended, and he was alone again. He was quite relieved when O'Brien soon followed.

"Well, what did you think of that trick?" Scudder said.

"Nicely done, nicely duh-done. A qu-quick word on Qu-Quantrill though."

"Billy?" Scudder asked. "What about him?"

"Juh-just remember he's very important to us. Israel Hands may wuh-well juh-join up with Duh-Dickens."

"Really?"

"Yes, at least at first. And we wuh-want a real tough man of our own."

"But Billy and I are great friends!"

"Aye, buh-but you are fuh-friends with everyone, Bradford. Qu-Quantrill's only fuh-friend is you."

"I've tried to help him make friends on his own," Scudder said. "Only he don't seem to take to no one."

"Wuh-well you should be luh-looking for wuh-ways to suh-single him out," O'Brien said. "You saw how Duh-Dickens has been chu-cheering him, we duh-don't want him getting no ideas."

Scudder laughed. "Don't worry none, Johnny. You didn't see us on that damned plantation. Those were hard times. If we stuck together then, we'll stick together now. He won't leave us for some tattooed baboon like Rob Dickens as long as I'm above ground."

6

Although everyone now knew that Apollo had set a northerly course as part of his Plot to surrender to the Portuguese, it became clear that this course also had a sound basis in seamanship. For when the *Saoirse* set a direct course for Java, the winds blew stubbornly into her face. Rios's and Yellow's measurements seldom agreed, but it was clear the *Saoirse* made little progress.

In the beginning, Scudder invited the crew to dine with him each night, but since he was eating the same food as everyone else (the fresh provisions having vanished shortly after being declared communal property), after the first week his invitations were only accepted by his supporters. Spry's men spent their time in the former gunroom, while Dickens and his men staked out the forecastle.

Dickens held daily Meetings. Participation started low and then diminished. The Meetings accomplished little, other than providing a forum for Dickens to compel Scudder and O'Brien to listen to his complaints, and for Spry to bring motions against men of Dickens's party, complaining that when Dickens's watch was on deck, the decks were not holystoned, or even swept, and when they were below deck, they did not do any work.

Eleven days after the Mutiny, the *Saoirse* was struck by a storm. Yellow's watch was on deck, and they were having such a riotous time, singing, shouting, stamping, that it was not the cries of alarm that alerted the men below of the danger, but rather the sudden stillness and silence.

The wind had come roaring over miles of dark water and sprinted into the side of the ship, catching the yards and sails and rigging and shoving them down, so the whole ship lurched forty-five degrees, and the men were thrown onto the deck and their chests and possessions slid and smacked into the beams.

Some cannon had not been properly secured after the toasts following the Mutiny, and those on the windward side snapped free and rumbled down the inclined deck. Each one of them eight hundred pounds, each one capable of smashing through the hull and sinking the ship. In the dark confusion, the pirates sought to restrain them with whatever they could as water poured through the hatches and soaked them.

Scudder staggered sideways out of his cabin and into the storm. The rain lashed down in sheets and the helmsmen spun the wheel, but it was too late, the *Saoirse* leaned farther to leeward, all her ropes and timbers groaning.

The sky lit up. An instant later it thundered as if it had broken.

The pirates bumped into each other, some climbing, others descending. The ship tipped farther and farther, and iron hoops and barrels and coils of rope, all manner of sundries, rolled and bounced and clattered along the deck and fell into the roiling sea. A numb, inanimate sense of strain tingled through every inch of the wooden ship as she tilted farther still.

Scudder ran forward, without any clear goal, but the ship had leaned so far that he slid on the wet deck and banged up against the rail.

Another brilliant burst of lightning. Another rumbling snap of thunder.

The tips of the yardarms touched the waves, and water streamed into the open hatches. Before his eyes a man fell into the hungry water and vanished.

Now that the ship had tilted so far to leeward that she lay upon her side, the deck was sheltered, somewhat, from the wind and rain.

Scudder shouted, and the men turned to look at him, for he was the Captain, but he found that he had no idea what to say.

"Cut the masts down!" someone yelled, brandishing an axe. "Cut down the masts!"

"No!" a powerful voice shouted.

Hornigold, up the main companionway: "Let go all the halliards!"

"We must chop down the masts!" the panicky man screamed.

"We're in the middle of the bloody Pacific," Hornigold shouted back, "and if we want a new mast, we shall have to whistle for it. The ballast is secure, it was stowed by Apollo, and it shall pull us to rights. Let go the halliards, shut up the hatches, and leave the masts be."

"Do as he says," Scudder shouted, and the halliards were let go and the sheets ran down and the men stretched canvas over the companionways and nailed them shut to stem the flow of water. They waited, as the ship groaned, heavy with water; they knew that if the ballast shifted, the *Saoirse* would never come right again.

But the ballast did not shift, and the gravity of the ship pulled her back up. The wind hit them head-on, and the ship moved backwards, wailing like a grandmother in mourning. The useless rudder strained, and water ploughed into the stern windows and threatened to break them. But Hornigold shouted directions and the sails were trimmed and the bow fell off the wind and the ship turned so the wind was at her back and her sails filled again. Hornigold gave more orders, and the men swarmed up the shrouds and ran out over the cracked and damaged yards and dangled in the watery air, wrestling with the soaking, flailing canvas while lightning lanced in little arcs. Water ran out of the scuppers in thick streams, back into the sea. Thunder crashed as they ran on into the dark.

7

Scudder ran down to the lower deck. The lanterns had been smashed and doused and it was very dark, yet the men had found some light and had lashed the cannons back into place, double- and triple-secured, and the newly appointed caulker was hard at work at the ports, some of which had not been sealed.

"Ten feet of water in the well, sir," the carpenter said to Scudder.

"Are there men at the pumps?" Scudder cried. "To the pumps, to the pumps! Who is with me?"

He led the way, tramping down the wet, slippery stairs into the blackness of the orlop and the pump room. The pump was worked by means of a horizontal iron bar. A dozen men took their places and heaved and the chain rattled up from the well and the water spurted out of the scuppers.

"Heave-ho, men!" Scudder cried. "All together now!"

They strained together, pushing and pulling, and the big Irishman, Connor, sang out in Gaelic, and Scudder felt his heart lifting. Why, they'd made it through, hadn't they? A blow like this was just the thing to bring the crew together, show everyone that they had a common interest despite their differences . . .

A hand on his shoulder, a voice shouting in his ear. Davies's unpleasant face.

"Come up, come up!" Davies shouted. "It's going to come to blows!"

"What?" Scudder said.

"The Meeting, it's going to come to blows!"

"What Meeting?" Scudder said. "Take my place."

Davies pressed against the bulkhead and then stepped in to the pumps when Scudder squeezed past.

Up the companionway he went, into a tangled mass of men, shoving and struggling. Only two lanterns and all was a seething mass of shadows. Scudder took such a deep breath the air went down to his toes, and then he shouted with such force as to be heard over the shouting and the storm alike.

"Belay that you goddamned sons of bitches! Oy there! You leave off fighting right this moment or I'll hang the lot of you for Mutiny!"

Some of the men turned towards him, but those at the core of the dark struggle continued to shout.

"Silence!" Scudder cried. "Order, order! I'll have order, you dogs, or I'll hang the lot of you!"

The voices dimmed, and then Dickens shouted:

"Get these men off of me, I had the floor! I know my rights! I have the floor!"

"The fucking floor?" Scudder shouted. "Goddamn your soul to Hell, Robert, I knew you was a Sea Lawyer, but I never thought you'd call a fucking Meeting at a time like this."

"There was a quorum," Spry said.

"Fuck your quorum," Scudder said. "What are you doing calling a Meeting when your own Captain is at the pumps? Mr. Dickens, go down below and take your turn, and that's an order."

"I will not!" Dickens said. "I had the bloody floor, you tyrant! And it weren't me that—"

"Billy," Scudder said.

Quantrill loomed, suddenly, out of the darkness, ploughed through the mob, shoving men aside, and caught Dickens by his collar.

"You can't do this!" Dickens said. "Unhand me! I demand my rights!"

Quantrill propelled Dickens down the companionway.

"This Meeting is suspended," Scudder said.

"It's up to the Quartermaster when Meetings are called or adjourned," Ironside protested.

"Well I'm the Captain," Scudder said. "And I say you can have your goddamned Meeting when the ship is safe, and not before. I see many a man from Yellow's watch. You ought to be on deck! And those of you that ain't needed on deck have plenty to do below. Now off with you!"

Spry seemed as if he wished to say something, but Scudder cut him off.

"So the Meeting's adjourned then?" Ironside asked. "You won't bring no motions without us?"

"No, of course not!" Scudder said. "Go to your duty!"

"Well, it's irregular," Ironside said. "But I suppose we'll see what the Company has to think of it."

"I suppose we will," Scudder snapped. "Where's O'Brien?"

"Huh-here," O'Brien said, and stepped forward from a place by the foremast.

"Imagine the cheek of that bastard," Scudder said. "Calling a Meeting at a time like this."

"Duh-Dickens duh-didn't cuh-call the Muh-Meeting," O'Brien said. "Suh-Spry did."

"What?"

"There was a qu-qu-quorum," O'Brien said. "And so Spry called a Muh-Meeting."

"To do what?"

"To puh-puh-punish Yellow for negligence."

"Why that's a damn dirty trick," Scudder said. "Why didn't you do something?"

"I duh-didn't do anything."

"I know that," Scudder said. "Why *didn't* you do something?"

"Well, Buh-Buh-Bradford, he fuh-followed the ruh-rules, and it suh-seemed a good chance to ruh-ruh-remove Yuh-Yellow buh-buh-before he kills us all."

"Nothing will ever come of such a dirty trick," Scudder said. "I am surprised, John, you don't see it for yourself."

O'Brien shrugged, shifted, looked away. Scudder left him and went on deck.

8

Hours later, Scudder awoke, swinging back and forth in his lonely hammock, so much like a coffin. He dressed and went out upon the quarterdeck. The storm still raged, and the *Saoirse* ran before it, propelled by a double-reefed topsail, no more. The bow smashed into dark waves that rushed the length of the deck.

Coffin had the watch, and he nodded to Scudder as he came out of his cabin.

"Good afternoon, Captain," Coffin said.

"Afternoon?" Scudder cried.

"Aye," Coffin said. "Four bells of the afternoon watch."

"Goodness me," Scudder said. He almost asked: Why did no one wake me?

Rain slashed and the wind blew. The ship rose, and fell, rose, and fell.

"No more than eighteen inches in the well," Coffin said. "Cannon double-fastened and the gunports sealed, hatches battened down. She's as dry as can be expected. The bosun and the carpenter have done what they could, but there's more work to be done in fairer weather."

"Well then," Scudder said, and cleared his throat.

Coffin watched him with his large eyes.

There was something about Coffin that made a man a little nervous, the way he looked at you, so Scudder smiled and went below. The upper deck was mostly empty, save for the forecastle where the Negroes had lit the galley stove and where Lewis was striking an anvil with his hammer. Scudder continued down to the snug dark of the lower deck. It was packed with men and smelled very close. Dozens of lanterns hung from the beams and the hammocks had been stowed, so the men sat cross-legged and worked among the clutter of all the equipment and supplies, some of which clattered as the ship pitched and rolled. The men stitched sails and mended rope and picked oakum. They looked at him, and some friendly faces smiled or nodded, but most turned back to their work.

"Captain," a voice said.

Scudder turned and looked behind him to see Alfie.

"Hello Alfie," Scudder said. "How are you, Brother?"

"May we speak with you?" Alfie asked.

"In a moment, Alfie," Scudder said.

He picked his way through the men, nodding, attempting to seem Captain-like, until he found the bosun, who was in discussion with Hornigold.

Both men nodded.

"Captain," Hornigold said.

"What's happening?" Scudder said.

"Well, we pumped the ship dry, and she's not taking on much water," Hornigold said. "The launch was lost, of course, and the bowsprit has cracked, and the foremast—"

"Why wasn't I woken?"

"Well sir," Hornigold said, "you might ask Yellow or Dickens or Coffin, or someone, about that. But it seemed you had a long go at the pumps, and the crisis had passed, and there's not much needs doing until it grows fair."

"All right," Scudder said, and looked around at all the men. "Well."

Hornigold regarded him, deferential and wary.

"Good work then, good work," Scudder said, and made his way aft where Alfie and the other Negroes waited.

"What was it you was needing, Alfie?"

"May we speak in your cabin, sir?" Alfie asked.

"I suppose so," he said.

They went up, into the rain, past Coffin, who watched the Captain pass without nodding or saluting, and then into the Great Cabin.

"Have a seat, Brothers. Tell me what's on your mind," Scudder said.

But Alfie was looking at the small iron stove in the corner. "The fire is out," he said.

"Don't trouble yourself about that," he said.

But the Negroes were already speaking in Igbo, quick and low, and they left and returned with firewood, fresh water, and a coffee pot.

"Is there still some coffee, then?" Scudder said.

"We saved it."

"Now Alfie, that's against the rules."

"If we did not save it, it would all be gone."

"Well, we should serve it out to all the men," Scudder said.

Alfie took on that polite disapproving look, which Scudder found strangely intimidating.

"We'll table that for now," Scudder said. "What's this all about?"

"The weather, sir," Alfie said.

"Damned inconvenient, ain't it?" Scudder said.

A knock at the door, and O'Brien entered.

"Hello John," Scudder said. "Come in and have some coffee. Alfie and I were just discussing the weather."

"We have found the witch," Alfie said.

"Pardon me?" Scudder said.

"The person making the storm?" Alfie repeated. "You call this person a witch? Or a Jonah? We say *ndi amoosu.*"

"Ah," Scudder said, and glanced at O'Brien.

"We have discussed it, and we are sure, the witch is Coffin."

"Now see here—" Scudder began.

O'Brien cut him off. "You know Cuh-Coffin's buh-buh-been elected the mate of the Captain's watch."

"Oh, he is not a *bad* man," Alfie said. "It is good to have a mate who has these powers. But perhaps you should speak to him and ask him why he has brought the storm. Or perhaps if you put him in the orlop he will make the weather stop. I do not know."

"Thank you for buh-bringing this to our attention," O'Brien said. "We will take cuh-care of it."

One of the other Negroes spoke with a thick accent. "You must lock him up," he said. "That will make him stop."

"We'll duh-deal with him," O'Brien said.

Alfie poured out two cups, one for O'Brien and one for Scudder, but none of the Negroes would accept any for themselves and they left.

"Now John, see here, is it really wise to tell 'em we'd deal with this? It's bunkum, is what it is. Anyway, I don't have the authority under the Articles."

"Let's thuh-think it oh-over," O'Brien said. "But that's not why I came to see you. I have it on guh-good auh-authority there shuh-shall be a muh-motion of non-confidence brought against you."

"For what?" Scudder cried.

"Wuh-well, Spry and his lot want stricter duh-discipline on the ship. They're saying we're shuh-sure to duh-drown, and they ain't happy you adjourned their Muh-Meeting, given they had a quorum. And Duh-Dickens is saying Hornigold is acting like an officer, duh-despite of his oath, harping on about that suh-spy, how they're still puh-plotting to give up thc ship."

"Oh, rubbish," Scudder said.

"Well, how many muh-men can you cuh-count on? I mean really count on."

"The crew likes me, I think."

"Shuh-sure," O'Brien said, sipping his coffee and then holding the cup level as the ship rolled. "But if Spry and Duh-Dickens unite against you, do we have the vuh-vuh-votes?"

Scudder didn't answer.

"This brings us to the Nuh-Negroes. You were always kind to them, and they never forget a kindness."

"I can't lock a man in the hold for sorcery!"

"All the muh-men already thuh-think he's a Juh-Jonah."

"I don't have the authority!"

"Well, how about thuh-this," O'Brien said. "How about wuh-we say that the ship is in action, and so you huh-have the authority to order everyone about."

"But we ain't in action."

"Why not?"

"Well, action means in battle. Don't it?"

"No, buh-battle means battle. Action muh-means action. A storm could mean we wuh-was in action. And then you cuh-could say you weren't locking him up for witchcraft, but only duh-doing an investigation."

"Damn it, I don't know, John." Scudder sipped his coffee, then said, "I don't feel right drinking this. You know, John, when I went below, just now, I felt like there was a difference."

"Aye, it's a luh-lonely thing, command," O'Brien said.

Scudder swirled his coffee, and thought. "John, what were you on about last night?"

"What's thuh-that?"

"Why didn't you send for me straight away when Spry started up that Meeting?"

"Well, I thuh-thought about it," O'Brien said. "But I duh-didn't want to be seen to be tuh-taking sides."

"Taking sides? I'm the Captain—I have to be there for the Meetings. Don't let it happen again."

"Sorry, Buh-Bradford," O'Brien said.

Scudder shook his head.

"Get Quantrill to bring in Coffin."

9

While he waited, he toasted a slice of cheese over the portable stove. The knock came, and he glanced in the mirror, drew himself up straight behind his great table, and said: "Come in."

Coffin entered, followed by the looming Quantrill.

"Have a seat, both of you," Scudder said, assuming an air of awful dignity.

"Is there something wrong, Captain?" Coffin asked.

"Brother Coffin," Scudder said. "Serious charges have been brought against you."

"Charges?" Coffin said. He was wearing a tarpaulin hat and he removed it now. "What charges, sir?"

"It is alleged, Brother, that you are a sorcerer, and that through your sorcery you have brought upon us the present inclement weather."

Coffin opened his mouth. He looked at Quantrill, who only glared. He said, "Who hath accused me?"

"That information is confidential, Brother."

"What is the evidence against me?"

"Brother Coffin, this is not a trial, but only an investigation. Do you have anything to say for yourself?"

"I am no sorcerer, Captain. I am a Christian."

"What evidence do you have, Brother, that you ain't a sorcerer?"

"I do not know," Coffin said.

"So you have nothing to say for yourself?" Scudder said. "You do not make it easy for me."

"What is the evidence against me, for the love of God?" Coffin said.

Scudder drummed his fingers on the desk. "Very well then," he said. "Since you can't say one word in your own defence, you shall be confined in the orlop until the investigation is complete."

"What about a trial?" Coffin asked.

"You haven't been charged," Scudder said. "I do not know whether you will be charged. That is why we are having an investigation."

"How long must I stay in the orlop?"

"Until the investigation is concluded."

"How long will that take?"

"I cannot say. Quantrill, please escort Brother Coffin to the sail room."

"But Captain," Coffin said.

Quantrill's hand clamped on Coffin's shoulder. "Come now," Quantrill said, not gently, but not roughly neither, and led him away.

Scudder was alone again. So much room!

One of the perquisites of Scudder's position as Captain was to keep a small keg of rum in the Great Cabin. This keg was the ship's communal property, and anyone could come in and drink it. However, no one did; they could get rum other places.

And so, Scudder spent the afternoon getting drunk by himself, and rooting through Kavanagh's remaining possessions. Most of what was left was what you might call domestic items, lace doilies and cotton napkins and a few fine tablecloths, and best of all, locked up in a wooden box and packed in newspaper, a porcelain tea set. It was the real stuff, from China, for Scudder's mother had taught him to tell the difference, as thin as eggshells and white as bleached bone.

Scudder's father had been the youngest son of a baronet, his mother a milkmaid of heart-stopping beauty, and it had always been an open question as to who had seduced whom. His earliest memories were of high-stakes visits to his grandfather, when it had been impressed upon him that his fortunes entirely depended upon making a good impression. He had been trying to make such an impression ever since, in the Royal Navy, with Bellamy, now here.

As he drank, he handled the cups with exaggerated care, and his maudlin imagination turned to his mother, and what she was doing now, and whether she ever thought of him. In his loneliness, an idea occurred to him. He would use this lovely porcelain, along with Kavanagh's silver, to serve up salt beef and biscuit!

Scudder summoned the Negroes and instructed them to set the table. Alfie suggested that perhaps they ought to wait for better weather, but Scudder would hear none of it, although he was dismayed each time the ship lurched and a cup fell and broke. O'Brien was summoned, and between them they drew up a list of men to invite, those whose loyalty was considered tenuous and whose votes O'Brien considered important.

Everything started off well, the china and crystal and silver making a favourable impression. The men laughed and drank and cheered and drank and ate and drank and made toasts and drank and all the time more and more china was broken and crystal was shattered and Scudder became more and more agitated and at last some rather hard words were said and the table was knocked over and all the china shattered and Scudder punched a man, and a knife was drawn, all of a sudden there was Quantrill, and a man was thrown off the stern gallery into the dead grey waves while the wind came inside shrieking, together with the cold rain.

Because, after all, outside the storm still raged.

O'Brien remonstrated with Scudder, and Scudder, now very drunk indeed, remonstrated right back, and then passed out in his hammock with the wind and rain still washing inside the cabin.

10

The next morning, the storm was over and the sun skewered Scudder's bloodshot eyes. The cabin was a ruin and O'Brien was standing at the door, telling him that the men had called a Meeting and if he was not out soon, it would be held in his absence.

Broken china pricked his soles as he rolled out of his hammock and stood. After he dug a little shard out of his callused foot, he looked around at the ruins of his cabin. The day before, he had wondered why Kavanagh had never used the good china during the dinners he gave for the crew. Now he knew.

Alfie came in with a basin of warm water, soap, a razor, and a mug.

"Alfie, I ain't sure there's time for that."

Alfie clucked and gestured. Scudder obeyed. He did feel better once he was washed and shaved. The mug was full of chicken broth; Lord knew where it came from, but once it was down, his stomach settled.

"You see the weather has improved," Alfie said, satisfied.

"Oh, damn it," Scudder said. "Alfie, would you tell someone to let Coffin out of the sail room?"

"Aye," Alfie said.

Stepping out of his cabin, he gasped, squinting in the glare, and it was a moment before he could see. The Company waited, sullen and impatient.

"There you are," Spry said. "I trust you are well enough for the Meeting."

A surge of a strange feeling in his chest, so strange, he was not sure what to call it.

"Going to top it the Holy Joe, are you?" Scudder said. "Because I was drinking last night? Bellamy always told me a sober man was likely to be in a Plot against the Company."

Spry frowned.

"Come to think of it, where's the rum?" Scudder said. "Before the Meeting, let's have a toast."

"Oy, enough stalling!" Dickens cried.

"Stalling?" Scudder said. "You men don't want a drink?"

Cries of rum, rum, greeted this. The Negroes brought up the barrels and the men stood in line for their drinks and the Meeting was delayed. By the time it got under way, many were drunk, and Scudder felt that feeling in his chest again. What was it?

Dickens called the Meeting to order. The first item of business was a motion of No Confidence against Captain Scudder brought by Brother Spry.

Spry allowed that Scudder was not the worst on the ship by a long shot, but the operation of a ship required discipline, and Scudder, everyone's friend, was not the man to impose it. Last night he'd been so drunk he'd killed one of his own party. The motion was seconded by Dickens, but for different reasons. He said that the captainship of Bradford Scudder was already marred by Tyranny: he had suspended a Meeting of the Company, he had killed a man in his cabin for breaking his crockery, and he had made Obed Coffin prisoner in the orlop without trial.

Scudder's supporters, prompted by O'Brien, shouted various objections. Scudder waited. The feeling grew. He realized what it was. It was contempt. Contempt for O'Brien's worried face. Contempt for the clumsy manoeuvrings of Dickens and Spry. And contempt for the Company, so easily misdirected, fooled, swayed. He was not used to feeling contempt. He liked people. He liked them as much as he wanted them to like him. That was his anchor. But it was hard to like men when you knew how their minds worked, how to pull their ropes and trim their sails and steer them whichever way you would, no matter whence the wind blew.

At last he spoke, his hands behind his back, his voice ringing down into the hatches.

"Well men, first thing, I'm damned sorry about last night. Let me put it to you plain as punch. We got damned, damned drunk. I don't remember it too clear. The best I can figure is Harry kept smashing my teacups, I said some choice words, and he drew his knife, and then Billy threw him out the window. And I'm damned sorry for it, he was a good mate, and I'm sorry he's dead. And if the shoe was on the other foot, lads, if it was Harry standing here, having killed me with his knife, he'd be saying the same thing. It wasn't no one's fault, Brothers, we were drunk. We're all Gentlemen of Fortune, and it's a hazard of our profession. What would you have me do? Take away the rum?

"No," Scudder continued, "it's a damned shame, but such is life when you're Upon the Account. A man can get as drunk as he pleases, when he's on a Cruise, so long as he ain't on duty. And that brings me to my second point. Every man here knows Yellow and his men was drunk and dancing when the storm hit us. And Brothers, if you're drunk on duty, you can't expect no mercy from your shipmates when a storm knocks over the damned ship. Now, well you might say, ain't you the Captain, Scudder? And ain't a Captain responsible for the ship? Why, in the Royal Navy, that might be true, although in the Royal Navy I could have Yellow whipped and turned before the mast. You lot ain't in the Royal Navy, are you? You're Upon the Account. And men Upon the Account do things by vote, and you lot all voted to determine your own watches and for each watch to elect its mate. So the only way I could have prevented that problem was by going against the will of the Company. And that I'll never do, gentlemen. When the ship is in action, the Captain's word is law, but elsewise it's the will of the Company, even if it drowns us all."

"You're one to talk!" Dickens cried. "What about Coffin?"

"Well," Scudder said. "I had some informants come to me, never mind who, only they were Africans, and tell me that Coffin was a sorcerer who'd brought on the bad weather. Now, I ain't saying he was a sorcerer. But what if he was? Hmm? He's a fine sailor and all, but you lot all named him Jonah when he came aboard. Ain't he the unluckiest-looking son of a bitch you've ever seen? Never taking a drink unless he's forced. And consider these were African sailors. I don't mean black fellows as grew up in the West Indies. Real Africans." He put special emphasis on this word. "Well, being as the ship was in action, I ordered him down to the orlop while we did our investigation. Afterwards, the storm stopped. Now gentlemen, I ask you, what do you make of that? The investigation didn't turn up more evidence, so there ain't no need for a trial. That's that."

"You had no right!" Dickens shouted.

"Why of course I did," Scudder said. "Just read the Articles. The ship was in action."

"There weren't a ship in sight!"

"If we'd meant 'a ship in sight,' we'd have written that," Scudder said. "By 'action,' I mean the ship was in danger, and we all had to follow orders until that danger had passed."

"Goddamn your eyes, you Sea Lawyer son of a bitch," Dickens said. "That ain't what we meant when we wrote the Articles. You can't lock up a man without a trial. You're a tyrant!"

"Tyrant?" Scudder said. "Didn't I always fight for all of you? Didn't I always have a kind word to say to every damned one of you? Didn't I? Don't you remember how I climbed up to the foremast, there?" He pointed. "Did you already forget?"

He paused.

"Brothers, if you let Spry take this ship, you'll be taking orders from

Hornigold and that lot, and if you let Dickens take it, we'll all go straight to Davy Jones."

After he'd said his piece, the debate continued. The men drank and drank, and bargained, and whispered back and forth, but when the vote was called, it failed to garner the requisite majority, though it was near enough.

"Well that's that," Scudder said.

"Three cheers for the Captain!" a drunken voice rang out.

Lewis asked if there was any more business, and O'Brien brought a motion that the mates be elected by the whole crew rather than their watch. A long, tedious debate followed, and many of the men went below decks or to the forecastle to dance, and the motion was passed. Yellow was replaced with Rios. Finally, Spry brought a motion of No Confidence against Dickens as Quartermaster. Dickens was narrowly deposed, and Spry elected.

Scudder did not feel much enjoyment in his triumph, and when he went to mingle with the Company, he found that they seemed uncomfortable. Whenever he approached, glances were exchanged. A less sensitive man might not have noticed or cared. But Scudder did notice and did care. After a while he made his excuses and returned to his cabin, where he was joined by a jubilant O'Brien, Quantrill, Davies, and a few other of their friends. Together they drank. Eventually, he was able to relax.

B ut that night in his dreams, he was back at Corso Castle, running for his life, the Fante howling after him, and the dying man grabbed his leg, but this time he did not jerk free, this time he fell, and he turned and looked and it was Tom Apollo holding him, all bloody and hacked up, and he was grinning as he had never grinned in life.

Scudder was screaming and kicking and screaming and black hands were on him and he struggled and thrashed but he was in a coffin, the bastards had buried him, and then his eyes finally saw it was only Alfie, gentle Alfie, shaking him awake, and he was in his hammock.

"Captain, Captain," Alfie was saying. "It is enough, it is enough. You are awake. It is enough."

"Oh," Scudder said. "Oh God."

Alfie smiled, patted him on the shoulder.

"What's cooking?" Scudder asked. "Something smells nice."

"Rats," Alfie said.

And there was Israel Hands in the Great Cabin, cooking rats upon the portable stove. The hides, tails, and viscera in a nauseating clump. He looked at Scudder without acknowledging him. In another man it might have been a challenge; such considerations, somehow, did not apply to Israel. As devoid of evil as a fox. In his way as innocent as a child.

Scudder noticed that Israel had been newly tattooed, his face superimposed with the maw of a shark. Dickens's work. So, he had joined his party.

"Good morning," Scudder said.

Israel wolfed down the rats without offering to share, crunching on the bones, and then threw the remaining mess out a porthole. Afterwards he looked at Scudder as if just seeing him.

"What was you dreaming of?" Israel asked.

"The battle at Corso Castle," Scudder said.

Israel nodded.

"I bore up well enough at the time," Scudder said. "But it is different in your dreams."

"Of course," Israel said. "You're starting to remind me of him, you know."

Scudder began to ask who, but he knew who, so he didn't.

"I wouldn't have credited it," Israel said, and left.

Alfie wiped the floor and put on the coffee. Scudder had little appetite. He wanted to go out, to see everyone, but he was afraid of a cool reception. While he picked at his biscuits, the rats still fragrant on the air, O'Brien came in.

"Good morning, Brother," O'Brien said. "Something smells good."

"Have some coffee," Scudder said.

O'Brien sat down, sipped the coffee, and said, "Thuh-there's been some tuh-talk. Among Dickens's buh-boys, especially, saying that if they cuh-can't win an election, puh-perhaps they'll just have to guh get rid of you. Duh-Dickens was tuh-telling everyone he wouldn't let himself be tyrannized."

"They've been drinking."

"Even so, it might be wuh-wise to stay aft for a while. My muh-man couldn't get all of it."

"What man?" Scudder said.

"My informer," O'Brien said.

"Your informer? Who's that?"

"Why, Cuh-Captain, I tuh-trust you, of course, only I guh-gave my word not to tuh-tell."

"Hmm," Scudder said. "This ain't the same spy as was spying on us before?"

"I can't talk about that, Buh-Brother."

"You never really explained how it was you got Billy onto the stern gallery," Scudder went on. "He ain't that much of a swimmer."

"Well, Buh-Brother," O'Brien said. "If I don't tuh-tell you, if anyone asks, you wuh-won't have to luh-lie."

Let him have his secrets, Scudder thought. But he could not stay on the quarterdeck all day. He felt false, an imposter. A little before noon he walked to the foremast, greeting everyone by name, and offering to lend a hand. He climbed to the foretop and spoke to his old mates. They, at any rate, were happy to see him, although they would not play dice while he watched. He climbed still higher, to the crosstrees, and sat there for a while, alone, staring down past the canvas to where the bow ploughed the sea.

On the way back to his cabin, he met Kenneth Jacobs, the one called Goldie by the men. Goldie was a natural idiot, and he seemed agitated, and wanted Scudder to follow him. Scudder did, grateful to have someone require his assistance. They went down the aft companionway, and greeted Spry and his followers in the wardroom, who returned the greeting very cordially.

Down on the orlop, Scudder looked around. Goldie had carried no lantern, and so the only light was what streamed through the hatches and the gratings, and it was dark and smelled close.

"What was it you wanted to show me, Goldie?" Scudder asked.

The men on deck heard a sudden pounding of feet, shouting, and a thin and horrible scream. When they rushed down (mostly of Spry's party) they could not make out much more than a mass of men pressed against the hull. Scudder and Goldie were surrounded by men armed with knives, and Scudder was stabbed over and over, fast and hard. Spry and his people rushed in, shouting, and though they were unarmed save for pocket knives, they outnumbered the assassins, and a few of the killers were killed.

Goldie let out a long, despairing bray.

At last a lantern arrived and its yellow light revealed Scudder cruelly stabbed, blood spurting with frightful speed, his eyes wide and shocked.

A deep, thundering wail as Quantrill smashed his way through the crowd and scooped him up and hugged him tight so he was covered with blood and Quantrill howled and howled. No one had ever seen him so affected and it added considerably to the shock and horror of the scene.

"The surgeon, Billy!" Spry urged. "Get him to the damned surgeon!"

"It's no use, they've killed me, lads!" Scudder cried. "Oh, they've murdered me!"

Quantrill stumbled up, blubbering like a huge and insane infant, knocking the men out of his way who tried to tell him the surgeon was behind him, fucking behind him. At last Quantrill was restrained and Scudder taken to the sick bay and Quantrill sat on his haunches and wept, his big shoulders going up and down, up and down, up and down.

The dark, narrow space was crowded, and men slipped on the bloody deck and no one knew who was supposed to be in charge. Spry raised his voice and ordered everyone out unless they had a damned reason to be there.

"And throw some fucking sand down," he said. "Get some sand on these boards."

Goldie was smeared with blood but unharmed, and no one could make him speak. Spry tried to separate witnesses from suspects from rescuers, while others examined the corpses under the swinging lanterns. Above them, the drum was beating. When the men came up on deck, they found that the quarterdeck had been secured with armed men loyal to Scudder and O'Brien.

Men shouted questions: Was the Captain alive? Who had done it? Why had he gone below? Was the Captain alive? How had it happened? Who had been there? Who had done it? How was the Captain? Was he alive?

O'Brien called for order again and again. The men were pale, agitated, not violent, not disorderly, but all talking at once.

At last the surgeon, Devereux, came up on deck with the news. Scudder clung to life by a thread.

O'Brien called again for order, as Dickens complained about the armed men on the quarterdeck, and a furious drunk voice shouted for him to shut up, shut the fuck up, that everyone knew his men had done this and he should shut his fucking mouth. Finally, O'Brien fired a pistol in the air. All eyes were upon him. He was shaking. He took out a sheet of paper and read from it without lifting his eyes.

"Buh-Brother Puh-Pirates, fuh-fuh-first luh-let muh-me explain muh-my actions. I huh-heard Suh-Scudder yuh-yell out and I suh-saw thuh-that thuh-the suh-stairs and the huh-hatch wuh-were cuh-crowded with muh-men and I didn't nuh-know wuh-whether it was a puh-personal qu-quarrel or wuh-whether it was a Muh-Mutiny whereby a fuh-fuh-faction wuh-was attempting to seize cuh-control of the ship. Suh-straight away I tuh-took steps to secure the qu-quarterdeck. I duh-do not know what huh-happened duh-down below as I wuh-was on duh-deck at the tuh-time. I only nuh-know fuh-from suh-speaking to wuh-witnesses that a guh-group of muh-men attempted to kill Cuh-Captain Scudder."

"Well what happened?" someone shouted. "Who saw it?"

"Buh-Buh-Brothers, puh-puh-please," O'Brien said, and went back to his paper. "Here is wuh-what I puh-puh-propose: the Cuh-Company puh-proclaim that the shuh-ship is in action and shuh-shall be cuh-considered to be in action until an investigation is cuh-complete, or until tuh-tomorrow at nuh-noon, at which tuh-time the Investigating Cuh-Committee shall report on its fuh-findings."

"Action?" Dickens said. "Action?" With a wave of his hand he encompassed the blue sea, the clear skies, the fair winds, the empty horizon. "State of Action?"

"Wuh-well," O'Brien said. "There are uh-external enemies, and internal ones. Suh-someone tried to kill the Cuh-Captain. Thu-that is a crime against the Articles."

"No one can say I don't care about the Articles," Dickens said. "I'm the only damned one of you that does."

"You're the one that fucking done it!" someone shouted.

"I am not!" Dickens said. "It weren't on my side of the ship, now was it? It's those spies as were never caught! Oh yes, they're still out there. They might be anyone. Anyway, bring out the witnesses and let's do it as a crew. Bring out the witnesses one at a time."

"Duh-damn you for a fuh-fuh-fool," O'Brien shouted, red in the face, finally losing his temper. "It's only for wuh-wuh-one duh-day."

"Dickens don't want an investigation," Spry said. "It'll show he done it, mark my words. It weren't any of my men—we rushed down there and saved the man."

"Who is to be Captain?" Dickens cried. "You didn't answer that."

"Wuh-we cuh-cannot have an election until thuh-there has buh-been an investigation," O'Brien said. "Wuh-we shuh-should leave the mates in place until tuh-tomorrow, appoint a Buh-Buh-Board to manage the ship, with the two muh-mates, the Quartermaster, and myself as suh-secretary."

The shouting escalated. O'Brien was unable to impose order and eventually fell silent, frozen except for his eyes, which blinked and flicked all over.

Eventually, Spry and Dickens stopped fighting and blaming long enough to agree that the motion should be defeated so they could put forward their own ideas. So sure was Spry that he did not call for a show of hands or run down the roster but merely said: "All those in favour, say aye." Somewhere between two-thirds and three-fourths of the men called out aye.

"What?" Dickens said.

"All opposed?" Spry managed.

"Nay!" some men shouted, so loud that they made almost as much noise as those who had called aye. But the result of the vote was obvious.

"That ain't right," Spry said. "That can't be right!"

"A recount!" Dickens said.

"The motion carried," O'Brien said.

"That can't be right!" Dickens insisted. "Damn you, do it properly, have the men raise their hands."

"All those in favour," Spry said, but the hands were already shooting up in the back, and Dickens stood, dumbfounded, looking around him at the forest of hands.

"Davey, what the fuck are you thinking, man?" Dickens said to one man, one of his more peripheral supporters.

"The motion is carried," O'Brien said. Unable to conceal his triumph, he called an immediate meeting of the Board in the Great Cabin.

As they all took their seats around the table, O'Brien confided to Davies, "I thought we wuh-wuh-were duh-duh-done for. They were ruh-ripping us to shreds."

But, of course, only thirty or forty men had been making all the noise at the Meeting. The rest, shoved to the back, pressed up against the rails, or sitting on the spars with their legs dangling down, had been silent. And the more Spry and Dickens shouted, those silent men became, somehow, still more silent. Their expressions sour and disapproving, their eyes vacant and bored.

Davies smiled his empty smile.

OLIGARCHY

A government by the few.

(Merriam-Webster)

JOHN O'BRIEN, SECRETARY OF THE BOARD

1

A less sanguine man might have found the faces around the table uninspiring. Coffin, newly released from the sail room, with large, haunted eyes, still skinny except for his belly. Yellow, with one of his eyes staring up at nothing. Spry, harried and edgy. Last was Davies, O'Brien's clerk, licking the nib of a quill with small, repulsive flicks of his pasty tongue. But O'Brien was radiant from his unexpected victory. He took his watch out of its case, wound it up with his key so that it went ticktick-ticktick, set the time very, very carefully, then watched the gears march round and round. Tiny chains (handmade by orphans), golden cogs and wheels, every piece finely engraved.

He'd taken it with Rackham, just after they'd voted out Vane and set him ashore with Dickens and his few loyalists. Seized a merchantman within sight of the pedestrians in Port Royal, twenty thousand pounds of plunder, including these watches. The boys had been so confident more was to come that after a few bowls of punch they'd set to frying the watches in a pan. Sadly, they'd been surprised in their revelry and lost all the stuff. O'Brien might have sold this one for a pretty penny, but it was a memento of those days.

Alfie set down a pot of coffee. O'Brien clicked his watch shut and left it, ticking on the table.

"I didn't know there was any left," Yellow remarked, raising his eyebrows at the coffee.

Alfie laughed and nodded, as if he did not speak English.

O'Brien drank. The brew tasted like mud. Still his mood was undaunted.

"Let us cuh-call this Board Muh-Meeting to order," he said.

Davies dipped his quill in the ink.

"All members of the Buh-Board are puh-present, save Rios, who has the wuh-watch. The time is six bells of the muh-morning watch. First order of buh-business is to form a Committee to investigate the attempt on the life of the Cuh-Captain."

Davies's pen scratched.

"Well, Secretary," Spry said. "I am willing to sit on the Committee if you wish. Or I can recuse myself, if you prefer."

O'Brien had a list of the crew before him; his lips moved as he thought. He said: "Wuh-what about . . . Matthew Lewis, Israel Hands, and Duh-Davies?"

"Israel?" Yellow said.

"I would like to have a muh-member of Dickens's party," O'Brien said.

"Is he eligible?" Spry said. "As a half-share man?"

"Who will object?" O'Brien asked. "Everyone tuh-trusts Lewis. Then you have wuh-one man from Duh-Dickens's party and wuh-one from Scudder's."

Davies smiled and nodded. O'Brien knew that many men did not like him, and it was true he was somehow unpleasant. He had the oddest habit of always looking you right in the eye, not in a firm, gentlemanly way, but rather as if he was too weak to look anywhere else. However, O'Brien had found him loyal and useful. As for Lewis, he was an easy choice, and O'Brien was keen to make an overture to Israel Hands, who he knew would switch loyalties without a second thought.

The door to the cabin swung open and Quantrill trooped in, covered in blood, his face unreadable. He had not been invited.

"Any other cuh-comments?" O'Brien asked.

"Comments on what?" Quantrill said.

"The Cuh-Cuh-Committee to investigate the attempted assassination."

"Who else have you got on it?" Quantrill asked.

It took O'Brien a moment to understand. "We puh-put Lewis, Hands, and Duh-Davies on the Committee."

"Well, put me on."

"Buh-Bill, on account of your cuh-close relationship to Buh-Bradford, we cuh-can't have you on the Cuh-Committee."

Quantrill flushed and scowled. "Damn you, you're always cutting me out. I won't vote for this unless you put me on the Committee."

O'Brien opened his mouth to tell Quantrill that his vote was not needed but stopped himself in time. He was forgetting himself. "Well Billy, the second order of buh-business, after the formation of the Cuh-Committee, ought to be security for the Cuh-Captain. Would you like that responsibility? You could also be the Muh-Muh-Master-at-Arms."

"I can think, um, of none better," Davies said.

Quantrill folded his arms and sneered.

"All in favour?"

Both motions were carried.

"Well then," O'Brien said. "The Board is adjourned."

They left, but O'Brien was not alone for long. A knock at the door, and the Negroes came back in, Alfie leading the way, head bobbing, a razor and a bowl of warm water in his hands, the others following with mops and buckets. "Cuh-Come now, that ain't necessary," O'Brien began, but Alfie tut-tutted, smiling, and O'Brien leaned back and submitted to the razor. He did feel more comfortable with them in the room, cleaning and organizing.

From below he heard Scudder begin to scream, weakly.

"No, don't! No, Billy, don't! Don't do it, don't do it!"

O'Brien rushed out, and was jammed with the other men at the companionway, but Quantrill was coming up the stairs, bearing the Captain in his arms, smooth and graceful, no lurches or sudden movements, Scudder's blond head on his shoulder, his face pale, horribly young.

"Handsomely, handsomely," Scudder wept. "Oh, handsomely, now."

Into the Captain's cabin. Connor had come up with Quantrill, leading the way, and he put a hand on the hammock to steady it.

Quantrill bent over, slowly, slowly, slowly.

"Handsomely," Scudder whispered.

"It's done," Quantrill said.

So it was, so gently Scudder had not realized.

Quantrill tucked in Scudder's blankets. Lifted his head with one enormous hand and slipped a pillow underneath. Then he stepped out and closed the door. Nodded at Connor, who O'Brien now noticed held a musket.

"I suh-say," O'Brien began, then swallowed his words. It was poor optics to give one of Tulip's Irishmen the job of guarding the Captain, but it was worse to argue in front of the crew.

O'Brien went to the door of the Captain's cabin, but Quantrill gripped his shoulder.

"Surgeon says he needs rest," he said.

"Of course," O'Brien said.

He went through the dining cabin into the Great Cabin. Before long, Quantrill posted a Guard in there as well.

2

It was marvellous what the Negroes could cook up without any fresh provisions of any sort. They had smashed up biscuits and made a sort of pie with salt beef and dried peas, and of course there was fish caught by Benjamin. The Board ate a hearty dinner, the Committee having spent all day taking evidence. Davies had gone so far as to draft up affidavits for the witnesses to sign, and they were prettily done, each one witnessed by all three members of the Committee (sworn before us, the Investigative Committee, etc.) and stamped with a seal found in the Taoiseach's desk.

O'Brien read through them. The first were from Spry's supporters, who deposed that three men, two members of Dickens's party and a lascar called Muhammad, had attacked Scudder. All three were dead. Goldie had been present, but he had been unarmed, and he had not been attacking Scudder. Finally, one George Beard had also been present, a Negro, born and raised in London, and an Able Sailor. The affidavits were divided on whether Beard had been involved.

After the failure of the non-confidence motion, Dickens's party (including the two dead men) had become black drunk and declared that the ship was doomed with Scudder as Captain. Other witnesses had testified that Dickens had sworn he would not be tyrannized by that lubber, Captain or no.

Two of Goldie's messmates had also given evidence. They managed Goldie's affairs, which is to say Goldie gave them all his money and they spent it. They both swore, up and down, that Goldie could not have known anything about the Plot, that Goldie had loved the Captain as much as anyone, everyone knew it, and moreover everyone knew that Goldie was a damned Honest Fellow that was always faithful to his friends. If he'd been mixed up in this, someone must have tricked him, and they hoped the Committee wouldn't be too damn harsh on him as Goldie was easily tricked and they both could testify to that.

"No doubt they could," O'Brien murmured, and Davies laughed, too heartily.

But who might have tricked Goldie? During the motion he had apparently been excited, and talking to many people, including the three dead assassins, and also Hornigold.

"Hornigold," O'Brien said. "How interesting."

The Negroes produced a bottle of port from somewhere. O'Brien looked at Yellow and Israel, but neither batted an eye, both accepting this little luxury as their due. Lewis made some token remark, yet even he took a glass.

Well and good!

From above came the stomp of feet and O'Brien started in his chair. But then he heard Quantrill's voice, and he realized what was happening. Quantrill had put together a group of men he was calling the Captain's Guard, and he was drilling them in the use of their weapons on the poop deck. That would keep him out of the way.

"Let us go see Goldie," O'Brien said.

The Committee, along with O'Brien, went down to the orlop, and threw open a trap door leading to the section of the hold that contained the firewood. Dozens of rats fled, a noise like a fluttering fan. When the light from the lantern fell upon Goldie, he gasped. It stank this close to the bilge, and Goldie had soiled himself. His hair stood in every direction and he was bloody with stabs and scratches. One of his eyes was swollen shut.

He asked for water, and whether the Captain was alive.

When asked why he had taken Scudder down into the hold, he said to show him something.

When asked what that something was, he replied he could not remember.

They pressed him again: what had he wanted to show the Captain?

Goldie rubbed his reddened eyes and asked if he was to be hanged.

"Well now," Lewis said, stroking his beard. "It don't look good for you, Goldie. But everyone knows you're an Honest Fellow. Maybe someone tricked you."

Yes, Goldie said, someone tricked me.

"Who?" Lewis asked.

Someone, Goldie said.

"Was it Dickens?" Davies asked.

"Yes," Goldie said. "He called Scudder a tyrant. Everyone had been calling Scudder a tyrant. Even if a man was your good friend, you might have to kill him if he was a tyrant."

"Did Dickens specifically instruct you to kill Scudder?"

"Yes," Goldie said. "He did. I was leading him down into the hold to kill him, where no one would see, when those men came and attacked me."

A pause.

"The men attacked you?" Lewis asked.

"Yes."

"They weren't working with you?" Lewis asked.

"I can't remember."

"Did you tell Dickens your plan?" Lewis asked.

"Yes," Goldie said.

"Do you think the men were working with Dickens?" Lewis asked.

"Yes."

"When did you have this conversation with Dickens?" Lewis said.

"What conversation?" Goldie said.

"Where Dickens told you to kill Scudder, and you told him your plan."

"I don't remember."

"Come now, you must remember."

"Well, it was dark."

"Dark?"

"In the middle of the night."

"And he told you to kill Scudder?"

"Yes."

"And you told him your plan?"

"Yes."

"And the next day when you carried out your plan, the men attacked you?"

"Yes."

Goldie was becoming more certain.

"How's this then?" O'Brien asked the other men. "Duh-Dickens sends Goldie to do the job. Then the others are to kill Goldie before he can tell who put him up to it."

"Yes," Goldie said confidently.

"That weren't a question for you," Israel said.

"Sorry," Goldie said.

"No worries, mate," Israel said.

Lewis was unsure. He asked Goldie: "Why would you kill Scudder? Wasn't he always good to you?"

"Yes, he was," Goldie said. "Scudder was a good man."

"So why did you plan to kill him?"

"Everyone was saying he was a tyrant."

"But you voted against the No Confidence motion."

"Yes."

"Why was that?"

"Well, Scudder was always good to me, so I voted for him. But afterwards everyone was saying he was a tyrant."

"Did anyone else hear Dickens tell you to kill Scudder?" Lewis asked.

Goldie hesitated, then said he didn't know.

"Do you have anything else to tell us about what happened?"

"Can I go to the head?" Goldie said. "Can I change my trousers?"

"Davies," O'Brien said. "Draw up an affidavit and commission it."

The Board met that evening and voted unanimously to end the investigation and recommend that charges of Mutiny, conspiracy, and murder be brought against Goldie, George Beard, and Robert Dickens.

3

O'Brien instructed Davies to make copies of all the affidavits, and he was doing so, scratching his pen over the parchment and licking it more than seemed necessary, when O'Brien went to visit Scudder. He first tried to go through the door in the Great Cabin, but it was locked from the other side. He went onto the quarterdeck, where he found two of Quantrill's Guard barring the entrance.

"Duh-Damn your eyes," O'Brien said. "I muh-must suh-speak with him."

"No one in or out," one Guard said, a particularly useless Portuguese who had joined the Company after they had taken their great prize.

"It's all right." Scudder's voice came weakly.

"No one in or out," the Guard repeated.

"Are you muh-muh-muh-mad?" O'Brien said. "That's your duh-damn Cuh-Captain suh-speaking! This is Muh-Mutiny. Open the duh-door."

The Guard pulled his head into his shoulders like a turtle and glared. Suddenly he looked past O'Brien with fear. O'Brien turned; it was Quantrill.

"Buh-Billy, I know I told you to kuh-keep the Captain safe . . ." O'Brien said.

"It's all right, Bill," Scudder called.

"Open the door," Quantrill said.

O'Brien and Quantrill went in.

How wasted Scudder looked! How pale, how young!

"You were right, Johnny," Scudder said as Quantrill closed the door behind him.

"Ah well," O'Brien said, smiling, taking one of Scudder's hands. "That's what cuh-comes of not listening to Clever Johnny."

Good Lord, that beautiful boy, it was as if the better part of him had drained away.

"Duh-do you feel well enough to give any evidence?" O'Brien asked.

Scudder did, but he remembered very little. In particular, he was not sure whether Beard had been one of the assassins, or their lookout, or simply a bystander.

"Thank you, Captain," O'Brien said. "Duh-Davies will bring you an affidavit later. In the meantime, you ought to nuh-know how things are puh-proceeding. And you too, Buh-Billy," he said to Quantrill.

O'Brien gave them a thorough account of the investigation.

"So it was Dickens, then," Quantrill grumbled. "I ought to wring his neck."

"Nuh-no, no," O'Brien said. "We muh-must have a tuh-trial. They'd nuh-never stand for it if we didn't have a tuh-trial."

"He's right, Bill," Scudder said.

Quantrill did not look happy at being contradicted.

"Nuh-now, we duh-don't want no more elections till you're back on your fuh-feet," O'Brien continued. "And you leave that to me, mate. I ain't sure wuh-whether we'll hang Dickens, but you can be damn sure once I'm done tuh-tomorrow we'll be seeing no more of his tricks. And Billy here is watching you night and day. You can hear how vuh-vigilant the men are outside."

"Of course, he always takes care of me," Scudder said. "I only wish I'd listened to you, John, when you warned me to stay in my cabin."

"Well, think nuh-nothing of it," O'Brien said, with a sudden queasy feeling about where this was heading.

"Who was it, then, that warned you?" Scudder said.

"Ah wuh-well," O'Brien said, conscious of Quantrill at his back. "You remember before, you said you wished you'd tuh-tuh-taken my advice? Well, take it now. You don't nuh-need to know that, Brother."

"Is it the spy?" Scudder said.

"If it were, wuh-wuh-would you want to know about it?"

"They'll think I know about it, whether I do or don't."

"Take my advice," O'Brien said. "You don't need to know everything. It's buh-better if you don't."

Scudder's exhausted eyes remained on O'Brien a moment longer. Then he coughed, painful convulsions he resisted as best he could, and Quantrill's heavy hand fell on O'Brien's shoulder, and the interview was over.

4

At the Meeting, beer was served, but no rum. O'Brien chaired it, standing with the Board in a group upon the quarterdeck, dressed in clothes that had been mended, cleaned, and pressed by the Negroes. The findings of the Committee sat upon a table by the mizzen-mast watched by two members of the Captain's Guard, where any man could look at them. Some had already done so, and a restrained murmur moved among the men until O'Brien called for silence. The Company was quiet, attentive, straining to hear, and anyone who interrupted was hissed down.

Lewis presented the Committee's findings and recommendations, including that Beard, Goldie, and Dickens all be tried for Mutiny.

Dickens argued that the Committee had been biased against him, that they'd not asked the right questions, and before the Company decided who should be tried, he should be granted an opportunity to cross-examine the deponents. Disputes began, shouting and tumult, but O'Brien ordered the bell rung and called for order.

While the men waited, muttering, tense, mostly silent, O'Brien discussed the matter with the Board. At last he ruled Dickens might have a limited right of cross-examination, but only to determine whether a trial should take place, and not to establish his innocence, which was properly the subject of his trial.

Dickens wasted no time in summoning Goldie. Goldie was dirty and disordered and at first he was a little confused, but the more questions he was asked, the more confident he grew.

Dickens was loud, but not angry.

"Hello Goldie. You know me, right?"

"Yes, you're Robert Dickens."

"All right. Now, you sailed with Hornigold aboard the *Ranger*, didn't you?"

"Yes, I did."

"And he's a good captain, ain't he?"

"Yes, he was a good captain."

"And you speak to him sometimes, aboard this ship, don't you?"

"Sometimes, yes."

"And yesterday morning, d'you remember when you was walking across the deck to see Scudder, you saw Hornigold, didn't you?"

"I don't remember."

"Well now, see here Goldie, your mate Harry testified that. Here's his sworn affidavy. Do you remember now?"

"Yes, I remember now."

"And then he told you to take the Captain down in the hold, didn't he, Goldie?"

"Yes. I remember."

A roar. Hornigold turned white.

"Objection!" O'Brien screeched.

"On what grounds?" Dickens said.

"You luh-luh-led him into saying that."

"A course I did, it's a bleeding cross-examination, ain't it?" Dickens said. He turned to the crowd. "Anyway, you all heard him! You heard what he said! Put Hornigold on trial, that's what I say, there's as much evidence against him as me."

"Do not address the Company until your cross-examination is finished," Lewis said to Dickens.

"You just muh-made that up, duh-didn't you?" O'Brien shouted at Goldie.

"No," Goldie said. "I never did."

"Cuh-cuh-come now, you don't have to say it just because Duh-Dickens told you to."

"It was Hornigold and Dickens working together," Goldie said. "They're the spies."

A greater roar, like thunder.

Men drew their weapons. Goldie was rushed into the Great Cabin. Quantrill, followed by the Guard, waded between the two factions and laid low a man on each side with a heavy punch. He then insisted they all disarm, but they refused. Some rushed below decks, others climbed the rigging.

The Committee re-interviewed Goldie, to little avail. Mostly he claimed he did not remember, but once he could be prevailed upon to remember something, he would never change his story, but only add to it. Hornigold and Dickens were both spies, he said, and the three of them would often meet in the cable tier and Plot to take over the ship.

5

O'Brien was rattled, but his mind was working. It was all right; it was all right. Likely they never would have convicted Dickens in any case. The evidence against Hornigold might even present some advantage. He just had to think it through. Everyone at the table was looking at him, even Spry, to salvage this. He put away his watch, with which he had been fiddling; he could do this.

Start with what we know.

"Juh-Gentlemen," he said. "A few puh-points. First, while Duh-Dickens may not be innocent of this Puh-Plot, I put it to you that Guh-Guh-Goldie's testimony is worthless, from an evidentiary point of view."

"Quite," Spry said.

"I am not sure I agree?" Rios said.

"I am sorry, Buh-Brother, but it is true," O'Brien said. "Not even an English juh-juh-judge would take his word."

"Shouldn't it be up to the men?" Rios pursued.

"Well, that buh-brings me to my second puh-point," O'Brien said. "We cuh-cannot say how the men will vuh-vote, but it will likely be along puh-partisan lines. Third, buh-both sides will refuse to accept a vuh-verdict they do not like, guh-guilty or not. Fourth, I cannot say whether Quantrill's Guh-Guard will prevail should the matter come to buh-blows. Now the qu-question is: what we should do?"

No one said anything. From below came a happy, barking noise; a party had broken into the spirits room and were becoming drunk. O'Brien forced himself to stop thinking. He directed his attention to his breath. He looked out at the sea. Don't think, he told himself. Stop, stop thinking. He inhaled, exhaled. It came to him unbidden.

"What if," he said, "both Hornigold and Dickens were to plead guilty to some lesser crime?"

The suggestion was so odd no one replied.

O'Brien went on:

"Both men deny Guh-Goldie's story, and his evidence is discarded. But Duh-Dickens admits fault for speaking ill of the Captain. And Hornigold admits fault as well, first by violating the tuh-terms of his Pardon by taking command in the storm, and next for negligence in the matter of the assassination attempt."

"How would they be punished?" Spry asked.

"Buh-because they accept blame, formally, their sole punishment is to be rebuked by the Company," O'Brien said. "And that is an end to it."

Into the silence, he said, "Do you see? It gives everyone an opportunity to stand duh-down."

"I suppose," Spry said, dubious.

The Board emerged into the white sunlight and despite the beer and the heat and the hard words and the drawn swords, the Company grew still and expectant and strained to hear.

O'Brien lifted his prepared remarks and began to read.

"Buh-Brother Pirates, it is the opinion of the Buh-Board that Brother Guh-Goldie's evidence is of no value. However, that duh-does not end the muh-matter, for there is still suh-significant circumstantial evidence against Brother Duh-Dickens. Specifically, his threatening and intemperate language after the Nuh-No Confidence motion, which verged upon Mutiny."

"Mutiny?" Dickens cried. "It's a free ship, ain't it? Can't I say what I like?"

"Brother Dickens," O'Brien said, and at last his voice acquired a measure of strength. "You brought your No Confidence motion yesterday. It failed not because of deceit or Tuh-Tyranny, but because it did not garner the requisite number of votes. Because you seem incapable of understanding this, I shall make it plain. That is not Tyranny, that is Duh-Duh-Democracy."

"Hear him!" someone shouted, and a murmur of approval swept the crowd.

"If men are a goddamn lot of puppies," Dickens said, "then they may well vote in a tyrant."

"A tuh-tyrant like Scudder?"

"Yes, Brothers."

"You call the Cuh-Captain a tyrant, sir?"

"I do."

"Though he won the vote?"

"Yes."

"Tuh-Tyranny is a failure to follow the will of the majority of the Cuh-Company," O'Brien said. "And attempting or advocating to overturn the wuh-will of the majority is Mutiny."

"That ain't right!" Dickens said. "Just because you won an election don't mean that men can't speak their mind."

"We will see what the Cuh-Cuh-Company has to say," O'Brien said. He then turned from Dickens and said: "Brother Hornigold, you were seen by numerous witnesses to speak with Guh-Goldie before he approached the Captain."

"Yes," Hornigold said.

"And a few days before, you seized cuh-command of the ship."

"I beg your pardon?"

"Brother Hornigold," O'Brien said. "This Cuh-Company was presented with significant evidence that you colluded with Kuh-Kavanagh in his Puh-Puh-Plot. Your life was spared subject to certain cuh-conditions, the most important of which was that you were forbidden from assuming a position of authority upon the ship. Now you have not only done so, without any authority from the Company, but have cuh-colluded with certain other members of the crew to assume, *ipso facto*, a position as a mate of the ship."

"I only acted to preserve the ship during a storm," Hornigold said. "For the good of the Company."

"For the guh-guh-good of the Company," O'Brien said. "What a wonderful thing is the good of the Company! It can be made to suit any purpose. When you are in command, then orders must be obeyed quickly, for the good of the Company! But when you are not in command, they may be disregarded or overridden, all for the good of the Company."

To this, Hornigold had no answer.

"Buh-Brother Pirates," O'Brien said. "As I said, the Board has grave reservations about the evidence of Brother Goldie, and in the suh-circumstances, we do not believe there is enough evidence to convict the two men he has named, Rob Dickens and Ben Hornigold. However, in buh-both cases, their conduct has cuh-contributed to a mutinous spirit which indirectly caused the recent disturbances. In the circumstances, we buh-believe both men ought to disclaim their former behaviour and sign affidavits of self-censure, but should suffer no further puh-punishment."

"I ain't signing no damn statement," Dickens shouted, but around him the mood of the Company was darkening like storm clouds spilling across a clear sky.

It was a brilliant stroke. Aimed neither at those who hated Dickens (who would always vote against him) nor those who loved him (who would always support him) but that elusive, ethereal group in the centre. And the stroke landed. The motion was carried.

The look on Dickens's face was, to O'Brien, without price. It brought him back to those last few days under Vane. For all his talk of Democracy, Vane had never really understood it, or even believed in it. Well, this was Democracy, real Democracy, a viper that could turn on you in an instant.

The subject of the debate turned to the content of the statements. Dickens, red-faced, teeth clenched, discussed the matter with his followers, and in the end they settled upon the following:

I, Robert Dickens, crew member of the *Saoirse*, hereby MAKE OATH AND SAY:

The charges brought against me by Kenneth Jacobs, called "Goldie," are false.

However, I admit that the night before the Captain was assaulted I did say to my shipmates that I would rather die than serve under a tyrant (hereinafter, the "Remarks").

I specifically deny that the Remarks constitutes Mutiny. However, I hereby admit the error of making the Remarks. First, while the statement was not made in secrecy, all political discussion should be made at a Meeting of the Company or nailed to the mast. Second, I confirm that as long as the Captain follows the Articles and is supported by the Company, any violence against his person is mutinous and illegitimate.

Sworn before me, Secretary of the Board, a commissioner, etc.

This statement was accepted by the Company. Davies drafted it and Dickens signed it, to scattered applause. Dickens was not called upon to speak. With this done, attention turned to Hornigold, but despite a long and hushed conversation, neither he nor his allies had prepared a draft.

Lewis asked him whether he wished the Board to take the first turn.

"No," Hornigold said. "I won't sign."

"The Cuh-Company has spoken," O'Brien said. "You muh-must abide by the will of the Company."

Hornigold looked to the stern of the *Saoirse*, and the colours of the Commonwealth that flew there. They were none of them as young as they used to be, but Benjamin Hornigold was forty-two and looked older, the reddish hair now a washed-out orange, the crags in his face deep, the lines around his eyes tired and sad. He held on to a backstay and rocked with the motion of the sea. He said: "No."

"You muh-muh-must sign it," O'Brien said. "To duh-defy the wuh-will of the crew is Muh-Mutiny."

"No," Hornigold said.

"The Cuh-Company has passed a muh-motion, and you will be hanged for Muh-Mutiny," O'Brien said.

"Then hang me," Hornigold said. "I know your tricks, O'Brien. If I give in to you now, I am doomed in any case. I will not sign."

Silence, whispering, then everyone was shouting.

O'Brien looked at the Board; they were looking at him—fury from Rios, alarm from Spry, blankness from Coffin.

The wheels spun furiously. To hang Hornigold they needed two-thirds of the Company. Did they have the numbers? What would happen if they did not?

Dickens was bellowing, hectoring, jabbing with his finger. Why would Hornigold not sign? Did he believe he was not subject to the will of the Company?

O'Brien turned to the Board. "Puh-puh-perhaps we could censor him by way of muh-motion?"

"Too late for that," Spry said, shaking his head.

"It is insufficient," Rios said primly.

"Goddamn you puppies!" Dickens shouted. "Didn't I sign your damn paper? Hornigold must do as we say or swing, and that's the long and the short of it."

A motion passed for Hornigold to sign the self-censure statement or hang, but with only a Simple Majority. Dickens howled and hectored the crowd and called for a new vote. Now Spry was speaking up, and it was unclear whether it was in his role of Quartermaster or as a member of the Board, and he stated that a man could not be tried twice for the same offence when there was no new evidence. O'Brien was frozen, crowds of words jamming in his throat, until at last Lewis declared another adjournment.

6

Hornigold was brought into the Great Cabin; he was the calmest man in the room.

"In a wuh-wuh-week we'll buh-buh-buh-be in Buh-Buh-Buh-Buh-Buh . . ."

"Batavia," Hornigold said.

"Sign the damn statement!"

"No," Hornigold said. His eyes were the only part of him that did not look old. They roamed. The sound of shouting from outside did not lessen.

"Wuh-wuh-why?"

"You know why, O'Brien," Hornigold said.

And indeed, he did. O'Brien remembered the last days of the Commonwealth, when it had finally assumed its true form. He remembered Hornigold's trial, the beatings, the humiliation, the imprisonment. None of it so severe, really, in one way of looking at it. Nothing that would have left any permanent physical damage. And yet. Did O'Brien know why Hornigold would not sign a statement? Certainly, he did.

Scudder was carried in.

"Benjamin," he said, hoarse and quiet. "Be reasonable. It ain't how I would have done things, but it's done now. You must sign the damned paper."

"I signed papers like that in Nassau," Hornigold said. "You know I did, O'Brien. You remember. And—"

"Duh-Damn you!" O'Brien said. "Wu-we're almost at Buh-Buh-Buh-Buh . . ."

"—as I sat in your dungeon, I swore I'd never sign 'em again."

"It's a cuh-cuh-compromise," O'Brien said.

"Compromise," Hornigold said. "These things never stop till someone stops 'em. I'm stopping you now."

"Benjamin," Scudder said. "This ain't like that."

Hornigold smiled. "Oh no?"

"You have my word of honour," Scudder said. "You have my word as a Gentleman of Fortune. I'll never let it go that far."

"I would rather die," Hornigold said.

Finally, Quantrill stepped forward, his face black with rage, and gripped Hornigold by the upper arm.

"Sign it now," he said. "Or you're going out the fucking window."

"No," Hornigold said.

"Very good then," Quantrill said.

Two massive steps, Quantrill dragging Hornigold, and the two were on the stern deck. Quantrill pivoted and threw and Benjamin Hornigold, last of the great pirate captains of Nassau, soared over the rail and vanished into the churning white wake of the *Saoirse*.

7

O'Brien screeched womanishly and lost his head. Scudder clapped the heels of his hands into his eyes and said nothing. Spry shouted that Quantrill was a murderer and would have to face a trial. Quantrill sneered and told Spry to watch his mouth or he would be out for a little swim with his mate.

Word spread of what had occurred and the noise redoubled.

O'Brien's brain strained and raced. There was not enough time! There were only a few moments! On his best day he could not . . .

O'Brien tried to breathe, to breathe.

He took out his watch and wound it and listened to it *tickticktick*. Breathe.

His eye fell upon a copy of the Articles, which he reviewed, just as a way of calming his mind. His eye snagged on something, and stuck.

He looked at Scudder. Scudder was looking right back.

"Cuh-can you stand?" O'Brien asked.

Scudder did not reply.

"I have something, Brad. But I think it must come from you."

O'Brien's hands were shaking; Davies drafted the resolution. Spry, alone, refused to sign; he looked furious and nauseated.

They went outside into the cheerful sun and faced the Company.

Scudder could not stand, but with tremendous effort he could sit upright in a chair.

"Brother Hornigold's refusal to obey a duly passed resolution created an emergency," Scudder said. "In the circumstances, it was my sad duty to sentence him to death after a summary trial."

"Summary trial?" Dickens shrieked.

"When the ship is in action, the Captain has ultimate authority," Scudder said.

"Damn you, you drafted the Articles, which state no man shall be killed without a two-thirds majority."

"No," Scudder said. "It states that no man shall be *hanged* or *shot* without a two-thirds majority, but it is silent upon other forms of execution, including being obliged to walk the plank."

A large section of the Company actually screamed.

"Goddamn you, you Sea Lawyering son of a bitch!" Dickens said. "That weren't what we meant when we drafted that."

"You have it buh-backwards," O'Brien said. "We use the wuh-wording of the Articles to determine the intention of the Cuh-Company. Here the relevant puh-principle of statutory interpretation is *expression unis est exclusion alterius.* That is, the expression of one thuh-thing is the exclusion of the other. Had it been the intention of the Cuh-Company to exclude all forms of execution, then that would have been puh-plainly stated. The listing of specific forms of execution implies that other forms might require less than a two-thirds muh-majority. In this case, once an emergency arose, the Cuh-Captain, and the Board, had the lawful authority to execute Hornigold, so long as a means other than shooting or hanging was employed."

"Now Robby," Scudder said. "I tried to give him a way out, only he wouldn't take it. You've spoken out against the two-thirds rule many a time. You was saying a minute ago how you'd kill him yourself. We all heard you. You're loud enough. Now this is done with. I ain't well enough to go back and forth all day. Let's have the trials for Goldie and Beard, and put an end to all this."

Dickens ranted a little longer, but he had been shouting so loud for Hornigold to be killed, vote or no, that his objections seemed hollow. O'Brien moved that the Meeting be adjourned so the trial could begin. Spry shouted that Quantrill should be tried too, but the motion for an adjournment took precedence.

A show of hands was called, and a majority of the pirates, black, white, and brown, tattooed, puckered with scars, jammed in shoulder to shoulder in the waist and on the gangplanks, raised their hands. The Meeting ended.

8

Beard was tried first, but he had little to add to the evidence he had already given, and he could not shake the testimony of his accusers, who grew more certain as time passed. At last he was reduced to pleading to the Company: "Ain't no one going to help me?" he said. "Ain't there one of you that's going to speak up for me?"

He looked over the faces gathered there, the men he had supped with cheek by jowl for months, with whom he had fought and drank and chopped wood and filled casks of water and reefed sails. And what a coldness there was now in those assembled countenances! What hardness! What lack of recognition!

"Harold . . ." he began, but Hutchins looked away, quick as if he was scalded, and so did Coffin and his other messmates. Beard swallowed, his throat bobbing. "I was just down there because I didn't want to use the head! Damn it, men. Ain't none of you got something to say?"

Goldie was a little more fortunate; his two mates did their best. But it was no use. Both Goldie and Beard were convicted.

When he understood he was to be hanged, Goldie cried like a child, great deep miserable sobs. Goldie's mates made one last attempt to save his life, pleading that he be marooned rather than killed, for someone must have led him astray. This motion was not seconded. Beard, terrified, reversed course, and admitted his guilt but claimed to have not acted alone, and offered to name the other conspirators in exchange for his life. His voice fluttered with panic, and he was disbelieved.

Both men had their arms tied behind them and hoods put over their heads and nooses round their necks and then the ropes were hauled, and they rose, kicking, into the air, up, and up, until they were high above the deck. They kicked for a long time, a smattering of urine and feces dripping beneath them, and then they stopped. The decks were mopped and the corpses consigned to the sea.

Everyone went back to the business of sailing the ship.

O'Brien retired to the Great Cabin. Davies accompanied him. O'Brien wanted to send him away but was not sure how. Above him, he heard Quantrill tramping on the poop deck and his low voice growling at someone. Quantrill's recruits were not an inspiring lot since he'd chosen those whose position aboard the ship was most tenuous—the worst seamen, the men without friends, those who had only a half share. In his first day as Master-At-Arms, he had already dismissed several men for what he called "smart talk."

At last, when the sun was setting, O'Brien told Davies to go below decks, and he did, still smiling. O'Brien lay on the chaise longue and closed his eyes. He was awoken in the middle watch by men screaming in a foreign language, sounding like cats. He rushed out, so did the Guard, and found one man dead, another dying, the rest having fled by dropping down into the waist and scattering in the dark.

The wounded man was awash in blood; no one could understand him. On O'Brien's instructions he was carried into the dining room and laid on the table. The surgeon, Devereux, was summoned from his cabin on the orlop.

It was some time before a translator could be found; normally, it would have been Muhammad, but he had been killed in the attack on Scudder. The man who was finally produced informed the Guard that while he did not speak the language of these lascars, they had another language in common, which neither one spoke particularly well.

From the man's confused answers, it was clear that he had only dimly grasped the purpose of all the Meetings and shouting and voting and threatened violence over the past three days, and he believed the ship to be very poorly managed. Upon Muhammad's advice, he and his friends had voted in favour of the non-confidence motion, largely on their understanding that it was sure to pass. Once it failed, Muhammad had been convinced that Scudder would be very angry with those who had attempted to depose him, and he had sworn to make things right.

Since the death of Muhammad, the lascars had seen the Committee conducting its interviews but, not speaking English, had no idea of what was going to happen, other than that it would inevitably lead to them. The dying man had decided to come and make a clean breast of it to the Board, one of his friends had violently disagreed, and so they had fought.

Incredulous questions from O'Brien. Shouting back and forth in the shaky light. Blood everywhere.

"Gentlemen, please, please, a little room," Devereux said.

The nameless lascar had no more to say. His eyes rolled up to the ceiling, the whites orange, and then closed. He whispered a prayer and grew still.

O'Brien slept little that night.

9

After five days of clear sailing, with no Meetings, the *Saoirse* arrived at the Sunda Strait, where the land closed in, and they passed little islands, some black and foreboding masses of volcanic rock, some green and Edenic, some swarming with birds. The strait narrowed and narrowed, till it was scarcely fifteen miles across, and the water became shallow, so the men could see the bottom, and the ships that had wrecked there. Rios had consulted Governor Rogers's charts for hours before their arrival, and now he acted as pilot, climbing the foremast and shouting directions to the men below, who in turn shouted them aft to Coffin, who held the wheel.

At a critical moment the wind deserted them, and the ship's momentum slackened, and she drifted, and the rocky sea floor rose towards them. The straits were thick with little native craft, some of them having approached the ship and offered fruit, trinkets, monkeys, and the services of pilots and whores. Three proas approached from Sumatra that bore no wares, cast no nets and lines, and were thick with men. The little double-hulled canoes sailed into the wind, switching tacks as easily as a carriage, and as they grew closer, their guns and swords glinted in the sun.

The little merchants and fishermen scattered. Quantrill assembled the Guard on the poop deck and the call went out for all hands to beat to quarters. But the wind returned, and the sails filled, and the proas retreated to the shelter of Sumatra's shore.

Two days later, they sailed into Jakarta Bay, where thirteen rivers flowed into the Java Sea. Beyond the walls of Batavia they saw the spires of churches and the dome of a mosque. The great anchor dropped into the sea, a cheer erupted, and the men threw their hats in the air. The remnants of the beer and rum were produced and the fiddles came to life, and the drums and trumpets, and the men danced on the deck, arm in arm.

Two men-of-war were in the docks, but they did not look seaworthy. A twenty-six-gun ship was moored closer to the harbour, along with two Dutch Indiamen. The rest of the ships were little, nothing bigger than twelve guns, mostly native craft, little canoes, rafts, proas, fishermen casting their nets and divers plunging into the water.

Scudder emerged from the cabin, and he was greeted by another cheer. He was pale and thin and his eyes yellowing, but he could stand and his teeth were all there and he showed them his famous grin and raised his good hand in a wave as Quantrill supported him and the Guard stood ramrod straight behind.

"We've done it, lads," Scudder said, lifting a cup. "You've all done it. Drink with me, shipmates. To the *Saoirse*."

They all drank.

"Speech, speech," they called.

"I still ain't in no shape to give a speech," Scudder said, his smile receding, "so I'll keep it short. Dutch ports have always been friendly to Gentlemen of Fortune, but we're a lawful prize for every ship on the sea and so we must send a boat ashore to make sure all is well. After that, we'll vote on what to do. In the meantime, I don't doubt the locals will bring us the pleasures of shore. Everything today is out of my Captain's share."

Laughter, applause, backslapping. A man already drunk ran along a spar and dove headfirst into the sea.

"As for the boat's crew," Scudder said, "that's Spry's prerogative. That's all then, boys, have a drink! You damn well earned it." Aside: "Take me back, Johnny."

Spry selected Quaque as coxswain and brought along O'Brien to help him manage the money. At O'Brien's suggestion, he also took Dickens and a few of his supporters. They brought an iron strongbox filled with gold and silver, and Spry wore a moneybelt with a hundred golden gilders, and all were armed with pistols and knives.

They rowed against the current, into the wind, and it was hard going for two miles. Around them hills rose like a great green bowl. They passed canoes sailing easy with the wind, some loaded with fruits and vegetables, and others with bottles and kegs, and others with native women of all sizes and ages, plump and thin, painted grandmothers and thin girls. They shouted and waved, and one boat followed them for a while as a boy, in shrill Dutch, extolled the virtues of a nearby village with better prices than Batavia.

At last they moored and hauled up the heavy cash box, which was entrusted to Dickens.

"Where'll you go, lads?" Spry asked.

"Don't know," Dickens said, surly.

"Remember, always one man with the box."

"I ain't a fool," Dickens said.

O'Brien felt a sudden affection for Dickens. "It's done, Ruh-Robby," he said. "It's duh-duh-done. We've made it, and you and I will be quits for good."

To this Dickens did not reply, merely took up the cash box with another man and walked into a tavern.

Spry received directions to the harbourmaster's office, and he and O'Brien walked along the stone streets, crossed a bridge over the canal, and entered the fort. They were left to stare at a great portrait of William of Orange in an antechamber with other petitioners, but not for long, as their bedraggled appearance made their profession and purpose clear.

The harbourmaster's expression was one of naked greed beneath a veneer of severity. Business was conducted in English. A show was made of inspecting the ship's papers. The harbourmaster invoked regulations, Spry inquired whether some special provision could be made, the harbourmaster named a price, Spry made a show of protest. The moneybelt was emptied onto the table; it would not even be necessary to use the funds in the cash box.

Business being concluded, the harbourmaster leaned back, looking satisfied, as well he might. Jenever and coffee were provided, along with bread and fruit, and they made conversation until they were interrupted by cannon fire.

10

Dickens led Quaque and the others into a tavern, and found therein a few determined drunks, a man sleeping on a bench with a fiddle on his bare chest, a half-witted Mardijker boy pushing a broom, and a Chinaman behind the bar.

"Right," Dickens said.

First order of business: kick the fiddler awake and hold a Spanish ten-dollar coin in front of his eyes. The wink of light from the little wheel of gold stirred the fiddler like the call of a bugle, and soon music drifted out the open window and over the canal.

Dickens approached the sweeper, whose wits had visibly sharpened from one-half to three-quarters, gave him a smaller coin and instructions to bring something to eat. The boy did not ask for any specific direction; he was gone before his broom hit the floor.

Last, Dickens went to the bar, dumped the contents of his pockets in front of the Chinaman, and ordered a round for the house. Two of the men with him did likewise.

Quaque had brought no money, and he asked whether he should take his share from the box. Dickens's face flared with anger, but then he gritted his teeth and said:

"By the Powers, you lubber, you'd take money from the Common without permission of the Quartermaster, would you? That's the lowest thing a Gentleman of Fortune can do, save poaching his Brothers. You ought to ask for a small share when you're at sea, so as to make sure you ain't never caught short if you find a chance to go ashore."

The Negro stammered and asked if then he might trouble one of the white men for a loan.

"A loan?" Dickens howled, now almost anguished. "Like I'm a damned Jew moneylender? Like I'm to stand here drinking when my own ship-mate can't? Even if he is a Negro?"

One of the other men shook his head, disgusted.

The Chinaman was filling up glasses and the drunks had taken places along the bar in expectation.

"When we're drinking ashore," Dickens snarled at Quaque, "what's mine is yours, and if it was the other way around, it'd be you standing me, that's the way it is among Gentlemen of Fortune. Pay me back indeed, damn your eyes, you sooty-skinned son of salamander. That's what you've learned from your time aboard our damned ship, goddamned lot of swine."

All of them raised their glasses and drank, Quaque too. The other pirates coughed and spat and asked for rum, but Dickens liked the jenever. The astringent taste suited his mood, and it was colder than it had a right to be. The drunks smiled and bobbed their heads and waited as patient as spiders. The music of the fiddler had attracted the peddlers and they came streaming inside bearing bunches of fruit, armloads of neck-laces, monkeys and serpents and feathered hats and shrunken heads. Someone bought a monkey and gave it a drink and soon it was dancing upon the bar.

The whores came in next, a great gaggle of Javanese and Chinese women and girls, and they sat together at a table with a bored, expectant air, followed by layabout sailors, and the room was soon crowded, and Dickens shoved forward another stack of gold and signalled for a round for the whole bar again and the Chinaman beamed and there was a cheer and an old woman broke into song, startlingly sweet, like a bird.

The sweeper returned with a fishmonger and a magnificent yellowfin tuna so big two men strained to carry it. Quaque's eyes lit up and he hacked off a dense strip of its solid purple flesh and ate it raw, silver skin and all, and the Chinaman and the fishmonger haggled with one another and a brazier was fired and large hunks of the tuna were rubbed with spices and seared.

Dickens took the blue bottle and poured himself another glass and drank it and poured another and drank it and poured another. He felt as if he was chasing something that was running away. If the Dutch learned they were not here to fence stolen goods but were instead laden down with specie, he doubted they would be content with gouging. Perhaps they should sail for a smaller port, but to spend any more time afloat bore its own risks. And anyway, what was next? Say they paid out his share, all in gold. Say for a moment the money wasn't seized by some greedy magistrate the moment he tried to buy something. What was he supposed to buy? A sugar plantation? He'd not the faintest notion what to do with a fucking plantation. He could hire a manager, but what was to stop the manager from fleecing him? A tavern? Like this damned Chinaman? Pouring out drinks and throwing sawdust on the puke and breaking up fights? A merchant? Sailing back out on the open seas with all the risks that came with that, not the least of which was fucking piracy? If he bought a little cottage and put the money in the bank or bought an annuity, how would he know which was a solid bank and which might fail? And what would he do with himself, other than drink?

The fish seared over the hot coals and thick steaks of tuna, still raw in the middle, were distributed. A trio of Dutch soldiers sallied with the whores, and another sailor bought a round of drinks. By this time even stray dogs and cats were jumping in through the windows, the dogs barking and chasing, the cats rubbing against the legs of the patrons and sauntering on the tables. The monkey climbed to the top of the shelf behind the bar and drained the bottle of jenever and fell with a limp thump.

It was only the present moment you could count on, Dickens finally reflected. The past was gone, and the future was a dungheap. He looked around him and felt a fierce kinship with every single person he saw. They were all in it together, weren't they? All of them! Even this Negro, yes, even O'Brien, all of them. Brothers of the Coast. That feeling of fellowship, so transitory, that was the best feeling of all. He shoved forward more coins and bought another round and filled his glass and shouted for silence, and the whores, their rough shifts stained purple with wine, waved their handkerchiefs, and the men cried for a speech. Dickens looked at their faces and his mind, swimming with gin, turned slippery on him, so he could not get a hold on it.

At last:

"To fellowship!" he cried. "To fraternity! For ain't we all shipmates, after all? Shipmates sailing to the grave."

The assembled crowd, momentarily solemn, raised their cups in salute, and in the silence that followed, when all assembled drank, a voice rang out from the door:

"Well said, Brother! Well said, upon my soul, prettily said, a fine toast from the finest figure of a Gentleman of Fortune that ever sailed upon the seven seas."

All eyes turned to the figure at the door, short, wiry, hatless, spiked hair, scarred lips, a loose shirt, and a crude tattoo of a naked woman on his neck.

George Lowther.

Dickens froze and the revellers, watching, froze with him.

Lowther roughly pressed through the crowd, smiling, a half-dozen roughnecks following him. He smacked his hand on the bar and was provided with a tin cup of rum, which he raised to the ceiling:

"To the *Saoirse*! The ship that took the richest prize in the world."

No one drank. Even the cats and dogs stood stock-still.

"You know what they call the ship that took the richest prize in the world?" Lowther asked.

Dickens did not reply. Under the pretext of scratching his back, he put his hand on the hilt of his knife.

"They call it," Lowther said, "the richest prize in the world."

11

O'Brien and Spry ran out of the fort. The *Saoirse* was firing her guns at the small craft clustered around her. A brawl raged by the docks; a tavern was on fire. The bridge over the canal was clogged with people fleeing to the fort. In the brown water of the harbour, a Javanese labourer sat in a small canoe. Spry dropped a handful of gold and silver coins into the boat and pointed his pistol. The Javanese gathered the coins and leapt into the filth, and Spry and O'Brien jumped into the boat.

Spry plied the oars. O'Brien sat in the bow with his pistol at the ready. They paddled over the flat, greasy water to the main river, and once they reached the open sea, they turned along the docks. It was not clear who was fighting, although they could see the blue coats of Dutch soldiers. Spry weaved the canoe through the fleeing boats until they saw Dickens crouched behind a row of barrels, pouring powder from his flask down the barrel of his pistol. Spry whistled. Dickens holstered his weapon and helped up Quaque, who was wounded. Practically carrying the man over his shoulder, Dickens sprinted into the scummy water, with its vile covering of green algae and human waste. They nearly tipped the canoe bringing them aboard. Quaque took up an oar and though he was wounded, still they fairly leapt away with the tide.

A grey curtain of gun smoke hung over the *Saoirse*; through it could be seen a tangle of men and winking steel swords. The wreckage of at least two proas was scattered over the water, broken planks and burning canvas and shattered men. However, still more proas had attached themselves to the ship, and the natives were clambering over the gunwales. The anchor cables had been cut and the ship was drifting out of the bay.

"Make sure all them pistols is loaded," Spry said.

Before their eyes, the mizzen-mast was brought down and crashed into the sea, but that was the high mark of the attack. By the time they arrived, the pirates had triumphed, though the wounded screamed like livestock half-slaughtered as they were hauled down to the sick bay. Everywhere men hacked at the ropes until the mizzen-mast came loose, then they salvaged what they could, ropes and spars and metal fastenings.

At last they were under way. No ships followed. A Meeting was called. The men stood in the mud made by sand thrown upon blood. Stories were exchanged. The men aboard the ship told of the sharp little knives in the hands of the whores, the blunderbusses and pistols and the fire and the axes, the swift approach of proas, so overloaded that armed men clung to the sides, kicking their feet in the sea. Dickens told of meeting Lowther in the tavern. O'Brien noted, for the record he said, that he could not verify Dickens's account of what happened in the tavern, and Dickens asked whether O'Brien was calling him a liar, but the argument petered out.

"That traitor Lowther called us the richest prize in the world," Dickens said. "They was waiting for us. He's told everyone about us, except the goddamned Dutch."

"How did he know where to find us?" O'Brien asked.

"How should I know?" Dickens said.

"You spoke with him for a long time in Madagascar."

"Damn you, that was before we voted where to go!" Dickens cried, wiping the blood out of his eyes. "Take a look at me! Do I look like a man in a Plot?"

Batavia receded.

The men looked at each other. In the sick bay a man screamed, don't, don't, as an arm was sawn off, while the loblolly boy soothed him, loudly, as if speaking to a half-deaf baby.

"Well, Brothers," O'Brien said. "Does anyone wish to take the floor?"

The discussion was informal, with many men shouting. Some were for heading west, towards Africa, but passing through the straits would be no easy task, and word of their success must have spread through the entire Indian Ocean. It might be unknown farther east, and as they had done no harm to the Spanish, the governors of the Philippines might well be amenable. The bosun warned that the ship was leaking and needed to be careened as soon as possible. They were also low on supplies, including fresh water, and of course the ship now had only two masts.

The lookout sang out; a sail had appeared on the horizon behind them. A twenty-eight-gun ship, it was Lowther's vessel, the *Happy Delivery*, which had been hiding behind an island.

The men voted to sail east. Before the Meeting could be adjourned, Quantrill was granted the floor.

"I want to commend the Captain's Guard," he said. "While the rest of the men was drinking and taking their leisure, they stayed ready, and if it weren't for them, I don't doubt we'd have lost the ship."

Quantrill produced gold medallions, which he must have minted himself out of gold coins taken from his share of the general treasury, for they were of embarrassing crudity, and pinned them to the chests of four men who, in his estimation, had particularly distinguished themselves, including the Irishman Connor.

It was a welcome distraction, and some men applauded, while others catcalled.

Quantrill flushed and said, "Well, I am not one for talking."

"Nor goldsmithing neither," someone shouted, to general laughter.

The Meeting was adjourned, but all hands remained on deck to set up a jury-rigged stump as a mizzen-mast.

12

The wind blew from the east-southeast; the *Saoirse* sailed north. The nimble *Happy Delivery* might have caught her, but she was outgunned, and content to follow in sight but out of range. In a day they were within sight of Borneo, and they turned east and sailed upon a bowline, although tacking was dangerous in this shallow sea. Upon one occasion, when they were obliged to wear ship, they sighted dozens of crowded proas bedangled with human heads like hellish trees bearing terrible fruit, staying just out of range, sailing into the wind like rowboats.

Towards evening, they turned due south to engage the *Happy Delivery* and leave the proas behind. But howsoever far they sailed from Borneo, the proas followed.

Night fell. The *Saoirse* adjusted her course and doused every lantern, so the only light came from the slender shard of the moon, which cast a streak of pale light upon the black deep. The only sounds were the groan of the ropes and the moan of the wood, yet evidently these sounds were too much, and a wild and terrible cry arose from the north, and flaming missiles lit up the air and fell upon the deck. The pirates doused the fires quickly, but in that blackness even the smallest flicker was visible for miles, and the loon-like cries of the Dayak reverberated over the waves.

They fired the *Saoirse*'s cannons, a rough, irregular broadside, and on the seventh shot a proa was smashed and the men roared to see it burn upon the black ocean. But the survivors swam to other ships, and the ragged fleet approached in a broad arc, jangling long poles from which hung both their alien standards and the heads of their enemies. The men fired more cannons, and destroyed more proas, yet still more came. For the last round they fired grape and pulped men into tripe. Yet still the Dayak came. The riflemen on the yardarms fired down and men spun and dropped. Yet still they came, climbing up the ship, or diving into the water and swimming under her and coming up the other side.

Quantrill ran along the rails with an axe in each hand, hacking off the fingers of the Dayak as they gripped the rails and butting down with his enormous head like a goat, and pistols cracked in the darkness, the flashes revealing a tableau of wooden masks, and noses pierced with bone, and teeth sharpened to points, and faces painted blue and green and white. The boarders carved out a space upon the forecastle and came up in a great swarm and the pirates were forced back.

The *Happy Delivery* emerged from the darkness and now fired her cannon, great white flashes, a full broadside into the sails and rigging, and flames licked up and down the tarry ropes and dropped in great sizzling gobbets onto the deck.

The Dayak blew their horns and fought with bravery and skill. The sails were now alight, the whole battle lit up as if it were high noon.

An arrow had struck Quantrill in the hip and he snapped off the shaft and fought on and everywhere he fought, an empty space formed around him. At his side were the two surviving Irishmen and they cried out: *Fág an bealach*! And: *Éirinn go brách*! And: *Saoirse*! And: *Taoiseach*!

The *Happy Delivery* then rammed the *Saoirse* so hard that every man aboard, the pirates and the Dayak alike, was knocked to the ground, and then Lowther's men swarmed onto the decks with pipers and drummers and the flag of the Commonwealth above their heads.

A champion rose up from among the Dayak, a man larger even than Quantrill, his hair clotted with some thickening agent so it stood like the arms of a cactus and a great mask of teak over his face, and he wielded a great war mace and a shield carved with the faces of animals. With two swipes of his weapon he knocked the Irish away, and then, kicking Quantrill in his wound, he forced him to the deck. He raised the mace above his head, bellowing, illuminated by the firelight, but a pistol rang out, and his mask was split in two and he tumbled back to the rail, stunned, and all men looked to see who it was that fired, and saw Scudder upon the quarterdeck, his face flushed with Fever and his blue eyes green with jaundice, and Scudder threw down the musket and drew his sword and shouted hoarsely, and the battle resumed.

Unexpected reinforcements had arrived, for the sea was alive with sharks, each one only just bigger than a man, with broad, blunt fins with white tips and mouths twelve inches wide lined with triangular teeth. They ripped at the dead and the dying, sometimes fleeing when the men splashed at them, and sometimes blasting forward, chomping and snapping and rolling in the darkness. The Dayak were accustomed to sharks, but the sheer amount of blood in the water pushed the monsters into a frenzy of bravery, and they attacked the sides of the boats and the ship, and they leapt out of the water like dolphins snapping at the climbing men and made horrible noises of hunger and madness.

Below decks, the gunners ripped another broadside into the water and men and sharks alike were slain and the morale of the Dayak crumbled, and boat after boat retreated to a safe distance.

But George Lowther led a Company of killers from all nations, English and French and Spanish and Malay and Chinese and Javanese and black Africans, all of them ready to die for the greatest prize they would, any of them, ever know. They fired a killing hail of bullets into the mass of men and charged. In the firelit chaos Lowther sought out Scudder and with one swipe of his sword he disarmed him and with another he ran him through, pinned him to the mainmast and set his free hand against the back of Scudder's head like a lover and leaned forward and was seen to whisper something in his ear, though what it was none would ever know. Scudder's expression was agonized but calm, and a dagger dropped out of his billowing sleeve into his hand and he jabbed it into Lowther's thigh and twisted and was rewarded with a shocking fountain of crimson blood. Lowther fell back, his dismayed face illuminated by firelight, and Scudder stabbed him in the neck.

The men who had been at the guns surged onto the deck, howling. First they drove any remaining Dayak over the rail into the maws of the sharks, and then they rounded on the men of the *Delivery*, the fighting bloody and close and perversely intimate. At last the outnumbered attackers fled, but those of their crew who had remained aboard the *Happy Delivery* had already cut her loose and were climbing the ropes and setting sail. Some of Lowther's crew jumped into the sea, heedless of the sharks, and others threw down their weapons, only to be hacked into meat by the vengeful men of the *Saoirse*.

Scudder lay in Quantrill's arms. He looked at the sails and ropes and wood burning, and he looked past the flames to the night sky of endless dark. He thought of his mother. He felt as if she was holding him, as if he was still a warm little boy. His eyes closed, his chest ceased to move, and his heart ceased to beat, and his body grew cold, and Quantrill wept.

The Java Sea.
June 7, 1722.

13

The ship drifted through charnel waters clogged with dead men and hysterical sharks, the rigging burning, yards tumbling to the deck, the jury-rigged mizzen-mast askew.

Coffin had been rather shy in the battle, but now he sprang into action, his voice urgent but soft, so that men quieted to hear him. He said little, but what he said was very direct and precise, and the men scrambled, replacing the burned and frayed rigging to ensure the masts, all interconnected, did not fall.

Men climbed up the swaying ratlines and struck the topgallant masts, and spliced rope in the dark, and hauled up great coils, while down below the dead were tossed to the sharks. As for the wounded, though some of them cried feebly and waved their arms, there was no time, no time, and their weeping comrades hurled them over the side too. It took three men to pry Quantrill from Scudder's mangled body, all of them sliding around in the mingled blood, and he howled like a dying dog as Scudder went over the side.

At last the *Saoirse* was sturdy enough to bear a scrap of canvas, and the men hauled and hoisted the yards and sheeted home the sail and she groaned, deep in her timbers, and began to move. The men cheered, exhausted and ragged.

Did O'Brien weep? No. He retired to the Great Cabin and marshalled his thoughts.

Scudder was dead. A Captain was needed. Rios? Incompetent and cowardly. The more you knew the man, the less you liked him. Coffin? A Quaker, a Jonah. Yellow, incompetent and still under Dickens's influence. There was no one. By the Powers, there was no one. And so, there could be no election. Not only for his own protection (to lose power now, to sling a hammock in the forecastle hold surrounded by his enemies!) but for the ship's. It would be one weak Captain after another.

A knock at the door, and Alfie entered, smiling, bobbing his head, with the bowl of warm water.

"No tuh-time," O'Brien said. "Please summon the Buh-Board."

Spry, Rios, and Davies were fetched (Coffin still had the management of the ship). The four men sat around the great table in the dark.

"Gentlemen," Rios said. "I put it to you that I am the only candidate."

Self-important fart, O'Brien thought. "I duh-don't duh-disagree you are the most qu-qualified," O'Brien said. "But an election in this environment wuh-would be very uncertain. I suggest that we call a Muh-Meeting and propose that until the ship is no longer in action, she shall be guh-governed by the Board, with Rios and Coffin remaining the muh-mates."

"But then who will be the Captain?" Rios asked.

"We shall not have a Captain," O'Brien said.

Spry laughed, sounding desperate. "Goddamn it, man, how can a ship not have a Captain?"

O'Brien turned to Spry, for if he could carry him, he would carry them all.

"Fuh-forget, for a moment, the Articles," O'Brien said. "Do you think the Company wuh-wuh-wants an election? With all that entails? For I do not. I buh-believe they would chuh-choose that things remain as they are, rather than to go to war with one another."

Silence.

O'Brien looked around the large table, which seemed larger with so few men sitting at it.

"Of course, if the motion fails, we can put Rios fuh-forward. Any man here can be a candidate."

Spry sighed, his loyal face tired. "Very well," he said.

A Meeting was called. How much space there was upon the gang-planks! In the past two days they had lost near on a hundred men. O'Brien presented the "unanimous resolution of the Board" and was met with a predictable and furious response from Dickens. But O'Brien had become more adept at handling Dickens. Whereas before he had sought to cut him short, now he let him talk, for the Company liked him less the more they heard. Wisdom and foolishness were bound up like a braid in Dickens, as in all men, and the same force that caused him to open his mouth stopped him from closing it, and he ranted and threatened and heaped invective upon hyperbole, and in so doing succeeded in convincing his Brothers that to hold an election would result in disaster.

When Ironside, Dickens's long-time supporter, was at last granted the floor, he brought a motion to amend, and suggested that O'Brien's motion expire, automatically, in one week, unless renewed by the Company. Ironside had not discussed the matter with Dickens, and the latter was shocked. But it was an effective tactic; the motion, as amended, passed easily. And so they sailed on.

14

The pirates worked four hours on, four hours off, sailing into the wind, often missing their stays and being obliged to wear. The hot weather loosened the caulking further, and oakum spewed from between the boards, and the ship leaked, and the men were obliged to work the pumps, sending the jets of warm and salty water over the side. Their pursuers—small native craft and the *Happy Delivery*—were rarely out of sight. Constant alarms, real and imagined, kept all hands on deck at all hours.

Worst of all, since the Company had celebrated liberally as they had approached Batavia, the rum was running low, along with the other stores, but they did not dare attempt to stop and re-provision.

Every evening, Benjamin came into the Great Cabin for his tipple before his evening fishing, and every night he told O'Brien the same story: Dickens constantly harangued the men, attacking O'Brien, saying he was no seaman, no fighter, he was a schemer and a Plotter, and what had his Plots amounted to? They were stranded in the Java Sea and sailing east, by the Powers.

Every evening, O'Brien asked: do they plan Mutiny? And every evening Benjamin shook his head. No, they await the election in a week.

Every day this selfsame tacking into the wind. Every day the measurements showing their slow progress. Every day more water in the well, despite the efforts of the carpenter on the outside and inside of the ship. Every day less rum in the spirits room. And every day the promised election drew closer.

And every evening, after Benjamin went out onto the stern deck and cast his line, O'Brien sat alone at the table. Quantrill was off with the Captain's Guard, drilling them upon the poop deck or lecturing them down in the lower deck, and O'Brien could not stomach Davies for long. The week felt short, but the days, the hours, the minutes, they all felt so long.

Dickens was planning something, he must be, and Benjamin was missing it. And even if he wasn't, O'Brien's nerves had snapped; he could not risk, or bear, an election. He knew how these things went; he'd seen it over and over. It had happened to Hornigold, to Vane, to Rackham, to Apollo. The only man he'd known to buck the trend had been Blackbeard, when the Taoiseach and Israel Hands had put down the Mutiny against him off the coast of Honduras. But how was he to do the same here?

He paced and paced, the Great Cabin feeling small, and thought. If only Dickens could be dealt with, but how? His mind raced over the past for some pretext. He remembered Dickens speaking to Lowther in Madagascar, then advocating for sailing to Batavia, then meeting Lowther in the tavern.

Was there something there? Dickens had fought the men of the *Delivery* with his usual courage. But what if, perhaps, Lowther had betrayed Dickens?

Two days before the deadline, O'Brien met with Davies and Quantrill in the Great Cabin. Outside, the men sought to change tacks. They felt the ship lose speed, and lose it more, the men screaming at one another, cursing, some hoarse and exhausted, some almost tearful. The ship hung, suspended, but then continued her movement through the eye of the wind. An angry, relieved cheer. O'Brien took it as a good omen.

"Buh-Brothers," he said. "I shall be fuh-frank. I believe Duh-Dickens is forming a Puh-Plot against the Cuh-Company, but my muh-man can bring me no proof."

"Fine," Quantrill said. "I'll deal with him."

"Nuh-nuh-no," O'Brien said. "Not without proof."

"I'll make 'im confess," Quantrill said.

"We cuh-cuh-cannot use hard methods," O'Brien said. "We will re-form the Investigation Committee. This time, Buh-Billy, you shall be on it."

Quantrill grunted. "Well, we'll try it your way."

Davies said nothing, only smiled, and demonstrated his suitability for his responsibilities by making a detailed note of these instructions in the logbook, and sprinkling sand over the wet ink.

15

The cabins on the upper and lower decks had been down since the Mutiny, but now the carpenter banged up the bulkheads on the upper deck, re-creating the gunroom. That was where O'Brien, Davies, and Quantrill met with Quaque for three hours. Word spread through the ship that something was afoot; the Guard let it be known that the Committee had re-formed. When two members of the Guard went out to fetch one of Dickens's chief supporters for questioning, the man refused, standing on his rights. The Guards accused him of Mutiny, and at last Dickens told the man to go, to answer all the questions, for they had nothing to hide. The man (whose name was Colin) was in the gunroom for two hours, and emerged drunk and unconcerned, and told everyone it had been a lot of nothing, O'Brien must be desperate, grasping at straws.

A second member of Dickens's party was summoned. This meeting was longer, and quieter, and when the man was released, he would not speak of the interview. Colin was re-summoned, and he went happily enough, expecting another drink, but instead was presented with two signed confessions—one from Quaque and the other from the second man. And O'Brien and Davies were grave, and unsmiling, and Quantrill was between him and the door.

Davies read out Quaque's confession first, in which Quaque alleged that Dickens had not been surprised when he had seen Lowther in Batavia, and that it had been clear, from their conversation, that they had planned this meeting and intended to seize the *Saoirse*. However, Lowther betrayed Dickens, and killed his mates, and only Quaque and Dickens escaped. Afterwards, Quaque remained silent for Dickens had threatened him.

The second confession alleged that Dickens had conspired with George Lowther at Madagascar to seize the ship, that he had signalled the *Saoirse*'s destination to the *Happy Delivery* with lanterns at night, and that he was plotting to seize the ship and deliver it to their pursuers.

The first confession had been easily obtained; Quaque had signed whatever was asked of him when he realized his life was at stake. The second had been obtained through trickery, as they had presented the man with both Quaque's confession and a forgery, which O'Brien had claimed had been signed by Colin during his first interview.

The sheer enormity of the charges knocked Colin off balance, and he looked for some sign that this was a joke.

"We have all the evidence we nuh-nuh-need to make you walk the plank," O'Brien said.

"I didn't do nothing!"

"Oh cuh-cuh-come now. Come, come. Are you denying that last night you were drinking with Dickens?"

"I was," Colin said. "But all them other things . . ."

"We'll come to them in a moment," O'Brien continued. "And you discussed the decisions of the Buh-Buh-Board?"

"I don't know what you mean by discussed."

"You duh-don't know what 'discussed' means?" O'Brien jeered.

Davies shook his head and made a note.

"We talked about it," Colin allowed.

"You know, of course, that it is contrary to the Custom of the Coast to discuss political matters in a private group?" O'Brien said.

"But everyone does it!"

"Do you know the Custom of the Cuh-Coast, shipmate?" O'Brien asked.

"You lot talk about it enough," Quantrill growled.

Colin wondered whether he should yell for help. But that beast Bill Quantrill was practically on top of him, his face rigid with frustration and contempt, not in on the joke, if joke it was. This was really happening.

"I know 'em," Colin said miserably.

"And Duh-Dickens admitted in his suh-suh-self-censure that such duh-discussions are improper. You remember that?"

"Yes."

"And you huh-heard Dickens say that the rule of the Board was Tyranny, and it would have to be overthrown?"

"I didn't say that."

"But you heard him say that?"

"I don't recall," Colin said.

"Our wuh-witness says that you were sitting right next to him," O'Brien said. "You laughed and said if Dickens kicked down the door, you'd be right behind him. That's what you said."

That was, in fact, what Colin had said (Benjamin had reported it), and he was shaken. He looked from O'Brien to Davies. "Don't do it to me, shipmates," he said.

To his own surprise, he found that his voice was wavering and his eyes were threatening to tear. It was worse than battle. He was afraid, but he also felt defiled. Much of what was contained in the confessions was true, and everyone knew it. The falsehood was the conclusion, that a Mutiny was planned, but that false conclusion flowed logically from the truth. This, combined with the fierce conviction of the three men around him, the ferociousness of their judgment, the rum, and the shattered windows at the stern of the ship, through which he might be thrown at any time, had a powerful effect.

"I ain't in no Plot," Colin insisted.

"Let me be frank with you, shipmate," O'Brien said. "We believe that you are an Honest Fuh-Fellow. But you're mixed up with a bad lot, Sea Lawyers, mutineers. If you make a cuh-cuh-confession, a full confession, and sign a self-censure, the Board may show clemency."

They began to badger him for a full accounting of the discussions of Dickens's party during the previous week. Colin was shocked at the quality of the intelligence. The spy, that damn spy! At first he tried to explain, but he was informed sternly that doing so called his repentance into question. Once all the details were established, and the man admitted that such conversations were contrary to the Custom of the Coast, O'Brien moved on to other discussions, which had taken place long before, often with men who were now dead.

Did you hear Dickens say this? What did you do? Do you remember when this happened?

The questioning continued for hours, and Colin was given nothing to drink, nor was he permitted to go to the head. O'Brien and Davies worked in shifts. By the time the interrogation ended, the man was exhausted, uncomfortable, frightened, humiliated. He signed his confession, initialling each paragraph, and was sent out of the cabin, blinking, into the evening sunlight, with strict instructions not to tell anyone what had been discussed, and a warning that howsoever safe he felt himself to be, he was always being watched.

16

A difficult night, hot, rainy, stinking, foul winds and false sightings, men rushing to the tops then bickering whether a sail had been seen. Israel Hands came into the Great Cabin to cook his rats, as was his habit, where his retreat was cut off by O'Brien and Quantrill and two members of the Guard. While O'Brien spoke, Israel stared in that queer way he had, like a wild animal, seeming both not to understand and to understand very well indeed.

The bells signalled the change of the watch, and some men went below, and Dickens came up the forward hatch, as he always did, but on his way to his accustomed position at the mainmast he was called by Israel Hands, and he came aft, where he was seized by Quantrill.

Dickens shouted, "Murder, murder!" Quantrill said not a word in return, and Dickens was taken through the dining room, the Great Cabin, and onto the stern gallery, where he was compelled to walk the plank.

The ship sailed too swiftly for a drowning man to catch, but not so fast that it did not linger in his sight, so that he was tormented by false hope of rescue. Dickens, unusual for a pirate, could swim well enough to keep his head above the warm waves, and he shouted at the stern of the *Saoirse*, calling the names of his friends, begging them to seize the ship or lower a boat. But nothing happened, nothing changed. A wave smacked him. The ship receded, farther and farther, and Dickens's powerful voice could not call it back again. Around him the sky met the sea, the whole world a seamless blue bowl, an infinite prison, where he waited to be claimed by a death of hideous loneliness.

Led by Ironside and Dickens's other supporters, the Company rushed aft and met a hedge of bayonets, swords, and muskets.

"Shuh-Shipmates," O'Brien shouted. "I was warned of a Puh-Plot to capture the ship and to surrender it to the *Happy Delivery*. We learned that Robert Duh-Dickens conspired with George Lowther in Madagascar to seize the *Saoirse*, and met together in a tuh-tuh-tavern in Batavia for that purpose."

"Lies, lies!" Ironside shouted. "You're a murderer, O'Brien!"

But now the three affiants faced the astonished crew. Quaque and two of Dickens's supporters, all three of them with bowed heads, slumped, defeated. They did not speak. Davies read their evidence, and only asked them, not whether something was true, but whether they had sworn it. Much of their evidence was known to be true; the rest could not be disproved. By the time Davies was finished, the shock and disorientation had transformed into gloomy confusion. On the one hand, the charges were fanciful. How could Dickens have been plotting with Lowther? Everyone had seen him fighting in the battle a few nights before. And yet, everyone had seen the two of them talking in Madagascar, and here was evidence from Quaque, the only man, save Dickens, who'd survived the tavern brawl in Batavia, and two of Dickens's closest friends! A dark, puzzling business.

"It's all bloody lies!" Ironside raged.

But how could it be a lie? It would be such a monstrous lie, too much to contemplate.

"You all heard him say a thousand tuh-tuh-times how he would not suffer under Tyranny," O'Brien said.

"You did this on account of the election, you son of a bitch!" Ironside said. "There weren't no Plot."

"You see how he acts, shuh-shipmates?" O'Brien said. "This is how we knew they would resist. Therefore, the Board carried out its sentence."

O'Brien's eyes scanned the men in the misty dark. He did not know what they were feeling; they mostly looked confused. Should he call a vote, or not?

No, he decided.

"It should be cuh-clear the ship remains in action. In addition to the weather, and the puh-puh-pirates, and the shortages of provisions, we must add another duh-danger. Mutiny. After all the Plots aboard this ship? First Kavanagh, then Apollo, then the attack upon Captain Scudder, now Lowther and Dickens. With these unfavourable winds, a fuh-faction could seize and surrender the ship in a few hours. But we shall never allow it. Nuh-never. We shall stand united as never before, we shall find a safe harbour, and all retire wealthy men. Brothers, those who are loyal to this Company, and its Articles, must not remain silent, but actively oppose Muh-Mutiny."

Ironside kept shouting, until at last Quantrill lunged for him, and there was a rush of pushing and shoving. Ironside went below decks, and O'Brien adjourned the Meeting.

It was, of course, all the men could talk about at their dinner, and yet they were restrained in their communications. The spy had never been captured; he might be anyone. Coffin's mess was much quieter without Beard, though the men muttered darkly. Most of them had trouble crediting the allegations, but so many Plots that had seemed incredible had proven true—the false log, the letter from the Archbishop—why was this one any different?

"What dost thou think, Brother?" Coffin asked Hutchins.

Hutchins did not answer, only flicked his eyes up, and then back down.

17

The *Saoirse*, jury-rigged, worm-infested, leaking, zigzagged across the Java Sea. Little progress was made. The weather was hot and muggy. Even the salted provisions were running low. The biscuits were so full of maggots that Benjamin laid his fish on top of the sacks to draw them out. The Board was obliged to ration the food and fresh water in addition to the liquor. O'Brien spoke out against hoarding and stealing at the Meeting where the decision was announced, and members of the Guard were posted at the entrance to the bread room.

Native craft flitted along the hazy horizon.

The weather always changed, O'Brien told himself. Outlast the calms and ride out the storms and fair winds shall return. Yet still the hot, wet wind blew from the east.

Every day he spoke to Benjamin, and Benjamin told him the same thing: that the men were low and dispirited but did nothing that fit even the most expansive definition of Mutiny.

"Cuh-cuh-come now," O'Brien said. "I nuh-know these men, duh-damn you. How can we suh-struggle like this without some of them combining into a Puh-Puh-Plot?"

"They know there's a spy," Benjamin said. "And, anyway, what would it serve to Mutiny now?"

"Why, they think they could do a buh-better job than us, that's what they think," O'Brien said.

"There's no Plot, O'Brien," Benjamin said.

"I have other suh-suh-sources, you know," O'Brien said. "If you are withholding anything from me, I shall discover it."

Benjamin's ugly face relaxed into vacancy, the mask of an idiot, and he left.

O'Brien regretted his outburst extremely; he was, in fact, dependent upon Benjamin. But he could not believe that there was no Plot. He was aware of his own failings, and he knew the sort of men down in the forecastle. Recently, he had become preoccupied with Spry. Not because Spry complained. On the contrary, he had become unusually silent, which could only mean that he was planning something. Spry could lead a Mutiny; he had done it against Stede Bonnet.

After an uneasy night of queer dreams, O'Brien sat alone in the Great Cabin, picking at a mouldering biscuit, crushing the weevils and flicking them away, when there came a knock and the Guard posted at the door escorted in Harold Hutchins, one of Spry's followers.

Hutchins twisted his hat in his hands.

"Yes?" O'Brien asked.

"Your pardon, sir," Hutchins said. "But I saw two men passing notes in the forecastle last night."

"Puh-passing notes?" O'Brien asked.

"Yes sir," Hutchins said.

"What duh-did the notes say?"

"Why, I don't rightly know, sir."

O'Brien said nothing. He thought.

Hutchins became nervous. "I ain't saying there's anything to it," he said. "But I know we ain't supposed to have no private communications."

"Hmm," O'Brien said.

"And I know others saw," Hutchins said. "And so someone was bound to come tell you."

"What others?"

"Why, most of the men of the watch, of course."

"Including Spry?"

"I don't know, sir."

"You duh-duh-don't know?"

"I think he might have."

O'Brien summoned Davies, and Hutchins repeated his story and signed an affidavit with a shaking hand, and then was locked in the orlop. Quantrill was summoned from the poop, where he was drilling the Guard in fencing, and ordered to place the two men who had passed the note under arrest.

"Whyn't get 'em all at once?" Quantrill asked.

"Guh-get who all at once?" O'Brien asked.

"I dunno," Quantrill said. "All of 'em."

"How can we 'get them' if we don't know who they are?" O'Brien asked. "We only have evidence against the man who puh-passed the note and the man who received it. We must speak to them first."

"I can pick up whoever I damn well please," Quantrill said.

"No," O'Brien said. "You cuh-cuh-cannot pick up whoever you damn well please. We need a pretext, a reason, to seize men, or else they shall Mutiny."

"Well, ah," Davies said.

Davies rarely spoke unless spoken to, and O'Brien was startled.

"All those men did, um, see the note pass, and none of them have come to tell us. That, ah, alone is reason to suspect they may have been involved in the Plot. Indeed, that alone arguably constitutes Mutiny.

Um, um, and if there is a Mutiny, by arresting the men in dribs and drabs, rather than all at once, we risk giving the conspirators time to collude on their evidence, or destroy documents, or even to seize the ship."

"I repeat my qu-question," O'Brien said, exasperated. "Who do you wuh-want to arrest?"

Quantrill glared.

Davies said, "Ah, um, perhaps we ought to make a list?"

And so a list of nine names was made.

"How will you suh-seize nine men?" O'Brien asked.

"Pah," Quantrill said.

He stomped out of the room and was heard roaring for certain of the Guard. They tramped forward in a body, and some of the pirates shouted, but their voices were wheedling, and in fifteen minutes Quantrill returned with the news that Spry and eight of his supporters were in the cable tier.

They were brought up one at a time, for interrogation.

Again, O'Brien conducted the interviews, with Davies taking notes and Quantrill pacing back and forth. Some of the men proved surprisingly recalcitrant. The note-passers claimed their communication was entirely innocent, something to do with gambling. However, Spry was broken. After three hours of questions, he confessed that he and his men had plotted to seize the ship when Coffin had the watch and sail the ship into a Dutch port and beg for mercy.

O'Brien took a break while Davies finalized the affidavit. After it was done, Davies also provided him with a new list of names. O'Brien frowned.

"I say," O'Brien said. "This is luh-luh-longer than I expected."

"Oh, ah, indeed," Davies said. "Shocking."

"We can't execute all these men," O'Brien said. "We need some of them. Tuh-Tuh-Tory is our last carpenter."

"No, no," Davies said. "I quite agree. Um, however, they must be dealt with somehow. Put on half shares, or clapped in irons and kept under guard."

O'Brien looked at Davies. Davies stared back with his usual fawning intensity. A queasy ripple went through O'Brien's guts.

Well. The thing was to get Spry out of the way, for good, and at last he would be safe.

18

The men were assembled and Spry, on the verge of tears, read out his confession. Some supporters shouted that it was a lie, a lie! But the fewer who shouted, the more conspicuous they were, and they soon stopped. The bulk of the Company did not know what to believe. All nine men had eventually confessed; none of them had been physically harmed. None of them were executed. Spry was locked up in the orlop, with a couple others, while the rest were released. A new crop of men was taken into custody, who in turn named other men. Some even began coming in early, to prove their loyalty.

O'Brien always conducted the initial interviews, and he became overwhelmed by the volume of information. He was not so naive as to believe that all, or even most, of what the men said was accurate. But surely some of it was, with the weather and the damage to the ship and the short rations. It could not all be false.

Yet day after day Benjamin claimed to have no evidence of any Mutiny. At last, O'Brien ordered him not to return until he had something to report. Benjamin put on his fool's face and departed, leaving

O'Brien all alone, listening to the timbers groan and feeling the deck lift and fall beneath his feet.

Through one hot, still day the glass dropped and as the setting sun blazed crimson behind them, they were set upon by a howling storm that pounded them westwards for two days and two nights, with all hands on deck, day and night, and every man taking a shift at the pumps to keep the listing ship afloat. When at last the storm ended, and it was possible to take a noon measurement, they found they had been blown backwards a dozen miles. The news spread through the ship by some silent osmosis.

Later, as O'Brien sat alone in his cabin, hungry, hot, frustrated, he heard two men fighting upon the quarterdeck. When he emerged from his cabin, he saw that it was Rios and Tory, the ship's last carpenter. The fished mizzen-mast had cracked, and now tilted crazily, yawing and straining against its tangle of ropes. Rios blamed Tory's workmanship; Tory blamed Rios's seamanship.

Tory screamed, his face purple, "Don't you know you must luff up handsomely? Goddamn, this ship is going to the dogs! There ain't no seaman worth tuppence aboard no longer!"

"Mutiny!" Rios cried. "Arrest this man!"

"I'm already on the goddamn list," Tory said, shaking with the extremity of his emotion. "Already clapped me in irons and stole my fucking share because of a pack of lies. By the Powers, if you ain't going to listen to me, I wish you'd leave me in the fucking orlop."

"Buh-Buh-Brothers, puh-please . . ."

Quantrill ascended the companionway, scowling. To O'Brien there did not seem to be a focus to his annoyance, but the carpenter thought differently. He drew his knife.

"I ain't going without a fight," he said.

"Puh-puh-put it duh-duh-down," O'Brien said.

"I won't!" the carpenter cried. "You're a goddamned murdering dog!"

Quantrill's face twisted; he drew a pistol.

"Go on and shoot me, you coward!"

"Puh-puh-put it duh-duh-duh . . ."

Quantrill's gaze fell upon O'Brien, and O'Brien saw therein something squirm, like a beetle under a rock.

"Go on, go on, shoot me!" the carpenter cried. "We'll all be dead soon! I'd rather—"

The man's head snapped back; a moment later the sound of the shot, and the smoke in the air.

"Nuh-Nuh-No!" O'Brien cried. "Wuh-Wuh-Why duh-duh-duh-duh . . ."

Quantrill glared at O'Brien as he tucked the smoking pistol into his trousers, then trooped downstairs. O'Brien returned to the Great Cabin to pace, back and forth, back and forth, clenching his fists.

The carpenter murdered! And him humiliated in front of the Company! But what could he do? He needed time, time, time. Time to think. To steady himself, he opened his watch so he could better hear it tick.

He needed the Guard to maintain control of the ship. That much was obvious. But he could not trust Quantrill. He needed to get rid of him. Seized, brought aft, a quick trial, then into the water. But whom could he trust? Who would help him? He ran through his supporters, those who had been Rackham's men, who had followed him aboard the ship. There were not many of them. But surely plenty of the Guards were not loyal to Quantrill. Surely some would jump at the chance to replace him. But which?

After dinner, he asked Benjamin about the Guard, but the response was not what he might have wished.

"I can't get near them," he said. "They eat by themselves, and they don't let no one come near, not even me."

"Cuh-come now, you can approach them at tuh-times other than meals," O'Brien said.

"Sure," Benjamin said. "But I ain't never heard any of 'em say one word against Quantrill. If they do, he kicks 'em out of the Guard."

"Duh-Does he? Who are some men he removed from the Guh-Guh-Guard?"

Benjamin listed a few names.

"Hands?" O'Brien said. "I didn't even know he was in the Guard."

"Aye," Benjamin said. "Though he didn't last long."

"Very guh-good," O'Brien said, rubbing his hands. "You must puh-pass him a muh-message for me."

"No," Benjamin said. "I only deal with you."

"Well, that has to chuh-change," O'Brien said.

"No."

"I can expose yuh-you!" O'Brien said.

"No," Benjamin said. "You can't." A cold look in his eyes.

So O'Brien worked on his own. He established a new Committee to improve the governance of the ship, and interviewed many men for this purpose, but he also sounded out men about removing Quantrill. His instincts were solid; almost every man he spoke to, including Israel Hands, agreed Quantrill had grown too powerful and promised to support his removal.

"I told the Taoiseach to cut his throat after I saw him go to work at Corso Castle," Israel said. "I knew he'd be trouble."

O'Brien's plans were well advanced when one night, as they sailed through the inky darkness, the ship ran aground upon a stone ridge that rose up from the deep like the appendage of some beast gigantic in size and appetite alike. It had been Rios's watch. At last the contrary winds helped them; they lowered the boats and backed the sails and were able to haul the *Saoirse* off the rock. The sea poured into the hold and the men scrambled in the dark to board up the hole and stem the flow of warm and greasy water as best they could with no carpenter.

While the men, tired and hungry, strained at the pumps, Quantrill, furious, arrested Rios for sabotage, and escorted him below decks to be clapped in irons.

O'Brien saw his chance. He summoned Davies and Israel Hands, along with some other men, while Quantrill was below and many of the Guard were busy at the pumps. O'Brien brought a motion to strip

Quantrill of his offices and dismantle the Board. To O'Brien's surprise, Davies objected, saying the Meeting was improper and the motion was out of order. Davies was restrained, and O'Brien entered the motion into the logbook.

O'Brien's men took up positions on the quarterdeck and around the hatches and shouted for the crew to rise against the Guard. Instead, the pirates ran below decks or scrambled up the rigging. Below them, the pumps were deserted and the ship took on water. The sails hung limp from the yards and the ropes flapped in the gentle breeze and the ship fell off her course.

"There he is!" a man cried from the forward companionway.

"Batten down the hatches!" O'Brien shouted, too late.

Muskets blazed, but Quantrill was seemingly impervious. Up the stairs he came, so fast for such a big man, all at once among the shooters like an angry bear, and O'Brien's men fell back to the quarterdeck and took shelter behind barrels and coils of rope and the masts. They were outnumbered, but they had the high ground and the powder and weapons.

O'Brien retreated into the Great Cabin, where Israel waited. The tattoos were skillfully done; in the dark he really did look like a monster.

"Well, Israel," he said. "If we can hold on, the men are sure to come round."

"How did you ever make anyone think you was clever?" Israel asked.

"Pardon me?" O'Brien asked.

Israel's knife swung in a quick, short arc. O'Brien's eyes flew open as if with divine revelation, as if now, at last, he understood. His life rushed out from between his hands while Israel came onto the quarterdeck with a brace of pistols and shot the remaining defenders in the back.

"There it is," Israel said. "It's done, Billy, it's all done."

Quantrill stepped onto the quarterdeck, nodded at Israel. Israel, smiling, handed him the bloody pocket watch as if in tribute. With a flick of his wrist, Quantrill sent it spinning into the deep.

TYRANNY

A government in which absolute power is vested in a single ruler.

(Merriam-Webster)

CAPTAIN BILLY QUANTRILL

1

The first image of Bill Quantrill's captaincy was a small forest of hands, dirty, bloody, waving like anemones—the surrender of O'Brien's pathetic faction. Quantrill looked them over and threw the grievously wounded over the side, along with O'Brien's corpse. Glancing at the slack rigging, the flapping sails, and the men peering down from the tops, he cupped his hands around his mouth and bellowed:

"You lot! It's over! Set all them ropes in order and get us moving!"

The men jumped to obey.

"What do we do with the rest of them?" Israel asked.

"Clap 'em in irons with Rios," Quantrill said. "And rouse all the men below. It's all hands on deck."

Quantrill stood next to the windward rail, his hands behind his back, scowling. To him, the men seemed awkward and slow about their work. Now and then he would shout: "You there! Look lively!"

After a while he grew bored and went alone into the Great Cabin and sat down in the chair in which the Taoiseach, Apollo, Scudder, and O'Brien had all sat before him, and feeling it creak and expand under him, a rare sense of satisfaction spread through his aching, wounded body.

He'd been born to a destitute mother in Liverpool, his patrimony as uncertain as the origins of the universe itself. His earliest memory was terrible pain from his ruined face. Of the injury itself he had no memory. He only remembered pulling on his mother's skirt and crying, while she pushed him away, saying she couldn't do nothing about it, until at last she struck him down into the dirt. There he lay for a thousand years, his burn radiating with unbearable pain, staring at the smoke-stained ceiling of their hovel while his nine siblings capered around him. Part of him lay there still.

In 1702 he'd been eleven years old, but nearly six feet tall, ungainly, ugly, unloved. Already he had formed the notion that he was a man of great natural talents that were being squandered by an ungrateful world. He volunteered for the Sea Service Regiment of Foot when Seymour's party came to Liverpool. He'd had a rough time of it at first, though things got easier after he killed four Spaniards upon the mole at Gibraltar.

He'd never had a True Friend, save for the boy Scudder. Since Scudder's death it had become clear he could not rely upon anyone but himself, for all the others were fools.

The ship being without a carpenter, the repair work was hard and awkward. The men fumbled below for hours in the dark of carpenter's walk, well below the waterline, struggling to nail planks to stem the inrush of the sea. Other men strained at the pumps, hour after hour, as the listing and sinking ship plodded on.

Once the ship was as seaworthy as she could be made, Quantrill called a Meeting. All the men were exhausted, almost inert.

"Well," Quantrill said. "I'm your Captain now. I ain't no prime seaman, nor am I a talker about rights and suchlike. What we need now's a man to set things right. Hands and Yellow shall be the mates, Davies shall be your Quartermaster. And to keep things in order, I believe I shall bring a few new men into the Captain's Guard."

Here he admitted various new men by calling their names, while expelling some few others for reasons that were unclear (an example, perhaps, but an example of what?).

"Dismissed," Quantrill said, and the Meeting was adjourned.

He met with Israel, Yellow, and Davies in the Great Cabin. Alfie came in with a bottle of Irish whiskey. God knew where he was hiding all this stuff. Quantrill accepted it, coldly, and poured out tumblers for the others. Also admitted was Benjamin, who skirted around the edges of the room, looked at Quantrill very searchingly, and went onto the stern gallery to fish.

"Well gentlemen," Quantrill said. "Any ideas?"

"Um, I have a list," Davies said, pushing a paper forward.

Scowling, Quantrill said, "I can't read."

"Oh," Davies said, his weak face startled. "Well, it is a list of men who conspired with O'Brien."

Quantrill grunted.

"Shall I read it out?"

He did; Quantrill nodded at all the names.

"Hands, take that paper below when you question Rios."

"All right," Israel said.

"No need to be gentle about it. And take care of Spry. I don't feel right with him still down there. Anything else?"

"Um, may I suggest, sir," Davies said, "that I take inventory of our supplies?"

"Fine," Quantrill said. "Get that black bastard Alfie to bring out all the things he's stashed as well. Now this Meeting is over."

Davies, Israel, and Yellow left, and Quantrill was alone, if you didn't count Benjamin on the stern gallery. That was the way he liked it.

2

The next morning, Rios was produced before the Company, crumpled and broken, and read out a confession. A collection of dull, dry eyes watched. Pirates so burned with the sun and wasted with hunger and illness they were like marionettes from a puppet show set during the Black Death. Rios was sentenced to be hanged, and the only man who spoke in his defence, hesitatingly, was Yellow, who suggested they were running low on men skilled in navigation. But Rios had no other defenders, whether they disliked the man, or whether they were affrighted of Quantrill, or whether they approved of the new regime. Which many did—for time and time again Quantrill had proven himself a stout, courageous man, and that was what was needed in this desperate hour.

That was what Hutchins told his messmates.

"Now, he ain't a much of a seaman, no one's saying he is," Hutchins said. "Nor is he one for Meetings and such. But it's folks like that as got us in this corner, and what we need now is a strong hand to keep everything in line. We'll pull through, mates, you may lay to that."

Coffin did not reply. Since his demotion from mate, his standing among the crew had fallen to new lows. But worse, somehow, was the feeling that grew on the boat. That greasy, ugly feeling when things began to go deeply wrong. Only, it was not precisely that they were going wrong, but that you realized they had never been right to begin with. As if some ghastly radiance shone upon them, and every man could see all the imperfections and weaknesses and flaws of every other. That unwelcome knowledge sapped something from the men, lessened them. Coffin had been to the very end of this dark road already, and he had no illusions about how it would end.

Rios was hanged, along with a few others, but Spry was gagged and thrown from the stern windows, vanishing without sign or sound. Davies had wanted to include him in Rios's trial, but Quantrill was sick of all the motions and bleating and liked Spry's end better. The wake swallowed up the troublemaker with scarcely a splash, not a line on paper to mark his passing, and then you didn't have to worry about him no more. Let all them Sea Lawyers guess what had become of him.

Each day, the men worked four hours on and four hours off, climbing the masts, hauling on ropes, straining at the pumps, tacking into the wind. Yet fewer of them worked now, as the Guard were exempted from sailors' duties. The bread ration was cut to half a pound a day. The beer being exhausted, they drank water, which had grown stagnant and foul, and men fell ill with the bloody flux and sat in the heads hunched and shivering, like wretched gargoyles brought to life, and shat blood down the bow, and if they raised their heads, none would meet their eyes.

The nearest European settlement was Makassar, on the island of Sulawesi, but it was home to a powerful Dutch fort, and Quantrill made the decision to sail for the farther port of Ambon in the Spice Islands. The *Saoirse* zigzagged across the Banda Sea, dotted with small islands of green rainforests and pure-white beaches, the men working to the point of exhaustion and then past it. Behind them still lurked a small armada of native craft, but the *Happy Delivery* was gone.

The winds at last grew favourable, and their speed increased, yet they did not arrive at Ambon, but some other massive land mass. It was clear that with Rios gone, and Coffin demoted, the reckonings had been done incorrectly. Yellow, terrified that he would be made to walk the plank, hid in the forecastle and had to be summoned twice before he would appear before his angry Captain.

Eventually it was decided to send a party ashore in search of provisions and fresh water. The ship dropped anchor and six men set off, including the cooper.

Their boat towed a line of empty casks towards the mouth of a river. As they grew closer, they realized that instead of a true shore, scrub and brush and even great trees grew from the brackish sea water, without solid ground in sight. The river was shallow and silty and blooming with strange algae. Bugs hummed, and birds sang in clipped bursts, and the trees were strangled with vines and dotted with orchids of startling colour and contorted form.

They rowed upstream for half an hour, the jungle closing in, then turned the boat to the larboard shore and steered through the trees and shrubs until the muddy water transformed into mud. They stepped out and sank past their ankles in the mire and swatted at the bugs and cursed. Nothing moved around them. The pirates picked their way through a diversity of ferns and stepped over roots and fallen trees, but the jungle was so thick as to be impassable and yet strangely sterile, with few animals and no fruits or nuts. They returned to their boat without so much as a berry and continued to paddle upriver.

They heard the chanting of the savages before they saw them, and so they were prepared when a long canoe rounded a bend and came into view. The savages paddled standing, the gunwales of their vessel only an inch above the water. At the sight of the pirates they let out wild cries, and their craft slowed and turned, and puffs of gun smoke rose above them. Some of the pirates returned fire. Since the savages had exposed the broadside of their vessel, they made easy targets and one was knocked into the water.

The canoe fled as the body floated towards them. A pirate caught it with the tip of his sabre and brought it on board. The corpse was heavily muscled, without a trace of fat. He had looping spirals of red and white painted over his legs and chest, and a curved bone through his septum, like the horns of an ox or a moustache. A wooden phallus was strapped over his genitals, but otherwise he was naked. His sole possession was a rawhide pouch filled with limestone powder. It was this, and not gun smoke, that they had seen in the air.

They threw the savage's body overboard and paddled farther upstream, looking for a place where they could at least fill their casks. Having found a short channel that suited their purpose, they followed it for a hundred yards until it ended in a secluded pool and there they tied the boat to a sickly mangrove tree.

On the other side of the pool, lurking among the trees and shrubs and reeds, was a mud-coloured saltwater crocodile, fat and ancient. Though only the creature's head was visible, it looked to be at least twenty feet long. Triangular scales in mottled shades of brown ran in thin ridges along its body. It would not look at them, though whether it was feigning lack of interest or they were truly beneath its notice, they could not say.

As the men slapped the bugs that hummed around them like vile halos and peeled the leeches from their legs, an arrow leapt from the trees and landed in the back of the cooper, who, surprised, barked out a fine mist of blood.

More arrows rained down from the trees, long and thin and tipped with arrowheads of bone and fletched with the shimmering feathers of birds of paradise. A war cry reverberated around the pool and the crocodile, still without sparing the pirates a glance, sank into the shallow, muddy water.

All at once the Otsjanep were upon them, dozens of them, coming through the dense forest like ghosts. They were painted white as if in mockery of the interlopers, and they wore bright feathers and their hair was done up in elaborate coiffures, and they wielded tall wooden shields of fine craftsmanship and design, and their long spears were tipped with the claws of cassowaries. The pirates fired their muskets, leapt for their boat, slashing the rope and shoving it out into the deeper water. Three of them made it aboard. The fourth was stabbed in the side, once, and then a dozen more times, and fell under the scummy surface of the stagnant pool. The fifth was raising himself over the gunwale when the crocodile exploded from the murk and locked its massive jaws around his torso and dragged him under before he could so much as exhale.

The bodies of the other two pirates were dragged over a brutal tangle of roots and vines and through the mud and the brack. The man who had been speared was dead, or nearly so, but the man who had been hit by the arrow was screeching and struggling. In the froth of dirty water and sweat, he slipped loose and scrambled halfway to his feet before he was clubbed back down. He spent his last moments panicked and thrashing in that lifeless jungle with the painted men around him on all sides, one sitting on his back, another jerking his hair to expose his throat. His last vision was of painted black legs, and his last sound their ecstatic cries of "Wo wo wo!" and the blowing of their bamboo horns.

A bone dagger cut his throat and his head was pressed back until the vertebrae cracked like the shell of a lobster. His struggles ceased, and the butchers crowded around him, and a broad, strong knife jabbed into him just above the anus. He was cut up to his neck, then to the armpit, then across the collarbone, and down his side. His ribs were cracked, his sternum ripped open, his legs hacked and twisted and pulled off, and his entrails spilled out into the murk.

Some of the other men had already started a fire. They scalped the dead and burned their hair, and made a kind of paste with the blood of the men and the ashes of the hair, which they rubbed over their bellies and genitals. The dead pirates' limbs were hung on spits and roasted, and eaten, and their brains were scooped out and wrapped in savoury leaves, and they were eaten also. Then they mixed the melted fat with sago flour and brought it back to the village, along with the heads.

This encounter, one of the first between Europeans and the Otsjanep, was of little import to the natives, yet it was never wholly forgotten. For that night a Bisj pole was carved and erected for the warriors who had been killed, and the skulls of the pirates were accorded all due ceremony and took their place in the bony pantheon of their fallen foes. The men who had killed the pirates told the story of those skulls to their sons, who in turn told their sons. And so they passed into legend as surely as all the rest, but a different legend, of a different people.

Papua New Guinea.

August 1, 1722.

3

When the boat returned, without provisions, without fresh water, without three of its party, without even the casks with which they had been entrusted, Quantrill's wrath was berserk. The three survivors were accused of sabotage and taken down into the spirits room, which, now wholly devoid of spirits, had been rigged up as a crude dungeon. They were never seen or heard from again.

Quantrill met with his officers and discussed how to proceed. Since the number and capability of the savages were unknown, and since no one on the ship could be even remotely described as a cooper, the decision was made to sail westwards, with the wind at their back, towards Ambon. Yellow was informed in no uncertain terms that another failure in navigation would not be tolerated.

For the first time in weeks, the breeze was abaft their beam, and yet it was no easy voyage. Six men died of disease, and the men always had to work the pumps, and because of Quantrill's insistence that they carry more and more sail (for the more sail the ship carried, the faster it would go), the ship listed and took on water and a yard was carried away.

Quantrill spent many hours alone in the cabin. The mismanagement of previous Captains had left him beset by bad luck, with a crippled ship and an empty larder. The weather was always against him. His men were against him, being either incompetent or disloyal, and frequently both. But could all the ship's problems be explained solely by bad luck? Were some sailors saboteurs, wreckers? It could not all be accidental. Indeed, if all these men were doing their duty, instead of shirking, there ought to be no accidents at all. So every time there was a problem—a sail split, or a rope snapped—Quantrill hauled in the culprits to interrogate them over their failure. If he did not like their answers, they were reassigned, or sent down to the spirits room.

At night he could not sleep. The flapping of the canvas that covered the shattered stern windows, the tread of the Guard on the poop deck, the wind and water, the groan of stretching rope, the bells: all of it presaged the assassins who would kill him. They would blame him, he knew, for every calamity, though none of this was his fault. How many men on this ship could he trust, could he truly trust, now that Scudder was dead? Trust had been Scudder's downfall, he had been too good for these accursed scoundrels. Could he even trust the Guards? Every time he closed his eyes, he imagined them climbing through the windows to kill him as he had killed Apollo, or picking the lock at his cabin door, or slitting the canvas that covered the skylight and dropping down in the darkness.

One night, a day's sail from Ambon according to Yellow's dubious calculations, the sound of a man picking at the lock woke Quantrill from opaque dreams of a large monster deep in the water. He screamed, unmanned by terror, and fell out of his hammock and floundered in the darkness till his hand fell on the pommel of his golden sword. With the dream banished and his courage restored, he stood to face the two Guards who raced inside with their loaded muskets and fixed bayonets. He snarled and raised his weapon, ready to fight, but they rushed past him looking for the assassins who were not there.

"Who was that picking at the lock?" Quantrill demanded.

"Ah, pardon?" the one Guard asked, a loutish lascar who spoke little English.

"Which one of you was picking at the fucking lock?"

Other Guards had arrived at the door, and Quantrill gestured and the first two Guards were seized and dragged away.

He retreated into the Great Cabin and barred the door and sat there with his head in his hands. They would depose him. He knew. He would drown like the others. Eventually the certainty of this prospect worked him up into a state of defiant courage. Quantrill's years in the marines had given him an appreciation of a neat turnout; he polished his boots, brushed off his clothes, and shaved himself as well as he could with cold salt water. Checking himself once in the mirror, he unlocked the door to the Great Cabin and went into his sleeping quarters.

There he found the Guards waiting for him, and in each of their countenances he saw an identical expression of poorly suppressed terror. Knowing his authority intact, he barked at them to rouse the men from their hammocks and call them out onto the deck.

On the quarterdeck, he asked Israel Hands: "Who was at the helm just now?"

"Coffin," Israel replied.

"Lock him up," Quantrill said.

The Company assembled, looking tired and frightened and much reduced, and the Guard lined the quarterdeck and crowded the poop.

Quantrill bellowed down at them: "Another conspiracy against my life this night. Failed, like all the rest."

He paced up and down the quarterdeck, shoving the Guard when they were in his way.

"One day out of Ambon. One fucking day!"

He stopped, his hands balled at his sides, so tight his nails cut his palms.

"But the traitors will never stop!" he said. "They won't be happy with their share of the treasure. They won't be happy doing their duty. No no. Not them! They won't stop till they've sold us out."

Quantrill stepped down and that whole body of men shrank from him, while trying to make it seem as if they were not shrinking from him.

"Why are you afraid?" Quantrill said to one of the men.

The man looked down.

"Why are you so shifty, shipmate?" Quantrill snarled. "Why won't you look your Brother Pirate in the eye?"

The man looked up. He'd sailed for decades, fighting a war without end, and never wept, but he was close to tears now. They all were, these grown men, heroes, killers, thieves. All terrified.

"Were you one of them?" Quantrill said.

"No sir," the man said. "No Captain. I ain't in a Plot."

"Someone's lying," Quantrill said. "One of you dogs is lying to me."

He paced down the ranks, daring every man to meet his eye.

"Who is it?" Quantrill said. "Who's the traitor? Who's the liar?"

No one spoke. Above, far away, the stars shone.

Quantrill shoved his way into the men, his heart jamming, expecting the knife at any moment, but he had to show them he was not afraid.

At last he came upon Hutchins.

"You," he said.

"I was in my hammock," Hutchins said. "Everyone saw me."

"Have your story all ready, do you?" Quantrill said, and caught Hutchins by the shoulder. A space had cleared around him. Everyone relieved it was not them.

"Down below you go," Quantrill said. "We'll get the truth from you." A couple of his Guards forced Hutchins down the aft companionway into the belly of the ship.

"The rest of you is dismissed," Quantrill said. "But this isn't the end." To Davies he said: "Come with me."

They went together out onto the stern gallery and stared out over the wake of the ship.

"Here's how I see it," Quantrill said after a time. "A man alone might kill the Captain, but he can't sail a ship. He must believe the crew will support him before he even tries. There must have been more of them."

"Yes," Davies said.

"How many men were loyal, at one time, to Kavanagh, Apollo, Dickens, O'Brien? How many? Almost all of them. How few can we trust?"

"Um, um, it's true," Davies said.

Quantrill leaned forward and gripped the taffrail. When he turned back to Davies, the latter flinched.

"Why are you so goddamn nervous?" Quantrill barked.

"I'm . . ."

"If you're innocent, why are you nervous? You think I'd kill an innocent man, is that what you think?"

"No, um, I don't," Davies said.

"I don't like to see a man close to me so damned nervous."

"I understand."

"D'you think we could kill Coffin or Lewis?"

Davies hesitated. Was it a test?

"Well, um," Davies said. "If we leave them alive, there's the danger the crew will support them for Captain. But if we kill them, Coffin especially, then Yellow's the only man as can navigate."

Quantrill grunted. For all his disdain for seamanship he had learned at some expense the importance of navigation.

"We have to change things up again," Quantrill said. "Think of some names."

"Ah, I can think of a few, sir," Davies said.

"You always can, can't you?" Quantrill said. "What's that say then? No matter how many cockroaches you stamp out, there's always another scuttling around somewhere, ain't there?"

"There is, sir."

"What's that say then?" Quantrill said.

"Um, um, well, I couldn't say, sir."

This was the truth. He could not. Neither of them could.

4

Around dozen were expelled from the Guard and were replaced with new men. Yellow was dismissed as an officer of the watch but given the role of Secretary and Master. The Master-at-Arms was demoted, and his position was added to Israel's responsibilities.

Still, Quantrill could not sleep. His nerves were as an old battle-ground, chewed up and littered with rusted iron. He could not trust anyone. The Taoiseach, Apollo, Scudder, O'Brien, Dickens—all vanished like stones dropped in water. Gone. They would do the same to him if they could. They would turn on him. They might be plotting even now.

Two men were overheard planning to desert the ship at the Spice Islands, even if it meant forfeiting their shares, and they were made to walk the plank.

Despite favourable winds, it took four days to reach the island of Ambon. The city was at the end of a bay ten miles long, and once again they had to sail into the wind without a pilot. To cross the distance took five hours, and when at last they arrived at that tiny hamlet, they found to their horrible shock that three Dutch ships were in the roads. Before their very eyes one weighed anchor, exploding into sail.

None of the pirates made a sound, save one, who screamed with laughter. The laughing pirate was thin, and his eyes were bloodshot, and he had lost many teeth to scurvy, and as his mirthless laughter accelerated, an empty space formed around him. Two Guards approached, but before they could lay a hand on him, he stepped up onto the gunwale and dropped into the sea.

The *Saoirse* had all three ships outgunned, but the Dutch had the weather gage. After a hurried conference, Quantrill gave the order to withdraw. The men shouted, the ropes were loosed, the wheel spun, and the ship turned her stern to the wind.

The schooner pursued them, and once they were out of the bay and turning north, it moved to intercept. But long before she could bring her little guns to bear, the *Saoirse* ripped off three furious broadsides in five minutes. None of her shots struck home, but the rate of fire intimidated the schooner, and she fell back.

Quantrill called another meeting of his officers in the Great Cabin. Yellow spread out the charts over the table. The question was where to go, but no one spoke. They only looked at Quantrill, who sat at the head of the table, ossified with rage. If a man looked at him, he demanded to know what they were staring at. If they looked away, he asked why they would not look him in the eye. If they spoke, he told them to shut up, and when they were silent, he demanded to know why no one said anything.

When Quantrill got up and walked to the window and stared at the canvas with his hands clasped behind his back, at last Yellow spoke.

"We need provisions, Captain. We ain't got enough to make it across the Pacific."

"You think I don't know that?" Quantrill said. "Damn your eyes. Where should we go? You're the goddamned navigator."

"Well," Yellow said. "We might try Manila. We ain't done nothing to the Spanish."

Davies spoke. "Captain, have you heard of the Sociable Islands?"

"Why would you ask me a stupid question like that?"

Davies lifted a logbook. "Um, it says here when Rogers sailed up to 'em, the natives were friendly. That's why Rogers called 'em the Sociable Islands. Sailed right up and traded for everything. Even the women, ah, sold themselves for iron nails."

"Why are you thinking of whores at a time like this?"

"Well, ah, um, if word's got around about our haul, I don't know that there's a civilized port anywhere in the East Indies where we'll be safe. And I don't know that we can trust the men, neither. Um, some of 'em'll desert. Others'll sell us down the river."

Quantrill grunted.

"But if we sail to the Sociable Islands, they'll have nowhere to run to, and no one to conspire with."

Yellow peered at the charts. "The Sociable Islands?" he said. "The Sociable Islands?"

"Are you deaf?" Quantrill said.

"It's . . ." Yellow began.

"It's what?"

"It looks to be more than four thousand miles, Captain."

"Then where?" Quantrill said.

Yellow shuffled through the papers, looked up, looked down, opened his mouth, closed it.

"How many days?" Quantrill asked.

"Ah, say forty-five, to be safe," Davies said.

"We have perhaps fifty-eight casks of biscuit and sixty-four casks of fresh water," Yellow said. "And there are nigh on two hundred and fifty men on the ship." His face grew constipated, his eyes closed, his lips moving. "A half a pound of biscuit a day. And a pint of water."

"More than enough," Quantrill said. "Fresh fruit and meat at the end of it."

Something about the plan struck a spark in his brain. The more he thought on it, the more sense it made. Out there, in the middle of the Pacific, that great ocean twice the size of the Atlantic, that great blank space on all the maps in the world, he would be hundreds of miles from any foreign power that might threaten him or tempt his crew.

5

The monsoon at last worked to their advantage, carrying them north till they were through the archipelago, and then obligingly shifted to the east, sending them into the great cyan void of the Pacific. The Board had informed the men they were headed to a settlement in North Maluku, but once the *Saoirse* had passed that island, the Company learned the ship's true destination.

Led by Ironside, some of the men staged a spontaneous and pathetic strike, refusing to come on deck at the change of the watch. Quantrill made no effort to coax them out but merely posted armed sentries and denied them water. A ring of Guards around the hatch, muskets and bayonets. Some of the strikers cursed the Guard and called for them to turn their guns around. Quantrill made no offer of clemency. Within eight hours the strike was broken. Ironside was obliged to walk the plank. The other ring-leaders (who included most of the remaining skilled tradesmen) were fitted with cruel metal bridles and beaten around the deck with canes. The next day they were put on trial and confessed their plan to surrender the ship to the Dutch, then were disappeared below decks, their fate unclear.

Suspicion fell upon Obed Coffin. Although he had taken no active part in the Mutiny (he had, in fact, been in custody at the time), it was natural that any conspiracy must involve him in some way. The Board met to decide his fate, and both Israel Hands and Yellow were in favour of putting him to death.

That had been Quantrill's first instinct as well. But now he began to suspect Israel and Yellow. It seemed to Quantrill that Yellow was over-eager to be the only navigator on board, to make himself indispensable. As for Israel, Quantrill grew suspicious that he was too loyal. The more Quantrill thought about it, the more unsure of his loyalty he became, and the more he cursed himself for showing Israel so much favour and putting him in a position to threaten his own authority.

Abruptly, he vetoed the execution of Coffin. Yellow was shocked into silence, a clear sign of guilt, while Israel took the rebuke as if he had expected it. Highly suspicious, the pair of them. Israel Hands was relieved of his position as mate, Connor was promoted, several Guards who it seemed to Quantrill were too loyal to Hands were dismissed and replaced by sailors not involved in the Mutiny, and both Israel and Yellow were ordered to deliver self-censure statements for insubordination. These statements were not delivered publicly but were noted in the logbook.

In the first week, it was discovered that Yellow's calculations had been wrong, and the rations of bread and water had to be reduced. Guards were dismissed or appointed every day. Since the Guards ate better than the jacks, and worked less, these appointments were of critical importance.

Progress was uneven, as the ship was short of rope, tar, sails, thread, needles, fastenings, fixtures, even oakum. However, the wind remained fair. Quantrill became concerned at all the time the men were spending below decks, and at Davies's suggestion daily Meetings were reinstituted.

The topic of these Meetings was the hunt for spies, traitors, and saboteurs. Quantrill reminded the men that there were, in all likelihood, still traitors aboard, men who sought to surrender the ship either to the Dutch or to the *Happy Delivery*. All men were required to report malingering, sabotage, or plotting to the Guard. Failure to report a suspected Mutiny made a man a mutineer himself. Men were also encouraged (at Davies's suggestion) to stand up and admit to any faults in their seamanship to forestall suspicions of deliberate sabotage.

Previously, Meetings had concluded with the unofficial anthem of the pirates, *did not you promise me / that you would marry me*. However, Davies brought a motion that the anthem, associated as it was with the Commonwealth, whose flagship had attacked them, be banned. In its place he proposed they sing a new song, dedicated to their leader Quantrill.

The song was to be sung to the tune of "God Save the King" and contained such lyrics as:

Quantrill, we thank thee,
Guardian of our liberty,
Of thee we sing!
Hero of the ocean wide!
Thou fillst our hearts with pride!
Let freedom ring!

And so forth.

Reports came in. A man sleeping in the maintop. Two men having a private conversation in the orlop. Another man who had tied a knot improperly. Men were not executed, so long as they confessed, which they always did. Instead, their rations were reduced, and they were assigned unpleasant duties.

They sailed and sailed and sailed. Twice they encountered moderate storms, twice they hove to and rode them out, with every empty barrel set open on the deck, every keg and cup and cask, and after they'd collected as much rainwater as they could, the men drank and drank, and washed themselves with the frenetic hopelessness of those whose uncleanliness ran to the core.

Upon the forty-fifth day, the biscuit was finished. The sundries had long been consumed, and the rats, and the ship was down to her last few casks of rainwater. Yet there was no sight of the Sociable Islands.

Somewhere in the Pacific.

September 24, 1722.

6

Quantrill met with his officers in the Great Cabin. None spoke. Everyone simply looked at Yellow, their expressions wrathful, pleading.

Yellow, thin and burned and dried out, with staring eyes and loosened teeth and bleeding gums, and with breath like an opened crypt, smiled at them, with a genuine, unfeigned warmth that set every man at ease. He told them the nature of the miscalculation, a minor oversight for which he was entirely responsible. New calculations had been done and checked and double-checked. He could state with complete certainty they were two days from the Sociable Islands.

Quantrill, much relieved, informed Yellow that he would have to admit his error to the crew. The cheerful radiance of Yellow's face dimmed, and he looked so downcast that Quantrill clapped him on the shoulder and told him to never mind, that he was a true Brother who had amply repaid the faith of his Captain. Yellow looked up, his eyes shining with tears, and thanked his Captain in a voice clogged with profound feeling.

At the morning Meeting, Yellow made his self-censure and sang the new anthem lustily.

Two days passed without so much as a crumb of bread for any man aboard the ship, and on the morning of the third day, when the sun rose without any land in sight, Yellow smiled at the Captain again with that same beatific serenity, and picked up a cannonball, walked over to the gunwale, and jumped, without a sound, into the sea.

There was a silence that only comes at such times and in such places, as if some hermetic dome had been punctured, and every noise had rushed out into that cold vacuum which lies without.

The Guard lined up on the quarterdeck while the officers retreated into the Great Cabin. Quantrill, anticipating an immediate revolt, barred the door.

On deck, the men were silent. They sat down, all of them, Guards and sailors alike, and tried to find shelter from the sun. The pumps were abandoned. Some men slept. The ship sailed on, slowly, under double-reefed topsails, rising and falling on the waves.

Israel Hands and Davies were silent while Quantrill paced, clenching his fists.

"Coffin," he said at last.

The door was not unbarred. Israel was hoisted up through the broken skylight, where he shouted at the lounging Guards to fetch Coffin. Coffin had been in the orlop, off and on, for over forty-five days. He was horribly reduced, and his body was covered with sores, and he cried out when the sunlight hit his eyes. The door to the Great Cabin was unbarred, and Yellow's logs were put in front of him.

Once he was given a little water, and recovered himself, he flipped through the pages. His review did not last long. He held up the book for the others.

There were pages and pages of question marks, exclamation points, and doodles, calculations done and crossed out and redone. This confused tangle continued for pages, until the past seven days, where Yellow had written no navigational information at all. Instead, every day he had twice written St. Patrick's prayer in an almost illegible hand:

Christ with me

Christ before me

Christ behind me

Christ in me

Christ beneath me

Christ above me

Christ on my right

Christ on my left

Christ when I lie down

Christ when I sit down

Christ when I arise

Christ in the heart of every man who thinks of me

Christ in the mouth of everyone who speaks of me

Christ in every eye that sees me

Christ in every ear that hears me

Silence in the Great Cabin. Silence on the deck. Silence, silence.

Quantrill's whole body clenched, a vicious rictus, and his eyes protruded. "Where are we now?" he said, like a man choking.

"I do not know," Coffin said.

"Take a measurement then."

"I cannot, until noon."

Quantrill leaned forward, slowly, and Coffin slunk back.

"We don't have until noon," Quantrill said, his breath stinking of scurvy and sweat.

"I . . . I must . . ."

"You must," Quantrill said, his voice as calm as purest death, "take a fucking measurement."

"I . . . I . . ."

Quantrill exploded to his feet, kicked Coffin to the deck, and rounded on the rest of the men.

"You're all against me!" he said. "Why wasn't none of you checking the fucking logbook? Damn your eyes!"

"Quiet, quiet," Davies said.

"Quiet! You'd fucking like that, eh? You'd fucking like that, wouldn't you? You'd like it if I were quiet so you could Plot against me!"

"We're all in this together," Davies said.

"You're fucking right about that," Quantrill said. "That's the one fucking thing you idiots got right. We are all fucking in this together now."

He stopped, panting.

Yes, they were all in it together. Not even a smudge of land on any horizon in any direction. Only the rolling sea, forever moving, infinitely powerful, unliving and uncaring.

Quantrill turned back to Coffin, who waited in a sort of crouch, looking at the ground with glassy eyes and muttering.

"Coffin."

"Aye."

"Which way should we sail until noon?"

"I don't know."

"Guess."

"We should go nowhere."

"Go nowhere?"

"All directions save one are wrong," he said. "But Captain, thou must know, the sextant will only tell us our latitude."

"What's latitude?"

"What's . . ." Coffin began, and looked around as if for assistance, but was met with expressions of careful neutrality. "Well, latitude is where we are on the globe, from north to south."

"And that's where we are?"

"Yes, but it doesn't tell us where we are east to west. That is longitude."

"Right," Quantrill said, frustration creeping into his voice. Why did these idiots make things so complicated? "How do we tell that?"

"Ah. There is, there is no way to tell our longitude."

"What?"

"There is no way to tell our longitude?" Coffin said, his voice rising, as if he was asking a question.

"What do you mean?" Quantrill said.

"The master begins with a fixed location," Coffin said. "And he notes the speed of the ship, and her direction, and, well, draws a line on the map, if you will. That is what is called dead reckoning."

"I don't see why you don't just figure out the damn longitude with your sextant," Quantrill said.

"I am sorry."

"So how will we find the Sociable Islands?"

"Well, I can tell the latitude."

"Right."

"At least, I can try. Thou should . . ."

"You'll find it," Quantrill said. "What then?"

"We can sail to the latitude of the Sociable Islands."

"What then?"

"Well," Coffin said. "Then we will hope we see them."

"And if we don't?"

"Well," Coffin said. "We will have to guess whether to go east or west."

Quantrill drew his pistol, pressed the barrel against Coffin's head, and cocked it.

"You have to do better than that."

And then the ringing call came from above:

"Sail ho!"

7

O
n deck a rush of feet. Quantrill pointed his pistol at the door, his lips pulled back from his teeth. "It's a trap," he said.

Israel lifted Davies on his shoulders so he could peer through the skylight.

"Nay!" Davies cried. "There's a native craft!"

"Davies, take a boat to them."

The davits had not been maintained and the boat had to be cut loose, crashing down into the water. Four Guards hauled on the oars while Davies waved a white flag. The native craft skimmed towards them, riding the waves beautifully, up and down. It was a double-hulled canoe and could reverse directions by untying the sail and bringing it to the other end of of the ship. As they approached, they saw the boat carried three men and five women, and contained fruit and wooden barrels of fresh water, and there was a little cabin on board where they might take shelter from the elements.

When they drew nearer and the natives saw the weapons of the Guard, they prepared to sail on. But Davies stood up and hollered out,

"Trade!" and flashed a polished marlinspike so it glinted in the sun. The natives stood on the deck of their ship with their spears ready, stern but unafraid.

Davies gave the marlinspike, along with a handful of nails, as a present, and the captain of the ship, a small, older man, very handsome, looked at them approvingly and gave everyone fresh water to drink and fruit to eat. Davies explained, with much difficulty and many gestures, that there was much more on the ship to trade for water and victuals, and the natives received this news with suppressed but visible excitement.

The leader of the natives motioned towards the horizon. Held up two fingers.

"Two days?" Davies said. "You can't be two days from land in this craft."

Two fingers, again.

The *Saoirse* followed the little craft for two days. There was no rain. Acute dehydration set in. Racking pain. Swollen tongues choking the throat. Searing Fever, delirium. Men sucked on stones and rope and bits of metal. Everything was crusted with white salt. The sun hammered. Men died and died and died with terrible swiftness, and there was no one with the strength to throw them overboard.

The ship's little supply of water and the fresh fruit were kept for the Guard and the Board. Coffin was confined to the Master's Cabin except when taking a measurement, and the water and fruit restored him somewhat. His only visitor was Benjamin, who was denied entry to the stern gallery and therefore did his fishing from different places, including the Master's Cabin. In these waters, he caught almost nothing.

The final night, there was hardly a breath of wind, so even though they spread every scrap of canvas they could, they made listless progress, and rose and fell on the swell, and drifted to the lee. Above them were alien constellations, and when the moon rose and lit up the dark waves, it was as if they were already dead, and had passed into a different world.

When the call of "land ho" went up, those who could walk staggered onto the deck, much of the Guard deserted their posts, and all pressed against the rail of the ship, burned and covered in sores, wobbly on their grotesque and bloated legs, croaking a cheer as best they could, their dry lips splitting and bleeding with the exertion. The Guard ordered them back to their posts, and there was much pushing and shoving among the weakened and starving men. The little canoes of the natives were already visible, paddling out from the shore loaded with goods for trade.

Quantrill watched the unfolding chaos from the quarterdeck, then called for Israel Hands and Davies. Despite the confusion, he felt elevated, lit up, electrified, suffused with power. He'd done it. By God, he'd done it. He'd brought the ship safe to the Sociable Islands, through his leadership, in the teeth of all those traitors and lazy bastards. No one else could have done it but him. Now they were safe and halfway home. Surely, surely, now his standing would at last be unchallenged. Which brought to mind one last thing.

"First things first," Quantrill said. "Coffin."

He was the only threat left.

Quantrill took a hatchet from the rack of weapons and went into the Master's Cabin. As he came in, Coffin pulled his head back from the window.

"Look down," Quantrill said. "It will be over in a moment."

Coffin's face, skeletal, burned, blistered, was twisted with some powerful emotion. Quantrill mistook it for fear.

"Look down, I said," Quantrill repeated.

Coffin did not move.

Quantrill grunted and stepped forward.

Coffin let out a little shriek.

As Quantrill grabbed Coffin by the neck and raised the axe with his other hand, Coffin pulled something from the back of his pants and swung it around. Quantrill did not have time to react. There was a bang; his face was full of smoke and powder and he felt a powerful, painless blow.

Quantrill lurched sideways and missed his stroke with the axe, and when he ordered his arms and hands to lift him up, they did not obey.

Instead he lay, trembling, and looked at the gun pointing at his face. He could not read what was engraved on the silver.

mes McIntyre, Esq.

The cabin door was smashed open.

Coffin squirmed out the window and dropped into the sea.

On deck, they saw Coffin swimming straight for the canoes, now only a hundred yards distant. Laden with mango and coconuts and tuna and living crabs, and monkeys and lizards in cages, and singing birds, as well as headdresses of red and green feathers, and wooden carvings of men and women and animals, and precious stones, and beautiful women with perfect skin and naked breasts, all of them singing and paddling and smiling.

A little craft skimmed to Coffin and he was hauled aboard. And then another man jumped down into the water, and then another, and all at once a wave of them splashed down, and there were angry cries from the deck, and a few musket shots, and then it was all of them, it seemed, jumping into the sea.

The natives witnessed this spectacle, motionless and uncomprehending, and their songs ended and their smiles vanished. At last they paddled, throwing their goods for trade into the sea, woven baskets of coconuts, bunches of bananas, shells that glowed like magic mirrors, all consigned to the deep, and they rescued the pirates in the water, every one, and then sailed for shore.

LEVIATHAN

For by Art is created that great LEVIATHAN called a
COMMON-WEALTH, or STATE, (in latine CIVITAS)
which is but an Artificiall Man; though of greater stature
and strength than the Naturall, for whose protection and
defence it was intended; and in which, the Soveraignty is an
Artificiall Soul, as giving life and motion to the whole body.

Thomas Hobbes

1

B y the time the exodus was complete, there were, perhaps, thirty able-bodied men left aboard the *Saoirse*. Quantrill wheezed out his last on the floor of the Great Cabin, unable to speak. Israel watched him die, a dim sparkle of arousal in the dark of his eyes.

"Where did he get the gun?" Davies wondered.

For Israel, first in the cabin, had thrown the mutilated musket out of the window. Fucking Benjamin. He could not help smiling, the corners of his mouth rising and rising, stretching muscles he had not used in years, ratcheting past his usual smirk and twisting his tattooed face into a thoroughly disconcerting grin.

Fucking Benjamin. Aboard the *Queen Anne's Revenge* they'd called him Donkey, and the enemies of the Taoiseach had kicked and spat at him whenever they'd a chance. Twisting his arm till he cried out "hee-haw, hee-haw." Never even came close to suspecting he was more than he appeared, and so he'd seen them all go under when they put down the Mutiny off Honduras. That mad black bastard, he was the maddest of them all, but maybe the smartest as well, for he'd live through this one too.

Kavanagh, Dickens, Spry, all gone under, now Quantrill, and Israel would follow soon enough, but not the Donkey. He'd live on. What a god-damned magnificent crazy son of a bitch.

Israel giggled, almost girlish, then realized they were all looking at him, like he was the Captain now, and this made him laugh harder.

"Well what are you fucking standing there for?" he said, laughing. "There's a hundred of those bloody bastards heading ashore, and we've no water or victuals. We have to follow them!"

Half a dozen men were appointed to hold the ship, including Davies. The cutter was crammed with two dozen armed pirates, with plenty of spare powder and shot. They rowed hard, as the tide was against them, and when they were three hundred yards from the shore, they saw that a mob awaited. Perhaps seventy men, all white, armed with short, slender wooden spears. They had flipped over the canoes of the natives to act as rude barricades, and they were led by Matthew Lewis.

"All right men," Israel said. "Steady the boats."

He stood up and raised his musket and pulled the trigger and missed, and then a wave collapsed under them and the bow of the little boat wobbled and darted to the right like a shy horse and they capsized and were swamped. The muskets and powder were soaked and two men were drowned. The rest straggled up through the coral and the waves towards Lewis.

"Do you dare?" Israel asked, calm and curious, pointing his cutlass at the crowd of men. "Do you finally have the guts?"

They did. He struck two of them down, then got greedy, lunging for Lewis, and was stabbed in the side. He died in the surf, pierced a dozen times, his corpse resembling an anemone. A few of the Guard attempted to surrender, but they were stabbed over and over and over, in a frenzy of vengeance. The boat and muskets were recovered. The pirates took possession of the island.

2

Coffin did not take part in the battle; he fled down a narrow jungle path, across the little island. He ran for hours, from that nightmare of sunburned and dehydrated men with blackened gums and protruding, starved bellies and sunken chests.

How life repeated itself! How it tracked around in circles! How evident, the hand of Providence. Not long ago he had been first mate of the *Puffin*, a fishy man to the bone, married to a beautiful wife at whom he had stared, day after day, across the Great Meeting Hall, until she had succumbed to that gaze, and they had been married. He left her behind with a baby son, and sailed for two years for a one-twentieth lay, but then a whale smashed the *Puffin* and sank it, and Coffin had been stranded in a whaling boat on that deep black sea, far in the southern latitudes, a thousand miles from land, without sails, without water, without food. No charts, no fishing lines, nothing with which to make a fire.

As they began to starve, Coffin had looked up at the roiling grey sky and prayed. Not for deliverance, but for strength. The child awaiting him in Nantucket was his second. The first, a girl, had lived three months and then died, red-faced, thin, screaming in pain. He had prayed for her deliverance and those prayers had not been answered and his faith had been shaken but had not fallen. It had not seemed to him impossible that a just and merciful and all-powerful God might call away his tiny daughter even if the reasons for that call were obscure. And when he had prayed for the strength to withstand that storm of grief, the strength had come. Now he prayed for the strength to resist this trial, but it did not come. It did not come, and so the men in his boat drew straws and every man who drew short was killed and eaten by the others, until only Coffin remained. After that he prayed no more. When his own daughter, the light of his life, had died, he had not lost his faith, but now his faith was gone. He did not require miracles, but he needed to believe in the primacy of the spirit and fifty-two days in the boat taught him that the body was the master of the soul. He did not need to believe in the goodness of God, but he needed to believe in the goodness of himself. And he could not so believe ever again.

He was rescued, and convalesced in the Cape Colony, but he could not return to his home. He could not face his wife and child. He could not go back. He was unclean, unlucky, a Jonah. He wanted more than anything to die, but he lacked the courage. No matter how much he hated himself, his desire to live was so strong. How disgusting it was! How repugnant! How the desire to live clung to him, wretchedly, as he heaped Sin upon Sin, and as the Cruise soured and maddened and transformed, again, into a lonely boat on an indifferent sea. But how hard it was to die! And the longer he lived, how much more degraded he became, how the very world around him became starved and wicked and debased.

In the end he had, again, violated the prime Commandment, murdering Quantrill rather than accepting death, damning his soul to preserve his wretched life. And it was this murder, more than anything else, that drove him on, that lashed him forward.

On the far side of the island, the natives lived in airy longhouses. They regarded him curiously; they had seen white men before, but did not know what to make of his behaviour. They fed him fruit and fish, and gave him a place to sleep.

He lived with them for three days, long enough to learn that they had no weapons, no warriors, no culture of violent honour. All disputes were resolved with a stick no thicker than a man's thumb, and ended at the first abrasion. They lived on the island in the harmony the Quakers dreamed of.

Coffin was floating on a hollow log with a sharpened stick, hunting fish, when Lewis came for him. The stocky armourer had shrunk; his beard now seemed bigger than his chest. Coffin paddled back to shore, then rolled off the log like a dog and dropped into the clear cyan water, warm as a bath, the sea floor radiant and pure and dappled with sun, and watched small and beautiful fishes of every colour darting away. Then he stood up and flung his hair back and looked at the pirate in front of him.

"We need you, Brother," Lewis said. "If you come without a struggle, you don't have to sign nothing, and we'll put you in the log as a forced man, but you still may have your share."

"Very well," Coffin said.

Lewis seemed to suspect a trick.

"I can't stay here," Coffin said, his voice thickening. He blinked away tears. For this was paradise, and he had chosen a damned life, and he must follow it to the end.

3

They took Coffin back to the ship, arriving after dusk. Lewis and his men had killed Davies but spared many others. Lewis told Coffin how the natives had wept at the violence and interposed themselves between the combatants. How a tall, powerful man with long hair sobbed and begged for the life of strangers.

Below decks, dozens of men were recovering from starvation and dehydration, including Harold Hutchins. The natives had the run of the ship, and they peered through spyglasses and tried on clothes and loaded up their satchels and baskets with iron nails and musket shot and good hemp rope. They took some coins as souvenirs but were uninterested in gold, the sole exception being the enormous golden cross, which Lewis gave to them as a present. In return they provided heaping baskets of smoked fish, steamed crabs, stubby red bananas, and sexual favours.

One night a hundred men met by the ruined stump of the mizzen-mast.

"Well lads," Lewis said. "Quite the Cruise, wasn't it?"

"It ain't over yet," a man said. "Not till I'm riding in my carriage."

"I suppose we ought to draft new Articles," another said. "Who's to chair the Meeting?"

"I'll chair it," Lewis said.

"Oughtn't we to have a vote?" someone asked.

Lewis sucked his pipe and looked around the circle of men. He exhaled and the smoke glowed in the soft yellow lamplight. Above, the stars burned bright, and below, they shone pale, dimly reflected on the surface of the water.

A woman reached for his pipe and he gave it to her.

"We don't need no vote," someone said. "Matthew, you can chair."

"Well lads," he said. "Let's keep the old Articles."

"Keep the old Articles!" a man cried.

"Keep 'em, I say," Lewis said.

"Now Matthew," the man said, "I ain't saying a word against you personally, you're a salt, you're an Honest Fellow, and when it comes time to vote for the Captain, I rather think you'll have my vote. But those Articles led straight to Tyranny."

"It was taking out duelling that done it," another man said.

"No, no," another interrupted. "It was all that damn talk of whether the ship was 'in action.'"

"Order! Order!" someone else said. "One at a time."

Lewis took his pipe back from the girl.

"I didn't mean to call order, that's for you, Lewis."

"It doesn't matter what goes in the fucking Articles," Lewis said with quiet vehemence. "A Sea Lawyer can twist anything."

"What will protect our rights?"

"I don't know," Lewis said. "The way a ship sails depends on the ballast, the rake of the masts, the sail plan. A thousand little things. So too the happiness of the Company. If you could bring the Kingdom of Heaven to earth with the proper constitution, we'd have done it by now."

From below decks came the sound of a woman laughing, along with one of the sick men, who was already sounding much restored.

4

They constructed a rough hulk from palm trees in the shallow water and towed the *Saoirse* and careened her hull and caulked the leaks and sawed planks and made new ropes. Over the days and weeks that followed, more and more men became disenchanted with island life, and straggled back into the pirate camp in twos and threes, where they signed the Articles and were put to work.

The air swarmed with flies, and the ground with ants, and it was very hot. Once the pirates had no metal left to trade, the women became less hospitable; the natives grew nervous as the pirates stayed longer and longer, though Lewis kept presenting them with gifts of fabrics and spices.

By this time, only thirty men intended to stay. They had set up an encampment on the far side of the island of rude lean-tos made from logs and palm fronds, and they spent their days scrounging for things to eat and drink, brewing vile brandy out of papaya, and trading with the natives. Coffin visited them with a party of armed men. Only ten pirates were in the encampment, along with two worthless-looking native men. All were very drunk. Around them were various projects they had begun, nets and spears and carvings, abandoned. The only man of them of any worth was Quaque. When Coffin offered all of them the chance to rejoin the Company, they all refused.

"You'll never spend a half dollar of that treasure," one of them said, shaking his head. "You're damned fools if you think otherwise."

"Quiet," another man said. "Let them go, there'll be more space for us."

"It don't square with my conscience," the first one said, very grave in his drunkenness. "You'll never spend a shilling of that money. Not a groat. Not tuppence. Not a penny. Not a halfpenny. Not a farthing. You mark my words."

One of the other men tittered, and then threw up on himself. Flies alighted upon him, and rubbed their legs, and then leapt up into the air, as if too excited to know where to begin.

"Is that thy final say?" Coffin asked.

"That is my final say, sir," the drunken spokesperson said. "Let us drink on it. Have a drink, there's an Honest Fellow."

The drink, a dark slurry of rotted fruit, sat in a haze of flies in a sack of tarred canvas, and they were using a coconut shell as a dipper. Coffin took up the shell and sniffed it.

"Been cooking eleven days," the man said proudly.

Coffin handed the dipper back. He looked at Quaque. Alone among the pirate settlers, Quaque had made a canoe and a fishing net. He was feeding most of the men here. Soon he would be married. One day he might be a chief. Still, Coffin's large, expressive eyes asked the question.

"It is you who should stay here, Brother," Quaque said. "What do you hope to find out there?"

The next day, the *Saoirse* weighed anchor and sailed south. For most of the first day the native craft followed them, criss-crossing their wake and waving and calling out. When the sun rose on the second day, they were gone.

Coffin was named Captain without a Meeting. That night, Alfie, smiling, brought him his dinner, crabs and fruit and yams. He also brought a bowl of warm water and a straight razor and, unbelievably, a pouch of tobacco. Coffin knew better than to offer any resistance.

The new Captain had a keen eye for anything amiss, and led by example, often staying up the whole night in rough weather. He rarely raised his voice, so he trained the men to listen for him, and he never swore or spoke chuffly, but only with great urgency, and disappointment, and in the chastened environment everyone leapt to obey. How quickly the fear and anger and resentment, and even grief, disappeared in the work. Climbing the shrouds, trimming the sails, polishing the decks, repairing the leaks, preparing meals and cleaning up, and sleep, no more than four hours at a stretch, and often less.

They planned to travel all the way to the westerlies to carry them around Cape Horn. The ship was making good time, a hundred and fifty miles a day, so that according to the charts they should reach the favourable winds in under a month. In their idle moments, of which there were not many, they made cold-weather clothes from the great rolls of fabric, pants and jackets, and they stitched together canvas hats, and ladled hot tar over them to make them waterproof.

After the first two weeks, Coffin came out onto the stern gallery while Benjamin fished. Benjamin looked at him with his faded, rheumy eyes, and then looked back to the sea.

Coffin leaned on the rail, and looked down upon his own work.

"Thou found me carving the taffrail, dost thou remember?"

Benjamin's eyes softened.

"Is it true that thou knew Kavanagh's father?"

"Aye," Benjamin said. "He was hanged for stirring up trouble." Benjamin tugged on his line. "He was a great one for liberty. Jimmy was always set on restoring what his father had lost."

"When did thou take up this act?"

"An overseer struck me when I was a boy," Benjamin said. "I nearly died, and the lady of the house made a pet of me. It was less work if they thought me a fool."

"Thou could stop this act."

"Thirty years is not an act," he said. "When I speak like this, that is the act."

"Thou art no fool, though."

"Oh," Benjamin said. "But I am."

From the Pacific Ocean to the Atlantic Ocean.

November 3, 1722.

5

In the southern latitudes the men saw their breath in the mornings, and the evenings, and through the night, and the stars were blue and cold and distant and very bright. The ship ran up and plunged down great waves the colour of slate, and the men lived and worked in a frigid, salty mist. Yet the winds were at their back, and the *Saoirse* crashed on, her timbers groaning, the water sloshing around their feet, the stars inching along their appointed trajectories far ahead, and they worked, and worked.

And at last they came upon the coast of Chile. One moment there was nothing, the next it was there, a thin smear of brown and green along the rim of the sea. The men screamed in triumph, and hugged each other, and danced, and they turned their ship to the north. After two hours the lookout called, "Sail ho!"

Coffin ascended the foremast with his telescope. The ship flew Spanish colours (as, in these waters, did the *Saoirse*), but she did not look Spanish, and she was too heavily manned to be a merchantman. As they sailed closer, the men quieted, the deck silent but for the shifting of the ropes and the water splashing. The ship came into focus.

When the men asked him what ship it was, Coffin found he could not speak.

"What ship is it?" a man said.

Coffin put away the spyglass and made his way down the shrouds to the deck.

"Who is it, sir?"

"The black flag!" someone called. "A fucking black flag!"

So it was, a black flag, with a white anatomy, in one hand a sword, in the other an hourglass. War and death and time.

The *Happy Delivery*.

For a long time, no one spoke.

Now thy death, Coffin thought, and he was ready, or he thought he was.

How fitting, how fitting, after all the crimes which thou piled upon thy first murder. Sin upon sin. Now thou shall receive the wages of sin: death.

But the eyes of the men were on him. He looked at them, and they looked at him, their Captain now. All of them, too, would they die? Surely they deserved it. Every man a pirate, a killer, a sinner. (Their eyes on him, Lewis and Devereux and Alfie and all the others.) Surely they deserved it as much as him. Death.

"Brothers," Coffin whispered. "Oh my Brothers. Was it for this? Was it for this we signed the Articles of the Taoiseach? Was it for this we stormed the beach at Corso Castle? Was it for this we took the *Nossa Senhora do Cabo*, and fought Lowther and the headhunters of Borneo, and drank piss and ate rats, and deposed Apollo and Quantrill alike? Nay, Brothers. Nay. Thou art meant for more than this."

His eyes moved from one face to the next, and a charge passed through the men, though none of them spoke.

"South," Coffin said.

And the command was conveyed along the length of the ship. The *Happy Delivery* turned to intercept, her yards swinging and ropes jerking.

As the day lengthened and the sun moved across the sky, all men saw how quickly the *Happy Delivery* sailed, how much cleaner was her hull, how empty her hold. They raced south and as the night came, they saw the *Happy Delivery* was almost due east, between them and the Atlantic.

In darkness they amended their course, now east-southeast, and every light aboard was extinguished, and all the metal rubbed with tar and dirt. The cold was bitter, the very air a sharp and hostile thing. There was no moon, nor stars, as the sky was overcast, and from beyond the edge of the visible world came the dim and frustrated sound of thunder. The sea rose higher and the ship pitched, so that everything on deck had to be secured, and when they struck the waves wrong, cold foam spread over the deck like a carpet of winter insects. Yet still they plunged into that unfathomable blackness, blindly racing before the wind.

A little after midnight, they heard singing and they saw a glimmer to the south. The helmsman made as if to sail north, to keep their distance, but Coffin was upon the quarterdeck and he grabbed the wheel and held it still. All was silent, save for the water against the hull and the ripples of the sail, and then, in a moment of dreamlike horror, they saw the *Happy Delivery*, to the north, appearing as abruptly as if she had just risen from the deep, for she too bore no lights and no one moved upon her deck and she was carrying very little sail and sailing to the west.

The lights still shone to the south, but it was a framework of lamps set up in one of the *Delivery*'s boats, like the bright lures of predators of the deep.

A primeval cry rose from *Happy Delivery*, and the pirates pressed up against the gunwales and fired their muskets. She turned south and her sails dropped and filled and strained against the ropes, too late to cut off the *Saoirse* but just in time to deliver a broadside. The cold wind moaned and the water shushed, shushed, shushed, and muskets popped and the two ships sailed closer, closer.

"Brace yourself men," Lewis cried.

The ships were less than a hundred yards apart when the cannons fired. The *Happy Delivery* aimed high, at the rigging and spars and masts and sails, and they fired chain-shot, the great metal balls orbiting each other like gears, and they shot cannonballs heated so they glowed pure white and left trails of sparks. Bright flashes lit up the scene and Coffin saw the *Happy Delivery* crowded with sailors of all races and all nations, three hundred, four hundred, easily, all of them laughing and swearing and shouting in their different languages, and snipers up in the rigging and upon the yardarms with their muskets, firing at the quarterdeck where he stood resolute, conscious of the eyes upon him, ignoring the musket balls as they smashed into the wood. Twelve cannons fired in five seconds, a noise like the bones of the earth shattering, and then the *Saoirse*'s deck lit up as the rigging and sails caught fire, and spars and yardarms tumbled down upon the deck.

The *Saoirse* fired low, to kill men, cannons loaded with grapeshot, and their handiwork was atrocious, and when it was done, it did not seem so much that the deck of the *Happy Delivery* was filled with the bodies of dead men as one enormous man had been blown to pieces.

The two ships passed, the *Saoirse* burning in that frigid dark like a beacon calling things from the depths, and the *Happy Delivery* coated with gore and echoing with the screams of the castrated and the crippled and the dying.

The Company formed a chain and passed up buckets of sand and water and doused the flames, while others hung from the spars and stitched the holes in the sails, and others with mouths full of iron nails hammered rude planks to plug leaks, and others untied knots and strung up fresh rope.

They all knew they could not outfight the *Happy Delivery*, so Coffin gave the order to throw overboard their cannon. The appointed carpenters moved below decks, feeling their way through the pitch-dark, and unscrewed the boards and shoved out the cannon one by one, each gun crew pushing their own weapon into the black deep, some men weeping for those weapons upon whose bores were inscribed the names of so many of their dead.

The *Saoirse* carried more sail than was quite safe for her battered spars in these heavy polar waters, and she rushed up waves and teetered upon the crest and then sledded down. They raced on, and on, into the dark, until at last the sun rose before them and the horizon lightened and when they looked back, they saw the *Happy Delivery*, carrying much sail, gaining upon them.

The casks were sprung, and their water dumped into the sea, and they threw overboard everything they could, the galley stove, the forge, all the shot, even their personal possessions, and then the fabrics, the silks and cotton, the casks of spices, but as the *Happy Delivery* grew taller against the bruised sky, they knew, without speaking, what they had to do. At last Coffin gave the order, and the gold and silver were thrown into the sea.

It rained then, and every man was soaked to the bone. No one had slept since the *Happy Delivery* had been sighted. They coughed as they worked and shivered and did not look one another in the eye. Now they were lightened, their speed was much increased, and the *Happy Delivery* did not look likely to overtake them before night, though she was still gaining. At sunset she fired her bow chasers at them and the shots dropped into the sea a dozen yards behind. There was no question of navigating through any of the straits, so they made directly for the open waters of the Drake Passage. The wind screamed about their ears and the whole ship leaned crazily so that the men walked tilted as they worked, and the waves were hard and cruel, so the ship rose and fell with terrible force and speed and the deck was swamped with cold water. Though they could not see them, they could hear icebergs around them, cracking and groaning from their great internal stress.

At last the darkness obscured all, and some men suggested to Coffin that they change course, but the seas were so high that if a wave struck their broadside the ship would be swamped. There was no choice but to run before the wind, the ship listing, the water rushing into the hold.

Around midnight, the *Happy Delivery* was again less than three hundred yards distant, so they could see the men crowded upon her forecastle, and watch the gunners as they went about their work. The only cannons left aboard the *Saoirse* were in the stern, and so the pirates returned fire, both ships blasting away in that roiling frozen dark, their hands blue with cold and their breath visible and ice on the ropes and the decks and the stairs so men slipped and fell and everyone was soaked with freezing water.

The cabin was shattered, along with the stern of the ship. When the *Saoirse* was in the trough of the great waves, her sails went limp and the ship lost speed, but when it was upon the crest and they were smashed with the full force of the howling winds, the masts jerked and moaned and were almost ripped loose of the ship.

Storm clouds came from behind and inked out the stars and the moon, and the *Happy Delivery* vanished in the blackness. The lamps were extinguished, and the cannons ceased to fire and the pirates worked in darkness. The sky thundered. The ship raced on. At last a bright burst of lightning, pure white, and the *Happy Delivery* appeared behind them, closer than ever, all its sails full and straining. The lightning came again, contemporaneous with the thunder, like the cry of a breaking world, and the *Happy Delivery* was at the top of a great wave, snow burning around her in a haze of light, and then all was darkness.

Soon the *Happy Delivery* resumed fire, and Coffin knelt, gripping the rail with one hand, so cold his flesh was seared by it, and he clenched his eyes shut against the snow and the night, and he listened for God, as he had sworn he would never do again.

Is this the end? Then so be it.

The snow made piles upon the sea water.

Was this the end of his cowardice then? Had he found his peace, at last?

He found his regrets draining away, save one.

His son, his little son.

The child who had lived.

What do you hope to find out there? Quaque had asked.

And a thought came to him.

All the times he had failed to destroy himself. All that he had done to survive, fighting, stealing, confessing to imaginary crimes. He had always thought it cowardice. But what if it had always been the braver thing to keep living? What if he had never turned away from God? What if it had been God telling him to hold on, all this time? What if that force, that will, to keep living—what if that was the Voice of God?

His men fired a shot, and then they were suddenly screaming, screaming and screaming, for the dark form of the *Happy Delivery* wobbled and changed, and a distant flash of lightning showed her in sepia, turning to one side, and then another bolt of lightning, this one an explosion of ozone and smoke and electricity turning the snow into a blinding prism of Holy fire, and the *Happy Delivery* had skidded around, exposing its broadside to the oncoming wave, and as everything was swallowed in darkness, Coffin saw her at the foot of a giant wave. When the next flash came, the *Happy Delivery* was gone.

The men were celebrating, cheering, saying they'd shot away a spar, knocked her off course. And perhaps they had, for all was dark and confused, yet Coffin swore that the ship had lunged upward as if something had struck her from beneath.

6

For a while they yelled, and pounded each other on the back, and then Coffin turned and saw that the man at the wheel was spinning it, with no effect on the direction of the ship.

Coffin clutched the frozen life ropes and crawled his way down the slanted, slippery deck to the companionway and rushed down to the lower deck, where it was black and cold water rushed around his ankles and water poured in through the stern. The rudder was smashed to bits and Lewis and some other men were desperately working to plug the hole.

"Captain, Captain! Ten feet of water in the well!"

The *Saoirse* ran helpless over the onyx waves.

Madly they worked as water rushed into the ship, and she sank lower. They nailed up what boards they could, and threw everything they could overboard, everything, down to the shingle. Then they took their spare sails and used them as a kind of rough patch. At last the flow of water was slowed. They would not sink, but they could not steer.

"Take down the mizzen-mast," Coffin called. "We must make an oar."

In this latitude the sun did not rise until almost noon, and then it hung low in the sky like a spider laden with eggs, and it was still very cold. The men were drenched through. In the madness of the chase Coffin had no idea where they were, but he knew they were headed east and they were south of fifty. There was no land at this latitude, and the seas were high and the wind was without mercy. Beneath the weak orange daylight the sea had turned a cold jade, and above their heads an albatross circled, twelve-foot wingspan, regal and carefree.

There would be, he knew, no more help from the Leviathan, and he asked for none. Discipline aboard the ship had not wavered. The men took turns at the pumps, worked sick and cold, hacking up mouthfuls of phlegm, climbing the rigging in the sharp winds. Without a carpenter the men struggled to transform the mizzen-mast and spare yards into a sort of oar, but it would not turn them far in these seas, and they could do nothing but run before the wind.

Days passed, and the seas gradually calmed, and at last they saw the islands, a brown-green smudge against the grey-green sea to the north.

Coffin shouted orders, and the oar was strapped onto the stern rail, and the men climbed the rigging and hauled on the ropes to brace the yards, and they dropped drogues into the water to larboard to turn them, and at last the oar was dipped down into the green water, sending showers of white salt spray down the length of the ship.

"Pull, men!" Coffin cried, his voice astonishingly loud when it needed to be, rising above the wind, the groaning of men and wood. "Pull, Brothers! Pull!"

The jury-rigged oar bent dangerously. A cracking noise.

All the men, pulling, pulling, white and black and brown and yellow, handsome and ugly, a wiry man without a tooth in his head, all of them hauled and hauled.

The oar snapped.

"Oh Jesus," someone said.

Coffin rushed forward. The ship pointed to windward of the islands. Was it enough?

The islands grew, and grew larger still, great looming mountains capped in white, and muddy green slopes with ferns and unhealthy grass and rushes, and dark-brown beaches, made up of mounds of smooth pebbles and teeming with penguins.

Closer, closer.

Then, at last, with a grinding blow the *Saoirse* ran up on some rocks, the men caught flat-footed and thrown onto their faces.

It took many trips with the remaining boats to get all the men ashore, where awaited a horde of penguins, staring at them, quite unafraid, for all the world like a committee of lawyers in suits.

Devereux's parrot screeched: "*Mon Dieu, les Espagnols me le payeront!*"

The Company sat on the stones, among the penguin droppings, and listened to their self-important squawking and watched them waddle to and fro. They spoke quietly in twos or threes, lay down and stared at the sky or the muted green and maroon and chocolate brown of the island or where their mighty ship was ruined in the bay, and all at once Devereux began to cackle, and the other conversations ceased and all turned to look at him. Devereux asked Coffin, when his laughter permitted, whether he remembered the speech he'd given them, that it was not for this that they'd fought the headhunters and it was not for this that they'd stormed the beaches, and so forth? Aye, Coffin said, he remembered. And Devereux asked, still cackling, well, *mon capitaine*, what *had* it been for? What, *par Dieu*, had it all been for?

Nantucket.

August 27, 1723.

7

Nantucket in the summer. Coffin stood upon the docks amid the bustle and looked up the hill, the houses getting grander and grander as they became closer to Heaven. His own about halfway up. He had been four years gone. Now he climbed, past men whittling on their stoops, past churches and inns, past great buildings constructed from half-disassembled hulks. He stood at the gate of his own yard and looked upon his own son, six years old now, unrecognizable to him, and he felt his face crumple, and he told himself to be strong, and the boy looked at him, and ran inside saying Mother, Mother, I told thou, he has come home. And Coffin followed his son inside and saw her, and she stared and then clapped her hands to her cheeks and dug her fingers in and she screamed and screamed, and then she fell.

Acknowledgments

I read many (too many?) books to help me write this one; I would like to mention a few here.

Published in 1724, *A General History of the Pirates*, by Captain Charles Johnston, is the most important historical source on the pirates of the "Golden Age." You can easily find a free copy online. Scudder's mock trial at Cape Coast Castle is closely based on the 'Mock Court of Judicature' in *A General History* (*the Design of my setting it down, is only to shew how these Fellows can jest upon Things, the Fear and Dread of which, should make them tremble*).

If you are interested in learning about sailing ships, and you are not proud, you are probably best served by reading *Steven Biesty's Cross-Sections: Man-Of-War*, a children's book. Otherwise, *Seamanship in the Age of Sail*, by John Harland, is the best book I found on the mechanics of sailing, with thorough, scientific explanations and excellent illustrations. However, it is not an easy read. *The Wooden World*, by N.A.M. Rodger, is the finest book I read on life afloat. Like all great books about one thing, it is really about everything; I would recommend it to anyone.

A Brief History of Mutiny, by Richard Woodman, also transcends its narrow subject matter.

Marcus Rediker is probably the world's foremost historian on the pirates of this era, and *Villains of All Nations* was very helpful. If you are interested in the "Pirate Commonwealth" of the Bahamas, I recommend *The Republic of Pirates* by Colin Woodward. And I would be remiss if I did not mention *The Sea-Rover's Practice*, by Benerson Little (a former Navy SEAL), a marvellous, meticulous book about the life of a pirate and pirate military tactics.

In the Heart of the Sea by Nathaniel Philbrick, the story of Nantucket whalers who had to resort to cannibalism, and the Aubrey-Maturin series by Patrick O'Brian, are obvious sources of inspiration.

Moving on to people, I would like to thank my agent, Carolyn Forde, for her patience and support. Thanks to the team at Random House Canada, and Penguin Random House Canada, for believing in me, and for all their help with this book, starting with my editor, Anne Collins, and also my copy-editor, John Sweet, and my cover designer, Lisa Jager.

Finally, I would like to thank my wonderful wife, Cathy. I wrote *The Winter Family* as a single man. I wrote this one as a father of two children under five, and I would not have been able to do so without her hard work and unfailing love.